Meet the elite. Four women. All vying for the English-speaking world's most glittering prize. The chance to trample 200 years of history – and become *The Times*'s first female editor.

The smart money's on sultry, sassy Zelda Lee Powers, ruthless victor of a thousand tabloid brawls. But mistress of deception Kiki Cox is an ice-cool blonde with a hotline to the people that matter. And flame-haired aristocrat Mira Freer Farmer has pull in high society – and push below the belt. How can overworked, underpaid Mandi Harry hope to compete with this high-powered trio as she melts down from sexual frustration?

This isn't office politics: this is war. There's a berserk stalker out there who will *kill* for the sexiest job on Fleet Street. Confronting the media maniac – and each other – forces all four contenders to face love and lust, life and death.

Welcome to the cruel, fast media world of sex, celebrities and money. A glamorous world where women make the rules and break the stories that shape your life. A world of passion where deadlines mean love is just another four-letter word for heartbreak – and where winning isn't the only thing...

It's everything.

WOW!

Amy Auden

MAINSTREAM
PUBLISHING

EDINBURGH AND LONDON

First published in Great Britain in 1994 by
MAINSTREAM PUBLISHING COMPANY
(EDINBURGH) LTD
7 Albany Street
Edinburgh EH1 3UG

ISBN 1 85158 694 6

A catalogue record for this book is available from the British Library

Typeset in Sabon by Litho Link Ltd, Welshpool, Wales
Printed in Finland by W.S.O.Y.

This book is fiction. All characters, situations, events, locales, dialogue
and other elements are fictitious – or used fictitiously.

To Alexia and Mia

1

At one minute past eleven on Wednesday morning, John Temple had been discussing a dead body.

Two minutes later he'd become one.

No-one saw the Editor of *The Times* die, but three people had heard him. Both Temple's long-suffering secretary, Joan Winterbloom, and his ambitious deputy Duncan Campbell, had been calling the hospital during Temple's final moments, equally outraged that no staff in its expensive private wing were at hand during the crisis. But Brett Collins, Temple's boss, had focused on the speaker phone that occupied the large desk dominating the Editor's office, listening to the gruesome sound of his death rattle. The way Collins saw it, there was nothing anyone in the room could do. Besides, he'd never actually heard anyone croak to death over a squawk box before.

Temple's death bore the hallmark that had distinguished his life – consideration. Things couldn't go on the way they had been at *The Times*, that was what Collins had come to tell Temple, in private, over the hotline that ran from the Editor's office to his hospital bed. His sudden demise had saved Brett the difficult job of firing him. There'd been nothing personal about his decision: even though the young Australian was responsible for running International News Europe, Brett Collins was answerable to a higher power. The man who'd built its parent company into the biggest, most powerful and successful media corporation on the planet: The Boss.

Brett's Uncle was unhappy about *The Times* – circulation was falling, morale low, advertising revenue in a desperate slump. Brett believed it needed a steady hand at the tiller, some firm leadership to bring the world's oldest and most venerable newspaper to a new audience. But The Boss had other ideas. Brett's Uncle wanted someone high-voltage; someone who'd drag the paper into the 21st century; someone utterly unlike any other Editor *The Times* had ever had before.

Someone who's here? Collins wondered, observing the group gathered at Temple's graveside. Three faces caught his roving eye among the crowd of mourners bundled up against the chill, biting wind and the occasional gusts of white snow.

There was Mandi Harry, rubbing her full lascivious lips with a stumpy finger, worried that the weather was bringing on a cold sore. A torn Pakamac shielded her legendary breasts and scruffy stiletto shoes concealed the blisters on the backs of her ankles. The dangerous curves of her petite body were blunted and bloated from too many sweet treats and long cocktails, and her flat-featured face – a combination of benign plausibility, rat-like guile and heavy foundation – completed the cut-out of everybody's image of the tabloid journalist from hell. And, Brett thought, what better place to find one?

His eyes flickered here and there like a snake's tongue, past the Prime Minister, past the former heavyweight boxing contender who'd once worked for the paper's sports desk, past the antediluvian authoress old enough to have been the dead man's mother – but who was actually his mistress – and on to Kiki Cox.

Cox cut a striking figure: a five-foot-ten ash-blonde in a sombre, custom-made cashmere coat. Her chic, long black suede gloves matched her eminently practical moonboots. Her small but wide, sharp-featured face was obscured by a dark shawl, and by the Marc O'Polo sunglasses she wore beneath her wide-brimmed black boater. A pallid, heartbreakingly handsome individual whom Brett recognised as Society decorator Crispian Frye held an umbrella above their collective heads.

Cox had exploded on to the British journalism scene four years ago when she'd thrashed out of nowhere to launch *Tasteful Living* Magazine. Her rise had been meteoric and her reputation was formidable: at an Australian Embassy party, Collins had seen his countrywoman's pale blue eyes turn shark-cold simply because a writer had dared to try and introduce herself. She hated writers:

they asked too many questions, knew too many answers. Cox organised *YES* Magazine, the weekly supplement produced by International News's biggest rival, Allied Media, like an army. An army that marched on other people's stomachs. Cox was all-round sensational. She had the looks; she had the talent; she had it all – except, perhaps, the heart. Maybe, Brett speculated, she kept it in her famous transparent fridge.

Zelda Lee Powers stood between the representative from Buckingham Palace and her husband, Sir Anthony George. She had arrived from Heathrow Airport, minutes before the service began, in a limo which was bigger than the hearse. She'd heard that a major power shift was taking place and, true to form, had jumped on the first plane outtathere to take advantage of it. Collins had never met her, but recognised Powers instantly. Who else would chew gum beneath a designer veiled hat? At 48, she was older than both Mandi and Kiki, but the New Yorker's snappy demeanour was that of a woman half their age. Her perfect, expensively textured skin was a glowing testament either to clean living or to the nimble skills of that élite band of cosmetic surgeons who create the knifestyles of the rich and famous. Everything about this living legend of American newspapers seemed sleek, lush, plush – from the deep, dark pile of her sable coat, through the power-polished, jewelled charms on her heavy 24-carat bracelet, right down to the gleaming soles of her Manolo Blahnik shoes. Her dark beauty was the kind that could've dragged a monk from a monastery, Brett thought – or driven a sane man right into one.

The Archbishop of Canterbury had begun a short reading: 'I have this in my blood, this is my blood, this is my family. We are all refugees, I have been wandering, we are all wandering, and I was alone in this strange place, but now I have come home.'

Brett noticed Zelda Lee Powers drawing a bead on the man in the funny hat, a curious gleam in her eye. Of course, she would take a special interest in the extract from *Full Moon On A Dark Night*; she had been married to O'Brien when, ten years ago, the man they called The Celtic Shakespeare had gone out to post a letter – and had never come back. Perhaps she too was wondering why Temple's mother had chosen a passage from Brendan O'Brien:

9

her son had despised drunkards, had irritated the Irish and had no time at all for communists – and O'Brien had been all three.

The Archbishop finished the reading, and asked for a moment's silence as a mark of respect for the soul of the departed. All was quiet, all were pensive, and the mourners composed their wind-chilled features into portraits of grief. Even the distant roar of traffic seemed to recede as Joan Winterbloom comforted Drucilla Temple. The Editor's mother, well into her seventies, was absolutely devastated. Brett tried to tune her out. The combination of emotional intensity and stiff formality at such events made him uncomfortable. Staring glumly into the middle distance, he felt trapped by emptiness and futility as Drucilla's sobs grew louder and more harrowing.

Suddenly, an alien vibration burst through the silence, shattering the solemn atmosphere of the cemetery. A mobile phone trilled a familiar shrill summons. Brr Brrr. Brr Brrr. Brr Brrr. Ask not for whom the bell tolls, thought Brett ruefully. Any wicked pleasure he might have drawn from his own wit evaporated into thin air as he realised people were turning round and staring at him. With horror, Brett realised that the shrilling phone was his own. Hurriedly, he began to nudge his way through the crowd.

'Uncle Ruprecht? Sorry, mate, it was difficult, they're just handing the bastard his final edition,' the brash young Australian said, as he walked away from the huddled throng. 'Jeez it's cold enough to dial Hong Kong on a witch's tit here, Unk, you and Auntie Tina are well out of it in Palm Springs . . . Yeah, the wreath was a ripper. His old mum told me she'd be writing to ya both. Put this one in 72-point Ironic Bold – they're not just burying the poor bastard within pissing distance of Karl Marx, but some bloody joker organised a reading from Brendan O'Brien. Yeah. O'Brien, the IRA bloke. Talking of terror, guess who else showed up? O'Brien's widow. The *New York Gazette* fired her? When? Oh, I see, I see – I'd thought she was just here on a jolly, waving the flag a bit for her husband. So Morty finally lost his patience with her, did he? Well, he is an impetuous son of a bitch. I thought Powers had done the right thing by him, the *Gazette* was a terrible rag . . . yeah, those weekly sex supplements she did brought in a lot of

10

Classified, turned it into a profit centre . . . I'm surprised . . . I've tapped Campbell as caretaker Editor till you give someone the nod . . . Nah, you're right Unk, Campbell's daggy . . . he's bored, he's lonely, I reckon his heart isn't in it anymore, mate. He couldn't find a grand piano in a one-room house. Did you see his pages yesterday? They were bloody dreadful. I've been more interested by the six-point on the back of a toothpaste packet . . . What? You're going to appoint a Sheila? You're kidding! You're going to put a duck on the pond at a place like *The Times?* Jeez, no, no, I'm sure it's OK, I'll mention it to him and get the bastard on the case the moment the service is finished. What? You want that Powers bird in it? OK, OK. Yeah, no sweat, mate, the candidate list will be in the overnight bag. OK, love to Auntie Tina.'

Brett folded the slim black cellular phone and slipped it back inside his overcoat pocket. As he returned, the Archbishop was giving the final blessing, and Collins resumed his position next to Duncan Campbell.

'The Boss wants a chick to edit *The Times*,' he whispered in his nearest ear. The acting Editor of the paper looked completely sand-bagged. 'What?' he said, his voice smeared with horror.

'Positive discrimination, mate.'

'Are you serious?'

'Me? I'm never serious. But my Uncle? The Boss is as serious as a second coronary.' Brett turned to the grave and smiled before adding: 'Hey, no disrespect, Sport.'

He savoured every syllable.

The mourners began to disperse.

'I don't care WHO the chairman's staying with. Get his goddamn ass on the phone,' Zelda Lee Powers commanded her husband, 'I've got my goddamn 9mm Gaugin gasgun in that bag.'

'How on earth did you get it through the X-ray machines?' her husband asked wearily.

'I put it in the hot roller box and left the rollers out so the security guy could inspect them, what do YOU care?' Zelda barked. 'Tony, it's a semi-automatic weapon. It's loaded, and all it would take is for the safety catch to click and it could blow up my entire suitcase. Maybe worse. I need that bag, you've GOT to call them. Plus, ALSO, how long will it take us to get to the West End?'

'In this weather the traffic could be difficult,' Sir Anthony George said.

He was dark, powerfully built, saturnine, with a chiselled, lived-in face. The blond highlights had been Zelda's idea. The laughter lines running into an expression of amused cynicism, and that knowing smile, were all his own. He slipped a battered leather hipflask from his mohair coat and took a pull.

'We'd better get going.'

Mandi Harry's make-up had run to reveal a small birthmark lurking on her chin. It looked like the stain from the dregs of a glass of port tossed in her face. Fortunately, Drucilla Temple – whom Mandi was trying to comfort, since no-one else seemed to be bothering – was too upset to notice.

Brett was on the cellular phone again. 'So do a statement – you know the form: "The Boss is deeply saddened by the tragic loss of an esteemed Editor, cherished personal friend, respected colleague, etc etc, but International News Europe is taking this opportunity to make sweeping changes to an established, traditional title that, that must, that . . . "'

Kiki Cox, so calm, collected and self-possessed, watched them closely, waiting for the right moment to approach Duncan Campbell and ask him if he could use a lift in her car to their lunch date.

'" . . . must nevertheless move with *The Times*?"'

'Very bloody witty, DC.'

'" . . . the specific appointment of a woman Editor, to orchestrate such improvements, he feels, is reflective of the attitudes of the age," point par. Then something about a short-list being drawn up, the appointment being announced on 7 March. Get it out to PA, AP, UK News, BBC and CNN with a strict embargo for seven a.m. Monday. We don't want some slimy little ratbag from the *Mail* or the *Express* getting wind of this and ruining everybody's Sunday lunch. Now, The Boss is pretty keen to tie in the announcement of the winner to our charity swimming gala, so . . . Jesus Christ, who the flaming hell is that?'

'Mirabelle Freer Farmer,' Campbell said.

'She edits *Verve*.'

Brett's expression betrayed his surprise as the ravishing redhead dressed in a lung-tight shiny black leather catsuit rose from the seat of a battered moped which had narrowly avoided sideswiping Sir Anthony's departing car.

Mira was cussing because she was late. Mira was kissing people, because everyone seemed to know her. Mira was giggling because she was sharing a joke with her ravishing half-brother Toby. Mira was always the centre of attention. Not simply because her Brazilian husband Mico videotaped her every last move, nor because, as one of Britain's richest, spunkiest heiresses, she was at the centre of a charmed and moneyed circle of talent, beauty and success – but because she was playful, curious, funny, confident and fascinated by the world around her. Mira had an ongoing love affair with life. She was a living, giving star, every inch, and to see her once was to be an enchanted acolyte, forever basking in her sparkling luminescence.

'*Verve*? She edits *Verve*?' said Brett. 'What – that asslickin' social glossy?'

Campbell smiled with all the enthusiasm of a tree in the Black Forest coming bark to face with a lumberjack brandishing a chainsaw.

'. . . That shiny bumwipe with all the artsy fartsy claptrap between the perfume ads?'

Campbell nodded.

Brett stared. 'Right. Make sure her name's above Zelda Lee Powers' on the list.' The acting Editor nodded and smiled. 'Oh, and Duncan, mate,' Campbell thought if he smiled any harder he'd need a truss, 'I'm a busy fellah. No more than four names, OK?'

2

The silver and black sign dominating the *Post*'s reception area proclaimed what Britain's first 24-hour, seven-day newspaper was all about: More News, More Stars, More Hits, More Fun.

Every Saturday, the *Sunday Post*'s offices buzzed like a beehive as its team raced to the peak of their week: a frenzied crescendo of action as they battled to serve up the scoop de jour and finish the paper before deadline. The journalists, that is. Management had other priorities.

At the end of a labyrinthine maze of corridors sat a glass corner office into which Managing Editor Nick Plant now called Mandi from her turbulent newsroom. 'It's about Kettle's exes, Mandi.'

'What about them?'

Three weeks earlier the *Post* had received an unusually hot tip about Lord Lucan. After a catastrophic night on the tables at Crockford's gambling club in Mayfair, the mysterious English peer had whacked his children's nanny with an axe – under the erroneous impression that his target was his shrewish estranged wife – which would presumably have made it all right. But it was all wrong. The nanny had died, and the enigmatic aristocrat hadn't been seen since 1971.

Ever since he'd disappeared, cranks and hoaxers had been calling in sightings of him from Southport to South Africa. Four months earlier, a former employee of a celebrated Mayfair gaming house had taken off to parts unknown with the casino's takings from a Bank Holiday weekend. Kettle, the *Post*'s scabrous crime correspondent, had succeeded in tracking down the fly-by-night manager. In return for not immediately informing the authorities of his vacational location, the croupier had passed the *Post* a hot exclusive tip: he knew where Lucan had been hiding.

It was what they call Newsesque – a speculative item about a mythical figure which was more than likely apocryphal but which, if it happened to be true, would make a sensational story. Mandi liked Newsesque. Little green men, dead rock idols, evaporating master criminals, hungry bimbos and starving starlets were all cheap to buy up, and they rarely sued.

But the Managing Editor, responsible for running the business side of the newspaper, didn't like Kettle's expenses. He didn't like it one little bit. When Kettle had returned from an abortive three-week pursuit across the Kalahari desert, he had filed an outrageous claim which had included: 'ITEM: To hiring Camel . . . £600'.

'Got a receipt for that then, have you, Kettle?'

'Look, Nigel, these guys were Bedouin tribesmen, OK? They don't speak English, they've never seen a receipt in their lives.'

Plant had decided to try another tack. 'OK, Kettle, let me put it to you this way. You bought a camel, right?'

'That's what it says.'

'Then you must've sold a camel.'

Kettle's facial features had reflexively composed themselves into characteristically wary cast. 'Must I?'

'So you didn't sell the camel?' the Managing Editor had said, a glint in his eye. 'Is that what you're telling me?'

'I didn't say that,' Kettle countered.

Plant had walked back behind his desk and sunk into the high-backed, G-plan-style, brown leather executive chair. 'OK then,' was his riposte. 'So where's the fucking camel, then?'

'What do you mean, where's the fucking camel?' Kettle had long ago learned the value of fielding awkward questions with a query of one's own. 'I don't follow.'

'You bought the camel, but you didn't sell the camel.' Plant had counted off both points on the fingers of his right hand. 'Therefore . . . where's the fucking camel?'

Realising that he had been outmanoeuvred, the hard-bitten veteran had looked momentarily crestfallen. The Managing Editor had pressed home his advantage.

'Said camel is, as I'm sure you appreciate, Kettle, still the property of International News Incorporated. So: produce the camel, I'll reimburse the claim, and we'll say no more about it. OK?'

Kettle had skulked away, clutching his rejected expenses slip. But this morning, Kettle had returned to the Managing Editor's office with a jauntier step – and a revised itemisation, which Plant now handed to Mandi. 'Come on, this is a sackable offence. Perhaps 20 years ago you could've got away with this sort of crap, but not anymore,' Plant reminded her. 'We're running a business, not a joke factory. Besides being grossly disrespectful to me, it's fraud. We could prosecute him for this.'

Mandi ran her eye down the expenses form. Among the usual melange of pumped-up, highly imaginative and rapacious entries, such as: 'To: Hotel, miscellaneous expenses; To: Porters, miscellaneous disembursements for information received; To: Purchase of Nintendo Game Boy, gift for confidential contact' – Mandi spotted the new item Kettle had added which had brought down her Managing Editor's wrath: 'ITEM: To hiring Camel . . . £600. ITEM: To burial of said Camel . . . £600.'

'OK, I'll deal with it,' Mandi said.

'Good,' Plant said. 'How's it going out there?'

'Deader than a wet Wednesday in Wales. The fashion looks like shit again . . . I mean, Lacroix . . . which of our readers can afford La-di-da-di-Croix? We've got to dump this liquorice posing pouch promotion, it's too tacky, even for us. And Ivor's gone mental . . .' – Ivor was the paper's top libel lawyer – '. . . about the Fifi Trixabelle-Macauley Culkin yarn.'

Plant's faced creased with curiosity. His remit was the commercial administration of the journalistic operation, not the actual newsgathering. 'Fifi Trixabelle and Macauley Culkin? What about them?'

'They've done a bunk to Gretna Green.'

'Those crazy kids,' said Plant, sardonic. 'What will they think of next?'

'They thought of signing the register in false names – Bob Geldof and Barbra Streisand.' She shrugged. 'Still, we got a snap. Although it's a bit blurry, I think it'll stand up.'

16

'Never let the facts get in the way of a good story, Mandi,' Plant reminded her.

'If I had a good story, I wouldn't, believe you me.'

Mandi stalked back to the newsroom, collected some layouts from an assistant editor, and had just begun to flick through them *en route* to her office when she noticed a sudden change in the atmosphere around her. A sharp drop in temperature, and then an incredible rise, as she felt the newsroom begin to steam like a rainforest. She stopped in her tracks and surveyed the floor. It was happening about 100 feet away from her.

'For Chrissakes, Steve, get that!' the foreign editor was shouting, standing up at his desk as those around him began to jump with adrenalin. 'Dave's on line one from Tampa, somebody get him up on screen, he's filing straight on to Copy.'

'Mike, check this out, NOW!' said a shirt-sleeved thirty-something. 'PA Flash, all wires!'

Mandi looked over the shoulder of the nearest hack. At the top of the black background of her ATEX computer screen, a line of green type flashed 'PA FLASH URGENT.'

Something big was breaking. Before she'd even had a chance to look up from the screen, a new message flashed up below the first: 'REUTERS FLASH URGENT.'

And another: 'AFN ALL WIRES URGENT.'

'What the f. . . what's happening?' Mandi said, going over to the foreign desk.

'Get CNN, get CNN!' the foreign editor was shouting.

'A plane's just smashed into Tampa stadium,' one of the reporters said.

'A plane crash?' Mandi asked.

What was all the fuss about?

'Fucking 747's gone down in Tampa stadium smack in the middle of the Superbowl.'

Phones were ringing. Faxes spewed paper. Computer screens flickered furiously. Everyone who wasn't zoning in on one of the dozens of TV screens scattered throughout the newsroom to watch the devastating carnage exploding before their eyes, was talking, shouting and typing simultaneously.

'Jesus, the casualties, how many people are in that stadium?'

'How the hell are the fire brigade going to get in there?'

'What kind of 747 is it?'

'A fucking big one.'

'Are there any celebrities at the game?'

'Where's Jenkins filing from? Is he on the spot in the stadium?'

'Use your loaf – if he was in the fucking stadium he'd be charcoal by now.'

'What was the score?' asked Bowles.

'You're sick,' snapped a female feature writer at the morose, unflappable deputy sports editor with a look that should have killed him. 'The whole fucking stadium's wiped out and you want to know the score?'

'Can we make edition?' Mandi barked at Worell, her number two.

'We'll make the splash,' he said, flicking through the photos pumping from the Press Association Leaffax machine. 'But it depends if Jenkins can get these pictures wired over in time.'

Mandi studied her deputy with a look he knew only too well. 'The splash?' she frowned.

'For Superbowl? Doesn't this belong to sport, on the back page?'

'A stadium that holds 70,000, a loaded British Airways Jumbo and a hole in Florida the size of Blackburn Lancashire – the biggest bloody air disaster in history, and Madame Editor wants to put it on the back page?'

'All right, all right,' Mandi said, up and moving again now. 'Don't get your frillies in a twist, Worell. Join me on the back bench, please. We're going to have to have a lightning rethink. Cut Culkin and Fifi to 800 words and run it on page four,' she said as her section heads gathered around her. 'Spread this Jumbo crash over the splash, two and three. Darren, get news to do a ring-round ASAP, push BA for a passenger list, the VIPs at the front of the plane at the very least. See if we can find anyone who missed the flight or cancelled at the last minute, and if it stands up before nine then drop the cobblers about Jerry Hall's fertility drugs from the spread and patch it with those bloody pics Jenkins was talking about – if they make it in time. Someone get Jimmy out of The Evil Star and have him tart up any spot stuff from the hospital that's coming off the wires.'

Mandi went into brilliant overdrive, snapping off commands and ideas with the smooth fluency of the seasoned professional, graceful under pressure and cool under fire.

'Send travel a message, ask Jack Travers to work up a box on flying by wires, a history of Jumbo crashes, were computers to blame, something authoritative from the CAA. How Safe Is Your Ticket To The Sun, right? Mike, check out that new European Superleague you were telling me about last week, get a line on the Brits who were in the stadium, any celebrities, human interest angles there. And pull the cuts on American sporting disasters, we'll run a box on that. How's that going to work on the page? Get a rift on, Worell, I want to see these layouts before I collect my pension. Vicci, find some bodies and get me a 1200-word backgrounder on The Accident Waiting To Happen, no, wait – Horror Hell That Had To Happen. Lift some background off the wires, what preparations for an emergency, how many ambulance crews did they have on standby, were the exits clear, that sort of thing.'

'The agencies don't seem to know yet,' the features editor began.

'Then make it up!' Mandi blazed. 'I need it ASAP, eight-thirty at the latest. What about that guy who used to test-pilot Concorde? Trubshaw or something. Get his number from Jack, ask him a couple of questions, bung him a grand and see if we've got a smudge we could use at the top of Travers's backgrounder. Worell, are you getting this down? Where are the new layouts?'

'Right here, Aitch,' said her deputy, handing her assorted sheets of paper with the hurriedly scribbled flatplans. 'What about Kettle's piece? I Married A One Legged Bigamist – And Lived With His Seven Other Wives?'

'Back of the book.'

'But there's no room,' Mandi's deputy protested. 'We're locked in!'

'Drop that ad,' Mandi said flinging the flatplan back at him. 'This is a newspaper, not a bloody department store.'

'Right you are, Chief.'

'Where is Kettle?'

'Down in The Evil Star, with Jimmy.'

'Right,' said Mandi, getting up. 'Get on with it. I'll be back in half an hour.'

'Mizz Harry,' her secretary said, 'This little old lady's still waiting. What shall I tell her?'

'That I've got a paper to put out tonight,' she said, collecting her bag. 'She'll have to come back on Tuesday.'

'But Mandi,' the secretary said, glancing at the frail, bony exhibit planted in his office, 'Look at her – I can't just throw her out.'

'Not now, Oscar,' she said, her voice firm, her stride brisk.

As she made her way out through the noise and bustle of the newsroom, she noticed the unflappable Bowles grab at a sports hack who was racing by. 'Hey,' he asked, all eyes and ears. 'What was the score?'

3

Kiki Cox shook the sleet from her umbrella and swept through the glass doors into Waiteley's restaurant. As her shiny flat-heeled pumps moved towards the trio of fierce-looking receptionists minding the austere antechamber like bejewelled Egyptian guard dogs, the slender Australian tucked her vast black crocodile holdall into her armpit. She refused, politely, to consign it to the care of those sabre-toothed bitches.

She ran her slim hands the thigh length of her grey silk pants and tugged at the hem of the exquisitely tailored jacket. The suit was brand new and on its first outing – she had picked it up at Neiman Marcus in New York the week before. She felt good in it. And she looked great.

Kiki wore such clothes well. Her legs were infamously the best in Fleet Street, though she would never say so herself. Those endless Barbie-doll limbs came in handy when she found herself, as was her wont, in airless meetings with hard-boiled executives. She would arrange and rearrange her pins with all the nonchalance of an insomniac Supermodel. It always had the desired effect. On short-skirt days she made sure she chose her underwear carefully. Cerise and violet were favourite shades. A flash of brightly coloured silk knicker worked wonders, she always found, and it certainly alleviated the boredom.

Kiki revelled in her enigmatic femininity and played it to the hilt. She would watch discreetly for stirrings in the zipper regions of her colleagues whenever her knees fleetingly parted company. Rarely was she disappointed, and from time to time she would excuse herself to make for the adjacent Ladies' room and finish what they had started. Jamming one fist in her mouth to muffle her pleasure, she would twirl the fingers of her other hand deliciously in the damp space until she felt her whole body blush. She derived her greatest sexual satisfaction from such illicit interludes, her climax all the more accentuated by the possibility that they could hear her.

While cleanliness may be next to godliness, even a freshly scrubbed Archbishop would find bagging a table at this white marble shrine to exquisite cuisine, elegant stylepower and astonishing prices, nigh on impossible. Sir Terence Conran, who had rebuilt the swank eatery on the site of a dilapidated bordello just six months earlier, had given his staff firm instructions to exercise the utmost care in the selection of Waiteley's clientèle. Only the indiscriminate might have mistaken it for snobbery.

'You're meeting Duncan Campbell? Fine, Ms Cox, Raoul will show you to your table.'

Kiki nodded at the black-jacketed greeters stationed by Siberia (as the area between the bar and the balcony that housed the overtly nouveau riche or less than fashionably dressed was known) and followed the sexy Castillian employee down the staircase. A lavish vista spread before her. Times like these reminded her how far she'd come from that boxy little house in the western suburbs of Sydney where she'd grown up.

'Jeez, it's like *Grand Hotel*,' Kiki said.

Raoul stopped and turned to her, his dark eyebrows raised. ''Scuse me, Madame?'

'It always reminds me of the film *Grand Hotel*,' Kiki said, 'this staircase, I mean.'

'If Madame says so,' responded Raoul with a haughty toss of his long dark ponytail. She watched his tightly clenched buttocks precede her, and admired same. For a moment she was lost in limbo, in thrall to a torrid sexual fantasy – Kiki was nothing if not a connoisseur of the tightly clenched buttock. But, incredibly, she thought, when she thought about it (which was rarely), she hadn't had sex with a man since she'd left Australia seven years ago.

Now they were walking through the heart-shaped centre of the restaurant, the sights and smells and the sheer volume of noise all around them brought the chic, athletic-looking blonde back to earth with a start. As her eye tracked across the tables of stuffed dates,

quails' eggs, satura and tempura lying before the ladies who lunch,
the dark-suited deal makers, the beautiful people, the glitz and cogs,
Raoul made a right, and she saw he was leading her to an enclave
hidden within the epicentre of the floorplan. He parted the fronds
of the palms, strategically placed so that only a few adjacent tables
– such as Dempster's – could see who entered this inner sanctum.

Inside were two tables. One was vacant. At the other, nursing
a glass of still mineral water, sat Duncan Campbell, still sporting
a smooth black suit, crisp white shirt and salmon and green club
tie. As he murmured into a tiny mobile telephone, the acting
Editor of *The Times* tapped at the keyboard of a granite-grey
Macintosh Powerbook. His fingers danced, Pavlova-nimble, and
his eyes sparkled. Then, glancing up to acknowledge Kiki, he
nodded at the plush red seat opposite, indicating that she should
sit on it. 'OK, Mike, that's fine. File it now and I'll put it above
the fold on Op Ed. I've got to sign off, my lunch has arrived.' He
hung up and stood up. 'Kiki, thank you for coming.'

Kiki had practised the art of shaking hands with men so that
her slender silky hand brushed theirs like a starling's wing. It
turned them on, and she revelled in this sexual power that she
could wield at arm's length.

'That was our man in Bosnia,' Campbell said. 'He's filing a
feature about the Holiday Inn there for Monday's paper. "Would
you like dinner now, or after the shelling?" Good little colour
piece.'

They made small talk about this for a while until a handsome
Irish waiter with a quirky smile and a glint in his Newman-blue
eyes took their order.

'John'll be sadly missed,' Kiki said pointlessly, after he'd left
them.

Campbell didn't respond.

'I know it can't be easy for you to come to terms with his
death,' Kiki pressed on.

'When I need your sympathy I'll hang out some black crepe
paper,' Campbell snarled. '"John'll be sadly missed."' Campbell
mocked her with cruel eyes as he mimicked her Sydneyside accent,
his pupils blazing. 'What right have you to say that? How could

you even begin to know the measure of a man like John Temple? You edit a vacuous little colour supplement stuffed with meaningless twaddle about aromatherapy and olive oil that fills in the gaps between cheap and nasty mail order ads. *YES* Magazine has about as much to do with real journalism as Nana Mouskouri has to do with concrete mixers. You're not one of us – and I resent your presumption that you ever could be. So don't patronise me with your Hallmark condolences, Miss Cox.'

Kiki was stunned by his outburst.

The first courses appeared. The uncomfortable silence continued.

'We haven't got off to a very good start here, have we?' Kiki ventured at last. 'You're not very happy about this, are you? Me being here now can't help. I should leave,' Kiki said, patting around her voluptuously pencilled-in mouth with her napkin and pushing back her chair.

'No, no,' Campbell said, laying a hand on her satisfyingly expensive sleeve and urging her to remain seated. As she settled back in her seat, Campbell spied a hint of peach satin and lace nestling in her modest cleavage. Small breasts. Small, pert, yet promising breasts. The deliciously skimpy bosom of some callous-toed ballerina. Campbell lost himself for a second, tripping over his middle-aged composure and tumbling, Alice-like, into the recesses of his memory, where he found himself: 19, gauche, bursting with equal amounts of virility and embarrassment, and sucking on a pair of hard, cold little apricots inside the sensible white cotton bra of a fellow undergraduate . . .

'I'm sorry,' he spluttered, a slight mauve flush seeping into his cheeks as he struggled to compose himself and ignore the erection which Kiki knew was there anyway – she could almost smell it. 'I had no right to indulge in an emotional outburst like that. It was quite uncalled-for. You're just the person sitting in front of me. Please don't take any of it personally. I am sorry.'

Campbell was in his late forties, bearded, with thin wisps of ginger hair receding at the crown to reveal pale and flaky skin. His complexion was newborn pink and drawn, and black rings accompanied the bags beneath his eyes. 'There's a lot of pressure,

uncertainty at work. To lose one of my best friends at a time like
this . . .'

'He was a friend as well as a colleague?' In common with
many Australians, Kiki's inflection rose at the end of her
sentences, leaving the listener in doubt as to whether she was
asking a question, or was just being tentative.

'God, yes,' Campbell exclaimed. 'I've known Temple for
more than 35 years. We were at St Johns together at Oxford.
When the milk round came, he went to work for the BBC and I
for *The Times*. While I was slaving away laying out the obituaries
in Printing House Square, he was covering the '68 riots in Paris,
being the glamour boy at Watergate, getting married to Polly on
the Embassy roof in Saigon. He never really got over losing her
like that . . . there's something rather ignominious about dying in
a traffic accident, isn't there?'

He seemed lost in thought for a moment. 'You know the only
reason Thatcher ran for the leadership in '78 was because Temple
found himself stuck in a hotel lift with her, jammed between the
34th and 35th floors during a conference in Tokyo?'

Kiki shook her head.

'He was the one who urged her to go for it. Temple's father
was a haberdasher, actually, but the man had ink in his blood. He
was a fantastic reporter, a great journalist, a wonderful judge of
people. He had a nose for the phoney, and a real enthusiasm for the
underdog. The sort of hack you see so rarely outside the provincial
press these days. Everyone on Fleet Street nowadays, they all want
to be celebrities themselves, plugging their own books, getting their
own TV shows. I remember when we worked on *Isis* together . . .
oh dear, I'm becoming rather maudlin, aren't I? The idea of a wake
is to celebrate the spirit of the departed – and my word, that man's
left us with plenty to raise our glasses to.'

The lead crystal chinked in mid-air. Campbell said I'm sorry,
did you want some wine, and Kiki said No, I don't drink, and
Campbell said It's Saturday, are you sure, I might have a glass
myself, and Kiki said Maybe later, I don't drink really, and
Campbell said That's OK, neither do I . . .

'I've always admired *The Times*'s consistency,' Kiki said. Her quinoa salad with scallop and mango butterflies was quite delicious, but she'd had to be firm when instructing the kitchen to serve her spatchcock peach-grilled rather than mesquite. 'Temple was a genius in keeping the core readers through the price war while managing to attract new readers from the *Mail* in the middle market,' she said.

'I know we arranged this lunch before John died,' Campbell said, 'so I presume you came to sound me out about the feature editor's slot.'

'Well . . .'

'Let me save you the trouble,' Campbell said briskly. 'You've got about as much chance of getting that job as I have of turning out for Bolivia's Under-21 subaqua squad.'

Kiki's almost pretty face fell.

'But something else has come up that I think you might be interested in.'

Kiki arched an eyebrow, and wondered wildly whether he meant the swelling in his pants by any chance.

'You came here to make a favourable impression on me, because you thought I might be your next boss,' said Campbell, smooth as soup. 'Actually, Kiki, the shoe's on the other foot.'

'How do you mean, exactly?' Kiki asked with a frown, when the Irish waiter had cleared their plates again.

'It's really I who should be greasing your wheels, Miss Cox. The Boss wants an editrix for *The Times* . . . and your name's on the list.'

Kiki looked at him long and hard. 'Really?' she managed to spurt, at last.

'Really,' Campbell replied wearily.

'So is this an interview?'

'Brett approached me after the service and told me to have a short list of four females on his desk by tonight. The Boss wants Zelda Lee Powers on the list, and Brett told me to add Mira Freer Farmer. That leaves two slots.'

'Am I in one of them?'

'You might be.'

'So who's the other?'

'Whom would you pick?'

Kiki named the ineffectual editor of a rival broadsheet's Style section.

'No! If Princess Diana arrived in her office tomorrow, she'd run a piece about how Court shoes were making a comeback. You're in the right area with a Sunday. But perhaps you're looking at the wrong end of the Street.'

'What do you mean?'

'Mandi Harry.'

'The woman who does the *Sunday Post*?'

'The same.'

Kiki's eyes doubled in size. 'Duncan . . . you're a respectable journalist. The *Post* isn't a newspaper – it's a crimewave. Just reading it makes my hands feel dirty.'

'She's a good little operator, is Mandi. You know the story about how she scooped the Yorkshire Ripper when she started on the *Sunday Mirror*? She'd bought up the widow, and had to drive her to the hotel where the *Mirror* was supposed to be keeping Mrs Ripper away from prying eyes and long lenses. But she was being pursued by a rat pack of competing hacks who had piled into another car. Mandi was trying to lose them, but got stuck at a red light. The pack pulled up behind her. Mandi got out of the car, motioned for the driver to wind down his window and said, "Look, it's ridiculous all of us chasing each other all over town like this. Suppose we agree to pool the story?" And when the driver turned round to ask the others what they thought, Mandi leaned in, snatched the ignition keys, threw them down a drain and spirited her quarry away.'

'How inventive,' Kiki sneered softly.

'That's the sort of guile a broadsheet Editor needs these days, Kiki. Fewer and fewer people are reading out there. We're in a declining market.'

'You're right,' Kiki agreed.

Only yesterday, the Group Managing Director Sir Donovan Dweasal had sent word that *YES* Magazine's budget was to be cut – yet again. But Kiki knew exactly how to put a stop to that. She enjoyed a close (intimate, some said) relationship with Allied Media's proprietor, Clifford Starsmeare, Earl of Lanchester. He had promised her a day at the races soon, and she meant to hold him to it.

'You may think it's odd that I'm being quite so straightforward with you about the situation. But frankly, I don't really care any more. One thing I've learned in this business is that few things really matter, and nothing matters that much at all. I've had my own ambitions – but it was not to be.'

'So what are your plans?'

'I'll be there to show the successful candidate the ropes and then, well, business as usual, I suppose. To paraphrase our old rock writer: you don't have to be a weather man to know which way to blow your nose. I've a good sense of which way things are going, so I'm just covering my back. When I retire I want that seven-figure payoff, so I can go away somewhere and shoot skeet, play with my computers and tell International News to go fuck themselves.'

After Duncan had helped her back into her cashmere, and then retrieved his own long black leather coat from the hat check rottweiler, Kiki smiled as she slipped on her sunglasses and swathed herself in her shawl. 'Thank you for the lunch, Duncan,' she breathed girlishly. 'I trust I can count on your support.'

'The world is a small place for a woman with a map, Kiki,' he smiled.

'I know.'

'Let me explain one key topographical feature in the lie of the land.' They were outside now, on the pavement. 'I've given 30 years of my life to *The Times*, man and boy: whoever gets this job is going to do things my way for a while . . .'

'You know what, Duncan? I reckon we'll get along just fine,' Kiki said, and curled her large waxy lips into something resembling a pout.

'Oh, would you fax your CV over to my office when you get home?'

She nodded and smiled. But inside Kiki was even more anxious than when she'd arrived at the restaurant. She didn't have a resumé. What she had were yawning great gaps in her life. There were things about Kiki Cox that you wouldn't want to know, that she didn't want you to know, that she would go to the greatest lengths for as long as she could to conceal from prying eyes and long lenses. It was vital that her secrets stay right off the record. As she strode back to her car as if on a mission, Kiki mused that the CV she had two hours to concoct would be the greatest story she'd ever written.

Campbell watched her as he headed for his own car. In spite of the fact that she had stirred raw sensations deep within him that he hadn't admitted to in a decade, his face was contorted with bitter and twisted rage. He didn't look as if he wanted to get along with anybody . . . not even a taut, feisty blonde with hard breasts and a your-place-or-mine smile.

4

Sir Anthony George sat behind the wheel of the highly polished racing green Morgan sportster. The engine of the two-seater convertible idled in the gridlocked West End traffic. Inside, the heater pumped out warm air. Outside, the traffic crawled across the gritted tarmac beneath a gunmetal sky.

Sir Anthony and Zelda Lee Powers were enjoying one of those 'discussions' that make married life so interesting.

'So who's holding the fort for you at the *Gazette*?' he asked, because he wanted to change the subject.

'Ah, Morty's editing it by remote control, same as ever.'

'When are you going back?'

'About the same time you get your third set of teeth.'

'What do you mean?'

'I'm not,' she said, matter-of-fact.

'What?'

'I'm not GOING back,' Zelda said. 'Colour me gone. Outtathere, history, cut, finito, kaputski, roll those credits. An editor dies, and a star is born. Goodbye baby and A-MEN.'

'What happened?' her husband asked.

'I resigned yesterday.'

They drove in silence for maybe half a minute, nudging forward in the stop-go traffic.

'You might have called me,' Anthony said eventually.

'Yeah, well, I was busy, packing up, you know how that is,' Zelda said, giving her gleaming teeth an energetic work-out on another stick of sugar-free gum.

'You seem to have had time to book the theatre for this absurd press conference,' Anthony said coldly.

'Look, I'm in crisis here and you're critiquing the colour of the ambulance,' Zelda said, her voice all snarky. 'I only heard the whisper about The Boss wanting a femme to helm *The Times* from a guy on the City desk while my assistant was clearing out my things. I had to JAM, Tony, I had to move right away. Everything's riding on this *Times* gig, baby. If I don't get it, I'll be through. If I'm successful, we'll make Harry Evans and Tina Brown look like they're running a salad bar.'

'Was it anything to do with this Morgan libel case, you leaving the *Gazette*?'

'Why do you always have to put such a negative spin on things, Tony?'

'I'm just asking a simple question,' he said.

'Did chilling the cocktails have anything to do with sinking the *Titanic*?' Zelda retorted. 'Over here, you call it tidying up the quotes. Over there, they call it actionable. If this Femi-Nazi whacademic makes me a party to her suit against the *Gazette*, Jesus . . .' She let the sentence hang in the warm, stifling air, and stared out at the traffic all around them.

Zelda was upset, worried about being dragged into the lawsuit, bruised by the shock of getting the bullet, by the stigma of blowing it. But her instincts told her that she couldn't open up to Anthony, show him the pain curdling inside her. Not now. They had to get to know each other all over again. Everyone said what a great couple they were, the brassy Brooklyn babe who'd brawled her way up from the gutter, and the handsome English Gentleman of Her Brittanic Majesty's Press Corps who knew the correct knife with which to carve up his rivals over dinner. The sex was great, and whenever she called him at three a.m for his take on the latest Royal scandal, he always had an amusing anecdote to murmur over the wire.

But now that she'd been deep-sixed by the *Gazette*, she wondered how their frantic, transatlantic show-marriage would play in the real world of bills, parking spaces and toothpaste-sharing. The balance of power in their relationship would undoubtedly shift: she needed him, not just to spin-doctor her career, but for emotional support, too. In New York, she'd drawn emotional sustenance from a series of delicious, ravishing, hardbodied guys with tight buttocks, all of whom eventually experienced 'Erectile Dysfunction', and all of whom Zelda had brought out of their closet. She'd treated them like girlfriends – they would gossip, and model clothes, and listen intently to each others' endless, aimless worries about which restaurant, which party in what outfit, which hot stock, which gorgeous guy and other crucial minutiae of Metropolitan life. But the libel case meant she wouldn't be shooting the breeze with any male models at the Russian Tea Room for a while. She had to fight her campaign in London.

From her monthly commutes across the pond for weekends of passion with her husband, she knew this grim, smoky city had 40 faces, some familiar, none to be relied on. All Zelda Lee had going for her was her reputation, her instincts, and her man.

'But hey,' she said, lobbing a tissue from the car window into the wicker bicycle basket of a passing Sloane Ranger, 'I don't have to tell you that for the purpose of getting hired by International News, we don't know Morgan and her stupid libel suit from a sack of shit, right? Don't even THINK about mentioning it.'

Anthony was fiddling with the radio, muttering about some Noel Coward programme.

'Where IS this fucking place?' Zelda said.

'Zelda, I don't think you understand. Doing something like this could be a terrible miscalculation. In New York, it might be kosher to hold a press conference to pitch for a job while the previous incumbent's still warm in the ground. But in this country it will seem in incredibly poor taste.'

'I lead from the front. And if they don't like it, they can suck my giblets. You know, Anthony, sometimes you just gotta ask for what you want, 'cos if you don't let people know what you want, how can you expect them to GIVE it to you?'

'But there are ways of asking. And times.'

'That's your problem, Tony. That's why you're editing that crappy little *Daily Sketch* rather than the *New York Daily News*. You could've HAD that job, I'd fixed Morty – it was yours for the asking. But you BLEW it. Never reinforce failure, Anthony. Didn't you say that to me one time?'

She sneezed again, and fumbled inside her Louis Vuitton tote for more tissues.

'You should've telephoned me and told me what was going on. I could've made some calls,' Anthony said, 'had a word in the right ear.'

'Tony, I gotta do what I gotta do. I'm not some little bimbo running to her sugar daddy to fight her battles for her.'

'But why hold it in a theatre, Zelda? The £18,000 hire fee is just a tad extravagant for someone who doesn't have a job.'

'I told you already, Morty gave me a hundred grand payoff. So I owe some money round town, what do I care? Either you're on the boat or you're off the boat.' Zelda dabbed more powder on her nose. 'Get with the programme, baby.'

'But don't you think you're being rather optimistic?' he persisted. 'It's Saturday. And while getting this job might be jolly important to you, in the scheme of things, most people couldn't care less who the next editor of *The Times* is going to be.'

'Tony, the place'll be packed to the rafters with hacks, SRO, trust me.'

'Look, I know this market, Zelda. This is a terrible blunder. It's not too late to pull out – just pay your respects to Temple and I'll come to some arrangement with the theatre management to cover the booking fee. We'll say there must've been a misunderstanding, that you were jetlagged.'

'Tony, getting a job like this is like running for OFFICE. You've got to CAMPAIGN. Get out, meet and greet, show some teeth, do a little aggressive hospitality. Press the flesh and flesh the press. You got those press packs?'

'They're in the boot, Zelda, you put them there yourself.'

He spotted a parking space, and swung the car towards it.

'Goddamn, it's cold,' Zelda said as Anthony took the press packs out of the boot.

'Zelda Lee Powers – Synergistic Editor Challenging The Times Into the 21st Century,' he read off the front cover. 'Did that ludicrous psychic of yours in New York make that up?'

'Tony,' she said firmly, as they made their way to the theatre, 'don't play me to the left, baby. I need you on my team.'

'Play me to the left?' said Sir Anthony, turning round to ask her what her latest vandalism of the Queen's English might actually mean. But Zelda wasn't there. He looked behind him, and saw her sitting on her bottom. 'Are you all right?'

'Shit,' she said, raising her derrière from the treacherous, slippery pavement, aided as if from nowhere by a passerby with short, gelled hair who was zipped into a purple ski jacket. 'Thanks,' she said, flashing him her best thousand-watt smile. 'Why don't they grit the fucking sidewalk?' she complained to her husband. 'If I'm injured, I'll sue the goddamn Council's ass off.'

'Don't worry, darling,' said Anthony, dying to get in from the cold. 'It was just a tumble.'

She followed him round to the theatre's stage door, cussing and flicking filthy slush from her expensive sable coat. Sir Anthony handed the press packs to a minion and introduced himself to the duty manager.

'I'm afraid not many people have pitched up,' he told the Editor apologetically.

'How many's not many?' Sir Anthony asked.

'Well, four, actually. There's a man from BBC radio, a couple of crew from CNN, and a nice Welsh woman from the *UK Press Gazette*, Jean someone.'

'Don't tell my wife. I'll get her straight out behind the podium.'

'Shit,' Zelda Lee said, examining the spectacles hanging from a diamante cord around her neck. 'I think I broke my glasses. Oh my GAAAAAAAAD. How am I gonna read off the autocue? Never mind, I'll busk it. Which way is Make-Up?'

'I don't think we've got time,' Sir Anthony sighed. 'Just go out there and do your stuff. I've arranged for someone to distribute the press packs.'

'OK, OK, don't hassle me, Tony. I've got to get centred.'

'But we're already ten minutes late! If you keep the hacks waiting they'll leave, and you won't . . .'

'Anthony, give me another fucking Kleenex and shut UP. I need to focus right now, give myself permission to empower the winningest me that I can be.' Zelda stood in the wings. 'Anthony, I want you to take a moment to share the ritual of energising my powerspace,' she commanded.

'Oh no,' he groaned, 'I'm not doing that bloody chanting again.'

'An-ton-eeee . . .' she warned.

He rolled his eyes. No one could see him. Zelda had made the cheerleading squad at High School. It had been one of the genuinely happier periods of her life, when the worst thing that had ever happened was when Brad Beauregarde, the school's star quarterback, had dumped her when he discovered she'd pulled a train for 35 of his fellow players on the football team. Brad was now running a Dodge dealership in Muskogee. Zelda had enormous belief in the power of chanting.

She began to execute a series of curious movements, half-chorus girl, half T'ai Chi trancedancer. 'Newspapers, newpapers, read 'em read 'em read 'em. Go get 'em, Zeelee Powers, and beat 'em beat 'em beat 'em,' she began intoning. Anthony stood rooted to the spot, exasperated with frustration and embarrassment. 'Anthony, you're clouding my focus,' she scolded, breaking off halfway through the second repetition.

Anthony recognised that voice, the whim of iron. He knew what would happen if he didn't fall in with her wishes: she would make his life indefinitely and utterly miserable. He closed his eyes, and with all the enthusiasm of a small boy threatened with a haircut before a visit to an elderly aunt, he began to mouth her mantra.

'You're not doing the STEPS, Anthony,' she cried. 'Come ON! You KNOW how I get if the ritual isn't done exactly right, I get anxious. And when I get anxious I want food. And when I want food I have to eat it. And when I've eaten it I get tense because of my diet. And when I get tense I get nauseous. And when I get nauseous I projectile-vomit until . . .'

'Miss Powers?' came a voice from the dank corridor.

'Who wants to know?' snapped Zelda, swinging round to face the stocky little man in the purple ski jacket who had helped her up in the street.

'Darren Clarkson, Lozanc Investigations,' he announced, handing her a piece of paper with a curl of red ribbon dangling from it.

Zelda stared at it, sitting in her hand. 'WAIT a moment . . .'

'Sorry,' he said flatly. 'Just doing my job.'

'What is it?' Sir Anthony asked, as the short-haired man walked out of the theatre back into the slushy streets.

'I'll give you three guesses, Tough Guy,' Zelda snarled, handing him the document and sneezing again. 'I feel lousy.'

'Look, Zelda, I'll just go out and apologise to the hacks, say you caught flu on the plane . . .'

'Goddamn it, NO, Tony,' Zelda said. 'Do you have any idea how much this means to me? Do you know how badly I want to edit *The Times*? I want it so bad I can taste it. I want it more than food, I want it more than sex, I want it and I mean to HAVE it. For the past 72 hours, for the past 5,000 miles, I've been thinking of nothing else, Tony, NOTHING. I'm tough. I've been around the block, I know all the angles. And that job's mine. No one's going to stop me, no crappy little private dick, no fascist rules that are so unspoken that no one's supposed to know them, nothing, nothing, NOTHING is gonna take it away from me. *Capisce?*'

She marched past him, stomped up the stairs and stormed on to the stage, leaving Anthony holding the paper with its dangling red ribbon as if it were some stranger's soiled baby. He turned it over. It was sealed. The lights came up and he heard *Thus Spake Zarathrustra* boom from the sound system . . .

Anthony broke the red seal and unfolded the sheet to read: 'Supreme Court of New York. Subpoena. You, Zelda Lee Powers, are hereby ordered to appear as defendant in the trial of Morgan versus Mortimer Media Communications Inc . . .'

5

Mandi nodded at Jim, the security guard who was always on watch each Saturday at the International News gatehouse. He'd once been. a dentist in Forest Hill. It was all a lifetime ago, before recession, depression, and the only way the poor could afford dental treatment was to opt for full and final extraction.

Ever since the pitched battles that had marked the opening of the new technology plant more than a decade ago, the Corporation's European headquarters had been protected by extensive, expensive security equipment. Yet somehow too many of the cranks, loonies and psychos who are unfathomably attracted to news organizations – perhaps by the dark flame of publicity – still managed to find their way through the elaborate net to the *Sunday Post*'s offices.

'How's the truth decay, Jim?'

'Mustn't grumble.'

'I know,' Mandi said, her smile revealing a smear of lipstick on her off-white teeth. 'If you did, it might get worse.'

As she headed for the High Road, the odour of manky drains and rank entropy assaulted her nostrils with customary savagery, and the East End's dank, wet, almost medieval desperation crept over her like a cold sweat. Out there were crumbly Victorian terraces, boarded-up shops with weather-beaten 'To Let' signs, Baptist temples made over into Mosques, market streets strewn with filthy cabbage leaves and cardboard boxes, and rack upon rack of the kind of cheap leggings and T-shirts she wouldn't even use to clean up after her cat. The thought had often flashed through her mind, but today, for some reason, the image was more vivid than ever: here she was, walking the same streets that

Jack the Ripper had once prowled. For all our valiant attempts to create mind-boggling technology that can simulate the actual thought patterns of the human brain, Mandi mused, we still haven't even come close to explaining the evil of the Ripper and his latter-day scions.

She crossed over the road and walked a hundred yards or so along a narrow pavement in the shadow of the high brick wall that guards the Royal Mint. Above and ahead of her, a filthy red, white and blue locomotive rumbled across the railway bridge that loomed over the potholed road. A few passengers stared vacantly through the grime-encrusted windows at the frozen sludge below. A wan, late winter sunlight strained through a grey, forbidding cloud blanket loaded with still more snow.

In the scowling sky a cloud caught her eye – its shape made Mandi think of a pregnant woman's breasts. One woman in particular, a woman she had known once, but had tried to wipe from her memory. A fresher, younger, more hopeful woman who came to her in those rare unguarded moments when everyone was out of her face, when she was undistracted by the pressing message, the familiar womb of home, or the rolling fury of the next deadline. That younger woman was Mandi herself, the way she once was: happy and hopeful, glad to be alive in this world, enthralled by the new life she carried within her. But her joy had been short-lived, and the baby wrenched from her arms before she had even grown used to the smell of it.

Now, as she strode through the dark tunnel below the bridge, yanking up the collar of her coat against the snarl of the north-easterly wind, that younger woman she had once been retreated into the shadows: silent, invisible, but always there, lurking, peering over her shoulder, above and below and around her every second of every day, as if waiting for something, always waiting . . .

Her stiletto heels reverberated on the dry flagstones of the tunnel, clickety clickety click. It was Saturday, so the traffic was light. But suddenly Mandi could detect a shape clattering towards her on the road. No-one lived here anymore, not since the War, when Hitler's bombs had blitzed the buildings to rubble. Later, the property developers had moved in on the dull dead end of the old dockside warehouses, and the area had begun to take shape as a thriving commercial district. Now that the train had passed, Mandi could hear the clip clop clip of hooves on the slushy road. She picked up the pace, her own heels clipping the pavement, click click, click click, click click. Now she heard it: the eerie toll of an oncoming bell. A dirty rag and bone man with half-loaded cart and half-starved horse oozed by. His accent was so thick she could barely make out the lyric of his cry. For a moment it sounded like 'Bring Out Your Dead.'

The wind blasted her face, chilling her skin to thin ice. She turned the corner into Pinchbeck Street where the wind flung the tavern's sign precariously to and fro. The flapping board depicted a magnificent golden bird soaring high and proud in the night sky, above letters which spelled out The Eagle Star. Nailed to the bricks was another notice, etched in brass and in need of a good polish. 'Members Only', it read.

Once upon another time this had been the local boozer. But 15 years ago The Boss had bought up some disused warehouse space and retooled it as the home of his London newspaper operation. Today, it housed two other tabloids as well as the *Post* and *The Times*. So now the Evil Star, as known to one and all, was a private drinking club for International News drones. One more deft move in the corporatisation of the planet, Mandi thought. Another dubious step in the transformation of Great Britain into UK PLC: a place where schools measured how cost-effective they could be at saturating young synapses with competitive, easily absorbed learn 'n' earn modules; where hospitals niche-marketed and cost-analysed themselves to treat only the most profitable diseases; a country in which people would soon start charging each other to say Hello! We're all accountants now, every man his own auditor. I've seen the future and it's tax-deductible, thought Mandi gloomily as she wondered how on earth she was going to deal with Kettle and his outrageous expenses.

She pushed open the door of the Evil Star with her fleshy shoulder and slipped with a smile and a wink past the dodgy, doddery commissionaire. She slithered easily among the fuggy crowd of hacks chitting and chatting about this and that and nothing at all at the tops of their voices, above some old Madonna track on the laser CD jukebox.

The Evil Star was warm. Press photographs dating back to the 1940s adorned the walls, and a dusty collection of some 30 or 40 neckties hung from a beam like colourful nooses. Somehow or other the capricious proprietor had established the right to remove the tie of any member or guest which took his fancy. He would wear it for a while – hours, sometimes weeks – before adding it to his collection. Since the recession, though, he hadn't bothered much.

Mandi navigated her way round a corner past Dinsdale Cheeseman, who'd been fired and retrieved by International News more times than the space shuttle, and nodded to Mungo Morgan, the paparazzo who'd grabbed the snatch shots of Fergie chatting with hunt saboteurs that the *Post* had splashed across page one last week. She turned the next corner into an area with tables and chairs where she saw Casper Reid, the oleaginous, perpetually ex-adolescent pop-hack on the *Post*'s six-day-a-week tabloid sister. What was he doing here on a Saturday, she wondered? Aha – talking to the manager of the latest acne and ecstasy band of chart-topping young bum bandits whose 'biography' he hoped to write in exchange for mega hype in the column he controlled. The column was called Wired, and it was weird. Not 'Doris-have-you-read-this?' weird, but 'rhymes-with-pony-and-trap' weird, because Reid had a nose not for news but for shopping-bags full of expensive, dusty, powdered white candy.

Finally, she found Kettle in a corner of the back room. He was playing cards with three other men: Jamie Stott, a PR at the Department of Trade; a *Sunday Times* environment reporter, and Adrian Lin, the *Sunday Post*'s local government writer. Every story Lin filed was about minor officials who had become transvestites or, occasionally, vampires. She knew that one day she would have to whack him. The prospect did not appeal: two or three times a year he would take her to an obscure Sichuan restaurant and order dishes that weren't on the menu in his native Cantonese. It was a tough call: on the one hand, he was the paper's only ethnic Chinese, and The Boss's minions had recently issued a crisp 16-page memo on the importance of multi-culturalism in staff composition. Lin was worth 25 PC points, easy. On the other hand, the *Post* never ran local government stories. What the *Post* ran was stories about sex, violence, celebrities, animals, kids and money, so Lin's lines never made the paper. He was going to have to go, Mandi thought, only not now.

'A word,' she whispered into Kettle's hair. He regarded her with a pained expression. She returned it with interest.

'Fold, check my stake in for the next round, OK boys?'

Mandi didn't like his attitude. 'I want you to hear this too, Lin,' she said. The other poker players suddenly remembered how thirsty they were getting. 'Kettle,' she began, 'Nigel's just been complaining about your expenses.'

'Has he, by Jove? Why?'

'Don't get up, Adrian,' Mandi commanded the Hong Kong refugee. She wanted him to hear this so he'd tell all the others, create a buzz in the newsroom that would get back to Plant, let him know she was on top of it. '"Item, Camel, burial of same,"' Mandi said, drawing up a chair. Kettle's expression was granite, stonewalling her. Mandi leaned forward, in his face, angry now. 'Don't you piss on my leg and try and tell me it's raining,' she hissed. 'This is fraud, Kettle, and you're getting a warning for it.'

Kettle launched into an explanation as convoluted as it was implausible. He was babbling on about how thirsty people get in the desert, so thirsty they'll drink anything: water from the car radiator, urine, blood . . .

'Shut up!' Mandi interrupted. 'Listen to me, Kettle, and listen good. If you're caught fiddling your swindle sheet, it's not just you who's suspect. There's mud on my column too. It's a question of trust, of credibility. You know the way the wind's blowing round here at the moment. Living in Lala Land is changing the way The Boss does business, and management are on the warpath. If I look bad, you're going to feel bad. Very bad.' She surveyed the poker chips disdainfully. 'If you want to piss your paypacket against a wall, that's your business. But don't expect me to subsidize it.'

Kettle looked at Lin, then at Mandi. 'This wouldn't have anything to do with there suddenly being an empty chair behind the Editor's desk at *The Times*,' he asked innocently, a twinkle in his bloodshot eye, 'would it?'

Mandi's eyes blazed like hot coals. Her pupils shrank to pinpoints. She took a deep breath. 'Make that a written warning,' she hissed, her tone level and measured. 'Your last.'

She caught Lin's eye and, with half a glance, told him to get lost. Kettle was staring into his beer. He looked up at her, and she noticed that his expression had changed. 'I'm sorry, Aitch,' he said. 'Really I am.'

The crime ace bit down on his bottom lip and stared dolefully up at her. Mandi sensed desperation. She could smell the fear seeping from his pores. 'It's Babs,' he said. 'The missus. I haven't told anyone at the shop because, well, you know . . .'

'Told them what?'

'Well, last year she started having these turns, you know, her arms and legs went to sleep, pins and needles, really bad, only they wouldn't wake up again. Then she started getting sick, spending all day in bed. It isn't like her, not Babs, but she wouldn't go to the doctor, see, not until just before Christmas one afternoon, she couldn't get out of bed. I called the ambulance. I took her to Harley Street the next day. They said . . . they said it's multiple sclerosis.'

She couldn't stand to see a grown man cry. Mandi fumbled in her battered Fendi bag, produced a shredded Kleenex, and squeezed his shoulder.

'Every day, it's another little thing,' he said. 'It just gets worse and worse. She's wasting away in front of my eyes, Aitch, I can't take it.' He gulped and looked at her, staring right inside her eyes. 'What it is, right, I bought this chair-lift so she can get up and down the stairs. When we moved from Osterley . . . she always wanted a bungalow near her mum. But then her mum died and I . . .' Kettle shook his head, silently pleading with his Editor. 'The bank, they said they'd bounce the mortgage cheque unless I covered it. I had to do something.'

'Is this true, Kettle?'

'On my mother's life, Aitch, swear to God,' he said, holding his hand up. 'Crate of Bibles.'

Neither of them spoke.

'I'm four months behind with the house payments now,' Kettle said eventually. 'But it's worth it. When I see her little face, 'cos she can get downstairs and make us a cup of tea . . .' He shook his head again. 'It's worth it.'

There was another silence.

'This lift, it's one of those things you attach to the banister, is it?'

'Yeah, something along those lines,' Kettle said, nodding vigorously. 'That's the ticket.'

'How much did it cost you?'

Kettle's face immediately assumed a pained expression. 'Seventeen hundred, all tolled,' he said. 'What with getting the engineer to install it and all the doings.'

Mandi searched his face, but found only the likely story that may or may not be true. Looking at him, deadpan, she fumbled around again inside her handbag. Cussing as she plonked her chequebook in a puddle of beer, she wrote out a cheque for £1700 and made it payable to him. Then she ripped at the perforations. 'If you say one word about this,' she warned, 'and I mean one word, to anyone, then I promise you, Kettle, you are a dead man.'

'Aitch,' he said, gazing at the cheque. 'Really? Are you sure?'

'A dead man,' she repeated. 'And I don't want any more shit from Plantlife about your exes.'

'No,' he said, folding the cheque and tucking it carefully into his wallet. 'There won't be. You can count on me.'

Mandi frowned. 'If you get into difficulties, come and see me. We'll secure a loan for you through the company, all right?'

He looked like an orphan clutching his first-ever birthday present. 'When do you need it back?'

'When you can pay me,' said Mandi almost kindly, and stared again at the poker chips. 'Good hand?'

Kettle shrugged. 'Depends,' he said, 'On what they've got. It's the pressure, see . . .'

Mandi turned the others' cards, then his. She spun around in her seat and caught Lin's eye. He came over. 'Kettle's cashing out.'

He looked at her. 'Thanks Mandi,' he said. 'Thanks. Really.'

'Don't mention it,' she said, getting up. 'Really.'

Mandi looked at the bromide on her desk. '747 HORROR HELL TOUCHDOWN IN TAMPA, 19,000 DEAD'. 'Is that official?' she asked.

'Well it's 18,215 actually,' Worell admitted, 'last time I looked.'

Mandi shook her head. 'Change that second deck: 23,000 – no, 25,000 Feared Dead in Jumbo Superbowl Disaster . . . Oh Christ, Oliver, what is it?'

'It'll be the fifth remake since the first edition went,' warned Worell. 'The Stone are going nuts down there.'

'That's what they're paid for,' Mandi retorted. 'They've no idea how many people are going to die, neither have we, neither have the punters. Dead people don't sue. If you won't get that page remade, I'll go down to the Stone and do it myself.'

'Yeah,' Worell said, backing away. 'Right.'

'Move!' Mandi shouted. Her secretary proffered a cup of strong black coffee. 'Thanks, Oscar.'

The secretary pointed outside. 'That old lady,' he said, hesitation clouding his voice. 'Aitch, she's still there. I've tried everything. But she won't go away. She keeps saying it's a matter of life and death.'

Mandi slammed her cup down on her desk and spilt hot coffee everywhere. 'Fuck fuck fuck, why is it always us?' she shouted. She stopped herself, closed her eyes for a moment and took a deep breath. 'OK,' she said, 'send her in.'

Her name, she said, was Pargeter, Emily Pargeter, and she'd travelled down from Cirencester. Bought a Senior Citizens' Superweekend Minibreak, and they were quite reasonable really, but you had to book seven days in advance, so it was fortunate that her grandson in Walthamstow had a spare room . . .

'Mrs Pargeter, I hope you won't think I'm being rude, but this is a Sunday newspaper and Saturday night is the busiest time of our week. Please tell me whatever it is you came to say.'

She seemed taken aback.

'It's Miss Pargeter. You see, I never married, during the War I was engaged to . . .' she began again in her well-spoken Cotswold tone.

The phone rang, mercifully, and Mandi said: '. . . then set it in Schoolbook, 72-point bold, Declaration of War, house style, what's the matter with you lot down there? Miss Pargeter, get to the point, will you please, I'm a very busy woman,' she said, turning back to her unwelcome visitor. Then Mandi's voice dropped to a whisper. 'Please.'

Just in time, she'd remembered the magic word.

She lived in a converted mill in Gloucestershire, it belonged to her nephew, the banker, but he was in the Bahamas now . . .

Mandi's mind was churning. The Midlands editions would have rolled out with 18,000 Dead . . . would they have gone yet? Was it worth holding them for the remake, risking the delay? She'd be into over-run and the papers might be late, and that could mean lost sales. But the *Mirror* had gained ground in the Midlands last week, the MD had told her to beef up their editions . . .

'. . . so I went outside and that was when I saw it,' the old dear was droning on. 'Hovering above the bottom of my garden.'

'What was?' Mandi asked. 'What, precisely, was hovering at the bottom of your garden?'

'The spaceship, of course,' Miss Pargeter explained patiently. 'I told you. That was when they gave me the message.'

'The message,' Mandi repeated.

'They had a message for us, all of us dwelling on this planet, the warning. The final warning.'

Mandi flopped back in her chair and considered . . . hedging, that was what she was doing, weighing off the revenue the *Sunday Post* might make by having the latest, bestest death toll on the newsstands in the Midlands as against the hard cash and possible lost sales if the updated paper missed the trains. Why hadn't they got the Dudley printing plant on-line by now? She'd told Patsy, the MD time and time again, she'd even taken Brett Collins aside at the conference at Cliveden last November. But would he listen? Would he fuck. No, they'd never listen, not until it was too late. Not until something like this happened. You try and do your superiors a favour, and end up taking the blame for their failure to act on your advice. No good turn goes unpunished . . .

'. . . and they said that unless we were ready to receive their transmissions through the television set, they'd destroy everything, everything in Britain. Then the world. My duty seems clear. I voted for Mrs Thatcher, you know. She had the stomach of a man and goodness, oh, what was that speech? I was a teacher during the War, I really ought to know. That was how I met Reginald, you see, he was stationed at . . .'

'Miss Pargeter,' Mandi cut in. She reached for her scrap pad. 'I'm very glad you came here. Really.' She lowered her tone and swivelled her eyes. 'This is clearly important, vital information. It is far too important for us to deal with. It's a matter of national security.'

'Yes . . .' the old lady said, leaning forward, adopting Mandi's confidential tone. 'Thank goodness I came. I'm so relieved. I can't tell you how relieved, this has been weighing so heavily on my mind, what one should do exactly . . .'

Mandi finished scribbling on the pad, tore off the sheet and placed it in the little old lady's hand. 'Go to this address. Ask for Security. They'll advise you exactly what steps we should take next.'

Miss Pargeter unfolded the paper with the agonizing slowness of the chronically arthritic. She peered at what Mandi had written there. '85 Vauxhall Cross? The big green building?' she said doubtfully. 'But that's the Ministry of Defence. The MI6 headquarters.'

'How do you know that?'

The old lady's face assumed a kindly, patient expression. 'Because,' she said, 'they were the ones who sent me here . . .'

6

Mira Freer Farmer arrived at Brands Hatch 90 minutes late – on a battered moped.

'That's her? The Editor of *Verve* magazine?' said the track's receptionist to Peter Watson, the square-jawed young PR man who was representing the sports car company. They could hardly believe their eyes.

Mira was wearing a well-weathered green parka with a moth-ravaged grey fur trim, square-toed black biker boots with silver buckles, and tortoise-shell Armani frames that were taped together with Elastoplast. The receptionist was genuinely puzzled: she read *Verve* magazine every month, had a copy on her desk, in fact she'd just been skimming through it, soaking up her monthly glamour allowance between bites of sandwich.

'I do hope so,' Watson said impatiently, glancing yet again at his Brietling wrist-watch. They'd have to get a move on, he thought, there was a Formula Three practice scheduled for two-thirty.

'She looks kinds of anoraky,' the receptionist giggled through a mouthful of cheese and pickle.

Pete Watson decided that what Mira looked like was kind of chunky, but he was far too well-bred to say so. The door of the hut flew open and the three-times winner of the Magazine Editor of the Year title stumbled in, knocking over an ashtray as she dropped her crash helmet on to one of the cracked brown leatherette chairs. 'Christ, it's cold out there,' she said, removing a leather mitten. 'Hi, you must be the guy from Cosworth. Mira Freer Farmer.'

Pete Watson realised that she was pumping his hand. He felt her firm dry grip, met her pixieish green eyes for a moment. Her cheeks were as rosy red as Cox's English Pippins.

'I don't suppose you've got such a thing as a Bloody Mary, have you?' Mira asked nicely. 'I'm fucking petrified.'

'Well there's nothing to be frightened of, I can assure you. Despite its reputation you'll find the new Vendetta is surprisingly user-friendly. Besides, I'll be with you all the way. But since we seem to be running a bit behind schedule . . .'

'Not petrified, frightened, thicko. Petrified as in petrified forest, as in stone bloody cold to the marrow of my bones. It's fucking freezing out there, wind chill factor 23, in case you haven't noticed.'

'I've arranged a little light lunch at the clubhouse after you've put her through her paces.'

'Her? Her?' snorted Mira. 'Why is it,' she demanded, turning to the girl at the desk, 'that men always humanise cars in the feminine gender?'

'I've got no idea,' stammered the girl.

'Something to do with penis extension, powerlessness,' Mira said, matter-of-fact, her eyes scanning the desk and alighting on a cheese sandwich with a dainty bitehole taken right from the middle. 'You don't mind, do you?' Mira had already swept the secondhand food straight to her mouth and was munching it down greedily. 'Can't eat breakfast, can never keep it down,' she said, scoffing. 'Always a bloody nightmare when you're on a job, all those happy eaters, makes me sick.'

'What are you doing?' Pete asked nervously. An anxious tone coloured his voice.

'What does it bloody look like?' Mira sneered, her mouth still full. She'd already kicked off her boots, and was now unzipping and stepping out of her baggy jeans. 'Oh by the way, this guy will probably turn up in a while with a camcorder. Frightfully common I know, but he is Brazilian and he is my husband, so do try to accommodate him, won't you?'

Pete watched as the parka joined the jeans in a crumpled heap on the floor. Mira sat down on the chair next to her helmet, put her boots back on and stood up again.

'That's it outside, isn't it?' she said, with a toss of her long, lustrous red hair. 'The black one.'

'Why are you . . . that is, I mean . . .' Pete stared uneasily at the vision before him. Mira was standing there as if dressed for a cocktail party or a First Night, in a short, sharp, shocking little black dress. Its sequins winked scornfully in the cold light. There were also black stockings, his weakness . . . She stared straight at him, and took off her glasses. In less than 60 seconds, she'd transformed herself from a snagged blue-stocking into a billion dollar babe. The receptionist looked up from her magazine, noticed the dress and wondered . . . hadn't she seen it somewhere before?

'I'm just dressing the way most of my readers would if they actually owned and drove the bloody thing, what are you gawping at?' She lit a Stuyvesant from the soft-pack she'd stashed between her breasts.

'It's just that most motoring correspondents don't quite, uh, dress with the same sense of style as you, Miss Freer Farmer,' Pete remarked as they made their way to the car.

'Don't expect many of them arrive on mopeds either,' Mira giggled, wrapping his coat around her. 'It's my husband's actually, my Triumph's in the shop, bloody camshaft's gone again, it's been there three bloody weeks, honestly, anyone'd think I'd asked them to give it a heart transplant. So,' she said, appraising the car they were now approaching, 'this it then, eh?'

'I'll give you the press pack over lunch,' Pete said. 'But broadly speaking, we're talking V-12 in line pushing 352 bhp at six and half revs. Del Mitchell from the *Indy* drove it this morning and told me it made the new Dodge Viper seem quite agricultural, very pedestrian indeed.'

They were facing each other over the roof of the gleaming, low-slung, smoothly angled black monster. Mira had contrived to work her way round to the driver's side, and was snapping her fingers. Pete looked at her. 'Keys,' she commanded.

'Don't you need your glasses? I think you might've left them . . .'

'Plain glass, darling. Nothing at all wrong with my eyes. They're just a prop.'

'Do you have your driving licence?' he asked, moving round to her side of the car. 'I need to have it for this ridiculous bumph . . .'

'Not with me, I'm afraid. But then again I don't have my passport either. That used to be a sackable offence when I worked on the *Telegraph*, not having your passport with you. This isn't going to be a problem, is it?'

'Miss Freer Farmer . . . Mira . . . you'll appreciate that only 20 Vendettas are going to be manufactured each year. This is nearly a quarter of million pounds worth of machinery. I realise it's a bit of a bore, but the insurance people insist that all the paperwork's in order . . .'

'Oh well, if that's your attitude we might as well all go home then, mightn't we?' Mira said, suddenly sounding very bored. 'Perhaps you'd be good enough to let me use the telephone. Johnny Hesketh has some nice little racers here, I could probably take one of them for a spin.' She was moving away from him, back towards the hut. 'Seems ridiculous to come all this way and not have a go.'

'Wait a moment,' Pete said, madly juggling pros and cons in his mind. If *Verve* magazine didn't bother to acknowledge the Vendetta's existence for its small but perfectly formed, not to mention ludicrously rich readership, the car might as well not exist, since the only people with enough money to buy it wouldn't know it was there.

'Oh, what is it now?' she said, folding her arms, thus forcing her décolletage into an even deeper ravine. The Stuyvesant packet promptly popped out. She bent down to retrieve it, and his coat slid from her shoulders. Pete surveyed the gorgeous scenery as her tight skirt rode up over her hard thighs and fabulously curvy bottom, and felt rather alarmed.

'Well?' she said. 'Hurry up. I'm bloody freezing.'

Pete produced the insurance company's liability waiver and his Mont Blanc fountain pen. 'Just sign here,' he said. 'I'm sure you can fax me through a copy of your licence when . . .'

'Good boy,' she breathed approvingly, taking the paperwork across to the car, where she used its roof as a makeshift desk in order to dash off a lightning scrawl. 'There you are,' she said with a flourish.

Pete raced round and opened the door for her. 'Right,' he began.

'Look, would you mind getting in? I really am jolly cold, actually.'

He was sitting next to her in the passenger seat, droning on about gear positions: '. . . this particular one's a bit sticky between fourth and fifth because, off the record, it's a demo car and at this level of the market all demos are just a glorified prototype, but if you drop it into third and then double declutch . . .'

He noticed Mira looking at him in an odd sort of way. He felt his mind wandering helplessly from the task at hand, to how the Editor of *Verve* might look bent backwards over a sofa . . .

'Now what I suggest we do is go round out of the car park here and then take the third turning on the right which leads us on to the nursery track . . .'

Mira lay back in the ergonomically designed red leather seat. She inhaled deeply its scented embrace. There's nothing like that new car smell, she thought. Jesus. 'Are you going to give me those bloody keys, or are we going to sit here all day in stroke mode?'

'It's just that . . .' Pete began, conscious that a note of anxiety had invaded his register. '. . . It's just that this is a rather expensive motorcar, you know, and I want to make quite sure you're comfortable with . . .'

Mira glanced at the tachometer, the tyre pressure gauge, the on-board, at-a-glance, all-system diagnostic troubleshooter, and snapped her fingers again.

'It's just that, should anything go wrong . . .'

'Have you ever changed the oil filter on a Triumph Bonneville?' Mira asked.

'I don't think . . .'

'For God's sakes, thicko, nothing's going to go wrong. You were the one in such a rush to get on with it.' She leaned sumptuously towards him. He caught a subtle whiff of Guerlain. She held out her open palm. Pete obediently handed her the keys. She inserted and turned. At once there was a high-pitched hum: well-behaved, discreet, but loaded, to the tutored ear, with a warning of forbidden pleasures and dangerous curves ahead.

'OK, now if we just turn her gently round out of . . .'

Mira touched the clutch, selected a gear, tapped at the

throttle. The hum rose to a low, throaty roar. The Vendetta shot backwards at 50 mph. There was a crash, a bump and a jerk as it smashed to a halt.

'Christ,' groaned Pete.

'I meant to do that,' Mira scoffed, releasing the handbrake and shifting gears. The car sprang forward like a temperamental thoroughbred from the stalls.

'What the . . .' Pete was turning, looking through the narrow slatted back window. 'Fuck! You've flattened your moped.'

'Relax, big boy,' Mira soothed, shifting up and spinning the car round in a storm of flying gravel.

'Stop!' Pete cried. 'Stop, for Christsakes, I've got to check the damage.'

'What bloody damage?' Mira said, smiling at him. 'What's the point of spending the best part of half a mill on a ride if it can't hack a teeny little ding? Anyway, I thought this thing had reactive back bumpers.'

'Yes, but . . .' Pete began, but Mira had changed up, then up again. The speedo was showing 80 mph, 128 clicks. 'Mira, we don't go on to the track here, not here, no . . .'

'Chill out, baby', Mira yelled as the Vendetta careered through a bush and plunged down a grassy bank towards the main circuit.

'The main track's the other . . .'

'I've driven round here before,' Mira said. 'Millions of times.'

The car bounced on to the asphalt, and she had to change right down and swerve hard to make the bend.

'Mira, we're supposed to be on the nursery circuit, we're not insured for . . .'

Mira put her foot down defiantly and selected fifth as they hit the straight. The Vendetta responded with a gratifyingly high-pitched whine of pure unadulterated acceleration. 'What's your name?' she said.

'Peter Watson. Pete.'

'Michael Orlando's stepson, right?'

Pete answered with a nod, pinned back in his seat, watching as the needles rocketed through the triple digit barrier again, hearing the motor sweeten as she hit top gear, 160 mph, 180, 192 . . .

'I knew this rocket scientist once,' Mira was shouting. 'He told me that the sound of a good engine burn . . .' She downshifted, took the bends in neat succession, running back up through the gearbox, '. . . is a very sexy sound, it's like the high-pitched gasp of a woman's orgasm, but there's a definite unsteadiness to it . . .' She shifted again, and that moment the Vendetta began backfiring. 'Like that,' she said, staring dreamily at him. 'It's turbulence. It creates an emotional response . . .' She negotiated the chicane, eased back up again through the gears.

'Well yes, I suppose it does,' said Pete helplessly, talking to stop his teeth chattering. Was it his imagination, or had it suddenly become very cold indeed? 'At this end of the market, cars are all about . . .'

'Aren't you going to ask me why I'm doing this?' she said. 'Why I didn't send a . . .'

'Look out for the . . .' Pete leaned cross and tried to grab the wheel but she'd anticipated him and had already corrected. The car spun off the track. Suddenly there were bales of hay bouncing off the bonnet and a crash barrier racing towards them. Mira declutched down, threw the car hard to the right and accelerated away. She saw he was staring at her breasts, torn frantically between lust and fear.

'Pete, darling,' she said, taking her eyes off the road to enjoy his discomfort in his face, 'would you mind just reaching in to get me a cigarette, please . . .?'

7

Around the next bend, the gables of the track's clubhouse loomed into view. Suddenly Mira swerved the car off the road and tore across the driveway, narrowly missing a small tree.

'Jesus Christ!' Pete started to say but never got to finish, because Mira was dragging him from the car by his jaunty scarf. Too taken aback to find the words to protest, he allowed himself to be led through into the stone-flagged vestibule and across the hallway into an oak-panelled library.

She'd been here before: she knew her way around without even looking. Her lips never left his. He struggled to speak, but something almost menacing behind the pretty twinkle of her green eyes reduced him to a pathetic palmful of putty. She printed his face all over with warm, moist kisses. He practically fainted with lust. His eyes rolled in his hollow face. He was powerless, all out of control.

'Look, if this is about advertising,' he managed to blurt, 'I don't control the budget . . .'

'You silly boy,' Mira whispered. 'This is about something much more interesting than advertising.'

'What could be more interesting than advertising?' he moaned, not realising how stupid he sounded. He was too preoccupied with the sensation of her cold fingertips, dancing like dry icicles on his cheek-bones, stroking his neck, poking inside his shirt, bursting open the buttons.

'It's all about keeping it in the family. Maybe you can finish what your stepfather started. Let's try you for size, shall we?'

Pete gasped. So Mira and his father had been lovers! But even as the thought mortified him, it turned him on. Mira drew a sharp breath. 'How is your father these days, anyway?'

Pete drooped for a moment. 'It's not good, I'm afraid. He retired to the place in Tuscany to do his memoirs some time ago – but he hasn't actually written a word. Been bed-ridden now for several months. Inexplicable wasting illness, the specialists can't put their finger on it. He's had every test money can buy and the medical profession has invented. He's fading away before their very eyes.'

He stopped talking now, because Mira was brushing her fingers back and forth over his pelvis with a gently persistent rhythm. Her nipples hardened. She dragged a well-schooled tongue the entire length of his body. Then she pulled him towards the hearth, stripping him of inconvenient garments with all the determined intensity of a rampaging storm tearing laundry from a washing line. Pete sank to his knees on the matted mustard hearth rug. Huge logs glowed in the stone fireplace, and a dry, woody scent pervaded the warm room. A dopy old red setter glanced up from its snooze, and as Mira tore Pete's belt buckle from its moorings and fumbled his zip into open submission, the dog beat a desultory path to a lumpy burgundy leather armchair.

Mira dribbled a stream of saliva into her palms, rubbed them together, and with delicious appreciation showed Pete's biggest asset some real interest.

'Oh, yes,' he moaned. 'Bigger, bigger, bigger.'

He was grinding his hips against Mira's wristbones, and didn't even realise he was doing it. She wedged her knees between his legs, prising them apart still further, sinking her fingers into secret places, grasping at him and pumping rhythmically like a baker dealing with a morning's supply of raw dough.

'Now, now, now, you bitch!' Pete's strangled throat could barely utter the words. Mira hated her prey to talk during the act. She plunged her breast into his mouth to shut him up. Then she yanked his joystick into overdrive and sank downwards.

'Move, move, move!' he gasped in a voice he couldn't recognise. Mira thrust her hipbones against his, thrashing him like cresting waves slamming against rock, again and again and again, going for the burn. Together they screeched towards the inevitable, blazing fire, foaming water, a sizzling hot metal furnace . . .

Mira stopped just short of the wall. How she managed it preoccupied Pete for days afterwards. 'What happened?' he said lamely at the time. 'What the fuck happened?'

'The same thing that always happens,' Mira said quietly, pulling away from him. 'Fucking nothing. So near, I get so close, I get so fucking close . . .' She looked away – a little sadly, he fancied. 'But this screaming red light comes on, I suddenly remember who I am, I can't, I can't . . .' She shook her gorgeous head. 'No man's ever got me there. No one . . .' She stared into his eyes, her face hard yet softly sensual; hungry, yet bewildered. 'No one, no man's ever got me that far, taken me so close to the edge. Not since your stepfather.'

'What?'

'I was very young, of course. I miss him dreadfully sometimes. God, it's like someone stole a piece of my jigsaw or something. Oh fuck, it's useless, I can't explain.'

'Frustration,' Pete said, lying back.

'God, men are such dickheads,' she said. 'You think the Grand Prix is the only ticket to ride?' She leaned against him, and he could feel her breath hot against his ear. 'There's more than one way to skin this kitten.'

'You'll have to show me sometime,' he said, annoyance creeping into his voice now.

'Be a good little boy and pour me a large wicked drink.'

'So what did Dad have that I haven't got?'

Mira wasn't listening. She was frozen to the spot. She'd caught sight of the last thing she'd expected to see: her face on the television set, which was mumbling away to itself on a mahogany stand in the corner of the room. Zelda Lee Powers, that New York bitch from hell, was giving a press conference about *The Times* editorship. And the reporter seemed to be suggesting that she, Mira, might be up for the job too. Where did they get that picture of her, she wondered, it's at least a decade old, I look much better now. Wait a minute, who was that? Mandi Harry, editor of the *Sunday Post*? And Kiki Cox, the Australian ice sculpture who helmed *YES* Magazine. Lord, can they be serious?

'. . . he wants a new kind of newspaper, I'll give him a new kind of newspaper. That means new thinking, new angles, new ways of doing things,' came the abrasive American voice that sounded as if it had a five-pack wedge of gum in each cheek.

That's why, Zelda Lee Powers was saying, she'd resigned from her plum post at the *New York Gazette* and had flown straight to London. '. . . it's about time *The Times* had a female editor and that female should be me. I've prepared a brief presentation . . .'

As Zelda pitched into what a wonderfully rounded person she was, how successful a photographer of international repute her blessed son was, Pete turned away from the set, looked Mira directly in the eye and said, 'Well?' Mira looked like a delicious nude in a painting. She was sprawled out on the rug, nothing to the imagination, silent, absorbed, contained. 'Tell me, Mira, damn it, I've a right to know.'

'Why?' she snorted, looking up at him with angry green eyes. 'What right?'

Pete saw something moving behind her eyes that he had never seen anywhere before. It was as if there were another person or even a wild animal inside her head, watching him and making calculations that could only spell the utmost danger for him. The animal was called Need.

'You want me to put you out of your misery? Or dig you deeper into it? *Post coitum omnes homines tristam* – all the same. It's so predictable. It's sad. Well,' she yawned, rising up on to her elbows, 'since you're asking, I'll tell you. The agony aunts say that size doesn't count, but it does. It counts big-time. All the way to the bank and back again. You and your stepfather? Marrow and mange-tout, darling. By the time Michael had managed to wedge that thing in, I was howling my way to seventh heaven. I didn't even need to move a muscle.'

'Oh,' said Pete, embarrassed now, and turning his pink face away from her to pour her another tumbler of neat Scotch. 'That's it then, I suppose.' He handed her the drink with a sigh.

'What's it?' she returned.

'Once you've had your sides stretched with something so grand, I suppose most guys' pricks feel like throwing a frankfurter up Oxford Street. Perhaps you should get yourself a nip and a tuck, Mira. A lot of women have that done after childbirth, best thing that ever happened to them.'

'I'd rather have a knuckleduster,' Mira said, looking coolly at him. 'Or receive all my guests through the tradesman's entrance.'

'You're kidding,' Pete said. 'That's the fastest way to get Aids, everyone knows . . .'

'Don't believe everything you read in the papers,' Mira said, taking another pull at her drink. 'You're the kind of boy who reads too much. Come here.' He moved towards her. 'Lower,' she commanded. 'Now cut the chat and put that babbling tongue to more constructive use.' Mira rolled over on to her naked back, raising and parting the smooth knees of her long, long legs. 'All yours,' she said, watching him harden again. He pulled away at first – he wasn't used to being bossed around like this by an older woman, even if she was a total babe. 'Get down buwoyy,' Mira gurgled in a pseudo-Jamaican patois. He hesitated, to her surprise – there was no instant obedience. She liked that. 'Or do we have to get that stupid old dog to teach you a new trick?'

'And how would you manage that?' Pete asked with a nervous laugh.

'Oh, silly boy, haven't you ever heard of a salt rub?' She laced her long fingers through the dark hair between her thighs.

But Pete wasn't watching. Something had distracted his attention. The dog, too, took notice, and padded over, it's nose wet, its tail wagging. Mira followed the animal's gaze to the window.

There stood Mico, her Brazilian husband, the red light glowing on the camcorder built into his hat. 'Don't stop,' he was saying excitedly. 'Please, don't stop . . .'

8

The days were getting longer – and wetter. It was the wettest March on record, the driver had said, and Mandi Harry had looked up from the 16-page memo on 'Our Multi-Cultural Workforce: a 21-point Action Plan' hot from The Boss's office in Los Angeles and pretended to be taken aback – 'Blimey, how do you know that then, Ronnie?' – even though, of course, she knew it already.

That was the trouble with editing a newspaper: you either had to know everything and be interested in if not obsessed with it – or be able to explain on the spot and in seven words or less why no-one else would be either. Even on a paper like the *Sunday Post*, which existed on a tabloid planet where they were never allowed to get in the way of a good story, facts were crucial.

On Planet Tabloid, there were news, hits and stars, plus a lot of advertising, and if the stories didn't make Mandi say 'Wow!', they might as well not have happened. Planet Tabloid was a parallel universe where every week the Royals faced a new crisis, and the Government was always on the brink of collapse following fresh and furious scandals; where close friends perpetually confided that their celebrity pals were devastated, vindicated or in hiding at a secret location following startling new revelations that would make your hair curl, drop out or grow back; where crooked businessmen quaffed drinks with slap-up meals before fleeing to suburban love nests into the arms of shapely ex-models and mums-of-two who'd perform disgusting, degrading or in extreme cases law-breaking acts of vice. No-one died on Planet Tab: they lost their final battle. No-one had babies there: childbirth was invariably 'a nappy event', and mothers produced, nine months after a stolen night of torrid passion, fragrant little bundles of joy.

And when brave, battling wives were finally reunited with have-a-go hero hubbies, they were invariably and immediately struck mute. The smile said it all.

When you lived, as Mandi did, in a world of hyper reality, where evil perverts stalked tiny golden-haired kids, where glamorous grannies announced to their neighbours, 'If I Can't Have Him, No One Will', where former telly stars could be arrested stark naked at any moment, you found consolation in facts. In prosaic concrete truths like rainfall figures and sports scores, because these were a salve for sanity, a reality check, a linkline to a life not driven by hysteria, banality, evil, and 44 double 'D' cup tits. But the trouble is, as Mandi had curtly told her leader-writer before moving on to a reporter's leaving do at the Evil Star earlier that evening, the trouble with omniscience is that nobody likes a know-all, do they?

The jet black Jaguar XJS cruised through the rain and took the exit to Loughton. Out there, Mandi thought, seeing the familiar spluttering pink neon letters blaring out the name of the local nightclub HOLLYWOOD'S against the dark sky, were her readers. First division footballers and second division villains; suburban gals in skintight stretch denim with big hair, high shoes and low IQs; the men who loved them, hard-faced blokes, unperfumed sweat in their armpits, who moved their lips when they read the paper, but mostly just looked at the pictures. Grannies and fannies; prannies and trannies; shopkeepers and shoplifters. All of them trapped in lives of quiet despair, and hungry for More News, More Hits, More Stars, More Fun. People, she thought ruefully, just like me . . .

The car splashed through a puddle and turned into a cul-de-sac, The Dene, a sweeping L-shaped drive of large, mock-Georgian houses less than 20 years old. Mandi's was the house on the U-bend at the bottom of the close. The estate agent had told her end-of-close houses kept their value best. Number six had a wide lawn sloping down from the road to the front of the brick and half-timber house – back in the 1970s, the architects had been liberal in their interpretation of 'Georgian' – where a wide driveway led to a double garage attached to the side of her wedge-roofed, five-bedroomed 'executive' home. Three of the bedrooms were unused and gathered dust. Only two people lived at 'Mandolin' – the name on the shingle was an amalgam of hers and that of her husband. Colin Harry would have laughed if you'd told him it was also the name of a lute-like musical instrument.

'Do you need a hand with those bags, luv?' asked the chauffeur.

'Nah, thanks, Ronnie, don't worry about it,' Mandi smiled, easing herself out of the car. 'See you tomorrow morning, OK?' She winked at her driver, and he winked back.

The bright beams of the security lights flooded out the dimmer bulbs of the carriage lamps fixed either side of the white-glossed wooden front door, illuminating the drive, the ornamental pond and the little willow tree cut neatly into the front lawn. Mandi inserted her key, and tottered across the threshold with a big bouquet of wilting daffs which had been languishing in the sink at work all day, and with her clutch of carrier bags. The names stamped on their sides were not those of petulant, expensive designers or hip 'n' trendy South Molton Street boutiques. They bore the all-too-familiar logos of Marks and Spencer, Debenhams and BHS.

'I doubt if any of those other toffee-nosed tarts would be caught dead in BHS,' Mandi mused. As she flipped through the post – record club, gas bill, insurance reminder, a Dixons catalogue and the usual raft of junk mail – and made her way down the hall, she wondered about the glamorous lives Mira Freer Farmer, Zelda Lee Powers and Kiki Cox must lead; how sophisticated their dinner parties were, how exciting their friends, how all-round fabulous life must be for them. She stopped at the living-room door. She realised that she was judging herself by her surroundings, and suddenly finding it all very humble by comparison, not at all up to the standards she presumed the other women lived up to.

A large copper hood covered the fake brick fireplace where an electric 'log effect' fire warmed the room. Everything was in place, the same as it ever was. Dusky pink velvet drapes hung precariously from their plastic rail to cover the nylon net curtains; the teak wall units were cluttered with Lladro porcelain, china trinkets and framed photos; the mahogany-boxed 29-inch TV was tuned to Eurosport; the middle-aged, balding husband was lying comatose on the leather settee from G-plan's top-of-the range three-piece 'Chesterfield' suite; there was the inevitable ensemble of debris on the carpet in front of him: overflowing ashtray, small mountain of crunkled snack food packs, half a dozen empty John Smith Bitter cans. Mandi stood still in the doorframe and looked at Colin. She watched the rhythmic rise and fall of his stomach, the undulations of pale hairy flesh protruding between the top of his grubby yellow acrylic shell-suit trousers and the frayed hem of his lurid 'Florida-Sunshine State' T-shirt. On the TV, a commentator was reviewing the progress of the Danish bobsleigh team. On the sofa, Colin snored like a pig.

At the leaving party earlier, in a private hired room above the Evil Star, about five minutes before she swallowed the inevitable One Too Many and started tap-dancing, Mandi remembered explaining to Nigel Plant that she hadn't fired Kettle because, for all his faults, the rat-like crime reporter was still capable of turning in what was referred to in and around the office as 'A Wow Read': the kind of story that made people say to their partners over the marmalade, 'Oh, wow, have you read this?'

'He's useful,' she said. 'Even when he's not turning over some hard-faced villain. He's the one all the younger hacks go to when they're stuck on a story. Besides, we couldn't have him crossing the street to the *People* or the *Mirror*.' But, she now admitted to herself, that had been a bare-faced lie. The real reason why she didn't fire Kettle was snoring gently on the sofa in front of her.

When Mandi had met Colin Harry eleven years earlier, she'd just got her first big break in Fleet Street, doing shifts paid by the day to dish the dirt for someone else's column on *The Sun*. He'd been chief sub-editor (Production) back then, an omniscient, omnipotent figure who, to Mandi, then a plausibly benign Gravesend girl from the *Hackney Gazette* out looking for a good time and a hard man, had seemed to straddle the corridors of power as easily as she wheeled her trolley round Tesco. But she'd always be ten years younger. And while she'd grafted her way to staff jobs on *The Sun*, the *News of the World* and the *Post*, accepting titles like section editor, assistant editor, and deputy editor before, finally landing the top spot after her predecessor suffered a nervous breakdown, Colin had been lagging miserably behind. He hadn't rolled with the punches. He didn't understand the new technology and made no secret of his contempt for many of his colleagues. Leaving a fresh turd in the desk of the Editor's brother after a reprimand had been the final straw. He'd got his pay-off, but he'd never work on Fleet Street again.

Listening to Colin talk throughout the years that followed, Mandi knew what getting whacked had done to him. Men of his generation who couldn't earn more than Her Indoors had no self-esteem, no ego, no hope. Colin had been right to the top, but he could never go back. The faces had changed, technology had changed, newspapers had changed. There were great tribes of men out there just like Colin, Mandi reflected. Ex-accountants who didn't add up to much; ex-middle managers who couldn't cope, let alone manage; lorry drivers who couldn't go the distance any more. Like Colin, they got up late and started drinking early, and were all too familiar with afternoon TV and the local bookie. These sad men who fantasised frenetically over coked-out assembly line goddesses baring their bits in porno mags couldn't get it up or get it on in real life. Because who they were was so tied up with what they did. And now that they did nothing they were no-no-people. Wounded men. Angry, redundant, relapsed.

Mandi flicked the couch commander through a soap ('. . . Something about that dress has triggered a memory in me . . .'), a talk-show ('. . . The last thing I remember was eating lunch on the 24th – the summer of '93 doesn't exist for me . . .') and found Lifestyle, a popular new channel targeted at women. Celia McNalty, a rather homely hostess, was showing how to cook with yoghurt ('. . . never serve your guests on warm plates,' she admonished sternly).

Mandi killed the sound, she couldn't take it – everyone at work wanting something, bouncing ideas and pleas and requests and threats off her as if she were a rubber wall, bouncing them right back at them again all day, being bombarded with people trying to sell you something, tell you something, show you something new, save you money or spend your last quid, load

your head all night with psychic data until you were set to explode
. . . Well, almost everyone.

Colin had woken up. He was yawning, rubbing his unshaven
chins, and asking what time it was. 'Blimey, I must've dropped
off,' he said when Mandi told him.

It was always going to be like this, Mandi realised. For the
first few years she'd tried to lift his spirits, build his confidence,
help him find a life, a purpose, get him to rediscover himself. Now,
it was as much as she could do to go through the motions of
practical matters. What was the point?

'Any messages?'

'Messages?'

'On the answerphone.'

'Nah.'

'Did you pay Del?'

'Nah, I forgot.'

Del was the man who ran the kennels where their greyhound,
Mr Bojangles, lived. Once, it seemed like a lifetime ago now,
they'd gone regularly to Walthamstow to watch him run, but now
he was nearing retirement age and Colin said why bother to get
another dog when he could watch his mates' mutts run for free?

'Did you tell my Mum we're coming down for her birthday?'

'Nah. Couldn't be fagged to call her back. I been feeling a bit
peaky today, I couldn't face her squawking on at me all afternoon.
I got enough aggro, you know?'

'Like what, Col?' she said. He was irritating her already. It never
took long. 'I've just done twelve hours with an office full of paranoid
shits. I almost had to sack someone for fiddling their exes . . .'

'Good on him! Who was it?'

Mandi began to tell Colin about what had happened with
Kettle, wondering as she talked why she'd focused on this out of
the thousands of items and incidents that cluttered up her day,
realising that it must be important to her somehow, though she
couldn't say why at the moment, for the life of her.

'A lot of good reporters need to be cajoled,' she said. 'You've
got to nurse them, coax them along . . .'

'Nah,' Colin retorted, scratching his greasy-grey, worn-out-

Brillo-pad hair. 'They're all farkin' cunts. I ought to know.'

The blinds were back down again, she thought, as her husband flicked back to Eurosport, pumping up the volume through the 'Stereosound' speakers.

'You want to go out?' she said pleasantly, trying to change the mood. 'We could just make the Chinky if we get a move on.'

'Football's on in a bit,' Colin said. 'You go out if you like. Makes no odds to me.'

Mandi sighed, and went into the open-plan kitchen to microwave a Lean Cuisine, changed her mind and had another Slimfast instead. She glanced at the ironing board – Mandi found ironing very therapeutic at the end of a hard day's thinking and drinking, and she always fantasised about sex. On the other hand, on those increasingly rare occasions when she and Colin actually had sex, she found herself thinking about the ironing . . .

Suddenly she heard a sound she knew. She looked down and saw a familiar little animal padding into the kitchen, making, as usual, a lot of noise. 'Hello, babe,' Mandi said, picking him up and tickling his furry tummy. The tiny kitten licked her face with his sandpaper tongue. Mandi had named her kitten Pinkee Poo after the cat in an essay she'd written at Gravesend Comprehensive when she was 14. 'Pinkee Poo was the naughtiest kitten in the whole wide world,' it had begun. She didn't remember the rest. After Miss Richards had awarded her the end-of-term prize for the essay, so much had happened that year: that man exposing himself to her on the bus, her brother's fatal accident, the school burning down . . . Pinkee Poo was everything that was good in her life, she thought.

'How's Mummy's best boy then?' she said, burying her nose in the cat's duck-down fur. Suddenly a voice inside pulled her up short. She put the kitten down gently and went over to check the Building Society calendar which hung on the wall next to the serving hatch. Yes, it was the 17th today, 17 February. How could she forget? she asked herself – and wondered if it was still there.

She went out through the kitchen door into the garage, past abandoned kitchen cabinets now filled with tools, plastic cartons of oil and garden paraphernalia, and climbed over a mouldy floral sun lounger and a folded whirligig washing line. She shivered, bunching her hands around her body for warmth. At the back of the garage she found it, still covered in heavy plastic sheeting and resting against a defunct fridge-freezer. Mandi reached into the covers, and put her hand right inside the pram. Her red-raw palm touched a piece of paper. It was exactly where she'd left it.

She tucked the crumpled photograph into her armpit and crept back into the house. Locking herself in the bathroom and squatting down beside the avocado-coloured bath, Mandi stared hard at the picture. There was a woman holding a newborn baby. The woman was Mandi. The baby was hers. She hadn't seen hide nor hair since the adoption people had taken the infant away, a quarter of an hour after a sweet young nurse had snapped the photo for her.

Every year, on the little girl's birthday, Mandi took out the picture and spent time with it. She wanted to remember. She needed to feel again how it felt to carry her, to be full of new life, to recall the bloody agony of birth. She thought back to the day she'd lost her virginity, and said something like a prayer for the little girl – young woman as she would be now, wherever she might be . . . Mandi prayed, please make her all right. Don't let her be ill, or sick, or crippled. Let someone love her, have someone look out for her, please see that there's someone there . . .

Just then, she heard a scratching on the door, and a thin miaow. Mandi opened the door and picked up the cat. She hid the picture in one of her handbags in the bedroom and took Pinkee Poo downstairs for some milk. She stroked and stroked him, and watched him as he lapped up his treat with a quick, darting tongue.

Colin popped his head round the kitchen door. He was not alone. Trev, a particularly dodgy mate of his, had just turned up. 'We're just going down Hollywood's for a swift half, it's Trev's sister's birthday, awright?'

Mandi was too pooped even to answer. He could fuck off to the North Pole in his knickers if he liked, what did she care? Pinkee Poo had finished his milk. She picked him up and felt the beat of his frail body against her cheek. Her mind was still racing: the Superbowl disaster . . . the Hermès scarf she had to get her mum for her birthday, 'Gotta be Hermès, the Queen wears them ones . . .' '. . . somehow, that dress triggers a memory deep inside me' . . . Mira, and Zelda Lee, and Kiki . . . the three bitches . . . the Bitches of Fleetwick . . . well, it made her laugh, if only for a second . . . the little girl she'd never met but would always love . . . the husband she saw every day of her life but couldn't even talk to. Mandi clutched the kitten to her big saggy bosom. Sometimes the best of everything just isn't enough, she thought, taking in all the mod-cons and expensive add-ons that surrounded her. But when it's all you've got, it's got to be enough, and that's the end of it.

Pinkee Poo mewed loudly, as if to say, hey, what about me? You've always got me. Mandi dreamed on about her long-lost little girl, and tears filled her eyes.

9

It only took a moment for Zelda Lee Powers to decide to leave her gas-powered 9mm semi-automatic Gaugin 'personal protection device' under that morning's copy of the *Daily Sketch*, its gunmetal snout poking from beneath the newspaper. As the rain poured down, Zelda locked up the Morgan sportster, and marched into the imposing, greystone building that dominated the Aldwych, the intersection where Fleet Street met the Strand. Noticing Zelda Lee getting out of the green sports car with its racy personal registration (the numberplates said SCOOP), a passing streetsweeper told her: 'I wouldn't park there if I were you, love.'

'Yeah?' Zelda snarled, snatching a honk from the inhaler in her handbag. Her morning had not begun well and she was in no mood for bogus Mary Poppins Cockney chirpiness. 'Well, you're NOT me. So why don't you go back to playing in the traffic, wise ass.'

Smurf, the *Sunday Post*'s court reporter, a short rheumy-eyed individual in a suit that fitted him like a bin liner, was swinging the lead, and smoking one of his toxic cigarellos. He spotted Zelda talking to The Emulsion Express. This hapless breed, this ragged pack, part freelance photographers, part freelance TV crews, had been stationed outside the court to cover a pop star's copyright case for longer than anyone could remember. Litigation would probably run well into the 21st century, long after the popster had been forgotten and most of the original defendants were dead.

'It's the double trouble shift,' one camera crewman was explaining to her. 'As well as old George in there, you've got the BNP in court 13 and the Animal Rights mob in court ten.'

'Who are the BNP?' said Zelda with a frown.

'Those Nazi guys?'

'Didn't I see you on TV?' Smurf said suddenly. 'You're Sir Anthony George's wife, aren't you?'

'He's my husband, yes,' Zelda said, shaking his hand. 'Zelda Lee Powers. My friends call me Zeelee, and I'm gonna be the next editor of *The Times*. What's up? You looking for a job?'

'So what brings you here then, Zelda?'

'Who did you say you were?'

'Mick Turner, the *Post*. You a friend of . . .?'

But Zelda had already clocked him as one of her competitors' foot soldiers. 'See you in the 19th century, tabloid scum man,' she sneered, and gave him the air.

Zelda walked through into the courts and, checking the Cartier wrist-watch Anthony had given her last Christmas in Val d'Isère, sat on a bench in the stone corridor outside court 14.

'You waiting for someone?' said a crop-haired youth in a black bomber jacket and Doc Martens, plonking himself down next to her.

'In the larger sense,' said Zelda, 'aren't we all?'

'Where you from, then?'

'New York,' she said, with an involuntary cough.

'That's a nasty tickle you got there,' said the skinhead.

'Goddamn weather, it's either snowed or rained every goddamn day since I got here. Maybe that's one reason this dump is so fucked up. Nothing works properly in this crappy country. I mean, take this morning, I wake up, I find my radio alarm that the airline finally condescended to bring over last night with my three suitcases which have, excuse ME, spent the last five days in a storage room in Delhi airport, and you know what? The goddamn thing is shorting out. So after I take a fire extinguisher to it, the guy arrives to install new phone lines only he's brought the wrong fucking equipment or something. I mean, why don't they know what they're supposed to be doing already? It's in MY time and on MY dime, and I don't see why I should pay some bunch of schnorers for a service I'm not getting, huh.'

'You a Yid?' the skinhead observed, standing up. He was a good six inches taller than Zelda and he was staring down at her, his mien far from friendly.

'A YID? Who do you think you are, asshole?' Zelda flared. She too was on her feet now. 'What's your fucking problem, Tough Guy?'

'You're the fucking problem, you people,' yelled the skinhead. His face was contorted with rage, and a pulsating vein bulged from the side of his neck. 'You run the media and the banks, your Zionist conspiracy is turning Great Britain into a shithole.'

'You know who I am? You know who you're messing with, you racist piece of shit?' Zelda was shouting too now, jabbing her fingers into his belly. 'My husband edits the *Daily Sketch*. You're going to wake up tomorrow and find you're one messy headline, motherfucker.'

'Don't touch me, you whore. You slag. You're trash. Hitler should've . . .'

The thug never got to finish his sentence, because Zelda drove her knee full steam into his groin. Another skinhead arrived on the scene, wrestling with two policewomen who were restraining him, one of whom now radioed for back-up.

'We'll get you,' the first skinhead shouted, his face a pitbull's on steroids, as more ball-point helmeted officers arrived to defuse the situation. 'We'll get you!'

At that moment, Sir Devnell Rumthrust QC emerged from court 14, removing his chalky wig, and spotted his glamorous, unmissable client. It was the work of a minute for him to whisk Zelda Lee away.

'What a fucking psycho,' Zelda babbled, wiping her mouth on a Kleenex as he steered her by the elbow. 'One minute the guy's hitting on me, the next he's a stormtrooper of the weeny Reich trying to get into a brawl.'

'Hitting on you?'

'Trying to pick me up, Dev. He said I had a nasty tickle. That's sexual, right?'

'I'm afraid people like that are too subterranean to concern me. Now, we have a conference, don't we?'

A lackey supplied the celebrated, corpulent lawyer with a black umbrella which he held for Zelda. He took her arm as they passed out of the law courts into the thronging hack pack.

'I don't know what's happened to this place these past couple of years, Dev,' Zelda whined. 'It's gone to hell in a handbasket. You got Blackshirts roaming the courts and I mean, can't these guys even speak real English, or what?'

They crossed the road at the top of Fleet Street and walked down past the beamed Tudor black-and-white frontage of the Wig and Pen Club.

'I thought you commuted over here regularly?'

'Yeah yeah yeah, but just for long weekends. Normally Tony and I go stay with someone in the country someplace, or we catch a couple of shows in the West End. Actually living here is a whole different deal. It's not just that everything's so squashed up, it's all those little details of urban survival. Like, none of my goddamn appliances work here, and the new ones are supplied without plugs. What the hell's THAT about? Plus, also, you can't get anything delivered, all the drycleaners have a real attitude problem . . . they're never OPEN. It takes days to get anything back, on and on and ON . . . and all these bomb threats are kinda scary. Plus, also, I'm getting some kind of influenza bug, but you can't buy proper vitamins anyplace, and, Dev, I could go ON, I could talk your goddamn wig off, if it were ON, but I guess you couldn't care less, right?'

Once inside Gray's Inn, they made for Rumthrust's chambers. 'It's kinda dingy in here,' moaned Zelda, wrinkling her nose at the musty whiff. 'How long you guys been here?'

'The set's been in Gray's Inn for 300 years.'

'Jeez, I woulda thought you guys could've spruced the place up a bit by now. Is that broccoli growing outta that wall?'

'Damp, I believe,' said the QC, collecting his messages from his clerk.

'It reminds me of this documentary I saw one time on PBS about your boarding schools. They said that's why Prince Charles is so fucked up. What is it they say? Never learned the difference between his ass and his elbow, or something. Does that mean he keeps putting his arm in the John? Jeez, Dev, this is like something out of DICKENS . . .'

'Ms Powers,' interrupted Rumthrust with barely concealed disdain, 'I must tell you that my colleagues and I have studied very closely your contract with the *Gazette.*' He had now sought sanctuary behind his enormous desk, and indicated a chair, into which she sank.

'And?'

'Our collective view, following a conference with our associates in New York who have also scrutinised your contract with your former employers, is that you are personally liable for any award the Supreme Court of New York may make in respect of a libel action of this nature.'

'You mean,' Zelda rasped, grabbing herself by the throat, 'if the *Gazette* loses the case, I have to pay this psycho-bitch 'cos some stupid asshole freelance jerk pepped up a few quotes?'

'That would appear to be the position, yes.'

'But she's asking for 40 million BUCKS! You mean my end could be HALF of that?'

'I'm afraid, so Miss Powers. I am so terribly sorry.'

'YOU are terribly sorry! YOU are! You – SORRY. Oh oh oh, OH my God, Heavens Demurgatroid,' Zelda said and swooned, passing out in the chair and sliding to the floor with a gentle thud.

When she came to, the QC's secretary was attempting to administer brandy and waft the office smelling salts against her nostrils at the same time. Rumthrust was suddenly nowhere to be seen. Zelda smacked the secretary away harshly.

'Oh Lordy,' Zelda moaned.

'Are you OK?'

'Oh . . . I do believe my stomach's taken a little turn. It's an allergy . . . why, you know, I just can't keep a teeny little mouthful down.'

'That accent . . . but I thought you were from New York . . .' the thirty-something, pinched-looking secretary faltered. 'Sir Devnell didn't say anything about you hailing from the South . . .'

'YOU seem to know a lot about the US of A all of a sudden,' Zelda snapped sarcastically, shifting back into New York mode as she picked herself up off the floor.

'Well . . . my boyfriend and I go to Florida every year . . .' she stammered, '. . . anyway, are you feeling better now?'

'FINE, thank you', said Zelda through clenched teeth. 'Fine, you hear? NO problem. You see, actually, my father was from the South . . . Virginia . . .'

'Are you sure you wouldn't like some more brandy?'

'Thanks, you know, but I don't really drink,' Zelda said, not looking at the girl. Her mind was elsewhere. She had just referred to her own father for the first time in years, and it had quite knocked her for six.

In truth, Zelda had never really known her father. Her big break into journalism had come 20 years ago when she was selling real estate, and a hot-schlonged Cuban client of hers, who'd somehow become her lover, had made her editor of *Teenybopper* Magazine to sweeten her, stop her exposing their scorching affair to his wife. Zelda had spent her first 45 minutes in magazine publishing firing all the old farts, and her next two days hiring demented chalk-cheeked teenagers who'd stay up all night long in the name of a deadline, and work for minimum wage. *Teenybopper* became a soaraway success and she went on to pen a column for *Harpers' Bazaar*. Next stop the fashion editor's chair at *Smart*, after which she was hired as a reporter-at-large by Jan Wenner at *Rolling Stone*. A three-day exclusive interview session with the eccentric Irish writer Brendan O'Brien – three days allowed by his PR on account of the fact that he was never sober enough to answer more than two straight questions in 24 hours, had resulted in her first marriage, and in the birth of their son Stone. Zelda, ever ambitious, and now anxious to match her husband's profile, progressed to a high-visibility column on the *New York Post* which evolved into the infamous Page Six, the city's must-read gossip slot. When Mortmedia launched the tonier *New York Gazette*, Zelda had towed her act uptown, relaunched her column as Bitch Inc, and been personally fêted by two Presidents. Rumour had it, as rumour would, that she'd slept with one of them – but which one? Meanwhile the paper was ailing, buckling under the dead weight of corporate debt. When the decision came down to relaunch it as a scrappy tabloid, it was Zelda Lee who came out on top. Her former boss had nothing but admiration for her. When a British aristo-hack by the name of Toby Freer Farmer had telephoned him on the pretext of sounding him out for an interview, Morty glowingly described his former protégé as 'Intense. The light's always on, the gears are always grinding, the engine room never shuts down.'

After O'Brien's untimely death Zelda had married, on the rebound, a hapless if distinguished-looking English journalist by the name of Tony George whom she had picked up on a girls' night out in an Italian restaurant in the East Village. He had been despatched to Gotham for five years to run the East Coast bureau of the London *Daily Sketch*, and happened to be dining alone after working late. Zelda had him on the steps of City Hall before he had half a chance to think about it. The knighthood had come later, after Tony's ascension to the Editor's throne at the *Sketch*. The handle was for services rendered by a grateful Conservative Government – the paper was unswervingly Blue with a loyal Tory heartland readership. It was to Anthony's infinite embarrassment that his wife had rushed directly to Coutts and Co to have her chequebooks redesigned in the format 'Lady George', even though she insisted on going by her maiden name in company. He had never worked out what all the fuss was about.

Now, as she made her way on to Fleet Street in a daze, she pulled up the hood of her sable to protect her hair from the driving rain. She crossed the road and got into Sir Anthony's Morgan. He had been perfectly happy to lend it to her, as he had the use of a chauffeured Daimler. As she prepared to do battle with the machine's volatile gearbox, and the still unfamiliar right-hand drive, she noticed that someone had pasted something right across the vehicle's windscreen, obscuring her view. Cussing, she got out of the car to rip it off.

'STOP!' it commanded in scarlet letters. 'THIS CAR HAS BEEN IMMOBILISED. DO NOT ATTEMPT TO MOVE IT.'

Zelda exhaled, kicked the off-side front tyre and noticed a gawdy yellow clamp hugging the wheel. Fuming, she trooped across the road to a row of telephone kiosks. One was occupied by a garrulous Asian woman in a pink sari. The second had been vandalised. She swiped her Visa card through the payphone inside the third, but a message flashed up to advise that it was accepting 999 calls or BT phonecards only – and of course, whaddya know, she didn't have one. She just beat a harassed-

looking man in a grey mac into the last call box. The booth stank
of urine and was festooned with fluorescent cards advertising the
services of Monica, 18 years old, New Blonde Model, 38-24-36,
Uniforms, Watersports, Sub-Dom. She dialled her husband's
private office line. A voice she didn't recognise told her that Sir
Anthony had a luncheon meeting at his club and was not
expected back until after three. Zelda knew better than to phone
Chambrun's – her husband's club was notoriously misogynous.
Chambers, the major domo or whatever they called him when he
wasn't at home, always assured you he would pass on the
message, but never ever did. She remembered Anthony once
telling her they had an unwritten rule that members would never
be interrupted by a gadget as vulgar as the telephone whilst in the
luncheon-room.

In frustration, she called home, to see if the maid might still
be there. But the line was busy. Zelda waited a couple of minutes,
a dripping nose thankfully protecting her olfactory tract from the
worst of the wine, urine and pong of the phone box. Zelda
pretended to talk animatedly, determined to hang on to her phone
box for as long as she needed it, and studiously ignored the glares
and vulgar gestures of the man in the grey mac outside.

She tried again. Still busy. OK, OK, so the car wasn't going
anywhere, she reasoned. On impulse, she leapt from the call box
and hailed a passing cab. 'Bond Street,' she instructed.

'You heard?' started the cab driver, swinging out from the
kerb. 'Them Irish bastards have only bombed the Channel Tunnel,
haven't they? It's just bin on the radio. My old Dad used to work
on the lump with some them paddies and every week they'd pass
the bucket round for contributions to the boys, you know, the
terrorists. Now my old man, he was a great old geezer, we used to
go to football together every Saturday and . . .'

'HEY!' interrupted Zelda. 'I had a fascinating childhood too,
but I hired you for a ride, not a biography.' She slammed the glass
partition shut.

When Zelda paid him off at Bond Street, the driver examined
the coins in his clammy hand and yelled: 'Oi! Aren't you going to
give me a tip then?'

Zelda stopped dead in her well-heeled tracks, breathed herself to her tallest and spun around to face the loud-mouth cabbie with a murderous smile. 'Yeah,' she replied. 'Just zip your gaddamn lip and concentrate on the driving, Pigfish. It's what you are FOR.'

Here, at last, she felt safe in familiar territory in the fragrantly reassuring world of Chanel and Armani, of Gucci and Yves St Laurent. Inside the gorgeous Hermès store, all was shiny and superb, opulent and irresistibly chic. Zelda wanted to buy up the whole store, now. She glanced around and recognised a TV weather girl, a couple of other *Hello!*-style celebrity faces she couldn't quite place, and the slick-looking black babe who was starring opposite Frank Bough and Robert de Niro in *Bounty!*, the West End premiere she'd attended with Anthony only last week.

'Did you hear about the Channel Tunnel? Looks like the terrorists have just blown themselves up again,' a horse-faced woman whah-whah-ed to an over-rouged friend. Drifting from counter to counter, Zelda pondered the unpredictability of the Irish, and found herself remembering the good times.

Times she'd been out on the tiles drinking New York dry with Brendan, her first husband, on endless trawls from bar to bar all over the Lower EastSide. *Danny Boy* always blaring from the jukebox, sending hard men misty-eyed about the auld country and getting them weeping into their Guinness. Zelda had learned a lot from her first husband about telling a story. The English, he'd said, approached language like favourite old clothes: something to slip into and forget about; the Americans, on the other hand, treated it like a power-tool: something you could customise to your needs in order to shape the world the way you wanted to see it. But Brendan, in common with many a fellow Irishman, played joyfully with language as if it were a new toy. To him, it was a precious, constantly newborn gift, something to cherish and relish and experiment with, to be refreshed and renewed by. It was endlessly, blessedly fascinating. At first, she couldn't see one bit of sense in all the fuss, but she grew to love the thing Brendan had loved most, just as she grew to love him. But that was then, before everything . . .

Zelda found herself rummaging through some end-of-season clearance stock at the scarf counter. Her eye alighted like a flickering butterfly on one particularly pretty pattern, but as she reached to examine the silk for flaws, the garment slithered from her grasp like a snake. When she looked up, there was a very determined hand attached to the end of it. 'Excuse ME, but I was looking at that,' said Zelda.

'First come, first served, love,' said the snatcher. She was a short, weighty brunette in her mid-thirties, dressed in a cheap short skirt and rather nasty stilettos. Zelda Lee noticed the scab of a departing cold sore next to her lip. EEEEUUUWW! The women looked each other over for a moment, a Can't-Quite-Place-You expression scanning their faces as they strained themselves to remember where they had seen each other before . . .

10

'Didn't I meet you at the *Bounty!* premiere on Friday?' Zelda said.

'No,' Mandi replied, 'it was the other day at John Temple's funeral. You rushed off to go to a press conference.'

'Honey, I rushed off to GIVE a press conference.'

'Same difference. Don't know why you bothered,' Mandi snorted. 'No-one takes any notice of them over here.'

'But the power players over THERE do. They take a lot of notice of who operates by their rules. Now, I think you better give me back my scarf.'

'Oh go and change your tampon or something,' Mandi snapped back, and made a bee-line for the cashdesk. But Zelda was all over her before she could find her credit card. One hell of a scrap ensued. In the end, the hapless sales assistant had to call the manageress to resolve the women's quarrel, which resulted in Mandi getting the Corgi scarf, and Zelda buying another from the full price line at a 20 per cent discount.

Zelda parked her used gum on the sparkling glass counter to emphasize the urgency of her need to telephone her husband again. But it was still the same old story: Sir Anthony George hadn't yet returned from luncheon, and the line into their home was still busy.

'Why isn't the goddamn Call Waiting working?' Zelda demanded of a harassed window dresser in the manageress's office. 'What IS it with this stupid tinpot little country anyway? Why can't you buy anything you want, WHEN you want? Why's everything cramped together? Why does nothing ever work properly?'

The manageress gently escorted her out on to the street.

A stone's throw away in a smart Mayfair town house, Society

decorator Crispian Frye sat bolt upright opposite his landlady. Both stared rather glumly at a Ouija board. 'Mneffwy?' he said. 'I don't see how that helps.'

The old woman's face was creased in thought, the wrinkles folding into her skin like gnarled elephant hide.

'I mean, what I really wanted to know,' Frye explained, '. . . was whether or not I should invite this Adonis to the cinema. Mneffwy? That doesn't help at all.'

The doorbell rang.

'Zelda! Sweetums! Kiss kiss kiss! How are you dahling? So what wafts this fragrant orchid-ette over the water to see little moi?' he asked eventually, when they'd finished embracing and exchanging trite-on talk so small it could've slithered unnoticed under the door.

'Crisp,' she said, refusing his offer of 'just a soupçon' of his landlady's sweet sherry, 'I've just flashed on something, on the way over here. And I want you to remodel the house.'

Frye's eyes lit up like fruit machines. 'When?' was all he could say, before pulling himself together and launching into babbling overdrive. 'I'm so frightfully busy you know, Zsa Zsa, all this corporate work is arse-paralysingly dreary, but they do pay fabulous spondoolicks for the most utterly banal things that, really, I can do with both legs tied behind my back . . .'

'And frequently do,' muttered Zelda under her breath. 'So what are you doing right now?'

'I'm having a meeting, well, more a series of little chats actually, with my textiles director . . .'

'C'mon over and check out the joint. It's vital for my emotional health that I establish a safe space in that house. I need my own turf. At the moment I feel like I'm an extra in someone else's movie.'

'Well,' Crispian sighed, 'I don't know . . .'

'C'mon Frye baby, I'll make it worth your while, cold cash,' she urged, producing a fat wedge of banknotes and rustling them suggestively.

'Ooooooooh, you're such a silver-tongued persuaderess, Zsa Zsa,' he said.

'Do you still have that funny little car of yours?'

'What, Daisy the Deux Cheveux? No, that was Michael's I'm afraid, and she's long gone, dear. Fret thee not, we'll catch a black bus.'

'Excuse me?'

'A taxi, darling, a coal-coloured cabette.'

From the moment he walked through the door of Sir Anthony's house off the King's Road, it was plain to the all-seeing, all-dancing decorator that there was considerable scope for improvement. 'What,' he demanded, waving a finger at a ceramic set of dubious origin that sat on a table in the vestibule, '. . . does that think it is?'

'I'm not sure . . . I think Tony once told me it was a Victorian chamber pot,' Zelda said lifting the hall telephone. No dialling tone . . . all she could hear was an unfamiliar noise . . . as if someone were dragging the telephone slowly through a quagmire . . .

'Oh, and that hideous sideboard,' Crispian cried with a theatrical shudder and a full-body grimace. 'All this Victorian kak is pure taste crime. Off with its head and straight into the skip with it, I say. And what is this beneath my tootsies? Why, I do believe it's carpet! Mon Dieu, how insufferably quaint. Nothing else for it, it'll all have to be torn up, it completely ruins the architectural resonance of the place.'

They started in the basement and worked their way up through the property. Sir Anthony had never got around to refurnishing properly after his first wife had died following a short illness years previously. Crispian grew increasingly indignant at the vulgar assault being perpetrated on his senses. 'Queen Anne!' he was heard to shriek. 'How vile, they must all be replaced by meridiennes immediately. Deary, deary moi, the very idea of temporary partitioning is positively barbaric. And such a particularly bilious example – those screens are so hopelessly bourgeois, how much did you part with for them?'

'I guess around four thousand eight hundred bucks a pop,' Zelda confessed. 'So figure around seventeen grand sterling.'

'Well,' soothed Crispian, '. . . think of it as the better kind of firewood, darling, and put it down to experience. You must replace them with dado rails, there, there and here . . .'

By the time the decorator had decided that the underlying problem was one of room proportion, or lack of: '. . . all these nasty little walls simply must be knocked down by brawny men with the most enormous hammers imaginable. I feel it in my bones. The house cries out to me . . . "Crispian, set me free from the tyranny of retaining walls – I want to be whole again . . ."'

Zelda Lee had finally succeeded in getting through to Richard Branson's private line on the decorator's mobile. She was always hustling, always busy, and busting-a-gut keen to sell Britain's maverick entrepreneur on her new schemes to put Marks and Spencer concessions on main Intercity train services.

'Configuration? What do you mean, configuration? Ricci, Ricci, this is Zee Lee talking at you . . . these are economy tariff passengers, babe, strictly steerage, rat class, get my drift . . . where's that old Can-Do spirit, huh? Rip the goddamn seats out! You're going to get more bang for your buck selling frillies to the toney end of the market than you are running goddamn cattle trucks into Clapham Junction. Ricci, babe, trust me, this is a whole new concept for in-flight entertainment, it goes on the trains, it'll soar on the planes . . . I see lingerie shows, I see Cindy Crawford, I smell big big bucks. What do you say we take a meeting, get this thing on track? OK, OK, OK, get back to me, babe, love you, Ricci, love you, sweetie, baby, cookie, honey, bye . . . MWAH MWAH . . . yeah, bye.'

In the upstairs sitting-room, Zelda snapped on the TV. An all-too-familiar image filled the screen: yellow number plates emblazoned with black letters that spelt SCOOP.

'. . . and within the last half hour, police have foiled a Loyalist terrorist attack in central London when bomb squad experts, in a controlled explosion, safely disposed of a suspicious vehicle parked opposite the High Court . . .' The camera panned back a couple of hundred yards to record the moment the Morgan sportster blew sky-high.

'Oh-My-GARD,' Zelda choked, her eyes fixed to the screen, as a police officer explained how tracker dogs had detected an explosive device concealed beneath a newspaper inside the car.

'My personal protector! My son sent it me from LA, this Israeli rapid fire gas gun, that's all it was, it was loaded, the dogs must've . . . SHIT, how am I gonna tell Tony about this? He's going to go into meltdown, he LOVES that goddamn fucking stupid car more than he loves ME. SHIT.'

'Well, whoop-dee-do,' Crispian said once he had grasped the serious nature of her offence. What's to say in these situations? 'Take some words of wisdom from Auntie Crispi, Zsa Zsa, sweetie, the nasty brute's sure to find out about it sooner rather than later. It'll look oodles better if you get in there first and break the ground. Trust me, dahling, I've been caught with my pants down more often than you've had hot ding-dong.'

'You're right, Crisp,' Zelda said, 'I've got to bite the bullet.'

She picked up the sitting-room extension, but the phone still sounded as if it were being used to mix paint. Wearily, the decorator again handed over his mobile, but Zelda's urgent pleas to be put through to her husband at his office appeared to be futile. 'Well, give me his goddamn assistant, what's her name? Hanni, put me through to Hanni.'

'I'm sorry, she's not at her desk either,' informed the voice at the other end.

'Jesus, what a bimbo,' snarled Zelda, and hung up.

'Now now, Zsa Zsa, don't have a period, Petal, it's just a silly old car, now, isn't it? Now look, this bathroom is an utter disgrace! You can't have *eau de nil* there, I positively forbid it! Have you never heard of cerulean blue? It's so civilized, so utterly millennial.'

'That's GOOD?' Zelda asked.

'It'll be gorgeous!' he replied. 'You'll see. What we could do is a lovely little sunken Roman *en suite* bath and bidet, surrounded by some hunky Corinthian columns, and then extend the motif right through this whole top floor. A very good friend of mine does the most divine friezes, we could run it all along the top here, through the wall and then right through this room here . . .'

He opened the door to the master bedroom. Too late.

'Oh, horrors!' he squealed as if in pain, his hands flying instinctively to cover his eyes. 'How squalid! Heterosexual intercourse!'

When Zelda peered over her friend's shoulder she saw her husband, Sir Anthony George, naked, lying flat on his back. On top of him, also naked, was a shapely off-beige girl who, Zelda noticed, in the way that one often absorbs apparently irrelevant details during moments of crisis, had a bell-shaped birthmark on her right buttock.

'Zelda!' gasped Sir Anthony.

'ANTHONY!' screamed Zelda.

'Christ!' wailed the unidentified flying chicklet, turning to stare at Lady George.

'So THAT'S why I couldn't get through,' Zelda growled. She could see a wire trailing upwards between the heartbreakingly firm thighs of her husband's lunchtime lover, whom she now recognised. It was Hanni, his personal assistant, of all slappers. Not at her desk, indeed . . . The wire was plastic-coated, and curly . . . a wire more usually associated with telephone handsets. What's more, it was still attached to one.

'Oh, poor telephone,' wailed the decorator. 'Doesn't that constitute some sort of domestic violence?'

'Domestic violence is something I take very, VERY seriously,' said Zelda murderously.

'Oh, don't know about you, I think I'm taking a turn. Crispi must have a large brandy.'

'Oh God, Tony,' whispered Hanni. 'Tony, I can't move.' The whisper became a wail. 'It's stuck.'

'Yeah,' growled Zelda, '. . . stuck on the WRONG FUCKING NUMBER.'

The first weapon that came to hand was a Victorian chamber pot, identical twin of the one in the hall. Zelda seized it, took careful aim, and launched it, very, very hard . . .

11

All the houses on the smart Chelsea terrace were painted white. Except one. It was covered with ivy. Milk bottles littered the front garden. This was the house where Mirabelle Freer Farmer, the Editor of *Verve*, lived. The house was set back from the others, an old brick wall ensuring splendid isolation from the end of the terrace on one side and, on the other, the lesbian motorbike club.

Mira's house had been built for a mistress by her paternal great-great-great-great-grandfather, the Duke of Datchet, and passed down among the poor relations of the family's cadet branch like a tainted heirloom. Mira liked to describe the interior of the house, sprawling over four floors, as 'eclectic'. The complex layout featured styles ranging from Arts and Crafts to seventeenth century; from Adam to Victorian Gothic. Stained glass was big. Carved wood was big. The chimney-piece in the drawing-room where Mira did most of her serious entertaining was very big. Well, about 14 feet high, anyway.

A man called Maurice Zeilinskov had been murdered in one of the guest bedrooms in 1929. Some people contended he was a Bulgarian who had forged the Zinoviev Letter, others that he was a New York Communist instrumental in orchestrating the Great Stock Market Crash. What was undeniable was that, despite all subsequent attempts to remodel the room in which Zeilinskov's throat had been cut, a bloodstain clung stubbornly to the polished boards of the new wooden floor.

Mira liked to joke about her home's idiosyncrasies. She was self-deprecating about its funny smells, the manky weeds that grew out of the cracks in the ceramic lavatory in the front garden, the noisy central heating her grandfather had installed. 'It was the first house in Chelsea to have central heating,' she would tell house guests with a certain pride. 'When the tradesmen came for the money, my grandfather told them to whistle for it. That's what the noise is, I suppose – the builders, whistling. Don't worry, you'll soon get used to it.'

Mira's other grandfather had ended his life in an asylum after his third wife had become embroiled in a celebrated Society divorce scandal in Kenya. Mira's father had disappeared, along with some of the family's more important 18th-century portraits, to South Africa. He couldn't pay his gaming debts. This turned out to be something of a personality trait – he'd moved through Australia and New Zealand before the tragic accident had finally closed his account during a game of Two Up in a bar just outside Manila.

Her mother had entangled herself with a series of rotters. When, during the summer of her 14th birthday, Mira had returned for the long holidays to the family estate in Sussex from her boarding school in Wiltshire, it had fallen to Wilkes the butler to tell her that Mummy was taking an extended holiday of her own in St Kitts, with an oilman called Max. Mira had never spoken to her since. There had been a letter with a Port-Au-Prince postmark, but its writer had seemed deranged, a stranger to her. Once she saw a woman in the background of a documentary about Bob Marley . . . she spent hours studying the freeze-frame, and in the end, decided it would be best to pretend she didn't know. After all, until she was six, she had firmly believed that her real mother was Nanny Culshaw.

Mira fumbled for the cordless telephone on her bedside table, hit the speed-dial for her assistant's private line at *Verve* and left a message on the Voicemail. She looked out of the window and saw that it was raining.

'Nadia, it's Mira. I'm not going to be in today, so please cancel all my appointments. Tell the German telly people I've had to fly to Biarritz at no notice, tell that frightful harridan from Glenwhatnot Promotions that I've got PMT, oh and get that guy for the features job to come in on Friday instead, tell him and the rest of the troops I'm working from home today on a frightfully urgent piece of copy, can't possibly be disturbed, etc etc. If that wretched flack from Cosworth rings about getting the Vendetta back, I'll speak to him at the end of the week. You can go to that Lacroix launch on my invite tonight if you like, take Hamish or James, you'll find the stiffie under that pile of Avedon trannies beside my fax. Hold the fort, but if anything mind-wogglingly must-do comes up, or there's a major crisis, call me on 9595, otherwise I'll see you tomorrow.'

She collapsed back into the soft mountain of bolsters and pillows at the head of her ancient four-poster bed, and was just drifting off to sleep when Mico started his hammering and drilling again. Then the doorbell went. She shouted out for her husband to answer it. Resigned to the fact that getting back to sleep was about the last thing she was going to accomplish, she contemplated dragging her weary carcass from the pit to see if the plumber had finally arrived. But she couldn't face the kitchen, or the huge pile of dirty dishes from the previous night's dinner party. So she turned to the stack of last Sunday's papers on the bedside table.

As she flicked through them she felt that familiar flush of angst and envy, of stimulation and irritation. Rory Tintagel had referred to it last night over the broached salmon as SPAS: Sunday Paper Aggravation Syndrome. As an environmentalist and the youngest Master of Foxhounds in the north of England, Rory was infuriated by the sheer volume of newsprint: the ten-section heavies, the leaflets and cards that fluttered from the supplements within magazines within papers like dead leaves; the punch-drunk sense of burn-out from absorbing too much information about global disaster, celebrity trends, prickly politicians on the make, corrupt clergy on the take, and gorblimey fury over the latest specious Royal scandal. The root of Mira's dissatisfaction was something slightly different. After all, she was a hack, and brought a trained eye to the foibles of her trade. As she waded through the *Sunday Post*, the *Sunday Times*, and the *Express on Sunday* which included the particularly bile-inducing *YES* Magazine, she found herself growing more and more depressed. All these big-name titles offering little more than sloppy journalism, predictable pictures, thin, unimaginative layouts and the craven, carping, familiar sneer that punctuated every piece which wasn't a flimsy plug for a bogus book, fatuous film, tedious TV show, superfluous shop or appalling new gadget.

Whatever happened to real journalism? Mira stabbed her first Peter Stuyvesant of the day on a hundred-year-old shell-shaped plate still smeared with the remains of Saturday's breakfast. She began composing a list in her head. Real Journalism Is . . . the time she'd chased a suspected child murderer through four miles of hedgerow as a cub reporter on the *Petersfield Post*; or the time when, on her first Fleet Street profile for the *Daily Telegraph*, she'd confronted a dubious hotel operator with a reputation for casual violence thus: 'What's the least amount of money you've ever had in your bank account?'; or the time, three years earlier, when she'd exposed as criminally duplicitous a Nobel-prize winning AIDS expert while editing the weekly *Cue* in New York . . . Mira was annoyed that her own carefully-planned stories were so often ruined by the Sunday editors' bulging chequebooks and the tawdry speculations of their minions. A fashion spread in the weekend magazine of one of the liberal heavies caught her eye: Giovanni Blanco was a diabolical photographer, he did too much skag, it was vile . . . sending him to the Seychelles to shoot those jumped-up, clapped-out teeny tyros Live Nude Girls! totally skewered the brilliant investigative piece she'd commissioned last week. But hers was a much better story: how the group's manager was using the girl group as a front for his involvement with a Columbian cocaine cartel.

What Mira really craved, she admitted to herself yet again, was to cover a real live war. Proximity to pain, preferably other people's, gave her a sexual high second to none. She could practically come at the smell of mortar-induced bloodshed. That closeness to death heightened her awareness of being fully alive, accelerated all six senses, exhilarated every nerve and fibre in her body. But it never seemed to work out like that, she reflected, as she padded down the dark staircase to the kitchen below. She'd been to Beirut, but the terrorists opened up a hotel rather than heavy mortar fire. She'd been to Sarajevo to meet a Society mercenary but just as she was about to board the plane a message came through that he'd sprained his groin, so could they please do the interview back at his mother's house in Hastings. Somalia had seemed a dead cert, but she arrived in the middle of a sudden ceasefire, and the closest she came to seeing action was a drunken argument at an Embassy reception with a Kiwi photographer who accused her of being a war groupie. The truth always hurts. In desperation, she'd sneaked off to Belfast the previous November with a scrappy snapper and Johnny Hoskins, veteran war correspondent, who'd been held hostage in Afghanistan for two years by the Mujaheddin. But Hoskins's contacts these days were distinctly pacifist, and they'd all found themselves an entangled laughing stock alongside Phil Collins, Paul Gascoigne, Gary Mason, Wincey Willis and Terry Waite in a Celebrities for Peace photo-op. Meanwhile every other day, or so it seemed, journalists all over the planet were being shot at by terrorists, stoned by freedom fighters, kidnapped by men in balaclavas and tortured by fragged-out militiamen. They managed to be in the right places at the right time but, try as she might, it never happened to her. Mira opened her shiny Westinghouse double fridge and saw she was out of milk. Perhaps it's the karma that comes from editing a glossy magazine, she mused, pouring black coffee from her Italian Gaggia machine. Maybe I should go freelance, she pondered . . . or get a job on a proper newspaper, where I could zoom off to write the occasional first-person piece when something really hot happened.

'PFWOOOOOARR!'

Mira spun round and found herself face to face with a tattooed skinhead who had to be the plumber. He was staring as if his life depended on it at the naked flesh revealed by her gaping silk dressing-gown. She could almost smell the saliva welling in the back of his throat. 'Bet you don't get too many of them to the pound, eh?'

Mira sneered at him as she covered up. 'Actually my husband's in the next room,' she said haughtily.

'E's a lucky feller then, innee?' leered the plumber.

'If you've anything to say about the boiler, tell him, I'm extremely busy,' Mira said briskly. Her tone of voice lowered the room temperature, which was already pretty chilly, because the central heating hadn't worked since September.

'Sorry, luv, no disrespect intended, but I tried to talk to him, see, but he's putting up them hooks, innee, and every time I try and have a word, he just smiles at me through them weird goggles of his, and sort of waves, you know?'

'Really,' mumbled Mira, securing her robe with strips of Sellotape torn from a roll she'd found in the fruitbowl on the kitchen table. 'So what's the problem?'

The plumber began to describe in excruciating detail how gaskets were worn and flange nuts corroded; he told of fractured and blocked base elbows, of misfitted flush bushing and copper-to-plastic transition fittings that, to be honest, a five-year-old wouldn't have installed, not unless he was trying to rip you off, but you never could tell with kids these days, could you?

She was thinking along different lines: about oily hands, greasy, big hands, dirty hair, body hair, sweat. Torn clothes. Men who left stains . . . and bruises.

Saved by the doorbell. The banging from the floor above stopped, and Mira heard Mico's clogs clattering down the stairs. As the plumber launched into a litany on the urgent need to build a new service tank in the attic and replace the boiler with what sounded to her untutored ear like the specifications for a small nuclear power station, Mira wondered who on earth her husband was expecting. 'This all sounds frightfully disruptive. How much will it cost exactly?' she said, staunching the boilerman's flow.

'Well, that depends on how you're paying. I mean, if the guvnor's got to put everything through the books, like, well . . . but I mean, if we're talking blue ones, we can probably do it a bit cheaper, like. But I'll tell you this for nothing, Mrs Lady, I wouldn't hang about if I were you, see, because water's boiling up in them transit pipes. Every time you use that waste disposal in there, you risk flooding the whole place out. See, what happens is, the water builds up in them pipes and when . . .'

'Yes, yes, I see', snapped Mira. 'Well, look, you'll have to tell your – guvnor – to send me a written estimate ASAP. I'll have to get the loot from my Trust fund, you see, and they're rather crusty about handing over my money without something in writing . . .'

Just then, Mico burst into the kitchen, still wearing his welding goggles underneath the old flying hat into which he had mounted a video camera. He was a sight for sore eyes. He was panting and waving his arms about like a banshee. 'Is the Vendetta man . . . I tell him boys steal it, ramrodder boys from Miabelle's photo-shoot, they done crash it into kebab shop, but he don't care!'

'Miss Freer Farmer?' enquired a jug-eared, spotty, bespectacled young man, as he entered her kitchen.

'Who in the hell are you?'

'Eric Phillpot, Madame, Regent Collection Agency. Reference unpaid bills for repairs to an Aga cooker. I'm empowered to seize goods and chattels to the value of £782.46 unless immediate payment is forthcoming.'

'But the bloody wretched people didn't fix it,' Mira exclaimed.

'Look, you can see for yourself, the bloody thing isn't working.'

'I'm sorry, Madame, that's not really my concern. Now will you be paying by cash or cheque?'

'Oh for fuck's sake,' Mira stormed. She had just noticed two burly figures who had appeared out of nowhere and were knocking on her wide-open front door.

'Now there's no need to adopt an objectionable tone,' the bailiff warned. 'I am merely following orders . . .'

'Hold on a minute!' Mira shrieked at him, 'And you,' she said, turning to the boilerman. 'My chequebook's upstairs. Will you wait a moment?'

'I think my guvnor would prefer cash if that's awright,' the plumber said, ogling her feet. 'How much?' Mira said. 'You still haven't told me how much.'

'Well, I'll just have another check around, make sure I ain't missed nothing, then I can tell you, OK?'

'Fine, fine,' said Mira. 'Now where was I? Oh yes, a chequebook.' The doorbell rang again. 'Mico, will you please answer the door, *Mi Amore*?' Brushing past the bouncing bailiffs, she hissed into her husband's ear: 'For God's sakes don't let them in if you don't know who they are, they might be the people from the bloody council.'

But the figure who threw his bowler hat at the hatstand in the hall, and missed – twice – was not a debt collector. He was family.

Toby Freer Farmer wore a grey Austin Reed overcoat, a white Turnbull and Asser shirt, a Chambrun Club tie, grey flannel trousers and black Oxfords. The lace-ups resembled any other pair of Oxfords, but had in fact been handmade to the last he kept at Lobb and Company. Toby wore hornrimmed spectacles. He had bushy brown eyebrows, thin, hairy wrists, and sported an almost permanent beaming smile which he now turned on his sister.

'Tobias!' shrieked Mira, embracing him. 'What are you doing here?'

'I telephoned your office but one of your minions told me you were here with a grave case of hives.'

'Why aren't you at *Commentary*?' Mira asked. Her brother edited a weekly magazine of robustly right-wing views and small circulation – all old school ties knotted together for posterity. At dinner the previous night, Peregrine Worsthorne had said he was certain it was financed by the CIA. What did he know?

'I have some splendid news.'

'Oh good. I'm always in the market for that. Oh, hang on a minute,' Mira said, remembering the pressing nature of her errand. 'Tobes, before you tell me, darling, come in here a moment.'

She dragged her brother into the library. The wood-panelled room was brimming with books. They lay on every horizontal surface; on the chaise longue, the sofa, on top of the TV set. Draped over a clothes-horse which blocked the television screen were a number of expensive-looking garments culled from the better *maisons de couture*, plus a couple by one or two of London's more thrusting young design talents. Toby recognised them from recent *Verve* covers. How they came to be in Mira's personal possession was something of a mystery to the uninitiated. Clothes would be lent by big-name designers from which the magazine's Celebrity Of The Month would select what to wear at the photo shoot. Then somewhere in transit, at the end of the shoot, some of said clothes would vanish – only to reappear with Mira inside them at subsequent Society events.

His sister had been a kleptomaniac ever since Toby could remember. As editor of *Commentary*, Toby prided himself on his firm views on personal morality. But as Mira's half-brother, he'd learned long ago that trying to control her was like trying to knit water.

'. . . So that bloody little man won't extend the overdraft until the next lot comes through from the Trust at the end of the month. Which leaves me in a bit of a jam. It's jolly lucky you've turned up, actually, because you always carry lots of wonga, don't you, darling? How much cash have you got on you?'

'Well, I'm a bit short actually,' Toby hesitated, his features clouding.

'I think I'm down to my last five hundred.'

'Would you be a positive angel and write me a cheque? You can have it back on the first, I promise.'

'Well . . .' Toby said.

'Please, Tobias. Just write me the cheque, then tell me your news.'

'I'll be two shakes,' she said, kissing him full on the lips as she seized his reluctant loan. She dashed back to the kitchen and Toby made his way out into the hall. He stared at the cracked floor tiles, the African masks on the wall, the abstract Bosnian Expressionist picture that appeared to have been executed almost entirely in oxblood, dumped beside the door to the lavatory just waiting for some inebriated foot to come crashing through it.

Mira reappeared. She was showing the bailiff and his henchmen the door. 'Oh, thank God that's over. It's just going to be one of those days, I can tell.'

'Mirabelle, you have one of those lives.'

'Come upstairs to the boudoir, darling. I can't wait to hear your news.'

Toby's expression brightened and he followed her up the staircase, stopping only to poke his head into the second-storey room where Mico had resumed his crashing and banging. 'What the hell is he doing?' Toby said, catching sight of his brother-in-law atop a painter's ladder, where he was drilling the last of a series of heavy duty grappling hooks into the ceiling of the bare room.

'It's all part of his new performance video,' Mira said, matter-of-fact. 'He did explain to me, but all I can remember is that he's going to string a cable across the hooks, suspend himself from a pulley and then cruise from one end to the other, shooting some malarky with a rhino.'

'A real rhinoceros?' Toby exclaimed.

'How extraordinary. You're going to let him have a rhinoceros in here?'

'What can I do? You know what he is. He's borrowing it from some zoo in the Ukraine that's gone broke.'

Toby shook his head incredulously. The antics of his bohemian relatives never ceased to amaze him. 'How the hell are you going to get it in there?'

'Don't ask me. Mico said something about one of his dodgy Brazilian buds having a crane.'

'Where are we going?' Toby said a few moments later, panting from the exertion of climbing three flights of stairs.

'I've got a heater in my bedroom, c'mon.'

Toby followed her through into the cosy master bedroom. Mira threw herself on to the four-poster, and beckoned him to join her. 'Now,' she said, conspiratorially, when Toby had dumped his overcoat and they had made themselves comfortable. '"Wonderful news," you said.'

'Really wonderful news, Mirabelle. Gizelle and I are to be married.'

There was a heartbeat of silence. Then Mira burst into fits of raucous laughter, rolled into a ball then started pounding the pillows with clenched fists. 'Brilliant, Toby, absolutely priceless,' she yelped, when she got her breath back. 'That blubbery Yank, that ball of fat in a T-shirt . . . Oh God, that's really brightened up my whole day. Too perfect, darling, excellent, you do still have a sense of humour! Now tell me your real news. Have International News offered you *The Times*?'

'Mirabelle,' Toby scolded. He sounded hurt.

'I'm serious.'

'You can't be,' she said flatly, her voice low and cold as an opponent's match point. She stared hard at her brother, her eyes probing his, trying to see right through his pupils. 'Oh Christ,' she murmured. 'You are, aren't you?' Time, and her heart, stood stock-still. She turned away from him so that he wouldn't see the tears welling up in her eyes.

'Anyway, they want a woman to edit *The Times*, didn't you

know?' he gabbled hastily. 'You should really think about applying, Mirabelle, honestly. I was talking to Brett Collins about it at the club the other night, and he said he was terribly impressed with *Verve.*'

Mira blew her nose on a dirty shred of tissue she'd found among the stale bedclothes, and turned to face her brother. 'Oh, don't be so silly. I'm such a minnow compared to those sharks at Wapping Wharf.'

'Are you upset about something?'

'It's nothing, really,' she said, wiping her face on her dressing-gown sleeve. 'Well, actually I had a few people round for dinner last night, and you remember that old luvvie I went out with? Michael Orlando?'

'Orlando . . .' He thought for a moment. 'Oh yes, Orlando, I seem to remember him doing rather a good Iago at Stratford when I was at Slough Comp.'

Toby always referred to his old school, Eton, as Slough Comp. He was the master of inverted snobbery, and was well-versed in the art of tactfully evading contentious subjects – such as his half-sister doing a bunk with an actor old enough to be her father. He remembered telling his parents' friends how disgusting it all was. He'd been twelve years old at the time and yet to experience his first orgasm, let alone the first flush of true lust.

'He's rather ill,' Mira said. 'Very ill, in fact. Could be handing in his Equity card at any moment. I wonder if I oughtn't to fly out to Italy again and see him.'

'Did you hear about the Morgan libel case?' Mira was pouting in a way that Toby had always found completely irresistible. It unnerved him, and he fiddled with his shirt buttons as Mira picked at her cigarette packet and shook her head. 'Zelda Lee Powers, the harridan from the *New York Gazette,* is for the high jump. Apparently the freelancer just made up some quotes for effect. It just goes to show that for all the Americans' fact-checkers and supposed scrutiny of material for objective verification, their journalists still have quite a bit to learn from Fleet Street. Why, I bet even a sub on a damp rag like *The Sun* or the *Daily Sketch* would've detected the false note in a minute.'

'Did you hear about Prince Randy's new girlfriend?'

'No, who is she?'

'That girl who plays opposite Frank Bough in *Bounty!*'

'Gizelle and I prefer more serious stuff actually.' The loaded silence hung in the room like a shroud. It was broken, eventually, by the familiar clump-clump of footsteps racing up the wooden stairs.

'Oh, hello Mico, how's it going?'

'Hiya Baby, hiya Toby. Hey, I'm finished, am ready to shoot when Mr Rhino arrives.'

'What's all this about a rhinoceros?' Toby asked.

At that moment the plumber knocked on the door, and stonked, uninvited, straight into the room. 'It's worse than I thought, I'm telling you, love, if you don't get those transit pipes seen to, this whole place could flood tomorrow. We're backed up till April, but I tell you what, you make it worth my while and I'll make sure you get to the top of the rota.'

'I've already explained, I've got to have something in writing to take to my trustees. Look, just have your boss fax an estimate through today and I'll see them this week, OK? What are we talking about here?'

'Well, what with everything that needs doing I can't see you getting away with much change out of ten grand. There's a lot of – Oi! What do you think you're doing, mate?'

'Hey,' said Mico, fondling the boilerman's jacket, '. . . is very fine, no, Miabelle? Is good physique, plenty muscle, am telling you . . .'

'Gerroff! Is 'e an iron or what?'

'I'm having a Barclays,' Mico said, unzipping himself. He was still wearing the peculiar hat with the videocamera mounted in it. 'Why don't you take Miabelle's clothes for him, Toby?'

'What the fuckin' 'ell is going on 'ere?' demanded the plumber.

'Don't look so Mr Party Pooper Pants, Toby, Miabelle tell me all about it, c'mon, I know you two do this before, keeping it all inside the family, eh, eh?'

'Fuck me!' exclaimed the plumber.

'Like, yes,' drooled Mico.

The Sellotape holding Mira's robe together had peeled open,

exposing large, terracotta-coloured nipples. She lay back on the bed, smiling like a centrefold, framed with her knees. She stared at them all expectantly.

12

Crispian Frye looked at his pocket watch. As the second hand touched twelve, he rang the doorbell of the Knightsbridge apartment block. He was precisely ten minutes late. He disliked arriving on time for anything, because only the lonely arrived on time. Crispian couldn't stand the idea of people thinking he was lonely. On the other hand, only the chronically disorganized were chronically tardy, and Crispian couldn't bear to have people think he was inefficient either. One just couldn't win – unless one could strike a happy compromise. Thus, fulfilling one of his New Year's resolutions, he had telephoned all his friends a few weeks earlier to tell them, in future, he'd be precisely ten minutes late for everything. The trouble was, this sometimes necessitated deliberate acts of procrastination on his part, which really went against the grain. For example, he'd just spent a quarter of an hour perusing Harrods' window displays in the freezing cold.

The door was opened by a Chinese houseboy who smiled but said nothing because he was mute. Crispian stalked into the flat, registering its decor with mixed emotions. Mon Dieu! The telephone in the hall wore a lacy pink cosy of the kind crocheted by old dears with lavender hair to keep teapots warm or spare loo rolls hidden. Quelle dilemma for this arbiter of interior sensibility! Was it, he wondered, as he wandered down through the minstrel's gallery which ran the length of the apartment, high camp kitsch (good), post-Tudorbethan ironic (possibly a startling new trend), or just hideously, arse-paralysingly suburban?

He landed in the drawing-room, and saw that a select few were already arranging themselves around a large table.

'You must be the Painter Man,' beamed a wide-haired blonde

in her late thirties. 'Hello, I'm Jennifer Mitchell Fox. This is my husband, David.' Crispian grimaced behind his spray-on smile. '. . . and this is Garth'.

'Oh, the Blank Cheque,' said Crispian, noticing the novelty name cards at each of the six places. His own was indeed a paintbrush. He was next to a creature called Tania Bryer, whose marker featured a coy illustration of a doe-eyed sun peeping out from behind fat, fluffy clouds. As they sat down, it was evident that Ms Bryer was not the only absentee. 'Where's cheeky Kiki?' Crispian said brightly. Might as well try to get into the swing of things.

'She left a message that she'd got caught up in a meeting with some Johnny from an ad agency,' the middle-aged man called David said, as the Chinese houseboy served steaming bowls of clear soup. There was something vaguely military about his manner, Crispian observed. 'Said we ought to tuck in while it's still piping hot, which is A-OK with yours truly,' David prattled on.

'What's on your card, then?' enquired Crispian politely. David turned it over to reveal what appeared to be . . . the decorator was too vain to wear his glasses and was much too squeamish even to dream about contact lenses . . . a knife. 'Oh! You're a butcher!'

'So they tell me, so they tell me,' David said with a bluff, hearty laugh. Crispian imagined him to be the sort of person who'd cheer loudly at rugby matches. A shiver ascended his spine like a high-speed lift. 'Actually I'm a medical man.'

'Really. A doctor? Oh – silly moi, you're a surgeon!'

'Well, so Miss Cox seems to believe, though I can't think why,' cut in the surgeon's wife, with a nervous titter.

'What is your speciality, you must tell me,' said Crispian with glee. One thing he shared with Kiki, he knew from the collection of weighty medical books wedged on the shelves above her computer at the far end of the room, was a deep fascination with health. David leaned slightly towards him.

'Actually I'm a proctologist,' he said.

'Oh,' croaked Crispian. 'Bottoms up!' But his smile began to harden at the edges. He was mentally running a mile. 'Then you,' he said quickly, turning his attention to another new face '. . . must be our millionaire!'

The man he now addressed was bespectacled and balding, the man called Garth who was seated next to Mitchell Fox. 'No, I'm just a bank manager actually,' Garth replied.

Kiki's new bank manager, of course. Did the woman have any real friends, Crispian wondered, apart from those she met professionally and who did this and that and the other for her? He didn't get the opportunity to ponder this further. Garth's views on interest rates and the difficulty in obtaining good quality recordings of the nightly shipping forecast (which he collected and on which he was, apparently, something of an authority) now that it had been moved to long wave, occupied the remainder of the first course.

'By the way, what's the sketch on Kiki's card?' Crispian asked, as the houseboy removed the empty plates. The doctor turned up the marker for inspection. It was blank.

'Tells us everything we need to know about her, doesn't it?' Crispian quipped. 'How do you two know her, anyway?' he asked the Mitchell Foxes.

'Actually, we've never met her,' Jennifer Mitchell Fox admitted, a little sheepishly. 'Well, just briefly when she came to deliver the invitation. We only moved in downstairs last week. How about yourself? Are you an old friend?'

'By her standards, practically palaeolithic, dear. I've known Kiki, gorgeous thing, since she hit these shores from Australia three or four years ago. But do you know, this is the first time she's invited me round to her flat. Her magazine did a big feature on my oeuvres last month, five pages no less, and since then the work's been absolutely flooding in, I can't tell you.'

No, he couldn't tell them. The truth was that people were either too cheap or too timorous to hire decorators of such exquisite sensitivity as he . . . or perhaps no-one who mattered actually read YES Magazine. The only call he'd received after the piece had appeared was from a man with a Scouse accent who'd asked him several fairly amusing questions about latex before descending into a rant of obscene gay-bashing. Crispian had rather enjoyed it, as a matter of fact, encouraging the caller to continue until he ran out of money for the phonebox.

As the houseboy disappeared with the soup plates, the central heating pipes suddenly gave the most alarming creak. Outside, wind whistled through the trees.

'Did you know,' the doctor said, apropos of nothing, '. . . that there's supposed to be a ghost in this square? It's one of the two most haunted squares in London, that was what the estate agent said, didn't he, darling? Isn't it funny, that an estate agent should use a ghost to sell us a property.'

No one laughed. The bank manager muttered something inconsequential about interest rates.

'Aren't her fish utterly lavish?' offered Crispian, vaguely. The others turned and looked at a large aquarium, set on an ornate stand. 'I think they're what Kiki loves most in all the world, probably the only thing she loves. Apart,' Crispian added, mainly for effect, '. . . from herself, of course.'

There was an uncomfortable silence. The central heating gave another eerie moan, like a delirious invalid. A door banged shut somewhere else in the flat. Crispian noticed with a start that the houseboy had silently materialised at his left shoulder. Startled, he twitched involuntarily, knocking the plate from the boy's hand. It hit the hardwood table, and, as everyone jerked to assist, Crispian's wine glass toppled, dumping Jacob's Creek bang in the crotch of his pink dungarees.

'Oh, quelle fucking drag,' the decorator said, leaping to his feet. Everyone watched as the dark stain spread across his groin. The houseboy was miming gestures of abject contrition, but Crispian ignored him, excusing himself from the table with an imperious eye-roll and a toss of his cowlick. As he made his way to the bathroom, the decorator noticed further small items that simultaneously disturbed and provoked him. Somehow they seemed incongruous in this gleamy, high-tech environment, with its state-of-the-smart, computer-entertainment-communication console and the barely stocked glass fridge. For all its aspirations, Crispian's highly developed senses detected a false note in Kiki's nest, a humming of plastics and laminates amidst the Opium strips and Peter Jones potpourri. It was something intangible, at the edge of reason: the coasters, the rouche curtains and doily set took his eye as having come from some other life, maybe not even hers. It was as if someone else secretly trod these stripped wooden floors when the flat's harsh lights were dimmed and the moon shone full.

The first door he tried was locked. Crispian went through into Kiki's lace-festooned, pink-tinged bedroom. A pot boiler lay open on the conch-coloured bedspread. Next to her bedside table was a child's sofa, crowded with teddy bears. Hmmm. Crispian found the *en suite* bathroom, and all but fell upon her collection of glass bottles and glossy cosmetics containers. Bliss! But he was supposed to be looking for some stain remover . . .

Crispian suddenly realised what was unusual about Kiki's boudoir. He couldn't see a mirror anywhere. Maybe it was built into the wall somewhere? Who could tell? Both his professional and sexual experience had taught him you could learn a lot about people from their bathrooms, and what they kept therein. Intrigued, he closed the door and began to rummage among the medicine bottles.

Back in the dining-room, Earth, Wind and Fire was playing on the CD. The other guests were discussing property prices and wondering when the main course might appear. Suddenly a long lean shadow fell across the table. They all looked up: there was a silhouette standing at the top of stairs.

Kiki stood straight as an empress in her minstrel's gallery, surveying her own scene. She wore a dark navy two-piece by Valentino, and discreet diamonds. Her skin was the colour of alabaster, her lips pale, her eyes shark-cold. She remembered, just in time, to smile. 'Good evening, everybody. So sorry that I got held up.'

'Age before beauty, Kiki. Well, that's what the wife always says.'

'Very droll, Garth,' said Kiki, tripping daintily down the spiral staircase into the dining-room. 'Did Crispian arrive yet?'

'He's just gone for a piddle, be right back.'

'Excuse me while I slip into something less comfortable,' said Kiki, still smiling. '. . . Oh, and don't worry – the next two courses will be here at any moment. Please, help yourselves to more wine.'

Kiki didn't go into her bedroom. Taking a key from her bag, she slipped inside the locked room and closed the door behind her.

This was Kiki's dressing-room – strictly out of bounds to all-comers. She threw off her Valentino suit, discarded her underwear and hastily selected a long gold Armani sheath and scarlet suede Jimmy Choo mules.

Back in the bathroom, Crispian was rifling through Kiki's stock of vitamin pills. Suddenly he heard her through the thin partition wall, bustling around in her dressing-room. 'Kiki, dahling,' he said wedging the door open.

'Christ, Crispi!' she yelled. 'I'm not decent!'

'That makes two of us, ducky. Seen it all before. Sorry, I'll see you at table. Red or white?'

'I'll give him red or white,' she fumed as she struggled to hook herself up at the nape of her neck.

In the second before she had blocked his view and banged the door shut, Crispian caught what he would later describe as 'the teeniest glimpsette' of Kiki's dressing-room. He saw three rows of pristine shrink-wrapped outfits hanging on rails; enough shoes to put Imelda Marcos back in business; a poster of Humphrey Bogart and Lauren Bacall in *Casablanca*; some framed photographs, the largest of which showed a powerfully built stud in speedos, holding up his surfboard – an old flame back home? – and a hat-stand dropping reams of scarves and handbags of every shape, size and colour known to man. As he walked back into the drawing-room, Crispian noticed that the doctor's wife was looking flustered, and that her husband was rising from his place, squaring up to a tall, bulky, Medusa-haired man as the Chinese houseboy attempted to serve the veal escalopes from silver tureens as if nothing at all was happening.

'Hey, good looking, what's cooking?' the decorator asked the newcomer.

'You're late, Paulo,' Kiki snapped from behind him.

'I'm late? What about the laminated cookery card offer *YES* Magazine is supposed to have put out with the Christmas issue?' he growled in a thick Lancashire accent, drawing away from the doctor and, to Crispian's total chagrin, ignoring him. 'That's twelve bloody weeks late, pet.'

The fax in Kiki's home infotainment centre began spewing paper.

'Don't get chippy with me, Paulo,' Kiki warned, stalking across the room to retrieve the message. 'It was very nice of you to . . .'

'I like that!' scoffed the unruly celebrity chef. 'I get all the way here and find I'm not even bloody well invited to stop for a bite to eat. Oh no, I only cooked the crap. What the fuck do you think I am? Some kind of up-market take-away service? You just bloody use people, Keek. I know your type,' he fumed.

'I don't actually need this attitude in front of my friends,' Kiki said coldly, looking up from her fax. 'I think you'd better leave.'

The chef snorted, petulantly lifted the tureen lid and spat in the veal. 'No, you fuck off!' he sneered.

'Paulo, really. Childish behaviour really doesn't become the middle-aged . . .'

Paulo wasn't listening. Observing the houseboy's hostile glare, Paulo grabbed him by the ponytail and shook the servant's head violently from side to side. '. . . and take your dumb waiter with you,' he said, and stormed out.

Kiki was sitting at her computer, making keystrokes. 'Hojo, are you OK?' she said over her shoulder.

The houseboy looked at her, tears leaking from his eyes, and nodded.

'Will you nip round to San Lorenzo and see if Maria can find a table for us? Then you can have the rest of the night off. Oh dear,' she said, reading the message in the Confidential E-mail file on the computer. There was only one person who could access that file: Clifford Starsmeare, the Earl of Lanchester. 'Folks,' she said, 'I'll be along later. I'll just have to pack. I've got to make a trip over the water tomorrow.'

13

Another frantic day in the life of the planet's busiest airport. Every year, some 48 million people pass through Heathrow. It has to be the ultimate stress zone: the roar of Jumbo jets taking off and landing, the hustle of luggage carousels, the crowded walkways, the packed duty-free shops, the overflowing transit lounges, the crammed restaurants, the queues and queues of bleary, weary travellers . . . oh, for an oasis of calm.

Zelda Lee Powers was in it. There she sat, in the Concorde VIP lounge, reclining in a plush leather armchair. 'HUH,' she snorted, so vehemently that all the charms on her bracelet rattled. She was scanning an article in the *Daily Sketch*, by the Editor, headlined 'Battered Husbands – Britain's Silent Victims Speak Out'. She looked up and registered a vaguely familiar figure shedding a cashmere shawl as she entered the windowless room. Zelda noted the chalk white hue of the woman's skin, then smugly fingered her own perfect honeydew complexion.

'. . . Sir Colin Marshall should've sent a fax to OK it,' Kiki Cox was saying, peering over her Armani sunglasses at the receptionist. Behind her, in breezed a stocky youth with acne who was inappropriately dressed in homeboy cut-off shorts and a Sexwax T-shirt. Across the lounge, Zelda waved frantically to the guy, pointing to the bar area and miming an instruction to meet her there in a second.

'Dennis, BABY, it's been a long time,' she pouted, kissing him on each spotty cheek.

'Oh, how are you?' responded Dennis. 'I haven't seen you in a while. Staying in shape?'

'You know how it is,' Zelda Lee said sheepishly. 'During the holidays I kind of lost the plot, there were so many parties to go to, and now I've relocated here to take up this fabulous new job. Are you still wowing them on the Westside?'

'Yeah, could say that. I just blew in to help Robert de Niro take off a few pounds for this new movie he's shooting here, *Good Sports.*'

'*Good Sports?*'

'It's about a bunch of gangsters in South Central LA, they're all in wheelchairs, and this guy they mug shows them how to play professional soccer.'

'Jeez,' Zelda said. 'You gave him hell? De Niro gets on my tits, the sonofabitch.'

'You better believe it,' the personal trainer grinned, pouring himself a huge orange juice. When Zelda was editing the *New York Gazette*, this Sydneyside stud had worked her out three times a week early each morning – usually on the polished floor of her Upper Westside apartment, tuning each other's pelvic muscles to old ZZ Top tunes.

'Hey, Denny, you see that chick who was at the reception desk when you came in?'

'Cute bird with the butt and the sunglasses?'

'Yeah, that's the one,' Zelda frowned, annoyed that Kiki had turned Dennis's eye.

'What about her?'

'Do you recognise her?'

'Nah, I don't think so. Why? Should I?'

'Don't know, I figured maybe you might make her from Sydney?'

Dennis took a surreptitious glance round the room in the mirror which ran along the wall, supporting the shelves or the glasses and bottles. '. . . Can't bloody see her anywhere,' he said.

A suspicious look passed down Zelda's face. 'Yeah?'

'But I reckon that if I'd seen her around, I'd know who she was. Why?'

'Oh, it doesn't matter, I guess,' Zelda said. The unlikely pair exchanged some more chitchat, and Zelda returned to her seat.

Before she'd caught her husband *in flagrante delicto* with the telephone and that little slut with the birthmarked ass on the receiving end, Anthony had told her there were only four hurdles between her getting her feet under the Editor's desk at *The Times*. The first was the deputy editor, Duncan Campbell. Zelda had plans for winning him over when she got back from her trip, during the course of which she'd take care of the other three. She wrote a list, recapping what she knew from the gossip Anthony had passed on to her.

1. Mira Freer Farmer. Ex-debutante, daughter of crazy Viscount, motorbike nut, rumoured substance abuser, nympho-maniac.
2. Mandi Harry. Blue-collar tabloid editor. Unsophisticated, sentimental, animal lover, married to a moron.
3. Kiki Cox.

Zelda paused for a moment, and put three mental question marks next to the last name. There was no point in sweating it, she thought, because by this time tomorrow the career prospects of all three at International News Incorporated would be history.

Zelda resumed her study of the papers. She was just settling down to a salacious page three story about a multiple sex murderer in the *Daily Telegraph* when, without warning, a shadow fell across her page.

'You're Zelda Lee Powers, aren't you? I thought I should come and introduce myself. Kiki Cox, *YES* Magazine.'

'HI!,' said Zelda with one of her speciality mouth-only smiles, getting up as Kiki bent down so that they could exchange a ritualised powerkiss: two sets of rouged cheeks brushing very visibly without ever actually touching. 'Oh, horrors!' thought Zelda, unconsciously mimicking Crispian's favourite expression, as she rapidly decided her usual '. . . but my friends call me Zeelee' line would be totally inappropriate here.

'So how are you? I recognized you from the funeral.'

'Wasn't it terrible about John?'

'Tragic, yes,' Kiki agreed. 'Such a loss to the journalistic community here. Such integrity, such a great champion of the underdog, a journalist's journalist . . .'

'Sure,' Zelda said. 'Terrible, just terrible, SO sad.'

Zelda guessed that Kiki hadn't actually known him either, but they don't employ bouncers at funerals.

'So,' Zelda said. Since she hadn't read it, she decided that complimenting Kiki on the last issue of YES wouldn't be the right move since it would give her rival the opening to ask her about the New York Gazette. 'So – you going over the pond, huh?'

'Well, just to France, actually. I promised a mate of mine I'd go racing with him at Longchamps.'

'The ponies, who needs it? It's like sex with my husband – a whole lotta talk then it's all over in two minutes.'

They both laughed thinly.

'So where are you heading for?' Kiki felt obliged to ask.

'I'm taking care of business in Manhattan, then I'm MGMing out to LA for a meeting.'

'MGMing?'

'MGM Grand Air, honey – it's the only way to fly.'

'Who are you meeting?'

Zelda had opened her handbag and taken out her compact to touch up her lipstick. 'You really want to know?'

'Sure,' Kiki shrugged.

'Since there's zip you can do about it anyways, I'll tell you,' Zelda said smugly, pursing her lips and snapping the compact shut. 'I'm having lunch with The Boss,' she said.

'Oh,' Kiki replied. 'How nice.'

Christ, the woman's a fucking iceberg, Zelda thought. Let's see if we can't turn her into a lettuce.

'Hey, Kiki – cute name, by the way – let me tell you something straight from the hip, OK? When I get this gig at The Times, I'm considering having you on my team. It takes a lot of moxie to just roll up to someone like me and say Howdy Doody Zeelee, what's shaking outside of my chins and cheeks. But I seen a coupla issues of YES Magazine, and the true story is – it really sucks. You guys kiss more ass than a toilet seat, you know that?'

'Sure,' Kiki said, her smile freezing into place, her accent stiffening a little. 'But at least I'm editing something,' she retorted, a dangerous edge to her voice. 'I heard what happened about the

Morgan case. Too bad you had to carry the can, eh, Zelda?'

'It's one of those things. It'll all blow over in a couple of weeks,' Zelda sneered. 'You been around hard news any length of time, some tough guy always wants to get into it, sue your ass off. But I guess you wouldn't really know about that, would ya?'

'Actually no-one's ever tried to sue me, even when I was a cadet on the Sydney *Daily Mirror*,' Kiki shrugged. 'But then I always make a point of reading every word that goes into the magazine before it's published. By the way,' she added, moving off, 'cute nosejob.'

'Yeah, right,' Zelda muttered at Kiki's slender, departing back. The only job I'd give YOU, honey, she was thinking, would involve a hatchet. She watched Kiki walk away and felt a pang of jealousy. The woman was beautiful. When I get this gig, Job Number One, she thought, is to bring a little ugliness into her life.

14

In France, they say, binoculars were invented not for watching the horses at the races, but for the discreet observation of those other fillies who parade around the paddock: the gigis, the elegant clothes-horses who put the *beau* before the *monde*. The coiffure of such thoroughbreds is as sleek as a groomed equine tail, the skin glossed to perfection, and the expensive legs seem to go on forever. For a Frenchman – or any discerning man, come to that – there are few more pleasing sights.

It was a familiar arena to Kiki Cox and she was as well-prepared as she was perfectly dressed for it. As chic as the most *soignée Française* in her flamingo suede Versace two-piece, Kiki sat as still as a waxwork in the back of the Citroën limousine which swiftly conveyed her from the Charles de Gaulle air terminal to the racecourse. The car swung through the gates towards the owners' private carpark beyond the paddock. The chauffeur opened her door and took her arm as she got out. Kiki leaned languorously against the vehicle for a moment, immersed in the spectacle. This was an environment which always aroused her.

Kiki waited while the driver scurried away to announce her arrival. She contemplated the bare trees and poked a steel heel into the springy turf. She'd been here often enough before to know the slanguage: the ground 'had some cut' in it, and all that.

A few hundred yards away, up in the owners' boxes about the finishing line, Gail Lanchester ripped up her pari-mutuels in disgust. 'Pathetic,' she snorted. 'He dropped his hands. The stupid little man wasn't even trying.'

Like Kiki, who unbeknown to her was waiting down by the car, Gail Lanchester had been around the track and back. The dizzy brunette, who had taken the decision to retain her face rather than her figure when she hit 50, had been the *Harper's Bazaar* model turned society wife turned rich man's bored and badly behaved chattel. During 30 childless years of marriage, the stern press baron and the flitsy socialite had come to accommodate one another as civilized people. They realised early on in their marriage that without mutual forebearance and a certain myopic tolerance, their lives would spin like gyroscopes in a confined space: all grinding, abrasive friction and irritating sparks. Thus Gail blithely turned a blind eye to her husband's wayward peccadilloes, the ones she called his 'snacks between meals'. And he, in turn, indulged her fripperous extravagances. It was one of those mutually satisfying arrangements: she was totally and lovingly loyal, and he was utterly discreet. What happened away from the prying public eye was between them and them alone. And fortunately for them, much of the public's vision could be blinkered by the eleventh Duke of Lanchester, Clifford Starsmeare himself, proprietor of Allied Newspapers. At least it had been, until the arrival of an impertinent parvenue buccaneering International News Incorporated.

One of the jaunty young swains Gail Lanchester liked to surround herself with whooped with delight as the victorious nag's number was displayed. The toy boy had picked a winner, and as Gail went with him to the mutuel window to shovel up the paydirt, she saw a flunky murmuring something to her husband, something to which she knew she must turn her infamous deaf ear.

His guest had arrived. The portly Lanchester slipped away, almost unnoticed, leaving behind a merry throng bubbling with good humour lubricated entirely by his vintage champagne.

Lanchester stalked directly to the stables, crossing a wide yard surrounded on three sides by low buildings arranged in a triangle. It was a very cold day and the stables seemed to shine with an iridescent brilliance.

'Kiki, dear darling Kiki.' Restraining himself even though he was all but champing at the bit at the sight of her, Lanchester brushed his lips stiffly against her hair. 'Come,' he said, cupping her elbow with a large hand, 'there's someone I want you to meet.'

Through the wooden doors of the closed stalls came muffled

animal sounds. Kiki's senses tingled at the sound of rustling straw, of twitching lips, of molars chomping on dry hay, of water slapping seductively in drinking pails, and found herself going weak at the knees at the prospect of the deliciously inevitable.

Lanchester flung open the first door they came to. Inside, the most handsome grey Kiki had ever seen reared his beautiful head to stare at them. He stood all of 17 hands high. His velvet brown eyes seemed to study them both expectantly. There was a certain haughtiness in his bearing – but he was clearly pleased to meet Kiki.

'Strewth,' gulped Kiki, 'the bastard's got five legs.'

'Two more than my three,' breathed Lanchester into her ear.

Kiki didn't dare move, she was rooted to the G-spot. 'How old is he?' Her voice trembled but her tone was as cool as she could keep it.

'Dunbar's Pride? He's four now. Magnificent animal. Unbeaten as a two-year-old. Ten races, netted me more than three hundred grand. Poor fellow took a bit of stick in the Derby but he's bounced right back, won the Coral Eclipse at Sandown, the King George VI at Ascot. We'll be retiring him soon. He'll probably make around five million at stud – lucky thing'll be on the job 'til he's twenty-odd.'

'Plenty of life in the old boy yet?' said Kiki with a knowing smile, right on cue.

'There should be a drink here for us somewhere . . . ah, here,' said Clifford, drawing her into the adjacent stable. She all but swooned at the scent of the place: the polished leather cruppers, suave saddles lubricated with English saddle oil; the bridles, their cloths freshly fragrant with Marseilles soap; the tingling fumes of newly burned wood; of violets, crushed barley and new oats; of Normandy Apples, clover and glowing cinders. Kiki felt her cold hand being pressed to Clifford's overheated crotch. He released his grip momentarily to retrieve a bottle of vintage Bollinger and two glasses from an ice bucket secreted away earlier.

Pulling off his boots, Clifford flopped heavily into the fragrant hay nest, pulling Kiki with him. She lost her balance and tripped into his meaningful embrace. Clifford moaned as he struggled to undo his buttons. As he reached the last one, his large manhood sprang free. Kiki's scarlet-slicked lips thrust themselves into an involuntary pout. She bent over it with a deep sigh, closed her eyes and softly kissed its tip, smearing it with her lipstick. She pumped him gently. Clifford surrendered to the agony and the ecstasy, his eyes half-closed. Reaching upwards, he wrenched roughly at her tight jacket. Unable to release it, he kneaded her breasts urgently through the suede.

'Suck me,' he pleaded, 'suck me.'

Kiki didn't need asking twice. This was a task she always relished. Taking him between thumb and forefinger, she slid her hand up and down as she spread her mouth lusciously.

'Oh, oh, oh,' he grunted. 'God, that is beautiful. Oh,' he moaned. 'Heaven, I'm in absolute heaven. I'll have to hurry you . . .'

'Not yet, Clifford, not here . . .' she started to murmur, hoping that they could continue this somewhere more private, where there was less chance of being caught red-handed by his wife. The atmosphere was charged, and heavy with sounds and smells: the dull splatter of droppings falling into straw, the nervous clinking of bit against soft pink flesh, snorting, husky whinnyings, the whipping of tails on hocks . . . Kiki saw the twitch in Dunbar's muscled flanks and sensed his agitation. But Clifford's hands were already inching up her thighs towards the slip of moist silk . . . She felt herself start to pant, she knew she couldn't wait, she had to feel him inside her now, before her flesh exploded . . . there was something she wanted, but she couldn't quite remember what it was . . . something she needed to ask him for . . . Kiki struggled desperately to keep control, she must say what was troubling her before she could let go. She pushed at his hands and bent to kiss him passionately while she wracked her brains feverishly.

Lanchester bit so hard on his lip that his teeth drew blood. He was ready for some real action, he wanted her now, and he didn't want to wait . . . and yet . . . and yet . . . Oh, God, almost there, Al-most there, this bitch was going to have to pay for this . . .

'Darling,' she drooled, spilling saliva over him, 'I've got a little project I want you to help me with . . .'

'Yes, Keek, anything, darling, only you're going to have to let me . . .'

'It's going to be very expensive, though, Clifford,' she teased, her mouth hovering above his. '. . . I'm going to have to get some very expensive new computer things at home, and the money isn't there in our budget . . .'

'Get any damned thing you want, don't do this to me, get on with it,' he growled. 'What is it, some new magazine?' he gasped.

She nodded. 'Sort of . . . I'll be honest with you, Clifford, we've always been honest with each other, haven't we? I've been offered the Editor's chair at *The Times* and I want to take it tabloid, but I've never edited a newspaper before, so if I'm going to make a fist of it, I've got to show them a dummy . . .'

'You weren't listening,' snapped Lanchester, his voice low with rising rage. 'While you are spending my money in your head – buy whatever you need, tell the Weasel to charge it to Special Projects – there's a little urgent business needs attending to right here. You asked for this . . .'

He slapped at her face to stun her, then grabbed her wrists, yanked them behind her back and jerked his knee into Kiki's spine with a sickening crack. Holding her face-down in the straw with one large red hand and ignoring her cries, he tore at the suede skirt with the other, forcing it up over her thighs and buttocks and exposing silk knickers the colour of tea roses, and stockings which held themselves up with elastic. Clifford laughed, but it didn't sound like Clifford laughing. Kiki felt him ripping the silk clean away, shoving his knees up between hers until she almost snapped like a wishbone, and prising the soft white flesh apart until she cried out in agony.

'No, Clifford, no, no, not like this!'

He didn't even hear her. The thunderous Niagra of lust pounding in his skull had deafened him.

Whimpering, helpless, horrified, Kiki realised what her hitherto gentle lover was about to do to her . . .

It was all over in a few seconds which felt to Kiki like an hour-long ordeal. But the pain, when it came, seared through her like a meat cleaver. And the sticky, hot, wet fluid which seeped from her battered body as he got up, hastily rearranged his clothing and stormed silently from the stable, had nothing to do with Clifford's desperately vengeful climax. It was blood.

15

Los Angeles shimmered in the morning sun like a desert mirage. Heat and smog rose from every pore. Zelda waited impatiently for the green light on Franklin and Cahuenga, picking at the armpits of her short-sleeved emerald silk two-piece. They were already damp, goddammit. How was she supposed to cope with these extremes in temperature? It had been snowing in London yesterday, for Chrissakes.

Suddenly a tiny man on a big Harley pulled up beside her limo. He made a hand signal, as if to say Hey! Wind down ya window, would ya please? Zelda hesitated for a second – who knows what kind of assholes around here would blow you away for just the contents of your purse? – but her curiosity, as usual, got the better of her.

'I need some scratch to go someplace,' he said, treating her to a big grin. Zelda groaned and reached forward to press the rear window button marked with an Up arrow. As she did so, something he said caught her ear. 'Watch what I'm gonna do . . . if ya like it, you can give me money,' the guy said cheekily.

The lights changed and the little man took off on his big bike with Zelda's limo in hot pursuit. At the next bend, his legs were up in the air. He launched into a sequence of flips and turns, all the while just managing to guide the motorcycle along the busy boulevard between cars and trucks racing every which way. They arrived at the next set of traffic lights. Zelda smiled, reached into her purse and posted a $20 bill through the gap at the top of the window. The little man on the big bike smiled back, mouthed her a warm 'Thank you' and was on his way.

Only in LA, Zelda thought. To most people, Los Angeles is the air-headed, psycho-babbling, bimbo-augmented, breast-implanted cult'n'car capital of the entire world. A city with more Porsches on its crowded freeways than the whole of Germany. A city where you can stop 20 people at random coming out of Vons Supermarket, ask how their treatment is coming along, and at least 18 of them will reply, 'Great . . . but what I really want to do is direct . . .'

Zelda Lee Powers knew this city of old. She knew that if you took the time to dig beneath its surface you would surely find . . . more surface. And earthquakes, droughts, floods, sex crimes, plagues, drive-by shootings, bikers dealing injectable methamphetamine in the parking lot of the 7-11; smog, insect infestations, pollutants raining from a clingy night sky; coked-out personal trainers who objected to your secondhand cigarette smoke, traffic jams, jack-knifed big rigs, schools that would make Haiti blush attended by armed pupils who had never, uh, like, really got into verbalising; toxic derailments, poisonous shellfish, mind-melting cults . . . and houses priced way beyond the sum of their unlisted telephone numbers. And that was in the good old days, Zelda thought.

The limo negotiated the 101 Hollywood Freeway exit. It cruised gracefully along the surface streets with a satisfying purr, made a turn and pulled up at the gates of the 21st Century Fox lot. After the most cursory of formalities, they were waved through into the compound.

Sunshine, blue sky, palm trees. Zelda felt like the bees-knees as she sashayed into the elegant reception area, tossing her sleek bob from side to side. She'd spent the entire morning working out at her hotel, and had succeeded in taking the edge off her jetlag. Her career felt hot, her forehead cool and the curves of her soul serene. She took a deep breath. Coming ready or not . . . She was coming.

'Zelda Lee Powers to see Ruprecht Pupkin.'

The receptionists were perched at a curved, monolithic silver desk in front of two shimmering columns which framed a large, wart-less oil painting of The Boss. They all looked ready to read the news at the drop of a hint. One of them ran her haemoglobin-red talon the length of a crisp computer print-out, reached for a receiver and tapped in a number. She shot Zelda a winning smile – the same smile that had helped her to the Miss Burma title the year before last. 'Would you take a seat please, Miz Powers?'

Zelda manoeuvred herself on to one of the delphinium-blue, low leather Roche Bobois sofas, and found herself sitting next to an athletic-looking man in a linen suit. He glanced up from *Black Enterprise* magazine and raised his caterpillar eyebrows at her, as if flashing his brights at a vehicle that had allowed him to pass first on a narrow street, then quickly resumed his reading. Zelda popped a cinnamon gum stick into her mouth. She shuffled the magazines on the glass table, tossed aside *Realities* and *Scientific American*, and picked up *Daily Variety*. Across the hall, a slender woman with long, cascading curls in Norma Kamali jeans and a pale silk blouse was whispering into a Sony cellular about step deals and ancillary rights. Zelda noticed that, like herself, she wore rings on four fingers. So what? So what was going on around here?

They always keep you waiting. Zelda raked around in the recesses of her mind for something to think about, while away the time. She suddenly remembered that her mother, the famous Broadway musical star Myrna Meitling, had screentested here with one of the last of the great Hollywood moguls. They still told stories about Zelda's mother, who now lived in a rest home for distressed dancers in Sarasota, Florida. The most famous concerned a call from her agent who'd told her that a rival mogul wanted to see her about a part in a Bogart picture. But she didn't have to turn up, her agent explained, '. . . because Mr Cohen has a terrible reputation for chasing nubile young actresses around his desk and tearing their dresses off'.

'Thanks for the tip,' Myrna had replied, 'I'll wear an old dress.'

Zelda's father had been a lavatory cisterns manufacturer in Des Moines, Iowa. But for years she'd preferred to believe that she had been conceived somewhere on the lot here: the scion of a siren with stars in her eyes on a screen test, and some rough, tough Texan lug who'd come to try his luck in the city of dreams . . .

As Zelda flicked through the showbiz newspaper, a tall,

skinny kid in his late teens – his very late teens, he was actually 21 – dressed in a Grateful Dead T-shirt and ripped'n'torn baggies, slouched in through the doors with something for Miss Burma to sign. His long stringy hair bopped to some internal rhythm. As he turned round, she intercepted his vacant stare.

'Mom!'

'Stone! My baby, let me LOOK at you! Oh my God, you look like some sort of hesher.'

'Hey Mom, chill out,' he said, disentangling himself from her embrace. 'What are you doing here?'

'Lunch with The Boss. What are YOU doing here? I thought you were working for the *National Enquirer*.'

'That kind of fell through. I got into a fist fight with Roseanne Arnold and they needed a scapegoat . . .'

'Oh Stone, not again. I thought you were going to get straight, be a mensch about this . . .'

'Things haven't been too hot for you either, last I heard. Everyone's been talking about the Morgan libel thing. She was on *Hard Copy* last night. How much, Mom?'

'TOO much, baby. Get off my case. Now tell me, what happened to Suzi Raggamuffin or whoever that schicksa was?'

'She split with a body-builder from Muscle Beach. They've gone to raise designer cows in Wyoming. How's Anthony?'

'Don't even ask. So you still taking pictures?'

'Soon I'm gonna be making pictures. This driving job's just a fill-in. I know, I know, you think I'm just another bum looking for a break in the wild wild West, but I've got it going on. Me and Charlie Sheen are working on this project – it's Virtual Reality sex . . .' He began to ramble on about fibre-optics, dildonic wet suits and off-shore tax havens. '. . . I mean, come on, you'd pay ten bucks to get laid by Errol Flynn, right? OK, so there are a lotta airheads out there who'd pay seven dollars fifty to get a blow job from Shannen Doherty, trust me.'

Zelda sighed. The beautiful and the innocent have no enemy but Time.

'Got any gum? Thanks. So,' he said, finally, 'why are you having lunch with The Boss?'

'I'm finalising the details of a job offer,' said Zelda. An idea suddenly struck her. 'Stone, baby, you got wheels?'

'Yeah, a Lincoln stretch,' he said, '. . . it's like, the company ride.'

'What are you doing this afternoon?'

'Oh, like, I'm really busy, I got people to do, things to see. Like I gotta meet with Rob, Rob Lowe, you know, we're doing a casting call over at Westwood. And . . .'

Zelda reached into her purse, took out a thousand dollar bill, and tore it in two. She gave one half to her son, and replaced the other next to her AT&T card. 'Come and get me at two-thirty, there's something we should talk about.'

Stone shrugged. Zelda kissed him. He grimaced and slouched off. Zelda knew he'd be back . . . her son had a lot of nerve, but most of it was located inside the hip pocket where he kept his wallet. Zelda checked her Cartier tank watch: 9:09, which meant that it was 1:09 PST, local time. She sat down and ran through her routine, the one she had mastered to 'energize her inner powerspace': 'I am big, I am strong, I play team games all day long, I am big, I am strong, I play team games all day long, I am big, I am strong, I play team games . . .'

'Zelda Lee? Hiiiiii!' drooled a perky young woman with perfect breasts, perfect legs, perfect clothes, perfect teeth, perfect nails and far too perfect hair. YEUCHHH. 'I'm Meghan . . . Meghan Wright, personal assistant to Jane Taylor, Mr Pupkin's senior executive assistant.'

Zelda got up, shook hands, prayed that everything was in place. If it wasn't by now, it never would be. This was it. No turning back.

'How are you this afternoon?'

'I've been better . . .' Zelda began, but realising that this was neither the time nor the place for self-deprecation, added quickly: '. . . but I've sure been worse. Why? What's it to you, Cupcake?' Despite her extensive self-preparation, this hostile streak to her native New Yorker personality would insist on asserting itself at the most inappropriate moments. 'I'm sorry,' Zelda said, 'I didn't mean to sound patronising, I mean talk down to you, it's just that I'm a little jetlagged . . .'

'Sure. Zelda, Ruprecht sends his most sincere apologies. He's been called away unexpectedly to an urgent meeting.'

'Meeting? WHAT meeting?' Zelda barked. Any attempt at mellow melted clean away.

'What meeting? Where IS this meeting?'

'Jakarta,' replied Meghan sweetly.

If looks could kill . . . Zelda supressed a violent urge to commit homicide, and vowed that when she became editor of *The Times* she'd initiate a campaign to make drawing smiley faces a felony. 'But I've just flown eight thousand fucking miles to have lunch with him!'

Meghan's expression chilled into a fridge-freezer of a smile. 'Miz Powers . . . Si Schultz, our director of corporate public relations, would be delighted if you could join him for lunch in the commissary. He's keen to meet with you and share his firsthand knowledge of some exciting projects we have going on here at 21st. If you'll follow me please . . .'

'SCREW the commissary,' Zelda exploded.

'This is outrageous! How could you let something like this HAPPEN, you addle-brained Barbie doll . . . who do you think you ARE? Do you know who I am? Do you . . . MEL! JOEL! Teenagers, how ARE you?' she cried, suddenly changing gear as she spotted Joel Silver and Mel Gibson striding into the studios. She all but hurled herself at them, hugging the film producer and kissing the film star on both cheeks. 'LOOK at you, honey,' she said. 'The big director. Who'da thunk it, eh, kid?'

She gave them both a couple of playful jabs in the ribs, so that everyone in the reception area would know how HOT she was. She gabbed at them for nearly 30 seconds, anxious not to let them get away before she'd got them to invite her for lunch. 'So, lunch?'

'We'd love to, honestly, but we have to process some suits,' said Mel Gibson almost sadly. 'You know what it's like. But maybe see you in the commissary, say 45 minutes, an hour?'

'Sure, fine, great, gorgeous, see ya,' Zelda said to their backs, and marched in their wake past the columns towards the studio's corporate canteen. A large hand suddenly blocked her progress. 'Excuse me, Ma'am, may I check your commissary pass, please?'

Zelda looked up at the security guard. He was almost seven feet tall, and carried a sidearm in his holster. 'Er, The Boss's secretary just invited me to lunch in the commissary. Didn't you see?'

'I'm sorry, Ma'am, no pass, no admission, studio rules.'

Zelda turned back to the reception desk. 'Get that goddam secretary on the line.'

'Which secretary?' asked a tall Nordic beauty who seemed to have replaced Miss Burma for the lunch shift.

'I don't know her goddamn name, what do you take me for, a telephone directory already?' Zelda screeched. 'Just get me The Boss's PA.'

'I have to know who you need to reach, otherwise I can't help you.'

'The one who just invited me to lunch!' Zelda choked, clenching every muscle to keep hold of her temper.

'One moment, please,' the Nordic goddess smiled. Zelda surveyed the reception hall. The man reading *Black Enterprise* peered back into his magazine, avoiding her stare.

'I'm sorry, Miz Wright has gone to lunch.'

'Goddamn it, I've got to get in there and meet Joel and Mel, we were in Aspen together when they greenlighted *Lethal Weapon* . . .'

'If you'd care to take a seat, please, I'll find someone who's available to assist you . . .'

'Just give me the goddamn pass!' Zelda fumed, almost peeing her pants with frustration.

'I'm afraid I can't do that at this time. If you'd wait just one moment . . .' she said, lifting a receiver.

'DO YOU KNOW WHO I AM!' bellowed Zelda at the top of her voice.

'Security,' the receptionist said into the phone.

'You're Zelda Lee Powers,' said a warm, reassuring voice from behind her, '. . . and I'd say you're having a bad day. Zac Barrett, pleased to meet you . . .'

Zelda found herself shaking hands with the man who'd been

120

studying *Black Enterprise* magazine.

'I run the in-studio counselling service here at 21st. I've been stood up, too. Why don't you come up to my office and let me help you work through your hostile feelings?'

* * *

The son of a bitch!' Zelda squeaked, huffily adjusting the moist collar of her jacket. She stared through the black windows. Out there was endless airport traffic edging down the 405, the cars stuffed with mannequins, automatons, glove puppets . . . everybody a somebody but ultimately nobody at all . . .

'You know what?' Stone said from the front of the car later, his mother tucked safely in the back with a bottle of vodka and a flask of ice cubes, which she was stuffing with tired abandon into her cleavage.

'What?'

'Maybe you're right.'

'What do I know? I'm only your mother. I'm just the entertainment here, I bump my gums, my son the jailbird laughs, I should be grateful. I opened, I got some notice. So maybe I didn't fly eight thousand miles for nothing.'

'No,' Stone said. 'That shit, you know, like breaking patterns, getting out of the gestalt, maybe you're right. Isn't it enough that I admit it to you?'

'It's a start,' Zelda said, '. . . is what it is. But what happens? I heard it all before. Everytime I'm there for you. Over and over, it's a cracked record, it's wearing me thin.'

'And I wasn't there for you,' Stone said, glancing at her in the rear-view mirror, '. . . when it really mattered?'

'Stone,' she said flatly, 'it happened. He's dead. We can't undo the past.'

'We could talk about it'.

'I don't WANT to talk about it,' she snapped, raising her voice. 'I'm conflicted. What happened was wrong . . . it was EVIL . . . but then again, what were our choices? We weren't the perpetrators, we were reacting to a difficult situation. You put anyone in that situation, they'd have done the same thing, I'd bet my life on it. What's to be gained from talking about it? Where's that gonna get us? It's done, Stone.'

'Who you flying with?'

'Virgin.'

They drove in silence for a while.

'My momma used to say to me, "Zelda, you make a mistake, you make a schlud of yourself, just carry on like nothing happened".'

'Hey, it's not like you missed a cue at Radio City,' Stone said. 'We're talking homicide, murder one, accessory after the fact. Kerrzap! What's that funky smell, Warden? Why, it's the O'Briens, to be sure, bejeezus, another tragic writing-related death, that was how . . .'

'SHUT UP!' Zelda screeched at him.

They pulled up at the terminal entrance. 'The white zone is for loading and unloading only . . .' repeated a mechanical voice over the tannoy.

'I'm being a mensch,' he said, handing over her Louis Vuitton luggage to the kerbside check-in staff. 'I'm admitting, Mom, that I am wrong and you are right about this. I should take a break, open myself up to some changes in my life. That's what you said, right?'

'I'm only your mother. What do I know?'

'I'm coming to London.'

'You're what?'

'I bet you my Polaroid against a first-class ticket, I'll be landing in London about, oh, say ten hours from now.'

'You out of your mind?' Zelda said. 'What are you going to DO in London?'

'Same shit as I do here. Pull babes, drink beer, study absorption rates of white powders.'

'For God's sakes, Stone, don't be ridiculous.'

'Hey, it don't bother me, I done the time to fit the crime already.'

'It was your own fault, that infantile episode. That's nothing to do with what happened to us. You want to bang jailbait, that's your funeral. You want to hang out with cookie creeps who get their kicks from drugging up twelve-year-olds, that's your problem . . .'

The airline baggage checker was following their conversation with some interest.

'. . . a mother can do so much. Despite all the shit you put me through, I'm still your mother, I still love you, though in God's name I sometimes wonder why, what is this I have spawned? Oh, is there no END to it?'

'No,' Stone said. 'There's no end to it. You're my mother, he was my Dad, and, hey . . .' he shrugged, 'I have the Polaroid. You're taking me to London.'

'What do you think you're going to do there? How do you plan on making a living? What about your big virtual sex scheme and Charlie and Rob and the car? Huh? What are you going to DO? Come on, I'm listening, Tough Guy.'

'Sir Anthony,' Stone said. 'You can get him to get me a job on the *Sketch*.'

'I don't think so. I'm not even speaking to him myself right now. You threaten me, and now you want favours? Oh, Stone . . .'

'C'mon, Mom, I've paid my dues. I had a picture in *Globe* last week, Shaq O'Neill wearing a dress.'

'I saw that. It was a charity gig.'

'OK, yesterday I was doorstepping Wesley Snipes . . .'

'I can't DO that, Stone. All the papparazzi in London, the top guns, are freelance. At your stage in the game, you shoot your frames, you sell 'em to the highest bidder. You got syndication?'

'Sure, Xanadu out in Westwood . . .'

'Never heard of them. Don't run before you can walk, baby, London's a very tough town. You got friends here, you got a nice place in the Hills, the girls love you, what do you want to throw it all away for?'

'Why won't you help me?'

'I've been commuting across the pond for three years now, Stone. Budgets are tight in London, I know from Tony that everyone's shaving a nickel here, a dime there. Money and time are running out for all of us. Don't ask me to give you what I haven't got, OK?'

'Then don't ask me to give you what I have got.'
'The Polaroid?'
'You want to, like, keep negotiations open, Mommy dearest, then you've gotta be the first one to give.' Stone stared brightly at the baggage man. 'I get my ticket inside or what?'

16

The club swimming pool was divided into two lanes, fast and slow. Mandi chose the latter, and jumped in. The cold slap of the water kick-started her sluggish body, and she breast-stroked towards the shallow end, taking care to keep her head above the surface. As a teenager at Gravesend Comprehensive, she'd once got water in her ears and it had stayed there for three days, the whooshing, sucking sound driving her crazy. She touched the tiles and was about to turn when a male voice said, 'Hi, Mandi.'

She recognized Sir Anthony George immediately. 'Oh, hello.'

She felt self-conscious. Suddenly she found herself wishing she'd made time to reapply the cover cream that she used to conceal the port wine stain on her face. Her body felt flabby, her hair a greasy, Medusa-like tangle.

He was one of the few people on Grub Street she'd ever found attractive. She thought of Sir Anthony and she thought 'Classy'. He was grey again – his barber on Curzon Street having quietly suggested that the blond highlights were not perhaps such a good idea on a gentleman of his age – and tanned, and clean. He looked expensive. Daddy had been an MP and Mummy had worked tirelessly for charity. To her, he seemed . . . noble. Not the sort of chap who'd grope his secretary. 'How's it going then? Practising for the Editors' swimming gala, eh?'

'Not really, I always try and slip in a few laps before the paper goes to bed. It's the most relaxing time of the day, I find. Soothing music, wash away the day's worries, clear the head before we go on edition.'

'I haven't seen you here before,' Mandi said.

'I normally go to the RAC Club.'

'So what brings you out this far east, then?'

Sir Anthony looked sheepish. 'Bit embarrassing,' he said, wincing. 'I jumped in the RAC pool last week, and this old codger had a heart attack. Thought I should, er, take the waters elsewhere for a while, till all the fuss dies down. So, what's this charity swimming thing about anyway?'

'The Boss has it every year in aid of the bloody literacy fund. Surely you've done it before? All the Editors have to get sponsors and . . .'

'Oh yes, I remember trickling along a few years ago. Got my secretary to swim for me in the last couple, but she's no longer with us, I'm afraid.'

'Oh?'

'She's going off to work for Duncan Campbell at *The Times*. At least, that's the plan.'

'No! Really?'

'That's where they're going to announce who's got it, aren't they?'

'Who's going to announce who's got what?' Mandi asked, confused.

'Editor of *The Times*.'

'Really?' Mandi exclaimed. 'At the swimming gala?'

'Don't pretend you didn't know,' Anthony smiled. 'My source works at Wapping Wharf.'

'Oh,' Mandi said. 'Well, yeah, I did, but . . . your wife's playing hard to get it, isn't she?'

'And you're not?' Anthony laughed. 'Mandi, really. When is this absurd gala?'

'What, two weeks?' Mandi said. '7 March.'

'You going?'

'What do you think?' Mandi giggled.

'A fortnight away. What are you doing to advance your cause?'

'Absolutely nothing,' shrugged Mandi.

'I don't hold with all this creeping around, sucking up to the big knobs. The Boss knows what I do, he reads it every Sunday. Either I'm good enough or I'm not. It's no skin off my nose either way.'

'I can't see some of your competitors adopting such a laissez-faire attitude.'

'You mean Zelda?'

'No,' he said, 'I was thinking more of Kiki Cox.'

'I try not to,' Mandi grimaced. 'After all, if I want to make myself sick, I can always stick my fingers down my throat.'

'She is an odd one,' Anthony agreed. 'Never quite sure who she thinks she is . . . so aloof . . . so aggressive, but such a sex bomb at the same time . . .'

'She wishes,' snorted Mandi, secretly annoyed that he should find Kiki attractive enough to refer to her in another woman's company as a 'sex bomb'. Honestly. 'What about her stupid sunglasses, and all the affected mannerisms . . . I wonder if it's all an act to try and draw attention to herself, create a spurious mystique . . .'

'Perhaps she's just paranoid. After all, she's reaching the level where people are going to be scrutinizing her journalistic credentials a little more closely.'

'That'd be like looking for a salt shaker in a snowstorm, if that bloody awful supplement of hers is anything to go by,' Mandi sneered.

'But she's driven, Mandi, she's driven. I was at a reception the other day and . . .' he mentioned the name of a star writer whose pieces hadn't run in the magazine since Kiki had taken over. 'Kiki just completely blanked her, turned her back and continued talking to me as if the woman wasn't even there. I'm not sure if it's because writers frighten her, or because she's really like that.'

'Like what?' Mandi asked.

'Like someone drove a splinter of glass into her heart at an early age,' Anthony said. 'I mean, she's sexy and she's got a certain something, but you can't quite get close to her . . .'

'Oh? So you've tried?'

'You know what I mean.'

'I think it's all an act,' Mandi retorted. 'Apart from the fact that she's got the news sense of a guinea pig and the morals of a gangster, there's something deeply suss about "Kinky".'

'It's that old film star trick of being a perfect blank screen,' Anthony mused, 'So people can project anything they like on to you. You can be all things to all people and you become an icon

127

. . . well, in Kiki's case, perhaps a bonnet ornament . . . You know Tracey Schwartz?' he said suddenly, changing the subject.

'You know I know her. She was working for us until you poached her. Don't rub it in.'

'She told me all about your legendary tap-dancing talents.'

'Ooo-er,' said Mandi. 'What else?'

'She mentioned something to me the other day. Someone who went round to dinner at Kiki Cox's flat, all very odd, no family pictures, very impersonal, a hi-tech sort of pad, but with weird suburban touches . . . you know, Franklin Mint plates on the wall, crochet, that sort of thing.'

'Sounds almost schizophrenic, doesn't it? What does Her Indoors think of her?'

'Zelda has been sweating blood and shitting bricks.'

'I had a bit of a run-in with her at Hermès in Bond Street the other day,' Mandi confessed with a self-conscious laugh.

'I heard about it,' chuckled Anthony. 'Funny, I'd never have taken you for Hermès clientèle.'

'Well it just shows you,' she replied with a knowing wink. 'I'm full of surprises, Anthony.'

'Of that I am in no doubt,' he said, feeling his eyes sinking deeply into Mandi's substantial cleavage. 'No doubt . . .' He was trying to picture her completely undressed. In particular he was fascinated by the idea of her nipples, and found himself wondering what they tasted like . . .

'So when did Zelda tell you about it?'

'Actually,' he said with a frown, 'I heard it from Jackie, our fashion editor. You see, I've had a bit of a run-in with Zelda too.'

'Oh,' said Mandi, inviting his confidence.

'Don't even ask,' Anthony replied, taking care not to be drawn.

'I've got to know . . . what happened to your face?' Anthony was sporting a beautiful blue shiner, a cut lip and a couple of jawline bruises from the attack launched upon him by Zelda on being caught red-handed before she'd stormed off to Los Angeles. 'Walk into a door?'

'Cut myself shaving,' he said, and Mandi saw she wasn't

going to get any more out of him about his private life. Too bad.

'Talking of blood,' Mandi said, 'what about Keith Richard's offer to donate a few red cells for Mother Teresa's transfusion fund? That gave all my lot a good laugh.'

'It's giving us a feature spread . . . Blood Ties: Britain's Top Twenty Celebrity Donors . . .'

'Go on, who've you got?' Mandi said, egging him on and, sensing his wariness, reassured him, 'Come on, cough, it's all right, it's too soon for us to nick. By Saturday, Keef's offer will look like a Max Clifford publicity wrinkle.'

'Or a new Keef facial one,' Anthony quipped. 'Well . . . Anne Rice for one.'

'No!'

'And Christopher Lee for another.'

'Blimey,' said Mandi. 'Would You Buy Used Plasma From This Man?'

'Don't, I've had to put up with a week of bloody awful jokes about blood donors in the same vein . . . cell outs, thin red lines, it's a bloody splash, boosting the circulation, been there, done it. Anyway, I suppose I must away, back to the Black Lubyanka.'

Until Clifford Starsmeare had sold it to a Saudi Arabian Pension Fund during a recent recession, the *Daily Sketch* had been based in a monumental black glass Art Deco building at the St Paul's end of Fleet Street, and its inmates had bestowed upon it the sobriquet of the doomed Russian liner.

Mandi watched Sir Anthony haul himself out of the pool. 'Oh,' she giggled, 'I like your trunks!'

He peered down at the once black garment, now greying with age, saggy and shapeless with wear. Tenuously supported by a drawstring chord at the waist, the costume looked as if it were ready to wrap itself around Charlton Heston and start asking demented questions about old age pensions. 'I know, I know,' Anthony grimaced. 'But this new-fangled synthetic sportswear just isn't me, Mandi. Zelda tries to keep forcing me into these ludicrous Speedo things, but they make me look like, well, not so much a Chippendale, more a chamber pot. And do I not like chamber pots . . .'

'What?'

'Oh, nothing. Private joke. It's just not my style.'

'What is your style, then?'

'Middle-aged white man in a suit,' he shrugged. 'I don't know, I've never thought much about it, to be honest . . . bossy, probably. Bit untrendy, bit tweedy perhaps.'

'Oh Anthony! You do yourself down.'

'I don't know why I bother,' he said, looking down at her now that she was leaning against the end of the pool. 'Zelda Lee does enough of that for the two of us.'

'She's giving you a bad time, isn't she?'

'Quite apart from having my car blown up by the bomb squad, and getting some screaming queen to turn my house into a replica of a particularly slushy Busby Berkeley film set and, well, various . . . no, things couldn't be peachier.'

Anthony surveyed her curvaceous figure, almost bursting from the shiny purple one-piece which encased it like coloured cling-film. He noted her warm brown skin, rounded bottom and gorgeous, pillowy bosoms. Maybe she did have a funny birthmark on her face. Maybe she was a little overweight, fat even, and somewhat stocky in build . . . and she was definitely no debutante . . . but there was something about her which told him that, however cold the British winter raged, there'd always be a heatwave, a tropical heatwave, in the groin of the lucky bastard who shared Mandi's duvet . . . 'Are you going to that reception at Number Ten the week after next?'

'Yeah,' said Mandi, 'I've been invited, of course. See you there?'

'Perhaps we could get together before. My wife's away at the moment.'

'Where?' said Mandi uncertainly. My wife's away, she was thinking. Huh! What kind of a come-on . . .? What did he take her for anyway?

'If you have lunch with me,' he said smoothly, the famous smile playing across his face, 'maybe I'll tell you . . .'

'And maybe you won't,' she pouted, finishing the sentence for him.

130

He instantly saw something of the coquette in the way she looked at him. It turned him on. 'Of course, people would talk,' he reflected.

'Then let's give them something to talk about,' said Mandi. 'Why don't we make it dinner instead of lunch?'

'When?' he said. She saw that he was serious. Interested. Seriously interested.

'I'll have to ask my husband,' she said coyly.

Sir Anthony shook his head, realizing that once again a woman had run rings around him. 'You Fleet Street *femmes fatales*,' he sighed, getting up. 'It's easier to understand Japanese sign language than make head or tail of you lot.'

Mandi laughed, and watched as he ambled back towards the changing-rooms. What was a man like him doing married to a woman like Zelda? Her bemusement switched quickly to silent amazement as Mandi felt a long-suppressed stirring. There is something devastatingly, irresistibly delicious about that middle-aged white man, she thought, as she turned back to swim another lap. Even in those ropy old swimming trunks.

17

Wednesday morning, and Mandi was looking for some clear nail varnish to mend the run in the Pretty Polly Nearly Black tights she'd torn on her gold ankle bracelet while she was leaning over a reporter's computer terminal. She opened her bottom left-hand desk drawer, where sundry odds and ends tended to lurk, and discovered a string posing pouch made from red liquorice, the one deemed too tacky even for the *Post* to use in a promotion. She grabbed a *Sunday Post* comp slip and scribbled hastily: 'To Hot Metal from a Cold Type.'

'Get this into a Jiffy bag,' she instructed her personal assistant, 'and over to Sir Anthony George at the *Daily Sketch* on a bike.'

'Will do,' said the secretary who was suitably decorative, even when typing at 100 wpm.

'Oh, and Oscar,' Mandi added, 'tell everyone I'm ready for conference.'

The section editors began to trickle into her office. Mandi crossed the room to the panoramic picture window. She was reflecting on her brief encounter with Sir Anthony, and how she hadn't felt that familiar urge in years. Mandi drank in the vista of London's skyline laid out before her. Some things, she decided, were simply unfathomable. There are a million stories out there in the naked city. The trouble is, she mused, most of them are a real drag.

As her crew filtered in, refuelled with caffeine, and got themselves seated and sorted, Mandi stared through the thick blue glass which all but hermetically sealed her from the organised chaos of the newsroom. She was half-listening to her news editor gossiping about an impossible rumour concerning the Duchess of York and some income tax fiddle.

Mandi's gimlet eye alighted on Kettle. She watched him flicking through an envelope or four, scribbling with a cheap ballpoint on a beat-up pad. For some reason it reminded her of her old dad, a retired milkman who was a volunteer at the British Legion and refereed Under-12s football matches. Her father was almost 70. He worked hard, played hard and was fond of boasting that he'd swallowed a glass of whisky 'every day of my adult life'. Kettle was 20 years younger but looked about the same age as her father. Back in Fleet Street's Glory, Glory Days, he had been one of the Happiness Boys, all at large and ever on the rampage. Mandi could remember, when she'd been a go-getting, nickel-spitting cub reporter about town, desperate to meet every face and be on every doorstep, Kettle had been one of the few established journalists generous enough to show her the ropes. He knew the pitfalls and the pratfalls, the lurks and the perks, and he'd pointed her in the right direction more than once. Spoon-fed her, helped her understand the esoteric machinations of the Old Bailey court ritual, all that – and he'd never once tried to touch her tits. Kettle had been voted Crime Reporter of the Year seven times in a career that scooped up gunmen, conmen, knife wielders, wife beaters and every kind of deviant sex fiend. He'd been publicly commended by Scotland Yard, had written *Hook, Line and Sucker*, the definitive bestseller on London's Escort Girls, and discreetly shepherded the heir to one of England's noblest fortunes into a rehabilitation clinic where His Lordship could clean up his heroin problem far from the madding eye.

That, mused Mandi, was when the rot had set in. Word on the Street was that the blue-blooded wastrel's grateful Papa had shown his appreciation by paying off Kettle's mortgage. He'd purchased a cottage in Devon three years ago and, since then, his fire, like his dreams, was behind him. His heart just wasn't in it. Now gamekeeper had turned poacher – Kettle had been caught stealing from the company. It pained Mandi to see him around the place, going through the motions. But I admired this man, I respected him once, she thought. He should have a chance to redeem himself. Everyone deserves a second chance. If he comes through, provided he keeps his nose clean, the sad old geezer can collect his pension. If he blows it, Mandi thought, I'll drop him like a bad habit.

Conference began to roll, and one by one the players put forward their ideas for stories. Each head of department outlined the week's agenda, highlighting likely sources of real news, bidding for turf and favour for big budget money and national exposure for their team's talent, while fighting off the snarkey asides and derogatory put-downs of competing space barons. As Mandi listened to sport on Mike Tyson's secret comeback campaign, to features talking about the latest American micro-bopper pop sensation, and to the fashion editor bidding for eight pages on The New Polyester, she realised she was on autopilot.

'. . . a contact of mine at *Underworld*, that girlie mag that's taking over from *Penthouse*, says they've got some pictures of a prominent Tory MP for their centrespread next month.'

'Who is it?' Mandi wanted to know.

'Well,' said the home affairs editor, 'I don't want it to go any further . . .'

'You know nothing that's said in this room goes outside this room unless it's into cold type.' Mandi said. 'Who is it?'

'Well, it's the Leisure Minister.'

'Got any smudges?'

The home affairs editor shook his head. 'They won't release them ahead of publication.'

There were lots of jokes about politicians being caught with their pants down, getting the right kind of exposure, being born with a silver staple in their stomachs.

'Don't believe the hype,' Mandi said, 'I'm not having that bunch of gangsters retiring on the proceeds of a libel suit against the *Sunday Post*.'

As Editor she was part referee, part coach, part playground supervisor. And she took it all in her stride. Whatever else she might be, she was bloody good at all this. 'Let me make it crystal clear to you again, ladies and gentlemen: no-one's becoming a millionaire litigant, not on my watch.'

And so it went: the stitch-ups, the hatchet jobs, the buy-outs, the doorsteps. All of it heading, Mandi thought, towards some sad geezer like Kettle. The ones who did the actual work of asking the army officer's wife just widowed by the terrorists, 'How do you feel, love?' Of impersonating a funeral director to steal tell-tale family pictures from a murder victim's mother while she composed herself under the pretext of making a cup of tea for the gentleman from the Co-Op. The actual graft of standing in a phone box with a pork pie in your gob while trying to file 900 words against deadline, starting: 'She looks like any other happy five-year-old . . .'

Mandi remembered the time she had been told: 'There's a hole on page fourteen, you're going to have to write 800 words about this book in 20 minutes, get on with it,' and looking at the book's title: *The Oxford Anthology of Stress*.

'OK, that's it, folks,' she said, waving them out of the room. It was only on Thursday, Friday and Saturday that this Sunday paper really came alive because, as Mandi well knew, the eleventh hour meant everything. Experienced of old in the way that significant events develop and mutate from instant to instant, journalists are inclined to be habitual procrastinators. Head waiters who would never commit themselves until the last possible moment: deadline. At the centre, all was chaos. No sense in knocking yourself out only to have it all knocked down around you.

Mandi picked up the latest edition of *Verve* from her desk and flicked through it. She'd never read it until now, assuming it was just another bossy, glossy jet-setting, arse-licking, ad-getting, polo-club Establishment vehicle. But she was taken aback by the high standard of reporting, the obvious breadth and depth of the magazine's contacts all over the world, the way the writing teased and crackled off the page, the ease with which the layout seduced the eye into contemplation of things you never would believe might have engaged you . . . Reading *Verve* was a bit like watching a movie: that confident assault on the senses suspended disbelief . . . reading it, Mandi felt (for a few moments, at least) that she was someone who inhabited that world of casual privilege and gifted amateurism; of endearing eccentricities and the intimacies of people who mattered; a rich universe of adorable shops and fascinating, frivolous experiences. If, Mandi thought, I'm going to go for this *Times* job, this Mira Freer Farmer bird is going to be my real enemy, the one to watch. She's good. Sickeningly brilliant. But then again, there was Zelda Lee Powers . . . She's a tough babe, Mandi conceded, they don't come any harder. Underestimating her would be a big mistake. She remembered their scuffle in Hermès. This was clearly a woman who'd never start a fight she couldn't finish . . . the kind of person who'd nurse a grudge the way others suckled a newborn; who'd watch and wait and, sensing your moment of weakness, would strike with all the tender compassion of a cross cobra . . .

And then there was Kiki Cox: the joker in the pack. Mandi knew only too well that ambition proceeds either on all-fours or on tiptoe . . . and that it's always the quiet ones you've got to worry about . . .

But what this is all about, Mandi mused, isn't them. It's me. I'm the highly paid Editor of the biggest-selling national newspaper in Europe . . . but my marriage is loveless and childless, I've no one to care for, and no one cares for me . . . What is my life about, she wondered. What was I put here for? To think up a bigger, brassier Oh-Wow! headline than last week's, to pander to the bookmakers of that overgrown baby masquerading as my husband, to get a bigger ulcer from trying to snare this *Times* job? Is that all I am? Kiki, Zelda, Mira, they've all got something going on in their lives. They've travelled, they take risks, they do things and they make things happen, she thought. They're not just empty shells for International News Inc. They're real people who feel pain and passion and pleasure. People who are connected to the world because they contribute something positive, something other people need. OK, I'm hard and I'm good at what I do, but could I be any more than that? Am I more than Hard-Woman Harry, the butcher of Wapping Wharf? Do I have anything to say that'll change people, stop people, make them think? As a person, can I reach high? As a woman, am I deep enough? Because the next Editor of *The Times* is going to have to be. That had to be the whole point of choosing a woman. Otherwise, she thought, she simply wouldn't fit.

Worell, her deputy, a man whose suits were too sharp and whose trendy buzz-cropped haircut made him look like a dodgy insurance salesman, rushed into her office. 'It's happened,' he panted, 'LA's been hit by the Big One.'

'Earthquake?' Mandy said. 'How big?'

'Humongous,' the news editor said. '8.1 on the Richter scale. We're talking 100,000-plus dead, stars' homes wiped off the map, a tidal wave ripping down Sunset Boulevard . . .'

'Where's Jenkins?'

'I can't get through to him . . . the lines are down.'

'We must have stringers out there . . . Get hold of Peter Sheridan . . . and what about that guy in Palm Springs? The one who keeps pushing the celebrity golf stuff, you know, the guy who did the thing about the smack dealer at the Betty Ford clinic . . .'

'Crane?'

'Yeah, that's it, Crane. Get him on the line, see if he can get himself into LA.'

'OK, Chief.'

Mandi wasn't going to sweat it: the dailies would be all over it like summer flies on melting butter, the story would be well-played by the time the *Post* hit the stands on Sunday.

'Oh, there's another thing, Aitch.'

'What?'

'Security have been on to us. Some loony's tried to break into our computer system to get your home address.'

'What else is new?' Mandi said.

'This seems to be a pretty determined punter,' the news editor said.

'OK, thanks,' she said, with a weary shrug. Suddenly she realised that Jerry, the picture editor, was still sitting in the corner of her office. 'Jerry, I'm sorry, I was preoccupied. I didn't realise you were still here. Did you want to talk to me about something?'

'Yeah. You know this rumour about the Prince and the showgirl?'

Mandi smiled. 'It's just the hottest story on the Street. If we could stand it up that Prince Charming is or isn't queerer than a bent corkscrew, we'd put on a million sales overnight.'

'Tell you what, Aitch,' the picture editor said. He was a paunchy, balding Cockney with the shifty mannerisms of an ageing greaser. 'It's true.'

'Pull the other one, Jerry.'

'Nah, it's straight up, Mandi . . . we've got a smudge of her.'

'You're kidding!'

Jerry handed her the contact sheet he'd been clutching all this time.

'Christ,' Mandi gasped. 'Who is she? I've seen her somewhere, I'm sure of it . . .'

'She stars with Frank Bough in *Bounty!*'

'That's right,' Mandi murmured, transfixed by the pictures. She held in her hands proof positive, if it were true, that the Royal Family – and everything else in the British Isles – was about to shake it on up. And how. If we can stand this one up, she thought, and it doesn't get my feet under the Editor's desk at *The Times*, the job's not worth bloody having.

The girl in the picture? She was black.

18

People had told Stone that London was played, that it was history, the capital of nowhere, tortured concrete rotting in grey rain. He didn't think so.

Within 72 hours of leaving LA, Stone had acquired a 1968 black and red Fender Stratocaster, a silver Harley 1200cc Fatboy motorbike, a Macintosh Duo computer, a black and red tattoo of a panther on his right shoulder, a Leica M6 with 17 interchangeable lenses and supporting accessory kit, £1400 worth of leather jacket, Gap jeans, a fortnight's supply of white T-shirts and sundry accessories . . . and a compact flat above a betting shop in Ladbroke Grove, W11.

It's amazing what you can pick up with your mother's credit cards. Like three girlfriends, for instance. Stone found it easy to attract women – especially in London, where he was, to all intents and purposes, a foreigner. The girl at *Verve*, the Asian babe, had stopped him *en route* to Mira Freer Farmer's office. 'Excuse me,' she'd said in her hi-tone Oxbridge accent. 'But where do you think you're going?'

'Out to dinner,' he'd replied. 'With you, tonight, wearing not more than three garments. The others you pay for.'

Natalie, the art assistant at *YES* Magazine, had taken a little longer. Two hours longer, in fact, in the photographic studio he had hired, before she started getting into the swing of the shoot and out of her clothes. Karen had been a cakewalk. He hadn't even had to pose as a motorbike messenger to meet her. Just used the press credentials he'd forged at the *National Enquirer* for the Roseanne Arnold job to wiggle his way past the doddery old commissionaire geezer at the Evil Star. When the DJ came on he simply started dancing with her and her mates.

'That's a great necklace,' he'd said.

'Naaaahgerrrofff!' Karen had yelled back in his ear over the pump-pump-pump of the techno-beat soundtrack. But she was smiling as she yelled it. And the moment they smiled, Stone was in like Flynn.

Compliments had always worked for him: he would compliment a girl on her necklace, her shoes, her orange polyester dress, her boyfriend . . . anything, really, whatever it took to get them talking, make them laugh, break down their defences. It wasn't just a crass act, because Stone genuinely liked women. He adored Nadia's sultry exoticism, Natalie's frilly girliness, Karen's rapacious sluttishness. The babes liked Stone because he was an all-out stud; for his zany humour, his off-beat charm, the way he'd listen, oh so intently, to their stories . . . and pay for everything. They adored his unusual genital jewellery, too, even though the ampallang piercing turned his dick into a watering can every time he went to the lav. For their part, the girls would tell him things; things about their bosses – where they lived, what they were like, who they were screwing, whose back they were stabbing, who was stabbing theirs . . . the fact, the fiction, all the irresistible little rumours . . .

Stone was definitely on to a winner. There was someone in his life who would kill for such information, and here he was giving it to her for nothing. He always got a kick out of his mother's excited voice whenever he called Zelda to tell her everything. Well, almost everything.

19

'Animula, vagula, blandula,
Hospes comesque corporis
Quae nunc abibis in loca
Pallidula, rigida, nudula,
Nec ut soles dabis jocos?'

The black-frocked priest chanted sadly to himself the dying words of Emperor Hadrian as he sponged his beloved English friend's blazing forehead. 'Soul of mine, pretty one, flitting one, guest and partner of my clay, whither wilt thou hie away, pallid one, rigid one, naked one, never to play again, never to play?'

A tear slipped from the priest's red eye into Michael Orlando's receding hairline. He smoothed it into the emaciated actor's skin as if anointing him with oil.

'. . . And finally,' Orlando gasped, struggling for breath, '. . . I would like to leave my collection of theatrical memorabilia . . .' The priest offered his friend the oxygen mask attached to a cylinder resting against the frame of his wooden bed. But the celebrated star of screen and stage waved it away.

'. . . memorabilia,' prompted Gubbins, the family lawyer.

'. . . yes, and esoterica, including the gold lamé jumpsuit once belonging to Elvis Presley, bequeathed to me by my dear friend Russell Harty, to the only woman . . .'

Even in the tranquil light of the shuttered room, Orlando's face, already ravaged and disfigured by disease, bulged with an awesome asymmetry. The priest sniffed into his sleeve.

'. . . to Mirabelle Freer Farmer, the only woman who . . .'

'Is that hyphenated?' enquired Gubbins, matter-of-fact. 'Freer Farmer? Is it . . .'

'No,' hissed family friend Gervaise de Groot. The strapping former combat officer was misty-eyed in spite of himself.

'. . . The only woman who ever truly understood me. Those who forced me, yea, forced me into this exile after our affair . . .' The priest coughed delicately. The actor seemed to rally. 'My life will come after them with a sharpened rake!' he cried, lifting himself painfully. There was a rattle, a nasty smell, and Orlando slumped back against the bolsters.

A flashbulb went off. 'Did ya get that, Harry?' the American woman hissed at her husband.

'Ssssch!' Harry whispered, pointing frantically at his camcorder. The priest, who was sobbing quietly, had already placed a couple of two hundred lire pieces over Orlando's eyes, folded the actor's hands across his heart and had begun to chant the last rites, a flaking Bible in his left hand.

Led by the lawyer, the small group descended the narrow, worn, stone staircase. They crossed the spartan kitchen and filed out into the dirty, narrow village street. The flood of bright sunlight was blinding.

'Fabulous, Gerv, just fabulous!' the American woman gabbled, unhooking a cotton surgical face mask from her ears. By the sound of her, she hailed from one of those rectangular states somewhere in the mid-West. 'Really, truly moving.'

'You know, last year we vacationed Utah for the Jackson execution,' the man called Harry said, holstering his camcorder. 'They still got firing squads out there.'

'It was intensely moving,' his wife agreed. 'Truly, a beautiful encounter.'

It was extraordinary: the American woman seemed so normal, so down-home, just a cookie-cutter stockbroker's yuppie wife from Dogpatch, USA. Not the kind of person one would have expected to see on a speciality travel excursion like this.

'Did you get everything you needed, Caro?' Gervaise de

Groot enquired of his short, plump friend in a ripped Versace microskirt and motorbike boots.

'Hey, Baby,' Caroline Buchanan, the magazine journalist, replied, '*Verve* are going to love this. The story I mean, not, you know . . .'

'Yeah, right,' de Groot said. When he'd returned from seeing his charges on their way, he commented: 'It's funny, you know, last week I was in Bosnia, shepherding a group of schoolteachers from East Grinstead . . .'

'They wanted to play Mercenary?'

De Groot nodded his chiselled, well-bred face and scuffed his shabby tassled Gucci loafers in the dirt and stones. 'It's funny . . . the carnage there, it was terrible. And I've seen some things in my time. But this was all kids with limbs and eyes missing, people being blown up all over the shop, everyone starving, shoving their hands into your face . . . yet somehow it didn't quite get to me the same way. It didn't hit me, you know, in the gut.'

'Perhaps because you knew Orlando personally, he was a friend,' Caro said, blowing on the large brass ring she wore on her wedding finger and rubbing it against her grubby Calvin Klein T-shirt.

'Friend of a friend,' de Groot corrected her, shoving his Ray-bans on to his nose. 'After all, he was Mira's friend really.'

'Bit more than a friend,' Caro corrected him as they wandered towards the village café. They had already been here ten days, waiting for Orlando to snuff it, and de Groot had established a substantial line of credit to pay for their drinks – 'while we wait for our money to arrive from London'. Now that the old roué had actually faced his final curtain, everything seemed a bit flat – that morning-after-the-party feeling.

'I suppose the police will have to close the file,' Caro remarked. 'It's a tragedy that someone with his amount of talent should have had his life blighted by petty suburban scruples.'

They sat down and de Groot ordered their first bottle of the day. Through frequent repetition, the patron's daughter had finally come to understand his rustic Italian. It was basic, very basic – he just repeated what he wanted over and over again, adding a vowel sound to the end of the English when in doubt.

'I don't know that it was that petty,' he said. 'After all, Mira was only 14 at the time.'

'Fourteen going on 25. By then she'd already run away from school twice to go and live with that ghastly French communist on his yacht. She was no Vestal Virgin, we all knew that. She used to joke that she'd lost it before she'd even been born.'

'OK, but the parentals hushed all that up, didn't they?' Gervaise said.

'They came unstuck with Orlando, though. Not only was he famous – he was a poofter.'

'He was married,' countered Gervaise, '. . . with children. You know Peter Watson?'

'Just because someone's got a Trouble and 2.4, doesn't mean they don't play with both feet,' Caroline said, wagging her finger in his face. 'You of all people . . . Orlando batted and he bowled; he scored for both sides, he was into the swingers and the roundabouts, he . . .'

'All right, all right.'

The wine arrived and de Groot swigged it straight from the bottle, downing more than a third of its contents before offering it to Caro. 'God, I'm parched,' he sighed. 'Death really takes it out of you, doesn't it?'

'Yeah, absolutely exhausting,' she agreed, tossing him a look of disgust as she took the bottle and sloshed wine into her glass.

'Are you going to tell Mira?'

'About Michael? I think she already knows, doesn't she? She must do.'

'I don't want to be the one to tell her,' Caro said, her face assuming the grotesque expression of some Hallowe'en fright mask.

'It'd be better coming from you.'

'Why?'

'You're . . .' De Groot searched for the right words. 'You are closer to her than I am . . .'

'Bollocks. I hate to be the bearer of bad tidings. Shoot the messenger and all that. They always assume that it's your fault. So where's the next stop on the itinerary?' Caro asked, as the patron's daughter fetched them a second bottle.

'Oh Christ, I'm supposed to cart them to Palermo. There's a museum of Mafia torture there that Head-Wound Harry's pretty keen to get his nose into. Thing is, Caro,' faltered de Groot, 'I think there might be a bit of a hassle.'

'About what, Baby?' Caro frowned.

'They called me last night from the office. The receivers are in.'

'Shit, no!' Caro exclaimed. 'What are we going to do? You still haven't paid the hotel bill, have you?'

'I think a covert tactical withdrawal is definitely in order,' Gervaise said.

'What about the Septics?' Caro said.

'Excess baggage.'

'Gervaise . . .' she scolded, 'you can't bloody leave them out here in the middle of nowhere, they're absolutely fucking helpless.'

'They're absolutely fucking sick,' he corrected her. 'They deserve all they get if you ask me.'

'Don't like it. Bad Karma,' Caro shook her head, 'I don't like it one bit.'

'OK, so we'll take them to the spa at Montecatini tomorrow and dump them there, they'll be well looked after. We'll tell the hotel we're coming back later for our stuff, and smuggle our luggage on to the jeep with theirs . . . I think I've got enough dosh to fuel up and get us to the airport. Don't worry, Caro – we're doing Harry and Mary Beth a huge favour. This'll give them a real adventure to boast about to the folks back home. With any luck, they'll be held hostage by kidnappers . . .'

'Have you got any loot to pay these people?' Caro asked.

De Groot shook his head. ''Fraid not,' he admitted. 'This could be get-your-knickers-off time. Since that bad run back in Monaco things have been a bit tight.'

'Look, Gerve, I don't want to rip them off too. I rather fancy our waitress. I was hoping to make time for a spot of muff diving later . . .'

'I thought as much,' drooled de Groot, rubbing his hands together and ordering up a bottle of best brandy. 'Can I watch?'

20

Hanni's hair was braided neatly into tight dreadlocks, exposing narrow stripes of scrubbed pink scalp. The navy blue skirt of her suit fell exactly to the mid-point of her calf. Her dark, discreetly patterned tights were fresh from the packet, and her black lace-up shoes were polished like dark mirrors. She wore the bare minimum of make-up.

Hanni was the picture of neatness and efficiency, her explosive sex appeal deliberately on hold. '. . . I understand that the most important thing is to protect you, Mr Campbell, to screen out all the pests and loonies who attempt to waste your time. I see my role as creating an environment in which you can do what you have to do as easily and as comfortably as possible.'

Campbell nodded, instantly recognising the smouldering siren cowering within this crisp, demure maiden before him, and liking what he saw. He coughed into his fist, and rubbed his dry lips together. 'I noticed you were limping when you came in. Do you have a disability?' he enquired.

'Only temporarily,' Hanni laughed apologetically. '. . . Umm, I sort of collided with a bedside lamp . . .'

'Oh,' The ginger-bearded man seemed deflated. 'Are you a Muslim?' he asked her, staring through his spectacles at 'Our Multi-Cultural Workforce: a 36-point Action Plan' direct from The Boss's office in Los Angeles.

'No!' Hanni exclaimed. 'Do I look like one? C of E, actually.'

'Mmmmmn,' Duncan Campbell replied, looking up from her resumé. 'I see there's no reference here to your status.'

'What status?'

'Uh, marital.'

'Definitely single,' she smiled.

Campbell leaned back in his chair. He seemed curiously relieved at her reply. Hanni studied his face, following his gaze to a large print of a hunting scene on the wall. 'Do you have, er, a boyfriend, Ms Slynn?'

'No!' she grinned, amused at the line of questioning and sparing a passing thought for Sir Anthony at the same time. 'Not really.'

'Another sort of partner, perhaps?' he asked eagerly, leaning towards her.

'Hey. Wait a minute,' Hanni said, frowning. 'I don't really see the relevance of all this. I mean, it's not like it affects my ability in the office or anything, is it? What exactly are you asking me here? If I'm a diesel dyke? A lipstick lesbian? If I go to lingerie parties and sleep over with my girlfriends, and do things that you'd pay to watch because you can't even begin to imagine them on your own? Is that it? What exactly are you getting at, Mr Campbell?'

Campbell seemed flustered by her directness. 'Erm, I'm simply trying to establish whether you're a person of alternate sexual preference.'

Hanni realised that her outburst had probably cost her the job, but she didn't care. Sod it! She didn't feel threatened any more, she felt free. This pompous asshole acting editor of *The Times* suddenly didn't seem as physically imposing as he had when she'd entered the room 15 minutes earlier. He was just a sad little man in a grubby tweed suit who wanted to be accepted by people who, even on his best day, would find him merely useful.

'Isn't that precisely the sort of question you're not supposed to ask job applicants these days?' she demanded, her courage mounting with her anger. 'As in non-politically correct?'

'Well, what would you like me to ask?'

'The same questions you've asked everyone else,' Hanni said.

'But I haven't seen anybody else.'

'Haven't you?'

'I'm probably not going to see anyone else.'

'Really?'

'You come very highly recommended . . . Sir Anthony George . . .'

They used to work on *The Times* Diary together, Hanni recalled.

'Then stop asking about me as a person . . . ask about me as a personal assistant. Ask me about my shorthand and typing speeds, my word processing skills, my languages, what sort of tea I make, even. I thought the idea was to be fair, to give everyone an equal chance.'

Campbell made a low grunting sound which she took to be his equivalent of Sir Anthony's thinking noise. 'Have you seen *Tribute*?' he asked, supporting his bearded chin on the steeples of his fingers.

'Wesley Snipes?'

'He directed it, yes. It's about a group of black nationalists who come over here and pillage a stately home. They take a hostage and . . .'

'. . . the reparations thing, yeah,' Hanni said. 'I've heard of it, but it isn't out yet, is it?'

'What do you think about the reparations issue?'

'I haven't seen the film, so it's hard to say,' Hanni shrugged.

'Put the film aside for a second. The issue itself.'

'Well, if people treat you fairly, I think you should let bygones be bygones.'

'Yes?' he said.

'You've got to draw the line somewhere, or everywhere would end up like Sarajevo, wouldn't it? What do you think?'

'I like Robin Givens,' Campbell said with a smile. 'But your answer's more interesting to me at this moment than the film. It's difficult, you see, because the sort of employee you'll make is indelibly linked to what sort of person you are.'

'But you know . . . it seems that Tony's told you enough about me already.'

'I prefer my observations on, and judgements of people, warm and first-hand . . . not prepackaged and reheated. Come with me, and I'll show you your desk.'

Two secretaries sat together in the next office, separating Campbell's unit from the unoccupied, more spacious Editor's quarters beyond.

'You'll work for both the Editor and myself. This is Joan Winterbloom.'

The severe, chignonned senior secretary looked up and gave a brusque acknowledgement. 'That's how I could end up if I don't find something else to do before my 30th birthday,' Hanni thought as Campbell introduced the two women.

'. . . and this is Alice.' Hanni couldn't see anyone.

'Oh, hi,' she said, bending slightly to shake hands. Alice was three feet ten inches tall.

'Katherine's away on holiday until next week,' she said.

'What system do you use here?'

'A-Text . . . all the INI titles run off the same system,' Alice told her. 'But Duncan has his own link into the Internet. That's why we have these Tandys.'

'I send a lot of E-Mail from my own laptop, but I like to take the paper's incoming in here. The message system on the A-Text isn't very secure.'

'I've used Tandy before,' Hanni said. 'But they don't have E-Mail at the Black Lubyanka.'

'It's easy,' Alice said, smiling. 'You'll pick it up in ten minutes. Well, I did, and I'm hopeless with technology.'

'Now, we've covered salary, holidays, BUPA,' Campbell resumed, back in his lair half an hour later. 'If you've any more questions about technicalities, just give Personnel a call.'

'Does this mean I've got the job?' Hanni asked him.

'Almost,' Campbell replied, fiddling with a paperweight. It was cylindrical, gleaming, shiny – a silver-plated shotgun cartridge which he kept beside the Apple Newton on his desk. 'But I'd like to know a little bit more about you personally before we actually sign on the dotted line,' he said. He opened up his face in a wide, almost attractive smile. 'Tell me about yourself.'

Not this again!

'How do you mean?' she asked him, faintly perplexed.

'Tell me who you really are.'

'I don't actually know,' Hanni confessed, to his surprise. 'It's not something I talk about much, but . . . well, you see my mother had me adopted when I was a baby. My real parents, the Slynns, lived in Hull. But when I was six, Dad's boat sank . . . he was a trawlerman . . . and my Mum had sort of a nervous breakdown, so I was taken into care. I fell in with a bad lot, and I was tripping from bad to worse . . . one night I met this guy in a nightclub in Manchester . . . a sort of talent agent. He got me into catalogue modelling. It was fun for a while . . . the actual modelling itself is a bit boring, and they all want more than their ten per cent, typical men, know what I mean? But I saw the world, as they say . . . well, Miami, Berlin and Scunthorpe, anyway. I knew it wouldn't last forever, so I saved some money to pay my way through secretarial college. Mum had always said shorthand and typing were a good thing to fall back on, that you'd always work.'

'But a girl with your beauty, your ability . . . why did you choose that?'

'Why does anyone choose anything? I don't know, it seemed like a good idea at the time. A way of putting things on hold, getting a safety net, hanging out with some of the students and extending my youth. I've got a sort of longing inside me, an empty space, a desire to know all about I don't know what . . . to have what I've never had. I suppose I thought if I could work my way up to become someone's PA, it would open doors . . . I think you learn a lot, you absorb and soak it all up and get the best of the people you are working for . . . and eventually it'll lead you into something else.'

She smiled, and shrugged. Had she said all the wrong things, talked her way out of the job again?

'It's better than laundry, scrubbing floors, or getting knocked up, isn't it?' she asked.

Campbell stood up as Joan Winterbloom came in.

'You'll be late for your lunch at Waiteley's, the car's waiting,' she said briskly, handing Campbell his overcoat.

'And when you get back, Mr Collins would like to discuss the Korean advertorial supplement with you.'

'Thank you, Mother,' said Campbell, winking at Hanni. A proud flush flooded Joan Winterbloom's face. Being indispensable to Duncan Campbell was the most important thing in her life. Well, ever since John died . . .

'Anything else you want to know?' Campbell asked, glancing back at Hanni. She was licking her top lip as she caught his gaze, and he wanted to kiss her so badly that he almost told her.

'When would you like me to start?'

21

Within his inner sanctum at Waiteley's restaurant, Duncan Campbell sat and waited. He didn't like waiting, but he'd had plenty of practice. In fact, Campbell had been waiting for years in the ante-room of his life's ambition. He'd been offered other jobs, sure: jobs with more glory, more guts and much, much more money; worthwhile jobs, less stressful jobs, jobs superficially less glamorous than his own but which, given time, would surely have proved more interesting. Bossier-titled jobs with bigger parking spaces and better perks in corner offices with panoramic views and furniture older than anyone who'd ever use it.

Campbell was good. He'd been flown to interviews in helicopters, fêted ten dozen times by poohbah proprietors over lavish lunches where the flattery flowed as freely as the vintage claret, and at the end of the meal the figures on the bill were preceded by the reassuring scrawl of triple digits. Offers had come in thick and fast over the years. They had been faxed by the *Straits Times*, Fedexed from the *Washington Post*, delivered by carrier pigeon on behalf of the *Daily Telegraph* and, in the case of a French daily which must remain nameless, showed up at his Belgravia flat on the lips of a heartbreakingly gorgeous call girl. Duncan Campbell had refused them all and, as he waited for Zelda Lee Powers to reappear from the bathroom, he had to wonder why. But only for a moment. The truth was that ever since he'd spotted the elated expression on his father's face 60 years earlier, when the paper had published the old Colonel's letter about hearing the first cuckoo of Spring, Duncan Campbell had always wanted to edit *The Times*.

And now he was doing so. He liked it, this feeling that it was, at last, his train set. That this time he was the one doing the interviewing. What he didn't like was that he was Brett Collins' peon, the acting editor. And how. Here he was, acting as his own executioner. He was interviewing a woman who might close down the daylight on his dream forever, leaving him a beached and gutted 52-year-old man stranded on the wrong side of his life's work.

'Everything all right?' he asked pleasantly as Zelda returned.

'Why, I'm happy as a bug in high cotton,' Zelda replied gaily, Southern-mode. 'Enjoying such a delightful little lunch with you, Duncan. Why do you ask, honey?'

'Nothing, nothing, I just thought you seemed a little . . . oh, never mind.'

'Stephen!' Zelda barked at the waiter, who emerged through the fronds surrounding Campbell's table, 'Is this tuna dolphin-friendly?'

'How do you mean exactly?' the waiter asked. His tone was cautious, his accent lilting County Connemara. During the first course, Zelda had made supercilious play of her first marriage to Brendan O'Brien, much to Campbell's disgust, not least because Zelda's babbling had caused his soup to be served cold.

'I MEAN, exactly, that these tuna weren't caught in dolphin-friendly nets, WERE they?'

'I could ask the kitchen . . .' stammered the tall, dark and handsome Irish waiter.

'FORGET it, I KNOW. A woman ALWAYS knows, we have sensitive antennae and I've just had an allergic reaction. Bring me the Teriyaki, would ya please, Stevie?'

She patted him on the bottom as he walked away. Then she turned to Campbell, who was simultaneously awed and repelled by Zelda Lee's apparent ability to switch from street-smart New Yorker to coy Southern Belle at the bat of a semi-permanent eyelash. Perhaps she took one of those personality pills, Prozac or something. He wondered how he could draw her out on this point. But Zelda was already talking in his face at full-on verbal velocity.

'. . . I'm real hot on environmental issues, and I think this is something significant that I can bring to *The Times*. With all due respect, Dunk, it's not enough just to have, like, an environment correspondent.'

'But we've got an environment reporter working with him. And general news pick up . . .'

'Pick up, schtick up,' Zelda interrupted impatiently.

'What does it MATTER so long as we're printed on recycled paper?'

'We're not,' said Campbell flatly. 'The presses couldn't handle . . .'

'Exactly, exactly, I can read your mind, honey. First we recalibrate the infrastructure, then we sensitize the troops in the trenches. Maybe it's because I was a dolphin in a previous life or something, but at the *Gazette* I had my team work Quality of Life angles right across the editorial agenda, like . . . you remember that Headless Woman in Topless Bar story a couple of years back? Well, last month I had our true-crime beat guys dig up a sensational new angle on it. Like, the barman said the TV was on all day at his work station, OK? So his lawyer said that all that exposure to electro-magnetic ray fields had driven the guy bazonkers, to the point that he wasn't wholly responsible for plugging the tootsie, you follow me? So we had incredible reader up-take, right? We instal this 0898 hot-line so everyone in the Tri-state area can call in their experience of aliens in their TV sets, but the stand-out angle was that we had more than 7,000 calls and all the aliens spoke ENGLISH! Spooky, huh? Haven't you ever wondered why aliens always speak English, Dunk? Or why they're so goddamn DULL? Anyways, the next day we get Leona Helmsley, who's a close personal friend of mine by the way . . . incidentally, you ever wanna stay at any of her properties just let me know, Dunkie, I'll get you a discount . . . so Leona blows up 7,000 TV sets on *Good Morning America* in front of the *Gazette* building, it was FABULOUS, the paper was name-checked on every local news bulletin on the Eastern Seaboard, I mean it was a RIOT for Godsakes, they had to call in the National Guard. REALLY! Now is that a result or WHAT?'

Campbell was utterly exhausted by her monologue.

Americans don't talk, they confide, he thought. For all her pretence towards uptown sophistication, her intimidating personality plus one, Zelda Lee Powers was not just naïve, but coming apart at the seams. If I can get her hired without damaging my own credibility, he thought, The Boss will fire her before she's even had a chance to wedge her size sixes under the table . . . and then they'll turn to me as the safe pair of hands, the sound candidate, the one to steady the ship, right the wrongs . . .

'Zelda,' he said calmly, 'for me, and for hundreds and thousands of English-speaking people, *The Times* is more than merely a newspaper. It is a national institution. An institution in which I have considerable emotional investment.'

'I hear ya, Dunks,' Zelda munched, through a small mouthful of Teriyaki. 'You just give me the nod, Babe, and I'll make sure you're taken care of. I'll take care of it myself.'

'Perhaps I'm not making myself clear, Ms Powers. Whilst no one could question your originality or enthusiasm,' Campbell said, the subtle pejorative completely passing his companion by, 'many might question the wisdom, in this conservative age, of handing over the stewardship of one of Britain's best-loved institutions to someone who is – and let me put this to you quite candidly . . .' Campbell's face assumed a brief, faint grimace of distaste, '. . . a foreigner.'

Zelda snorted. 'So whaddya think the man who owns International News Incorporated is?' she snapped. 'A fucking VIKING?'

'But debentures, differentials and liquidity speak a language without frontiers.'

'So does news, Dunkie, so does news. Hey, Stevie,' Zelda said, swivelling round to whisper into the fronds at the top of her lungs. 'Give me another Screaming Orgasm.'

'I beg your pardon,' Campbell spluttered.

'The drink! I need refuelling here, Babe,' she told the saturnine Irish serving lad.

'I take it Madame wants another Henri Special, the Deepening Chasm?'

'What Madame wants, Madame gets,' Zelda said, 'and call

me Zeelee, Stevie, all my friends call me Zeelee. Cute, huh?' she said, leaning forward and grasping Campbell's hand. 'When I land this gig, you can call me Zeelee too, Dunkie. But only in private. At work it's strictly Ms Powers.'

Campbell withdrew his hand with a loud hurrumph, and blew his nose into his handkerchief to cover his embarrassment.

'You see, DC, my take is that you've got to size up this property commercially. What The Boss wants, OK – and I have this from the inside – is that he's, like, bought up all these studios and these TV networks and he needs synergy between the print zone and the video zone. So, like, what I'm going to do is equip all the reporters with Hi-8s, OK, like, those bitching little camcorders that shoot in low light? The ones Manhattan One use to shoot all their cable news? YOU know . . . and then we'll pull the art off the V-tapes, 'cos, like, I'm gonna splash a lot of pics right through the paper, BIG, I mean it's the pictures that tell the story, right? The words are just, well, you know what a hassle writers are . . . anyways, then we can sell video back to 21st Century Fox at a mark-up, STILL beat the BBC and the other alphabets out there to the punch on breaking news – AND get *The Times* some free coast-to-coast promos. Plus, ALSO, people are cabling up all over Britain. In five years' time they'll be getting *The Times* off their TV screens, like it's video on demand. So what do you think, huh?'

'How very original,' Campbell said witheringly.

'THANK you,' smarmed Zelda.

'But of course that may not necessarily happen overnight,' Campbell said. 'While you're, er, retooling your infrastructure, how are your contacts here?'

'I got a Rolodex. I got an invitation to Number Ten Downing Street in a coupla weeks, press some flesh with your Prime Minister,' Zelda said. 'Plus, ALSO, I got a husband who edits the *Daily Sketch*. He knows where the bodies are buried. Fact is, he helped put a lot of them there himself.'

'Obviously I know Sir Anthony. I believe he briefly worked on *The Times* Diary – he was fired for wearing blue suede shoes, wasn't he?'

Zelda shrugged, taking a ladylike slurp of her neon-coloured cocktail.

'While, in a professional context, there's no gainsaying the enormous success that the *Sketch* is enjoying in mid-market,' Campbell continued condescendingly, 'with its relentless pandering to the prejudices of Suburban Little England, the relationship your husband has with, say, the Lord Chief Justice, just isn't quite on a par with that of the Editor of *The Times*. Let me give you an example, if I may. I was at university with David Frost, Peter Jay and the Prime Minister's wife. I know these people. We shoot together, we go to the same house parties at weekends, I'm godfather to their children. We share a common heritage, a personal history that binds us together. There's a *lingua franca*, and certain unspoken assumptions that an outsider, however talented . . .'

'Making an assumption makes an ass out of U and I,' Zelda interrupted, leaning across the table to grasp his hand with her own. As she had fixed him with a ravenous stare, he found it impossible to withdraw. Zelda's own hand was thin and scrawny. And although its grip was firmer than he'd expected – like the claw of some massive bird of prey, in fact – there was something bony and friable about it, as if her hand might crumble to dust in his were he to squeeze it back. 'Dunkie, you'd better get with the programme,' she said urgently. 'News values are changing. All this investigative shit is out. People don't want to have their world rocked, they got enough headaches. People are confused, they want to know how other folks are making out, they want media to SHOW them their place in life, not disrupt it. You ever read Daniel Boorstein on The Image?'

'Yes, some years ago . . .'

'OK, so you know where I'm coming from. We do newsesque, infotainment, handy hints in bite-size blips, cute packages, sprint reads. You know how I managed to heist the *Gazette* ahead of the *Post* and *Newsday*, huh?'

Campbell considered mentioning the Morgan libel case but quickly thought better of it. He caught the waiter's eye and stood up. He had wanted this over and done with, and Zelda Lee

Powers outside on the pavement, at three o'clock on the dot.

'What I did was devise a Q-score, so that staff can objectively measure how interesting an item is, against the seven components of a good story, the shit readers are interested in: celebrity, sex, violence, money, children and animals. So – Yoko Ono mugging up to a baby gorilla 'cos she's gifting the kids' petting zoo with half a mill, that's a good Q-score; people identify, they're interested.'

As they made their way towards the cloakroom, Campbell nodded to celebrated gossip columnist Nigel Dempster who was getting up to leave his own table outside the inner sanctum. Campbell allowed himself a small triumphant smile. 'By the way, you said there seven vectors to your Q-score but you only mentioned six . . . now let me see if I've got this right: celebrity, sex, violence, money, children and animals. So what's the seventh?'

'You know,' laughed Zelda, 'that indefinable something that makes a story a Must-Read. Like, say, Yoko turns out to be fucking the gorilla. Or it's actually Michael Jackson inside a gorilla suit. Or moments later, the gorilla runs amok and fucks Michael Jackson . . .'

'Ah,' said Campbell with a knowing wink, 'you mean the Wow Factor. That's what it's referred to over at Wapping Wharf.'

'I don't know, it was just a dumb hypothetical example. It's like "Hey, Doris, got a quarter? I GOTTA read THIS!"'

Campbell helped Zelda into her fur and then retrieved his own long black leather coat from the cloakroom attendant. Zelda thrust her glossy press pack into his hand. 'It's all laid out in the business plan at the back. Read it, you'll love it.'

'*The Times* they are a-changing, eh?' muttered Campbell. 'I'll, er, cast an eye over it when I get back to the office. I must say I'm surprised to see you wearing a fur after your passionate outburst in support of the animal kingdom.'

They went through the revolving door. Outside it was blowing a gale. 'Yeah, well,' blustered Zelda, 'fact is the sable were already dead, you know? Anyways, I got a steal of a deal on it at Bloomie's, couldn't let it go by.'

'I wonder what the Animal Rights activists would make of that,' said Campbell with a wry smile. At that moment Nigel Dempster came out on to the pavement to join them, and they all exchanged a few words.

'Nigel Dempster the diarist, right?' gushed Zelda, pumping his hand with both of hers. 'I'm your biggest fan! I see you on TV all the TIME over there . . .'

Duncan Campbell introduced Zelda, glancing down at his watch. One minute to three.

'Zeelee, PLEASE call me Zeelee, ALL my friends call me Zeelee . . .' she was saying as she turned to Campbell. Her voice dropped dramatically. 'If I were you I'd do more than just cast an eye over what I gave you just now . . . I'd study it REAL close. I'm a native New Yorker, and you fuck with me at your peril. The neighbourhood I grew up in, the day Carmine Russo became a faith healer, you couldn't find a cripple for 20 blocks. All he did was say seven magic words: "Walk . . . or I'll break both your legs."' She glanced at both men. 'I've got people checking out the opposition. All three of those bitches have got more than their share of skeletons in the closet. There are bats, werewolves, cemeteries and a George Romero crew scouting *Night of the Living Dead*. You'll find out very soon that I'm gonna be your next boss, Dunkie, so if you wanna get along, go along. *Capisce?*'

At that moment, something flew at them from the window of a passing car, which then made the fastest getaway in history, screeching round the next corner and out of sight. There was a soft splat, and Zelda screamed loud enough to wake the dead. There she stood, trembling from head to toe and absolutely dripping in blood. 'Oh, OH, JEE-zus,' she shrieked. Passers-by had frozen in their tracks, curious and appalled.

'Bloodbomb,' Campbell grimaced. 'Are you all right? Look, go back inside and have a brandy, put it on my tab, it's fine.'

'Let me get you a cab,' Dempster offered sympathetically.

Zelda was dabbing at bits of herself with the tips of her fingers. 'It's like some kind of plasma,' she said, her nose wrinkled.

'Paint probably, I think you'll find.'

'No, it's definitely blood,' Zelda said, carefully shedding the coat. 'SMELL it!' Campbell backed away. Zelda smiled. 'Maybe you're not as jaded as people say,' she cooed, nodding her head as she marched over to a litter bin and dumped the coat inside. 'Never liked it much anyway,' she snorted, turning back to Campbell. 'People in this town had better learn that it takes more than a bloodbomb to get the better of Zelda Lee Powers.'

She smiled a dangerous smile, and for a split second, Duncan Campbell was really scared. 'See you at the office, nine a.m., three weeks on Monday, OK, Dunks?'

22

The black, chauffeur-driven Jaguar splashed through a deep, muddy puddle and turned into The Dene. Mandi glanced up from the latest 48-page memo she'd been studying: 'News 2000: a 96-point Action Plan for Change', Fedexed direct to her desk from The Boss's office in Los Angeles. She saw the familiar sweeping L-shaped drive of large, mock Georgian houses. She realised she'd just been doodling all over the paper, miles away, not taking any of it in.

In fact, she had been fantasising about Sir Anthony. While she'd been urging Kettle on the trail of HRH's Dusky Delight, Anthony's PA had telephoned to ask if she wanted to buy some tickets for the Shaken Not Stirred charity ball which Sir Bob Geldof was organizing in aid of LA's earthquake victims. She'd been imagining how her life might change . . . all it would take was the punching of seven digits and the Yes-word. She only had to say it once . . . Because, of course, it wouldn't be possible to go with Colin. Oh no. Dinner jacket dos were not his scene in the slightest. In fact he'd never be seen dead at such an affair.

The Jaguar XJS rolled to a halt in front of Mandi's house on the U-bend at the end of the cul de sac. 'Tell your boy good luck for the game tomorrow,' she smiled at Ronnie, her driver.

'Thanks, Mandi.' He winked at her, and she winked back.

The bright security light beams flooded the dimmer bulbs of the carriage lamps fixed either side of the wooden front door, illuminating the drive, the ornamental pond and the little willow tree cut into the front lawn. Mandi let herself in and tottered across the threshold. She dumped her bags, flipped through the post: book club, electricity bill, insurance reminder, letter from the bank, a Next catalogue and the usual raft of junk mail, and made her way into the living-room. The electric log-effect fire warmed the room beneath the large copper hood over the fireplace. Everything was in place: the dusky pink velvet drapes covered the net curtains; the Lladro ornaments, the china figurines and framed photos still cluttered the wall units, gathering dust . . . but the teak-boxed 29-inch television set stood mute and dark.

'Col?' she called out.

No answer.

Mandi went into the kitchen, trying to imagine what Sir Anthony George would look like in his new red liquorice posing pouch. She could hear Pinkee Poo miaowing somewhere, he'd come to her in a minute. Mandi pulled a frozen Weight Watchers Lasagne from the fridge-freezer, dropped the packaging into the stinking, overflowing bin, and shoved the meal into the microwave. Then she went upstairs to change.

In the bedroom, she cleared the messages on the answering machine . . . one from her Mum asking if she and Colin were coming round for Sunday lunch . . . another from Colin, calling from a pub the other side of the M25, where he'd gone to meet someone about an earner. Mandi sighed, shuffled into the *en suite* bathroom, picked up the mushy pink bar of Camay soap on the side of the washbasin and turned on the tap. She rubbed furiously at the feet and crotch of the tights she had just taken off, then left them to soak in the water. She changed into worn leggings and a slack old jumper, and stared at herself in the mirror as she passed it.

What did she look like? A sight for sore eyes. Hair chopped in an uninteresting bob because it wouldn't behave; nails too long to disguise her stumpy fingers; ankles blistered, feet swollen and misshapen from the wearing of ill-fitting shoes with heels far too high for her build. They were supposed to compensate for her lack of height and her dumpy figure. Well, at least she tried. She'd try harder. She'd have to. What on earth must Anthony think?

Dejected, she went back down to the kitchen. The letter from the bank caught her eye: the statement wasn't due for a couple of weeks yet, but she noticed the Medway postmark. It wasn't a circular. She slit open the envelope with her finger, and sure enough it contained a letter written by a person rather than a machine . . . the writer had got her name right but spelt 'receipt' wrong. A machine would most likely have reversed the errors.

'We are unable to pay this sum because the handwriting indicating the payee's name appears to have been tampered with,' Mandi began to read, puzzled. 'After comparing it with the specimen signatures on file, we regret we cannot honour the cheque. Please contact us for . . .'

Ignoring the £28.50 levy the bank proposed to charge her for this act of terrorism, Mandi scrutinised the offending cheque. It was for £1700. It had originally been made out to 'J. Kettle,' but a crude alteration rendered it payable to 'Cashbox Club'. The Cashbox Club was in fact an all-night hosery; a lowest-of-the-low dive where Kettle picked up many of his stories from prostitutes, off-duty cops, barmen and other shady nocturnal creatures.

'The bastard . . .' Mandi thought. But she was suddenly distracted by a plaintive mewing nearby. She wondered where on earth her kitten could be and what he was doing . . . just then the microwave pinged to tell her dinner was done, and she saw that there wasn't a clean fork. She stuffed the letter from the bank into her Fendi bag on the side and went over to the sink, retrieving a used fork from the disgusting pile of cutlery and crockery on the draining board. She scraped cold pizza from the cleanest-looking plate and gave it a quick wipe with a tea-towel. Then she turned on the waste disposal unit . . .

The second she heard the hideous scream, something wet and awful flew into her face.

'Yeurghh!'

Mandi wiped her eyes, flicking her fingers . . . and saw the blood and fur splattering all over the white kitchen wall. The only sound she could hear was the tick-ticking of the electric wall clock. Then a car turned round outside the house in the bend of the cul-de-sac – she heard the crunch of a bad reverse gear. Mandi had sunk to the floor where she squatted in a crumpled heap. She began to sob, quietly at first, her grief soon gathering into uncontrollable hysteria until she knew she would vomit. Pinkee Poo, trapped inside the waste disposal unit . . . Her baby . . .

23

As the tattooed blonde in the leather bustier looked on, Joker and Gypsy stood at the bar watching their compadres from the Sons of Silence Motor Cycle Club playing snooker. One of the players potted the pink. He went outside with the tattooed blonde, and they heard a bike engine revving up.

'Hey, Baby, nice work,' said Caro, 'When you can get it.'

'This is nothing,' said Joker. 'You should come to some of our parties.'

Mira noticed that his gold tooth glinted in the low light as he smiled. When she and Caro had come into the pub, waiting for a mechanic to put the finishing touches to Mira's Triumph Bonneville, the two biker boys had tagged them immediately, picking up on the girls' black leather garb and the Chrome Hearts belt Caro wore. By way of a calling card, Joker had shown them the club name tattooed inside his lower lip. Gypsy said he had one on his dick too, if they were at all interested.

'It's wild,' Joker was saying. 'There are chicks being banged by four or five guys . . .'

'. . . guys rimming each other . . .' Gypsy put in.

'. . . some chick getting oral while she's strapped to this wheel,' Joker said.

'When are you next partying?' Caro asked.

'It never stops,' Gypsy said. 'Right now, if you want.'

'It's supposed to be consensual, isn't it?' Mira asked. 'I mean, if you go to one of these sex parties, you don't have to do anything you don't want to, do you?'

'Yeah,' Joker said. 'But people push it, you know?'

'I once licked out this chick on the rag,' said Gypsy.

'Hey – either of you birds called Mirror?' said the biker who'd lost the snooker game, coming over with two fistfuls of bottled beer.

Mira nodded.

'The guy fixing your bike rang in to say it was ready.'

'What's your ride?' asked Joker.

'Bonnie,' said Mira.

'Homemade or Septic?'

'British,' she said, knocking back the rest of the gin and tonic Gypsy had bought her.

'So what's the matter with it?'

'Camshaft,' she said, torching up another Marlboro.

'Tension spring gone?'

Mira nodded. 'And the head gasket,' she said. 'The bloody thing's leaking more oil than the *Exxon Valdez*. C'mon, Caro, we better hit the pale trail.'

'See you boys later,' smiled Caro.

'You know where to find us,' Gypsy replied, with a long, lecherous look.

'You don't have to come now, Caro. Actually, why don't you hang out with them a bit, see if you can get a line on these biker orgies. I think it'd make a terrific piece, especially if we could find some *Verve* people who were involved.'

'You mean like Ben Laverda?'

'Or Johnny Stokes,' Mira said. 'Go on, it's OK, I can handle it. I'll get the bike, then come and get you.'

'OK, Mira,' said Caro with a shrug, and went back to recapture the centre of attention at the bar.

Mira crossed the road and walked down the dark, narrow alley that lead to the mews. It was cold and foggy. She turned the corner and heard a dog barking. Inside the garage, the mechanic started up the Bonneville for her under a low-slung bare bulb. The room smelled of damp and oil and grease. Mira paid him, and was about to jump on and drive off to collect Caro when the mechanic handed her an envelope with her name typed on it.

'What's this?' she said. 'Didn't I give you enough?'

'Some bloke left it for you this afternoon, M'lady,' the

mechanic said. Mira, puzzled, opened the envelope. Inside was something . . . round, cylindrical, heavy . . . a bullet. It had been dipped in a sticky liquid. Then she noticed something else. Someone had printed her name on the side of the casing.

'Who left this?' she said.

'Some guy,' the mechanic said. 'I don't know who. Said he was a friend of yours, that it was important that you get the message.'

A bullet with my name on it, Mira thought. I get the message, all right. 'Who was he? What did he look like?'

'I didn't really clock him, M'lady,' he said.

'It's important,' Mira told him, her tone cool and urgent. 'Think.'

The mechanic furrowed his brow and for a minute or two he thought hard. But all he could tell Mira was that the man who left the envelope 'had a beard and a leather coat'. Mira couldn't immediately recognize any of her friends, ruling out some sick prank – a lot of her friends were practical jokers. So now she knew what this was about . . . the job at *The Times*.

She kick-started the engine, her face cold and determined. She intended to make it her business to identify the bearded man in the leather coat.

And then make him wish he'd never been born.

24

The wind whispered softly through the bare trees in the Knightsbridge square. It was late. But high in the imposing, smart Georgian apartments, a light bulb burned in the night. The home entertainment/communications console in the centre of the room was playing disjointed 'post-modern' digital cartoons on the big screen. The sound of Bizet's *Au Fond Du Temple Saint* emanated from the speakers beneath. To the untutored ear, the opera music might have sounded like a particularly gruelling scrap between two brawling alley cats. But Kiki Cox considered herself one of the cultural élite; the gifted few whose sensibilities were so finely attuned that they could genuinely appreciate the nuances of passion in opera.

She sat at the console of her computer working on her dummy for a tabloid version of *The Times*. Kiki sipped the last of her camomile tea. Tea without caffeine poured gentility on even the most troublesome waters, Kiki found, and camomile tea in particular seemed to soothe and relax her at the end of a hard working day. Although, she noticed, checking the time on the screen, her day was far from over yet.

She hit a key on her computer keyboard and the screen displayed a variety of symbols representing household objects. She selected and activated one and, a few minutes later, the electric kettle began to whistle.

Kiki had put the Earl of Lanchester's money to good use – although she was still smarting and limping from his violent attack in the Longchamps stable. Neither of them had ever referred to it again – but Kiki would certainly make him pay. One day, when he was least expecting it. That was a dish best eaten cold.

She walked over to the swish chrome eliptical wall units with their subtle louvred doors, of which she had taken delivery when she was still Editor of *Tasteful Living* magazine, and carefully measured out the precise amount of tea from the neat, tidy, methodically organized selection within. In another cupboard were a strange selection of decorative teapots. They had accumulated because, early in her career, Kiki had let it be known that decorative teapots were the only acceptable, gift from colleagues and professional acquaintances on those uncomfortable occasions, like anniversaries, Christmas parties and leaving dos, when the working world must assume a quasi-social patina. This calculated manoeuvre put paid to the possibility of people seeking to become over-familiar through the giving of gifts, and gave her a superficial interest to bring out and chatter about at drinks parties, right after she'd told them that she never drank. There were teapots shaped like bunny rabbits; teapots disguised as jokey little clowns with funny hats which served as the lid; teapots made to look like quaintly fanciful fairytale houses hand-baked in green and brown, yellow and orange; ceramic teapots, hand-painted, numbered in limited editions and personally signed, would you believe, by the artist. They had one thing in common: they all leaked. So Kiki never used any of them, preferring instead the brushed steel industrial model she'd bought from a designer kitchenware shop in Covent Garden.

She sipped her tea, dimmed the light in the room using her keyboard, and switched the machine from Household Operations mode back to the special project in hand.

She liked her new computer. Computers never made a mess, they didn't have periods, didn't depend on contraception, didn't require holidays, didn't answer back and – joy of joys – they never asked questions . . .

A message flashed at the top of her screen, indicating that someone had left E-mail in her confidential file. She knew that could only be one person – the only one to whom she would entrust its precious access code. Kiki opened the file to see what her aristocratic patron had to say to her.

HELP ME.

She dialled up Clifford's number on the modem. But the answerback told her Lanchester's machine was not receiving messages. It was disconnected because he was in Rome. He wasn't there. Message Waiting, said the command at the top of the screen. Kiki accessed her file again.

HELP ME. PLEASE HELP ME.

Kiki flashed through the protocol for identifying the caller. But the machine's search only revealed the answer: 'Code Not Recognized. Number Not Identified. Message Source Unknown.'

'Message waiting', said the command at the top of the screen. HELP ME, it said. There was a moaning sound. Must be the central heating playing up again, Kiki thought, dismissing fear.

HOW CAN I HELP YOU WHEN I DON'T KNOW WHO YOU ARE? she tapped out on the keyboard. She was about to tell the computer to send her communication to the last incoming number it had taken, when letters began to dance before her eyes, catching her off guard.

HELP ME, they said. I AM TRAPPED IN YOUR MEMORY.

'Jeez,' Kiki said out loud. WHAT CAN I DO FOR YOU? she typed.

There was a pause, lasting about a minute. Then suddenly up popped her screensaver – a graphic device that showed electronic images of tropical fish swimming across the screen, devised to prevent tube burn-out when the system was on but not in active use for periods of 20 minutes or more.

'What the . . .' Kiki began to say. As suddenly as it had appeared, the screen saver was replaced by the display of her E-mail system. Message Waiting. Kiki smacked down the access code keys.

NO, IT'S WHAT I CAN DO FOR YOU.

WHAT YOU CAN DO FOR ME IS GET OUT OF MY SYSTEM YOU LOUSY LITTLE HACKER she typed back.

CHEEKY KIKI.

A video graphic appeared in the bottom left-hand corner of her screen. Kiki's jaw dropped. She'd seen it before. It depicted a man taking down the pants of a teenage boy and smacking him across the bare buttocks. LEARN SOME RESPECT, flashed the display.

Kiki sat back. There'd been no Message Waiting command. This sleazebag was taking over her computer. She'd heard of things like this happening, but had never believed it – until now. ARE YOU A VIRUS? Kiki typed in

OR WHAT? snapped the answerback. She was now aware of a sound over and above the opera. Suddenly she realised what it was: the kettle was whistling. She rushed to the sink and unplugged it – it had nearly boiled dry.

'Oh my bloody oath,' Kiki said, and raced back to the screen. WHAT'S THE BIG IDEA? she began to type, but as she pressed the keys she saw that they were having no effect. Indeed, her own words were being wiped away.

At that moment the living-room lights went dim. She suddenly became aware of another sound – a sort of bubbling.

SHUT UP COX, the message said. I'M DOING THE TALKING.

She looked around her in panic. The bulb above began to buzz and suddenly flared into flattening luminescence, as if it were high noon on the equator within the room. Almost at once, it dimmed back down again, stranding her in shadows. The predator was working his way through her household command file. Something moved in the corner of her eye. Kiki spun around on her seat. With horror, she realised what was happening. The water in her tropical fish tank was bubbling and boiling over. The John Dory and female Angel Neon Tetra were flapping around uselessly on the floor. It was too late to save them, but Kiki rapidly slipped on the orange rubber gloves beside the kitchen sink and rescued the rest of the fish. It took too long. When she got back to the computer, there was another message waiting for her.

HOT ENOUGH FOR YOU? it said.

WHO ARE YOU? Kiki typed, her alabaster face registering little emotion. WHY ARE YOU FUCKING ME OVER LIKE THIS?

Suddenly the sound of opera cut out, as the TV screen went black, to a shorting-out, sparking sound.

DO I HAVE YOUR COMPLETE ATTENTION COX?

A video box on the bottom right hand side of the screen showed a line drawing of a schoolmaster in a mortar board and gown wagging his finger through some crude animatronic. Kiki could hear herself breathing. Wait a minute, she thought, and typed. SECURITY OVERRIDE: THIS SYSTEM WILL SHUT DOWN IN 30 SECONDS.

She waited, watching the clock. With seven seconds left to run the answer came back: HOW WOULD YOU LIKE ME TO SCRAMBLE YOUR SECURITY SYSTEM? THE ONE WITH THE PANIC BUTTONS TO KNIGHTSBRIDGE GREEN POLICE STATION? IT COULD GET DIFFICULT WHEN THEY FIND THE CHILD PORN I'VE LOADED ON TO YOUR SYSTEM.

FUCK YOU, Kiki typed.

WRONG ANSWER, said the predator. Almost immediately the opera on her CD player started playing again, the volume punched up to the max. Suddenly every electronic gadget in the house began functioning on its own accord. Her answering machine began playing back. The Magimix blended. The electric whisk spun wildly within its empty glass bowl, shattering it. The fax whirred, spewing out paper gibberish. Water began seeping from the fridge. The rings on the hotplate began to glow. She could see the lights in the bathroom and bedroom and hall flashing on and off. The noise in the place was deafening.

Kiki glanced out of the window. Lights were being turned on across the square. Groaning, she put her hands to her ears.

GIVE ME YOUR ATTENTION.

YOU'VE GOT IT, Kiki typed.

NOW SAY THE MAGIC WORDS, came the answer back.

P-L-E-A-S-E, Kiki typed.

WRONG ANSWER.

The light bulbs popped and the fluorescent tubes blew to smithereens. Kiki held up her arms to protect herself from the flying shards of glass. Suddenly all was darkness and silence . . .

TRY AGAIN.

Kiki was grinding her teeth, trying desperately not to cry.

WHAT DO YOU WANT? she typed.

A crappy graphic, of a man on a horse blowing a trumpet, dominated her screen. The sound of his tinny symphony came blasting through the computer speakers.

EXCELLENT NOW LISTEN . . .

Kiki waited.

THINK OF ME AS A FRIEND.

'Yeah, right, mate,' Kiki said to herself with a wry smile. But she was trembling, and her voice sounded very small.

YOUR DUMMY SUCKS. YOU'LL NEVER EDIT THE TIMES. GIVE IT UP NOW. BECAUSE IF YOU DON'T . . .

The display wiped itself, and the text was replaced by a blank screen. Kiki saw a subtle movement in the middle of it. It looked like a rip, a tear. As it expanded, something seemed to seep through it. Something red was oozing all over the inside of the computer screen.

'Jeez . . .' Kiki breathed, the rational part of her mind engaged despite the total terror which gripped her like a cold, dead hand. 'That's a ripper graphic. Uhhhh . . .'

The red was blood red. It WAS blood, congealing all over the inside of the screen. A message flashed up: YOU HAVE BEEN WARNED.

Kiki became aware of a sensation of heat around her fingers, all over her hands. She realised that the machine must be overloading. The keyboard was hot to the touch, scorching hot. With horror, she watched as the individual letter keys seemed to soften and, with a crackle, melt inwards on themselves, bubbling into an amorphous mass as the edges of the computer disintegrated and the screen imploded with a soft pop. Her brand new computer system congealed into a foul-smelling mass of broken glass and soft, smoking plastic.

Kiki slumped back in her chair. Outside, day began to dawn and birds began to sing in the mushy grey cloud of early morning. She remained motionless for about half an hour. Then she dialled a Mayfair number. It rang more than 30 times before it was answered.

'Hello,' murmured Crispian Frye.

25

Foursquare to the South Bank of the Thames stands one of the ugliest buildings in London: the headquarters of International News Incorporated's satellite station, Fab TV. Under the hot lights of studio three, a voice boomed down from the control room. 'OK, quiet please. Roll tape. Sixty seconds . . .'

Down below, the floor manager down-counted, swinging his arms for effect. The host was too vain to acknowledge his myopia, and the producer too craven to confront him, since he reckoned the guy was going to be fired at the end of the season anyway . . .

'Ten seconds and rolling . . . and five . . . four . . . three . . . two . . . one . . . and cue Dermot . . .'

'Gooooood evening,' gloated Dermot Chalmers. The words cascaded from his throat like a roller-coaster. 'I'm Dermot Chalmers – and you're not. Still, a warm welcome, ladies and gentlemen, to not just another edition of *Inside Media*. Tonight, we'll be taking a look at an issue which has left the chattering classes speechless, and is gushing through the glitterati grapevine like a geyser of molten hot gossip. We're talking, of course, about *the* job in newspapers today.

'Within the next 15 days or so, International News Europe's debonair, maverick CEO, Brett Collins, will tell a waiting world the name of the first ever woman to edit *The Times*. Will this mystery woman's elevation signify the death of the Grub Street Old Boy network? The birth of a new breed of media babe who can crash glass ceilings with a single bound? If the future of a paper steeped in the past is female – will it work?

'Tonight, *Inside Media* cuts through the PC psychobabble to take a long, hard look at the four frontrunners for Fleet Street's top slot and asks: is *The Times* the newspaper it used to be? And if not, does it matter? How do the women who hope to mastermind one of the most powerful prints on the planet see the paper's future? As ad revenues shrink and circulations plummet, will it take a woman to turn *The Times* around?

'Tonight, we'd planned a face-off with all four women down in the studio for a panel discussion in which we could identify an agenda, target the issues and get behind the hype to put contenders under the microscope. But we've junked all that boring po-faced crap-trap.

'Tonight, instead of our advertised programme, we're going to show you four of the most powerful females in print, down and dirty, head to head, toe to toe, *mano a mano* as only a concealed camera in the green room, 45 minutes before we go on air, can reveal them.

'So here, ladies and gentlemen for your delectation, live on tape, are the Fabulously Fractious Four in *Inside Media*'s "Fly in your Scoop de Jour" – Hitter Chicks Trade Dirty Tricks. Hit it . . .'

26

A big blonde finger squashed the punch button. The tape rolled.

'. . . we have a terrific energy in this room,' an American voice was saying. 'I'm getting some non-positive vibes, but we're all on the same trip here, right girls?' The camera picked up Zelda, chomping down on her Dentene. '. . . What I'd like to do is focus on establishing a safe space between us, where we can all resource to empower ourselves to be the bestest, most winningest people we can be . . .'

'Oh Jesus,' Mandi muttered. 'The Mothership's landed.'

'You know, four years ago, after my husband died in a tragic postal accident, I felt I'd hit bottom,' Zelda continued. 'There I was, a single Mom with a growing boy to put through college. The phone was ringing off the hook with psycho-penis people inside trying to repossess my car. I was bereft, hollow, empty inside. But one day, I experienced a life-transforming incident. I found myself at Debtors Anonymous, where my court-appointed social worker, Guru Marvin, suggested I create an interpretive dance for the group. Spontaneously I began to pep – it was a throwback to my old cheerleading days at Nôtre Dame. Slowly, I felt my way out of the foetal position, and there, in the . . .'

'Not another born-again personal growth story,' Mandi interrupted, 'for Christ's sake.'

'I'm trying to accomplish something constructive here. What are you doing? What's your contribution?'

'This is a TV show, not a sheltered workshop,' Mandi said. 'I can't stand all this pretentious crap, like we're supposed to be each other's friends . . . come on, we're all going after the same job – and only one of us can get it.'

'You are so mean-spirited – that came over when you snatched my scarf at Hermès. You know you got my husband's car blown up?'

'Your husband's car?' Mandi looked at the others. 'What the fuck is she on about?'

'You're a very hostile person, Mandi,' Zelda said. Her voice was level and measured.

'You've got a lot of negativity in you. You should perhaps consider seeking professional help. I think you've got some serious problems.'

Mira had arrived. She hung up her jacket and dumped a vast bouquet of cellophane-wrapped spring flowers which had been delivered by Interflora just as she was leaving her office. 'I think you've got some serious problems if anyone sees you trying to catch a cab outside in that coat,' she snorted in Zelda's direction.

Zelda glanced at her new fox fur, hanging next to Mira's black Johnson's studded leather biker jacket. 'Why's that, Lady Mirabelle?'

'There's a massive demonstration all day, PETA, it's going to be heavy – the ballpoints are tooled up. Didn't any of you catch it?'

Kiki sat, blank, impassive, scrolling through something on her Apple Newton.

'Excuse me?' Zelda said.

'The cops, to you . . .' Mira said, helping herself to some of the untouched white wine. '. . . They're armed, I heard on the radio when my brother was driving me over here. That's why I'm running a bit late. We took a short-cut through a police line and some of the demonstrators bottled us. Poor Tobe's Bristol's absolutely thrashed. I talked to one of them – surprisingly sweet little man, really. But there's always that mob element, isn't there?' She sipped, pulled a face, then held her glass at arm's length. 'Christ, I didn't realise Volvo made wine.'

'Who's Peter?' Zelda asked, puzzled. 'What's his beef?'

'People for the Ethical Treatment of Animals,' Mandi said with a sneer.

'It's the sort of thing it helps to know,' added Kiki, '. . . if you're planning on editing a national broadsheet.'

'Why?' Mandi asked. 'What would you do? Cover their flower arrangements?'

'You may sneer, but actually the question of whether the Animal Rights lobby will spread to plant rights may prove significant,' Kiki said. 'To those of us whose customers don't move their lips as they read the newspaper, anyway.'

'Oh, PETA . . . why didn't you say so? I'm with ASPCA myself, I went to their fund-raiser at Radio City the other day, FABULOUS – Joan Rivers, Diana Ross, Tom Hanks, Tony Hopkins, FABULOUS. Moschino did the party favours. Zal Zilcha, the ASPCA President, is an old friend of mine . . .'

'Zelda . . . isn't that vomit on your shirt?' Mira asked, her eyes squinting. Zelda froze, mortified, as Mira leaned forward, picked at it, and brushed away bits of caked sick. 'Are you bulimic, by any chance?' said Mira blithely. '. . . A friend of mine once threw up in Mick Jagger's lap. It's a frightfully funny story, actually. We were in Park Walk, and Piers Ballantine and Caro Buchanan were just leaving when Piers suddenly said, "Oh shit, my flies are undone", and he yanked up the zip, only he caught his willy in it, so he turned to what he thought was the waiter and said, "Would you point me at the lavs? I've got my tackle in a tangle." Only it wasn't the waiter, it was Mick Jagger, and he said "What do you think I am, some sort of bender, it's Brian you want." But he took one look at Caro and said, "Cor, I wouldn't mind taking your chick on, though. What about it, Babe?", and Caro was so drunk and excited and freaked that she parked a custard on his knob.'

Only Zelda seemed to recognise how frightfully funny this was. Her laugh was loud and raucous. 'That reminds me – one time I was at Area for this party with Keith and Charlie . . . they wouldn't let Bill come, and . . .'

'How edifying,' Kiki cut in with a theatrical yawn.

'Which part of Australia are you from, exactly?' Mira asked.
'All over.'

'I mean, town or country? I stayed with the Barbers, the squatty ones not the industrialists, for a whole summer when I was twelve. My parents were divorcing, it was a nightmare. They

178

gave great Bachelors and Spinsters parties every year at their place, about four cartons out of Newcastle. Ripping binges.'

'I come from a suburb you've never heard of, and wouldn't blink twice at if you blew through it,' Kiki said. 'But my great-grandmother had the stain.'

'The stain?' Zelda repeated.

'Really? What a coincidence,' Mira said, draining her glass and pouring herself another in spite of its disgusting taste. '. . . You see, back in the 18th century we had quite a few judges in the cadet branch on my maternal grandfather's side of the family. So one of my poor relations probably transported one of your poor relations.'

Kiki was absolutely impassive. She was toughing it out.

'There's something I've been meaning to ask you,' Mandi said to her.

'Must you? I think Zelda's right, can't we at least try and maintain the semblance of some personal dignity here?'

'Dignity?' Mandi snorted. 'Do you think you look dignified when you go around disguised as the Invisible Man?'

'I feel the cold here in winter,' Kiki shrugged. 'Anyway, how do you know about my personal habits outside office hours? I don't really see that it's any of your business.'

'Oh yes, that's going to look really impressive when you say that on camera,' Mandi said. 'Really inspire a lot of trust in readers, that will.'

'I'm allergic to British winters, it's not a crime,' retorted Kiki.

'I've got an allergy too,' said Zelda. 'I'm allergic to the carbonated water they serve here. It makes me nauseous.'

'Fizzy water's quite *outré*,' Kiki said. 'Everyone's drinking still water now. Lake Lomand Clear.'

'Not quite everyone,' Mira said. 'I think this whole water thing's hype. I was talking to the Minister of Agriculture at dinner last night, and he told me they're going to launch an enquiry into the whole scam. It's the most bogie rip-off . . .'

Hmmmmm, thought Mandi, mentally filing the information for the next day's conference.

'Excuse me,' Kiki interrupted, 'but this is a No-Smoking area.'

Mira exhaled a jet of blue fumes in her face.

'Right,' Zelda jumped in. 'Enough's enough. We're all womb-blessed human beings here. We should focus on the long-term view . . . whoever gets to edit *The Times* is making a radical stride on behalf of women all over the planet. We should be supportive and nurturing of each other. Bitching and sniping is just playing the psycho-penis people's power game. This is OUR moment – we have to smash through the glass ceiling.'

'Just make sure you don't get any splinters in your hair,' Mira murmured.

'Oh yeah?' Mandi said, with a sidelong glance at Zelda. 'And if anyone's buying that, I've got a chunk of London Bridge for sale.'

'Just what is your fucking problem, Mandi?' she demanded.

'It's such bullshit,' Mandi snapped. 'Women all over the world get to work twice as hard at shitty, boring jobs for 65 per cent of the money a man would earn, just so that one woman can edit *The Times*. That's progress? Who do you think you're kidding? Yourself? Because you're not fooling me.' She rounded on Kiki. 'I don't understand why a professional competition should engender such emotional insecurity. Jesus, have you listened to yourself? You're such a pompous windbag. You get those size twelves under the desk at Wapping Wharf, love, you're going to have to lighten up a bit. Even on *The Times* – much as it may amaze you – there are still a few bloody people with a sense of humour.'

'Passing off the *Sunday Post*'s bully-boy tactics under the guise of having a sense of humour is exactly the sort of moral bankruptcy *The Times* should be editorialising against,' Kiki sniped back. 'Our mission is to disturb the comfortable and comfort the disturbed.'

'I'll settle for getting the paper out on time and having a laugh on Saturday night.'

'I suspect the needs of *Times* readers are just a little more sophisticated,' Kiki said, her sexily pencilled-in lips clamping shut.

Mandi stuck out her teeth and pulled a grotesque face as Kiki looked away. But the gorgeous Australian Amazon saw her. She moved, Mandi jumped to her feet, jerked and waved the small crucifix dangling round her neck in Kiki's face. It was meant to be a joke, but Kiki jumped, and the others recoiled.

Kiki regained her composure long before the others had taken in what had happened. 'You've come a long way on a little petrol, mate,' she said, getting up. She towered, beautiful and cool, above the perspiring, diminutive Mandi. Her muscular voice dropped to a low growl. 'I'm warning you . . . don't push it.'

She turned and took another glass of still mineral water from the table behind them. Mandi put her index finger to her ear and rotated it. Even as she did so, she thought, I'm reverting to ridiculous playground tactics here. What is it about these people that's making me behave like a petulant child?

'You're invading her space,' Zelda was shouting.

'You're so fucked up, you're sick.'

'If you're healthy,' Mira sighed, 'I expect that's probably a compliment.'

'I don't like people sticking crosses in my face,' Kiki said. 'Or anything else, come to that. It's juvenile, and uncalled-for. Christ, I was persecuted enough when I was a kid, I don't expect this from grown women . . .'

'Were you a victim of Traumatic Childhood Abuse Syndrome too? God, it's always so affirming when I meet another survivor,' Zelda gushed, moving towards the drinks table. 'I knew right off that you weren't an integral person, because my father left home when I was six months old and I can remember devil men in black robes dancing round me naked beneath a full moon. We have to draw strength . . .' Zelda reached out to take Kiki's elbow.

'Don't touch me!' Kiki exclaimed, drawing back like a pinball ricocheting off a flipper.

'There you go – even a fucking Martian like her can see right through you!' Mandi said. 'You think we're stupid? No one's taken in by this West Coast Femi-Nazi-with-a-crystal crap. You're just a cheap hustler with a dodgy face-lift, and you don't get the jokes. And you can wipe that smile off your face, you posh bitch. None of you have got a hope in hell of getting this job, because none of you can edit a proper English newspaper. Every week we scoop the dailies, we scoop the broadsheets, and we scoop the telly and leave them for fucking dead! Take last week: Zombie Mum's Heartbreak Bedside Vigil – *Sunday Post*. Who sprung parole for the Hitman Dad Who Pleads "Cut Out My Heart and Save My Tina"? – *Sunday Post*. Week before last: Channel Tunnel Terror Target Horror. Who exposed the Muslim Fundamentalist Connection? – *Sunday Post*. Even our fucking supplement makes you lot look like you couldn't get arrested with the Crown Jewels. You know what we're running this week? Fergie's Royal Boudoir Tips: A Hundred and One Ways to Pull the Princely Hunk of Your Dreams, as told to Jilly Cooper with pics by Dave Hogan . . . topless. Stick that in your trophy case and mount it!'

There was a brief silence.

'You're very good at asking questions,' Kiki said. 'But not so good at answering them, are you?'

'What do you mean, Princess Kiki?'

'For God's sake,' Mira interrupted. 'Children, children . . .'

'As I was saying,' said Kiki, 'there are some questions I'd like answered. I don't know about anybody else.'

'Like what?' said Mira, puzzled.

'Like last night,' said Kiki. 'I was working on my computer at home when I was invaded.'

'Like,' Zelda asked, 'a home invasion?'

'You could say that. An electronic home invasion if you will. Someone dialled into my computer and menaced me. They hacked into my master system, deleted all my files and crashed the power into my flat. All my tropical fish died, and my £80,000 communication centre is a write-off.'

'That's weird,' Zelda said. 'Thanks for sharing that, Kiki. This is exactly what I mean. You know what happened to me? You heard?'

'I think we're about to,' Mira said, rolling her eyes and licking her fingers.

'OK, like I'm coming out of Waiteley's after lunch the other day, with Duncan Campbell, right, and someone throws a blood bomb at me.'

'A blood bomb?' Mira said. 'Oh, excellent!'

'Animal entrails and mulch and offal and shit.'

'Probably some loony psycho-penis from PETA,' Mandi giggled.

'Wait a minute.' Zelda cocked her head to one side and gave Mandi a hard look. Chomp chomp chomp, went her jaw. 'Why do you say that?'

'I don't know. I'm not like you. I don't run everything I say through a fucking computer.'

'I didn't tell you anything about wearing a fur coat.'

'Funny – I didn't say anything about you wearing a fur coat either.'

'But I WAS!' Chomp chomp chomp. 'How did you KNOW that?'

'I didn't. It was just a joke. I assumed that . . .'

'Assume anything you like, it only makes an ass out of U and Me. Only in this case, U.'

'Actually it is a bit weird, you know,' Mira interrupted. 'It's just a coincidence, but last week I was having my bike fixed and somebody delivered a bullet with my name on it.'

'You mean, like, literally?' Zelda said. 'At gunpoint?'

'No – it was just in an envelope at the bike man's shop. But now you come to mention it, it's creepy, isn't it? I mean, think about it. Whoever it was must have known where I'd be at that time. They went to a lot of trouble, I mean having my name printed on a shotgun cartridge. That's quite elaborate, isn't it? Quite considered, except . . .'

'What?'

'They spelt my name wrong.'

But she didn't take it any further. She left out the bit about the man with the beard and the leather coat.

'That's interesting, isn't it?' Kiki said. 'Three of us in the running for the same job. Three of us have been threatened.'

Mandi was thinking about an inscription she'd seen an hour earlier, when she'd gone to put flowers on Pinkee Poo's grave. It said: 'Gone for Long Walkies'.

'Look who's not talking,' Zelda's voice interrupted her reverie.

'Jesus,' Mandi said.

'How touching,' Kiki said. 'Our little tabloid battler's found God . . . but not, apparently, the power of speech.'

'Do you know where I've just been?' Mandi replied. 'Out to a place called Silverclere. Do you know what Silverclere is?'

'A target practice range?' Mira hazarded.

'It's a pet cemetery,' Mandi said. 'I went there because when I got home last week, I couldn't find my cat. So I did some washing-up, and when I turned on my waste-disposal unit, my cat was chewed to smithereens. Someone had stuffed Pinkee Poo down the gobbler.'

'Pinkee Poo?' Mira said, puzzled.

'My cat,' Mandi said, breaking down.

'Pinkee Poo?'

'HerHerHerHerHerHerHer,' chortled Kiki, like a machine-gun.

'What are you laughing at? What are you fucking laughing at, you cow? You don't understand what love is, do you? You bleached, dumb-breasted slag . . .'

'Girls, girls . . .' Zelda said.

'No, what I don't understand . . .' Kiki said, the mirthquake having subsided, the accusatory suspicion in its place on her face like a fast costume change in a movie, '. . . is exactly how you can fit a cat down a waste-disposal unit . . .' Her voice rose again at the end of the sentence.

'He was a kitten . . . just a little kitten . . . he was only eight weeks old . . .'

'Even so,' Mira said, 'stuffing a cat down the scoffer . . .'

'I know what you're thinking, Lady Mirabelle,' Zelda cut in. 'As my husband would say . . . it's all a bit thin, isn't it?'

'Reality check, bitch. Kiki's system's invaded, she can print the desktop, she can prove it.'

'I can't print the desk top because the whole thing's just sitting on what used to be my desk top at home like a heap of junk.'

'OK . . . Mira, baby, who gave you the bullet?'

'The man in the bike shop.'

'So she can prove it. And when I got blood-bombed by the psycho-penis, or maybe – let's not be sexist, maybe blood-bombed by the psycho-vaginas – they just missed Nigel Dempster. So I can prove it, too.'

'Col was . . . no, he wasn't home, someone rang him up and said they had a job for him in Colchester. But he saw me when he got back.'

'So you can prove . . .' Zelda said, lying back in the hospitality chair, folding her arms and legs, '. . . Jack Shit.'

'Who bottled out first?' Brett Collins asked the director sitting next to him in the control room.

'The Australian. Then the Yank wouldn't do it unless everybody else did. Mira just got up and left.'

'Free markets, I love 'em,' Brett said, standing up and rubbing his hands together. Watching Mira Freer Farmer had made him unbelievably horny. 'Some people will do anything to get a job.'

27

The old plasterwork on the white Georgian house was dilapidated. But within its crumbling walls the champagne was perfectly cold, the food deliciously spicy and the music a sultry, sensuous mixture of old reggae and young jazz. The elegantly furnished first-floor reception room was crammed with barristers and bankers, TV producers and MPs, all mouthing sweet noizak as they worked their jaws and chinked their glasses.

Mico was videoing it all.

'But why?' asked a minor Laird, whose kilt had been strategically attacked by a marauding pack of vicious moths.

Mico raised a finger to indicate silence, while Caro finished explaining a crucial style point to London's only Rastafarian tax QC. Then he turned to the Laird and said: 'It's because there are so many poor people, you know, in Africa and Asia and Russia . . . little children who is a luxury for to gather round the TV. You see, I am giving them my life. They can know what is like to be Mico, 'cos they can see my life on their TV. I can no give them food and is too hot for them to wear my clothes, or if in Russia is maybe too cold, but they can see TV, know what is like to live in privilege, go to all the parties, yeah? Is my gift to them . . . being me.'

Caro was becoming exasperated at having to explain yet again to some stumpingly thick Sloane Mama exactly why she was toting a live lobster on a jewelled leash. 'Hey, Baby, it's the year of the family, OK?' she said. 'So I'm making the bloody point that the whole planet is one big fucking family, yah? Geddit?'

'Yes, but what I don't quite understand is that if you're related to the lobster . . .' a petite blonde ventured.

'Stanley!' Caro snapped, lighting up another Benson and Hedges. 'He's got a bloody name you know.'

'. . . exactly why you're walking around with him on a leash,' said the blonde, ignoring Caro's outburst. 'I mean, I wouldn't bring my brother-in-law fr'instance to a drinks party in a cage . . .'

Caro rolled her eyes. Why did people have to be so bloody literal about these things?

Close by, Mira Freer Farmer was flirting outrageously with Gervaise de Groot, the former SAS officer who was still floundering while adapting to certain idiosyncrasies of civilian life – like earning a living. He found it bloody inconvenient, to tell the truth. It kept getting in the way of enjoying a good binge, of which there never seemed to be a shortage.

'I mean, the bloody little man expected me to turn up at nine a.m. wearing a bloody suit,' he'd explain, after yet another City gig arranged by one of his numerous ex-girlfriends or army muckers folded in his face. After his short-lived stint in the travel business with Exotic Excursions, which had taken him and the warped Americans to Tuscany in time to see the final departure of Michael Orlando, de Groot earned a brioche by turning out as an escort for an agency that specialised in supplying ex-military gentlemen and shop-worn sons of bankers, lawyers and the landed gentry to clients of uncertain age. But bookings had been rather thin of late, and Mira noticed de Groot's large, ungainly hands easing unseemly numbers of hors d'oeuvres into his pockets. 'So do you think I should take up Di's offer, then?' he was asking her.

'Is Jamie involved?' she enquired.

'Well, he's supposed to be their motoring correspondent, of course, but . . .'

'But he hasn't got a fucking driving licence!' Mira choked. 'The judge banned him from driving for life after . . .'

'He said he'd pay cash.'

'And you're supposed to be what, exactly: the security man?'

'Executive Director of Security Services, actually,' de Groot corrected her primly.

'Gervaise, I wouldn't touch it with a 50-foot bargepole. And that's the one I keep in reserve for dealing with people too slimy to touch with the 40-foot bargepole. Honestly, think about it, darling. What d'you think they expect you to actually do for four

187

hundred a week?'

'Well . . . secure things, I suppose. Stop Jamie flogging all the office equipment behind Di's back.'

'You'll probably end up pushing and pandering for them. Really, don't do it,' Mira begged him, squeezing his left bicep and kissing him full on the mouth. 'I could talk to Rupe, he might be able to find you something . . .'

Mira cared greatly for Gervaise. They were close friends, they knew each other of old; through parental ties, childhood tea parties and later, before Gervaise had gone up to Sandhurst, by having attended many of the same dances and coming-out balls.

'So Rupert . . . Rupert Stackridge, right? What's he doing now exactly?'

'He runs this extraordinary off-shore finance services company out of the Bahamas . . . I think it's called The First Bank of Gyno-America or something. It specialises in investing for discarded trophy wives,' Mira said, vaguely aware of a peripheral figure hovering around them, coughing politely, waiting to burst into chat. 'He did mention the other day he was looking for someone to sort out his visitors from the Middle East,' she said, turning her back on the interloper, '. . . so it's probably more pushing and pandering, but for a rather better class of person than Jamie and Di, I'd imagine.'

'Well, yes, I suppose . . .' said de Groot. 'I always thought this escort malarky was the bottom of the barrel, but when you pick the barrel up, there are Di and Jamie.'

Mira felt a tap on her shoulder. Much to her irritation, she found herself confronted by a man with a ginger beard. 'Good evening,' Duncan Campbell said. 'Mirabelle Freer Farmer?'

She spun round on him with a lash of her flame-red locks. No-one outside her family called her Mirabelle and lived. 'Good evening Good evening Good evening Good evening Good evening Good evening Good evening. Now let that last you the week,' she said.

'Duncan Campbell,' he persisted, 'Duncan Campbell of *The Times*.' He pronounced it as if it were in capital letters.

'And who might he be – Mr Suck Face?'

He grimaced, and a sardonic smile crept across his mouth as he blocked out de Groot – in itself no mean feat – and moved in on Mira. 'You strike me as a reluctant Faust, Ms Freer Farmer. You claim to want to sell your soul, but you have a curious way of haggling over the price.'

This was actually bravado. Campbell was concerned. He was supposed to have reported to Brett Collins on the three candidates who worked outside International News by last Tuesday.

'What are you talking about?' There was a flash of anger in those pixie green eyes.

'I've faxed you four times to set a lunch date in the past three weeks,' Campbell said, a touch of pique in his tone. 'You haven't even shown me the courtesy of a response.'

'OK then – No,' Mira said emphatically. 'All right? Now put an egg in your shoe and beat it.'

A crestfallen, bitter, angry Campbell turned on his heel and started to walk away. He heard a crunching sound, but paid it no attention. Campbell was thinking sour, dour thoughts. So he was surprised when, on collecting his coat, he found his exit blocked by Mira, Caro and her enormous escort in the hall.

'Ah,' Campbell said, 'So you've changed your mind then, Mira?'

'You murdered my girlfriend's lobster,' Gervaise accused him in the menacing tone that only a big man speaking softly in a small space can adequately command.

'Excuse me?' Duncan Campbell squeaked. In his agitation, he removed his spectacles and began polishing them on his scarf.

'My God,' Mira said. 'He's wearing a leather coat. A bearded man with a leather coat . . . Caro, it's him!'

'The usual satisfaction, I presume?' said de Groot.

'What are you talking about?'

'You killed Stanley!' shrieked Caro, flailing at him with the redundant bejewelled lead. In his confusion, Campbell looked down at the floor, where he noticed that his left shoe was covered with what appeared to be crab paté.

'All right, Caro,' Gervaise said, holding her back, 'I'll deal with this.'

'It's him,' Mira was hissing. 'He's the maniac, Gervaise, the one I told you about. He's threatened all of us. He's afraid we're going to get the job over his head. You creep!'

'I don't understand . . .' mumbled Campbell.

'Where and when?' de Groot barked.

'What?'

'What's your weapon?' de Groot demanded. 'I should warn you that I was the All-England épée champion four years running, and only missed the small-bore Olympic squad because of a misunderstanding with the local constabulary.'

'Have you people completely taken leave of your senses?' Campbell exclaimed. 'Are you on drugs? You're all barking mad. And I'm leaving.'

'Back trouble,' de Groot said knowingly to Caro and Mira. 'Big yellow streak from his neck to his arse. Leave him to me,' he said, grabbing the departing deputy editor by the collar of his leather coat and lifting him until the Campbell feet dangled an inch or two above the floor. 'You're leaving all right, matie,' he said, carrying the squirming newspaperman through the crowded room to a pair of French windows which led out on to the balcony. Using both hands, de Groot helped him out. This was quite spectacular, since the doors were closed at the time. Fortunately, Campbell's fall was broken by a Rolls Royce Silver Spur which some MP had thoughtfully parked outside.

'Frightfully sorry about the window,' de Groot grovelled to the hostess.

'You don't think,' Caro said, dabbing her eyes with an oil-smeared bandana, 'that might possibly hurt your chances at *The Times*?'

Mira snorted as she consumed her 17th double gin and tonic of the evening. 'Actually, Toby's ex-stepmother's sister is married to The Boss's brother,' she cooed, as the staff began to clear up the broken glass, '. . . so I doubt very much whether some frightful little yob like Duncan Campbell makes the slightest difference. You see, all I've got to do is find one good story and the job's mine for the asking. It's a question of loyalty, darling. People like us have to stick together . . .'

28

Within the labyrinthine maze of old cobbled streets near Buckingham Palace which comprise St James's, a discreet silver plate on an alley wall outside an immaculate, well-proportioned Georgian house alerted the curious to the existence of Chambrun's, the renowned English gentleman's club.

Chambrun's had been founded more than 250 years earlier, as a civilised alternative to City taverns; a place where one did not have to imbibe, as coffee was served to a like-minded group of fellows who gathered there to exchange views on the events of the day and collect one another's gambling debts. In 1838 it achieved a certain notoriety when Rags, the club's hound, had given birth to a litter of pups all over the then Prince of Wales. The club still honoured that event every year on the last day of February with a secretive, arcane ritual.

Chicks had never been admitted to Chambrun's. But the consumption of hog-whimperingly large amounts of liquor had been strongly encouraged since the Boer War, to both deaden the taste of the appalling food and encourage some semblance of congeniality among the members, most of whom had good reason to hate one another.

But lingering within the fug of cigar smoke, the aroma of fine Cognac and the warm, dull scent of overcooked beefsteak in the club's luncheon-room there was also, today, the distinct smell of expensive aftershave.

Sir Anthony George was enjoying, if that was the right word in these dank and gloomy surroundings, a festive lunch with an old college friend. News of old acquaintances had been exchanged and already forgotten, fresh views of current events aired and, lubricated by that conviviality that flows so easily between old pals after the third bottle of fine claret, the Editor of the *Daily Sketch* had begun unburdening himself on the trials of domestic life.

'Zelda's oiling up to me because, I suspect,' he said, 'she's running short of scratch. She seems to have a need to spend money in the same way that you or I have a need to breathe. She breezes in here from New York like some demented banshee and promptly institutes a sex strike, rents some grotty little flat in Ladbroke Grove and won't let me near her with a bargepole. Then last week she's back from LA and all over me like a rash.'

'Why?'

'Actually I was bonking my PA. Put my hands up to it. So I strayed . . . but let's keep it in perspective. Other men have a mid-life crisis and they invade Iran. Or attack a refugee camp or something . . .' Sir Anthony's tone had become somewhat melancholy. 'The other day Zelda double-parked my Morgan in the West End and the bomb squad blew it up.'

Perhaps they were having a mid-life crisis too, he thought to himself. His friend noticed that Sir Anthony seemed bemused. 'I can't think why I ever married the bitch,' he said forlornly. 'She makes my life utter hell.'

Above the hubbub of brusque masculine chatter, gruff guffawings and the subdued squeaking of fat bottoms on overstuffed leather chairs, a familiar, distinctly high-pitched voice was making itself audible close by.

'Duncan, dear boy, how are you?'

'On top of the bloody world, how does it look?'

'What happened?' Toby Freer Farmer asked him.

'I fell out of a bloody window, didn't I.'

'Fell out of a window?'

'Accidentally,' Campbell stressed. He had decided that his interests were best served by diplomacy. If Mira hadn't yet mentioned the débâcle at the drinks party to her brother, then she probably hadn't said a word to anybody else either. So perhaps the whole hateful fandango had been forgotten by everybody. Everybody, that is, Campbell thought ruefully, except me. 'I was drunk,' he told Toby, with a wan smile. 'Care to join me today? I need to pick your brains about something rather delicate.'

'Well, perhaps just a very quick one,' Toby hesitated. 'I've got to dash to meet Gizelle at the American Embassy.'

Campbell looked puzzled.

'Whole lot of ridiculous bumph to sort out there before we name the day,' elaborated Toby. 'You know: visas, what was your mother's blood group, batteries of medical tests and all that sort of bureaucratic nonsense.'

'So when is the happy day, then?' Campbell asked.

'I've just told you, we haven't named it yet. Now, what's on your mind?'

Campbell watched him ordering up a large brandy and soda from one of Chambrun's wrinkled retainers. Toby's horn-rimmed glasses, bushy brown eyebrows and beaky nose reminded *The Times*'s acting editor of many childhood hours passed spent studying ornithology. He's a curious bird though, Campbell thought. Always hanging around with older people. But perhaps his new American bride will loosen the young fogey up a little. Put a bit of an edge on him . . .

'I need to have lunch with your sister,' Campbell said.

'Mirabelle? Half-sister, actually. Well, ring her up and invite her.'

'I can never bloody get through,' Campbell moaned. 'I've written, phoned, faxed . . . I've even sent round a copyboy with flowers and a photocopy of my diary. Could you have a word? I mean, I only want to buy her a bloody lunch.'

'Why? Is it the job at your place?'

Campbell nodded. If he could talk Toby round, they could just have lunch as if nothing had happened. In time it might become a sort of joke between them. In the interim he'd be able to get the measure of her, see what sort of threat she represented to his ambitions.

'You see, I've talked to Kiki Cox and the madwoman from Manhattan, and Collins is pressing me to complete my report on the external candidates. The problem is, I can't do it until I've broken bread with your sis . . . with Mirabelle.'

'I don't know why Collins should concern you overmuch,'

said Toby. 'He's just an empty suit. He may be The Boss's nephew, but he's also a peon and a frightful parvenu. Absolutely no depth as a person, no moral intelligence at all. Somebody described him to me as being so crooked he eats soup with a corkscrew. People say he's supposed to have The Boss's ear, but I can't see anyone taking him seriously . . . can you?'

'I have to,' Campbell replied ruefully. 'He's my boss.'

'Just a minute . . . isn't there some other woman in the running?'

'Oh yes . . . the appalling harridan on the *Sunday Post*, what's her name? . . . Mandi Pandi . . . Mandi Harry . . . God, the more I see of women, the more I like used car salesmen. Actually, I don't have to worry about her, she works for INI already, so we've already sent her assessment over to Los Angeles. Christ, the prospect of that two-bit bimbo editing the paper . . . no, I can't begin to even contemplate it. The point is, Toby, if you could see your way clear to ask Mira if she could find time to fit in a lunch, I'd be inordinately grateful.'

'I don't think she'll come, you know,' Toby said. 'She seems to have got this bee in her bonnet that someone on the paper has got it in for her.'

'Really?' said Campbell, edging forward slightly in his armchair. 'What makes her think that?'

'Some lunatic sent her a blood-caked bullet,' he said. 'She seems to have got it into her head that they're following her. I don't know, it's probably just stress . . . you don't know anyone on the paper with a grudge against her, do you?'

Campbell shrugged.

'So you see, I don't think it's very likely that Mirabelle's going to have lunch with anyone from *The Times* for a while. Besides, why should she? If she wanted the job she'd just tell me and I'd tell my ex-stepmother, who'd tell her sister, and she'd tell her husband and he'd tell his brother, and Mirabelle would be appointed.'

'Would she?' said Campbell, trying to keep the alarm out of his voice. 'Why?'

'Because his brother is The Boss,' Toby said.

'I see,' said Campbell, his mouth glued into a forced smile.

'Besides,' added Tony, 'Mirabelle's the only one with . . . what's that clickword you use at Wapping?'

'The Wow Factor,' Campbell winced, forcing the syllables through his teeth.

'G'day,' said a preternaturally bouncy Australian in a loud checked suit. 'How's it going, ya dags?'

'I didn't know you were a member here, Collins,' said Toby with a certain brisk asperity.

'I'm not,' smiled Brett. 'But I am a member of the St Kilda Yacht Club in Melbourne and we've got reciprocal rights in this tip. Didn't you hear about Jason Donovan's cousin riding a Harley up the stairs in here and knocking over the Archdeacon of York? No? Your loss, fellers. What are you blokes drinking then?'

He never got to find out. For at that moment a group of men in monks' habits glided into the room bearing a plinth on their shoulders. Upon it was set a stuffed dog. Following up the rear was a man with a black hood over his head. His trouser legs were rolled up and he was shoeless. In his left hand he carried an ornately carved cleft stick. Immediately, much to the amazement of Brett Collins, every man in the room fell to his knees. A great hush fell over the place like a blanket of snow.

'What does she think she's doing?' chanted the hooded man, his voice solemn.

'She's a bitch, Sire, so she whelps as a bitch. The ways of whelping are all she knows,' the Chambrunians chanted back in unison.

Brett looked up, agog. And then the procession marched out as suddenly as it had appeared.

'What the bloody hell was all that about?' Brett exclaimed, as club stewards and members with their own teeth and hair helped older stalwarts of the club back into their bathchairs.

'It's 28 February,' said Campbell.

'Rags Day.'

'Rags Day?'

'Not something you'd know about at the St Kilda Yacht

Club, I'll wager,' said Toby.

Collins was none the wiser.

'Hello, Brett,' said Sir Anthony. His lunch guest had left, another victim of the Chambrun's suet pudding. 'Now, how many tickets would you like to the Shaken Not Stirred Ball? Shall I put you down for a table? Or would you prefer two, so you can accommodate all your closest friends?'

'You could fit all my pommy mates down the dunny, Tone. Is this that Bob Geldof lark next week?'

'He's a member of the committee, yes,' Sir Anthony said. 'I'm another. It's in aid of the LA earthquake victims. I'm sure you've heard.'

'If I can get to sit with Geldof and that ripping tart of his you can put me down for as many tables as you bloody well like,' Brett told him.

'Is that the time? Goodness, I must dash off to the Embassy. Sorry I couldn't help you out there, Duncan . . .' said Toby, staring at Brett Collins as if he had just crawled from beneath something heavy and damp.

'Before you go, Toby,' Campbell said, moving closer as he lowered his voice, 'I've just had a thought about the person who's been threatening your, er, half-sister.'

A bushy eyebrow rose.

'I did hear from a reliable source that Zelda Lee Powers has hired some sort of private detective fellow to dig up dirt on her competitors.'

Actually, Campbell hated to sabotage Zelda in this way. His view was that she'd be the easiest Editor to get rid of. But the situation was desperate.

'My understanding is that he's a freelance – could've got a little over-enthusiastic . . .'

'Good man,' Toby said. 'I'll mention it to her.'

'Could you have a word about our lun . . .' Campbell began, but Toby smiled and slicked away.

Sir Anthony George knew the source of Campbell's rumour about his wife. A secretary at *The Times* must have leaked it. Hannah . . . who had mentioned it to him in bed just three nights earlier. He hadn't mentioned a thing to Zelda, not least because the demands of editing a national newspaper, on top of juggling these two voracious women, left him little appetite or energy for intrigue. Well, just a little . . .

'Brett,' he said, 'if none of your female candidates work out, I'd just like you to know that I'm not altogether happy at the *Daily Sketch*.'

'I'm not bloody surprised,' laughed Brett. 'It's like something the cat fetched up. So what are you saying, mate? You want to make a run at *The Times* gig?'

'I might just be persuaded,' Sir Anthony replied.

'Can you get me on board with Sir Bob and Paula?' Brett asked, vaguely taunting him.

'It could be arranged . . .'

'Right. I'll talk to my Uncle about it,' Brett said, rubbing his hands together.

Sir Anthony made a mental note to ask Zelda about the private detective.

29

Party time. The Animal Rights protesters had fallen out with the anti-Royalists, and baton-wielding police charged at both to disperse the brick-slinging mobs besieging Berkeley Square. A news photographer from one of the Duke of Lanchester's Allied titles rejoined his fellow B-list paparazzo on the square's railings – only Richard Young, Dave Hogan and David Benett (the only photographers as famous as their victims) had been allowed inside the marquee, where a sign in the muddy ground proclaimed: SHAKEN NOT STIRRED . . . LONDON DISASTER RELIEF FOR LA'S EARTHQUAKE VICTIMS.

'It's getting nasty out there,' the photographer said in his Midlands accent. 'They're smashing up all the shop windows along Oxford Street. I got some great frames of this copper going ape with one of those new batons, and I think they arrested Morrissey. Hey, Stone, you should've been there, man.'

'I only do real celebrities,' retorted Stone. 'Celebrity babes. That's my diet, dude. Yo, check it, man,' he warned another lenser jostling him for position on the railings.

He turned to see who the pack was snapping; a pneumatic black babe had arrived dressed in African tribal gear that managed to be both politically correct and salacious at the same time. 'Who is she?' Stone asked the news photographer who'd been covering the West End rampage.

'That's Ethiopia,' he said. 'The girl who stars opposite Frank Bough in *Bounty!*'

'What have you done to your face?' the other snapper asked Stone. 'There's something different about it.'

'My beard's growing, I guess,' Stone said, 'and I got this new stud in my nose.'

'DIANA! DIANA!' the rat pack cried as a large limousine pulled up and disgorged that virtuoso player on the nation's heart-strings.

'My God, I never realised she was so tall,' Stone said when the feeding frenzy had abated and the Princess of Wales was finally allowed to enter the tent.

'Interesting,' his compadre remarked in that Black Country tone so flat you could have calibrated a spirit level on it. 'She wasn't wearing any tights. I can probably flog that to *Verve*.'

'Who do you deal with there?' Stone asked.

'Come off it,' the other guy snorted. 'I don't mind helping you out . . . hey, one day maybe you'll do the same for me. But I'm not giving you my fucking contacts book, Stone.'

'Chill out, man! I got my own in at *Verve*,' he said, contemplating Nadia's sultry loveliness with a rush of erotic pleasure.

'There are millions of faces here,' the other said. 'We're going to make a lot of wonga out of this.'

It was true. All British Society was there – the players who mattered, at least. The awfully entertaining and the entertainingly awful; the blue-blooded courtiers who formed the Royals' circle; the pretty, the witty and the terribly gay; former models now married to unsuitable dukes and earls; perpetually tanned Mediterranean playboys and rock stars with no underpants and jet slags on each arm; turf types and surf types and Polish Princes indistinguishable from each other in their dinner jackets; pivotal hostesses, power couples, taste-makers, contact brokers, home wreckers; première league flirts, showbiz moguls, bed-hopping gardeners and boffo movie studs; the genuinely titled and those who just had extra-long cheque books; social gurus and gynaecologists to the stars, dilated to meet you and at your cervix ma'am; food-and-mouth merchants and womanising philanthropists; the Season's most ravishing debutantes, hottest bi-coastal agents and most dangerous bisexual artists; greedy tycoons, scandal-tainted politicians and diplomats from chaotic nations; starlets busy sleeping their way to the top and well-born rakes bumping along the bottom, passing the time until they could fly away on some assignment with an object of desire, whether they peddled flesh in an Antiguan brothel, hit the right notes in an Acapulco bank or drilled for black gold in Alaska . . .

Even Alaska has to be warmer than this hole, thought Stone, bundling himself up against the cold. His gloved hands clasped his camera as he watched and waited, a bush shaman with a beeper, a wicker-whacked Druid in the fertile season, an acoylte at Delphi with a Leica, biding his time with silent incantations over his tools of ritual . . . waiting, waiting, waiting for still more celebrities to appear, materialising like spirits in the night . . .

Waiters in starched white coats scurried to and from the bar, bearing crystal goblets of sparkling drinks on silver platters with which to welcome new guests into the marquee. The Lester Lanin band played a medley of happy show tunes and Ethiopia, swathed in her baggy, vividly hued tribal outfit, made a big entrance. Mandi noticed her pristine white Reeboks, clearly visible beneath the black star's slit-legged, low-cut costume.

As she floated by, Mandi said to her, 'I love your outfit.'

'Thank you,' Ethiopia replied graciously, in an accent that was pure cut-glass Oxbridge.

'Where's it from?'

'A relation sent it from my homeland,' she replied. 'Nigeria. I'm an Igbo.'

As Ethiopia turned to receive accolades from a prettier admirer nearby, Mandi whispered to her escort, 'Chalk the shoes.'

'I clocked 'em,' said Kettle, trying to get comfortable in the new dinner jacket he'd acquired two hours earlier. 'She's fatter than in that picture, isn't she?'

'Mmmmn,' Mandi agreed, noticing, with an inward groan, that the expensive new Lacroix frock she'd hi-jacked from the fashion cupboard had already begun to crinkle around her ample rear. 'And she's obviously a bit of an operator too – by the end of the evening this ground will be so churned up and muddy, everyone else's smart little Charles Jourdan suede pumps will look like football boots.'

Ethiopia drifted from one schmooze to another. Here she was, smiling at Pierce Brosnan – all the 007 stars had been invited to the ball – and there she was, charming a new coterie of fans, drifting among the rustlings of new taffeta and old money like a bee flitting from the stamen of one exotic flower to another. Mandi couldn't fail to notice Ethiopia talking to Zelda Lee Powers, who had now resumed a tiff with her husband. Sir Anthony was wearing an eyepatch because, she assumed from rumours which had wafted her way, his shiner still hadn't quite healed.

'I don't see why I should pay for this bolt-hole in Ladbroke Grove if you won't tell me what you're doing there,' Anthony was saying.

'I told you already, it's business, for Chrissakes. At least when I tell you something's business, that's what it is – not doing the nasty with some cheap floozie and any goddamn household appliance that comes to hand.'

'If I can't see it, I won't pay for it, Zelda, it's as simple as that. If you expect me to pick up the tab, then give me a key.'

'Tony, I'm experimenting . . .' Zelda started to wail. But Sir Anthony had spotted Kettle and caught Mandi's eye. She joined them reluctantly.

'Blimey,' Mandi said, in spite of herself, taking in Zelda, 'where did you get that little lot? Bermans and Nathans?'

Zelda was wearing the frilly ball gown of a Southern Belle, circa 1860. But the *Gone With The Wind* effect was somewhat overplayed – she was also toting a jaunty 20-gallon stetson, two pearl-handled silver six-shooters on a weathered black gun belt and a Confederate flag flying from the top of her parasol.

'Or tell me,' Mandi continued mischievously, '. . . were the Ku Klux Klan having a boot sale?'

'Why, if it ain't alleged Editor Mandi Harry,' bitched Zelda in response. 'Thrown any good blood bombs lately, honey? Or are you just into melting down computers these days with all that white-hot intellect of yours?'

Before Mandi could reply, Sir Anthony had drawn her aside, out of his wife's range, by which time Zelda had spotted a Lord she had been wanting to chat up for ages and swanned off.

'I want to ask you a favour, Mandi,' he whispered urgently into her ear.

'Try me.'

'I want to borrow one of your hacks for a stakeout.'

'Sure,' Mandi shrugged. 'Why?'

'Office politics,' he said.

'Where's the doorstep?'

'Ladbroke Grove.'

'When?'

'ASAP.'

'Tomorrow morning OK?' she said, beckoning Kettle over. 'What's the address? OK, Kettle, got that?'

'What am I looking for?' Kettle asked Sir Anthony.

'Anything that moves,' Anthony replied.

'What about that other job?' Kettle whispered to Mandi, swivelling his eyes surreptitiously in Ethiopia's direction.

'Later,' Mandi said quickly. Kettle drifted away. In spite of herself, Mandi began to cry on Anthony's shoulder about her kitten, Pinkee Poo. Anthony watched as Brett Collins put his hand on Paula Yates's bottom. And Kiki Cox hovered like a locust behind them, just waiting to seize the opportunity to bend Brett's ear. Anthony had just begun to tell Mandi about a famous TV personality's collection of celebrity autopsy photographs when she noticed that Mira Freer Farmer was talking in a very animated fashion to Roger Daltrey, and that he had his hand on her left breast. 'What is that girl on?' she wondered to herself, trying desperately to place where she had seen Mira's ravishing turquoise dress before . . . but her rumination was interrupted by a jab in the ribs from Sir Anthony, as he addressed a newcomer in his polished baritone.

'Mr Campbell. Well, well, well.' There was a mischievous twinkle in his eye that gave him the air of a naughty schoolboy. 'Mandi here was just telling me a most distressing story – it seems that somebody deliberately trapped her kitten in her waste-disposal unit, so that when she turned it on, she killed her own cat. Nasty, eh?'

'My sincere condolences,' said Campbell, sounding shifty and not very sincere at all as he scanned the crowd for impressionable young heiresses who might be wafting about for the taking.

'Of course, as a tabloid editor myself, I can imagine the kind of security that would be attached to Mandi's home address,' Anthony said. 'But of course, as a senior International News man, you'd be able to circumvent that and just pull it off the computer system, wouldn't you?'

'Would I?' Campbell said with a frown, only half-listening as his gaze locked on to Caro Buchanan dancing mons to mons with a gorgeous Asian babe in a red silk dress. To die for . . .

'Then talking of computers,' Sir Anthony continued, 'everyone knows that you're a computer buff – you'd certainly have the technology to hack into Kiki Cox's system, even from your portable.'

'What are you trying to insinuate?' asked Campbell gruffly, fully engaged now, and frowning at Anthony.

'Insinuate? These are plain facts, dear boy, are they not? As is your well-known predilection for decimating the animal kingdom,' Anthony said, slipping an arm around Mandi's waist. 'It would take a certain knowledge of weaponry to have a name engraved on a bullet and, since you shoot every weekend, we can reasonably assume that . . .'

'I like your nose job honey,' came a voice like rush-hour traffic in Mandi's ear.

'I haven't had a . . .' Mandi began.

'Talk to a qualified professional,' Zelda said, with a catty smile. She turned to her husband, who had withdrawn his hand from Mandi's waistband. 'Why An-thony,' she drooled, switching into her sickly Mouth-from-the-South mode again, 'Ah don't believe that lil' slip of a girl behind the bar cares for me over much.'

'Why's that, Zelda?' said Anthony wearily.

Zelda pointed at the blue string dangling from her Bloody Mary. ''Cos, darlin', she just put a tampon in my drink . . .' Zelda said, tugging at it. Just as all eyes focussed on the cocktail from hell, the glass seemed to leap forward of its own volition, its dark red liquid cargo flooding Mandi's borrowed white dress.

'Farkin 'ell,' Mandi screeched, and moved in on Zelda, squaring up.

'That was completely uncalled for,' Sir Anthony snapped at his wife, shoving her aside. 'Are you OK?' he asked Mandi gently.

'This is a La fucking Croix original, on loan,' Mandi wailed. 'And now it's completely bloody ruined.'

'Bloody being the operative,' commented Campbell, enjoying the spectacle.

'Why, silly ME,' Zelda said, biting her bottom lip in mock-shame. 'Ah'm so careless, ain't I? Why, I just cain't BRING myself to begin to apologise to y'all.'

'I'm going to have to leave,' Mandi said to Anthony as Zelda tripped off to hug and smug with Jack Tinker from the *Daily Mail*. 'I can't walk around like this.'

'No, wait a minute Mandi, don't go,' Sir Anthony pleaded. He took her hand and glared at Zelda. 'It was her fault entirely. She's been drinking all afternoon. Look, Mandi, take my dinner jacket,' he offered, slipping out of it. 'Wear this. It'll look brilliant on you, you can change over there in the Portaloo.'

'Lay ONE finger on mah man,' hissed Zelda as she swished past, Tinker obediently in tow, as Mandi joined the loo queue, '. . . and I'll kick your ass so hard, your GRANDCHILDREN will be born dizzy. I'm warning you . . . Hey – is that champagne for me? Oh, you SHOULDN'T have, Brett, Baby!' Zelda seized his glass with one hand and grabbed Collins's tie with the other. The bow collapsed, and Zelda pulled at it, a flirtatious come-hither look lighting up her dark eyes.

'Jeez – my old mum warned me about girls like you,' Collins flirted back.

'It's all true, Sugar,' Zelda pouted wickedly, exchanging her empty glass for his full one. 'I'll be the WORLD to you, Baby – and you'll be on top.'

'But I bet your mother didn't warn you about Sheilas like me though,' said Kiki, resplendent in the bare minimum of black Donna Karan, swooping in and prising, with surprising force, The Boss's diminutive nephew from Zelda's vulpine clutches. Kiki whisked him away while Zelda could only stand and stare, speechless and goggle-eyed with rage.

'Jeez, thanks for getting me outta there. I think she's one over the eight, mate,' Brett said to Kiki, dusting himself down. 'Christ, that's quite a grip you've got there for one so slim, Keeks.'

'I stay in shape . . .' she smouldered down at him, tracing her inner top lip with a luscious lap of her tongue and brushing her left breast lightly with her hand.

Brett thought he would come on the spot. 'Err . . . right. Whatcha drinkin' there, sport?' he asked, his voice quivering. Any more of this and he was going to have to shag her. She wouldn't have said no either, he'd bet.

'Evian,' she winked. 'I drink it like water.'

'Slab?' he said, offering her a Winston and trying to sound cool.

Kiki shook her pale blonde head.

'Jeez . . . you don't drink, you don't smoke, so whatdya say to a little fuck?'

'Hello little fuck,' Kiki winked, kissing his damp forehead. 'Old joke, Brett.'

For all this horny-virgin-come-on stuff she sure is one defensive chick, Brett thought. He wondered if her mystique was calculated, or the defence mechanism of a paranoid whose journalistic credentials were beginning to be scrutinized just that little bit too closely for comfort as she tried to break into the upper echelons . . .

'I guess,' he said, 'I want to ask you a bit of a personal question, mate.'

Kiki shrugged as if to say, I'm all ears.

'I know you're from the lucky country, just like me, but no one I know seems to know anything about you. Where are you from? You must be a Sydneysider, aren't you?'

Kiki shrugged again, a hint of a smile playing across her sexy mouth. 'Bankstown,' she said.

'What did your dad do?'

Kiki crossed her arms. Brett noticed that she had a large, heavy bag tucked into her armpit. 'He was sort of an undertaker,' Kiki said, choosing her words carefully. 'I never knew him very well. He was killed in an air crash when I was three.'

'Jeez, I'm sorry to hear that. What about your mum? You do the right thing and get over and see her at Chrissy, then?'

'My mother died when I was about 15 . . . she'd been ill for some years,' Kiki said, sounding as though she were reading the price of wool off an autocue. 'I was looked after by foster parents until I was old enough to leave home. That relationship, I'm afraid, has not stood the test of time.'

'So don't you stay in touch with anyone from Down Under?' Brett said, smiling at Mira and Toby as they breezed by with a barrel-chested, big-shouldered, lanky young fellow with startlingly long blond hair.

'Well, only Wayne and Shane really,' Kiki said. 'My young cousins . . . they're out near Darwin.'

'Can't stand the NT,' Brett said with a grimace. 'All those mozzies.'

'Have you seen my dummy yet?' she asked, changing the subject.

'Well, Kiki, I know it's there. I just haven't got round to sending it yet, but it's . . .'

'Look at it,' she urged him, squeezing his forearm. 'It's superb . . . if I say so myself.'

'Oh, OK, clickety click, will do.'

'What are you doing next Sunday?'

'No idea.'

'I have a very good one,' Kiki smiled. 'It's my 40th birthday party at Sorrell's in Covent Garden. Feel free to drop by, anytime after eight.'

'Yeah . . . well, come to think of it, I've . . .'

'I'll have that glass of Evian now if you don't mind, Brett.'

'OK, I'll shoot through and get it,' he said, backing away . . . straight into a barrel-chested, big-shouldered, lanky young fellow with startlingly long blond hair. 'Ah, 'scuse I, mate, gotta see a fellah about some water.'

'No worries,' replied the hunk.

'Bloody hell,' Brett said, staring up at him, 'there are more fair dinkum blokes here than at Geelong Grammar Open Day. Brett Collins,' he said, offering his hand.

'I'm a Kiwi if truth be told,' said the blond, accepting the handshake. He said his name was Ian Something or Other.

'Yeah, I picked that up,' Brett said. 'One thing about these

206

pommie bastards, they know how to throw a thrash, eh?'

'Too right,' said Ian Something or Other.

'I had my picture taken with Sir Bob,' said Brett. 'That's one for the old den wall, I'd say.'

'Good on yer, mate – so did I.'

'No shit?' Brett's face fell a little. 'What did they hit you up for then?'

'How d'you mean, mate?'

'I had to fill half a dozen tables at two grand sterling a plate. How many notes did you burn?'

'Nothing,' the other replied, puzzled. 'They just took the picture.'

'Oh,' said Brett flatly. He was silent . . . but only for a moment. 'I'll tell you what, though, I could do some serious bloody damage to the skirt here. I feel hornier than a nun with a porn mag. That Mira bird you're with . . . FWOARRRGH! I wouldn't mind giving her a ride on the old love rocket, too right, eh?'

As he nudged the blond Adonis in the ribs, Ian said: 'I don't think you've met my partner.'

'Oooooh, such an insufferably manly handshake, it's making all my ganglions resonate deeply,' Crispian Frye swooned.

'What the fuck do you look like?' exclaimed Collins, realising his mistake.

'I'm a continental fruit plate, luvvie,' said Frye, his metallic-coated Smokey Sage one-piece polyester dungaree dinner suit shimmering quite fetchingly beneath his Carmen Miranda hat. 'And when this is all over, someone's going to eat me up and lick me clean!'

Just then Mira and Toby Freer Farmer joined them with an American blonde whose understated dress suggested the simplicity that only really big money can buy. Mira introduced her half-sister-in-law-to-be Gizelle to everybody, and Toby asked after his step-cousin-in-law, Brett's father.

'So how d'ya go at the Embassy then, mate? Everything rigdi didge?'

'Terrible bureaucratic nonsense,' Toby said, shaking his head.

'Jeez, what about that club of yours? I couldn't believe it

when all those old codgers started dropping on their knees and barking like a pack of wild dingoes.'

'Oh, that'd be the Chambrun, right?' said Gizelle.

'It could be a bloody loony bin for all I know,' Brett said. 'I've never seen anything like it! You must be as mad as a meat axe to hang around that dump.'

Toby was about to say something, but Mira fixed him with a look that would chill an iced vodkatini.

'So tell me again what it is that you're studying, Gazelle?' she asked sweetly.

'The role of diphthong neutrality in the North Icelandic Saga,' replied the beautiful girl with a smile.

'Jeez . . . as the captain of the *Titanic* once said, that breaks the ice at parties,' chuckled Brett, popping another tin of Heineken. Toby's fiancée ran counter to one of his stereotypes – that educated women tended to be thinner. 'Most of the birds I know,' said Brett Collins, chugging on the golden vitamin pill, '. . . their favourite author is the guy who wrote "Pull tab to open".' He wiped his mouth on the back of his sleeve. 'So where's the old ball-and-chain tonight, Mira?'

'Mico? Oh, he's at home, working on his video. You must join us actually, Brett, we're going to have an intimate little breakfast after the ball.'

'. . . the thing is,' Crispian was saying to his boyfriend, who was actually an internationally famous model, 'Kiki can seem like such a robot at times, but she's got this positive obsession with transparency. Do you know what she asked me to do last night? No, not that. Convert the cistern into a transparent tank so she can put some more fish in it. Honestly, Ian, don't you find it all just un petit peu infra-dig?'

'No,' said his luscious companion. 'Why, should I?'

'Well, why is she so obsessed with transparency? It's as if she's trying to say she's got nothing to hide . . .'

'Well, maybe she's trying too hard . . .'

'People like her, they always give themselves away,' Crispian mused. 'You mark my words. There's more to her than meets the eye . . .'

Across the tent, Zelda broke off her conversation with a rich Society psychic as she saw Mandi reappear wearing her husband's DJ.

Mandi sidled up to Kettle. 'Her secret love's no secret anymore.'

'Who, Ethiopia?'

Mandi made a shushing sound. 'No – Julie Andrews, you plonker – yes, of course Ethiopia! She was blabbing her mouth off in the Ladies.'

'What?'

'She says,' Mandi said, 'that they sometimes stay at the Portobello Hotel.'

'You want me to cover it?'

Mandi shook her head. 'Do a number on this stakeout for Sir Anthony tomorrow.'

Kettle looked sullen.

'You owe me one, Kettle,' she reminded him. 'Don't let me down.'

'No, no way, Aitch,' he promised. 'Look, are you sure you don't want me to case the Portobello? It's just round the corner from Ladbroke Grove, and I know that sometimes . . .'

'I've got a good reason for doing this one on my own,' Mandi said, closing the subject.

'My God,' interrupted Sir Anthony, 'you look absolutely stunning.'

'Thank you,' said Mandi, and she blushed. She felt like a schoolgirl. About 50 feet away Zelda felt ready to explode. 'No-one gets outta here alive,' she muttered to no-one in particular, taking another pull on the bottle of Jack Daniels she'd just stolen from behind the bar. But her words were lost in the noizak of the best of times, the worst of times, that were being had by one and all. Zelda took one of the pearl-handled pistols out of her holster, twirled it round her finger and made for the door.

30

Stone saw his mother leave the tent but pretended to be absorbed by his Leica as she tried surreptitiously to attract his attention. She marched over to her son. 'Why, you must be the famous paparazzo Stone Z. O'Brien,' said Zelda, her tone a meld of sweetness and sarcasm. 'May I have a moment of your very valuable time, please?'

'Mom,' he hissed as they walked away from the other lensers, 'I don't believe you did that!'

'Did you really have to describe me as the Wicked Witch of the Upper Westside to that Neanderthal?' she hissed back.

'Check it,' Stone said. 'I'm freezing my butt off out here.'

'Why aren't you wearing that scarf I got you from Liberty's? Nearly 80 bucks it cost me, and a night like this you come out in a singlet and bitch about being cold. Take it someplace else.'

'I don't wear the scarf 'cos it's, like, passmodius,' he said.

'Huh?'

'Scarves are for cool guys, you know?'

'But don't you wanna be a cool guy,' she said, puzzled, 'or at least a WARM guy?'

'Mom,' said Stone, stopping dead and raising his eyebrows to the stars, 'a cool guy is a really uncool guy who thinks he's really cool. Give it up, will ya?'

'Well,' said Zelda, 'I'm so goddamned PLEASED that you've inherited your father's fascination with language.'

They stood looking at each other. The air was as cold as an undertaker's handshake.

'You gotta do something for me.'

'Newsflash,' said Stone, looking from side to side, snarkasm flooding his tone.

Zelda hiccuped. 'Take out Mandi Harry's car.'

'I don't think so,' Stone said with a sneer, and turned to walk away.

'Where are you going?'

'I'm bailing,' he snapped back at her.

'Stone, you're NOT! You can't let me down, you CAN'T! I've flown you 8,000 miles, I've spent more than $30,000 on you these past two weeks . . .'

'Hey,' said Stone, stopping in his tracks, 'I pull my weight.'

'Disable her car if you know what's good for you. NOW.'

Stone made a low noise that was halfway between a snort and a sigh. He looked at her, looked round the square and said: 'You hosing me?'

Zelda hiccuped again and wished she'd brought her new mink out with her. But the queue at the cloakroom had been too long. Plus, ALSO, she didn't want to attract attention from anyone who might assume she was going home. Alone. 'Don't you sass me,' she warned.

'I'm not . . . I, like, don't even know which one her car is, OK?'

'It's a Jaguar,' she smiled. 'It said so on the detective's reports.'

'Great,' said Stone, indicating with his forehead the long row of dark, identical, chauffeur-driven Jaguars parked against the kerb.

'Okay,' said Zelda, trying to get to grips with his unanticipated aspect of the situation which had somehow eluded her. 'Then trash Tony's instead. The green Merc over there.'

'The rental?'

'Yup.'

'You are totally reality-impaired.'

'I'm also your mother,' Zelda reminded him.

'Oh Jeez. Mom, will you please stop playing with the gun? It's stressing me out.'

Zelda put the pearl-handled pistol back in its holster.

'Anyways, I can't just walk over and beat up the Benzo,' he said. 'There are like a million cops around.'

'I'm not ASKING you to beat it up,' Zelda said. 'Just make sure the goddamn motor won't start.'

'How am I supposed to do that?'

'Didn't they teach you ANYTHING in that Reform school?'

'Sheee-it!' Stone yelled. 'I'm trying to go straight, and my mother, get this, my Mom, wants me to start breaking up Uncle Tony's ride. I don't believe this, I'm gonna call Oprah, Donahue, Sally Jesse Raphael at least. No wonder I'm a total fuck-up . . .'

'No, no, Stone,' she soothed sarcastically, '. . . it's strictly a *Suzanne Somers Special*: Weak Boys Who Blackmail The Moms That Spoil Them.'

Stone shrugged. 'It's cold,' he said. 'I hate this place. I'm pissed at doing shitty jobs for you, I'm pissed at never having any fucking money unless I come crawling to you, and I'm pissed to the max with this cretin maggot weather . . .'

'Don't be so naïve, Stone. We're all on the same trip, we might as well help each other out.'

'That's what you call it?' he said, incredulously, 'Help? I can think of better words.'

'We've got a deal,' Zelda reminded him.

'Wrong, Ma,' he said. 'I've got a Polaroid picture, and you've got Dad's bank. What we've got is a problem.'

'Sure, honey, sure . . . until you let me have the Polaroid, we've got a problem,' Zelda nodded. 'I couldn't agree with you more.'

'Don't even think about asking. I'm not giving it to you, not even on your best day.'

'Why not?' Zelda cried. 'It's worth ten grand sterling, cash in palm, tomorrow.' He shook his head. 'Cash,' she repeated tantalisingly.

'Everyone in your generation is like, L-twelve.'

'L-twelve?' She remembered him saying that to her once before, but couldn't recollect what it meant.

'Stupid times twelve. It's like you all took some stupidity drug back in the Sixties.'

'Gimme the Polaroid,' she demanded, holding out her hand. 'NOW.'

Stone stared at her, shaking his head slowly. 'I do Tony's car, that's it. You're overdrawn at the favour bank.'

'Why don't you give me . . .' Zelda hiccuped again, and cussed. 'Why won't you even SELL me that Polaroid?'

'Because it's my insurance policy for getting back all the money you jacked off Dad.'

'Like you weren't involved?' Zelda said. 'Yeah, right.'

'It's like a chicken and egg situation, OK?'

'No,' said Zelda, correcting him, 'YOU mean it's like chicken and PIG. If I'm eating bacon and eggs, the chicken's involved, but the pig's committed.'

Stone shifted around uneasily, grinding his muddy Caterpillar boots against the pavement. Zelda stared at him, her son. Baggy, pierced and on the make. So precious and only slightly flawed. He drove her crazy – but she loved him so much, only she couldn't tell him anymore – too much had gone down, too much was happening between them. And that Polaroid was too dangerous . . .

'Listen, if you don't hit Tony's car before he gets outtathere, everything we've done will be wasted, down the pan.'

'Why?' frowned Stone.

'Because Mommy says so,' Zelda replied. 'How about I know just a little more than a 21-year-old professional failure who knows everything?'

'Where do you get off, coming on like you're an adult or something? Has Mommy Dearest really thought this one through? I mean, if I whack out Tony's Benzo, how's Mommy gonna get home?'

'Brett Collins'll give me a ride,' Zelda said confidently.

'He's totally in thrall to me. And if not, I'll take a cab.'

'What about those cops?'

'I'll keep them busy,' Zelda said. 'You just make sure they can't leave in Tony's car, OK?'

'Wait a minute,' Stone said. 'Suppose they leave in *her* car?'

'They won't,' Zelda smiled. 'Trust me. That little shit may have a balcony you could do Shakespeare on, but she's way too uptight to let her chauffeur know she's banging some sleazebag like Tony.'

'Why you dissing him like that? What kind of a way is that to talk about my stepfather?'

213

'Like you care so much for Tony all of a sudden? Stone – please. It's your mother you're talking to. And hey – I'm the Mommy, I do the lectures,' Zelda said. 'Let me talk straight to you. Your allowance is terminated, as of now. Do his car and maybe – just MAYBE – I'll think about reinstating it.'

'Fuck you,' Stone said, in spite of himself.

'Just watch me,' Zelda retorted, and walked over to a group of policemen, positioning herself to talk to them so that their backs would be turned on her husband's car.

Stone moved fast. Using the Swiss army knife he kept in his camera bag, he managed to catch the spring that opened the bonnet. Taking a brightly-coloured scarf from his camera case, he executed a series of simple, practised movements, removed the fanbelt and stuffed it into his case. He slapped the bonnet shut again and walked away quickly.

'You missed that guy from *Eastenders* trying to snog David Bowie,' the Midlands snapper said gleefully. 'It were wicked, they got into some right fisticuffs. Hey – who was that strange woman you were yappin' to? The one got up like a space cowboy?'

'My mother,' Stone said flatly.

'Gerroff!' the other said.

'OK, OK, it's some mad Editor I used to work for in New York. She's like – what do you guys say? – bonkers. Yeah, that's it, totally fucking bonkers.'

Stone watched Zelda stagger back towards the tent. She and her stetson had parted company somewhere along the way. The way tonight was panning out, Stone fully expected to see one of the policemen wearing it.

'You know what she's going to do next?' Stone said to his pal.

'No – what?'

'She's gonna go around and spike herself up with whatever's left to drink on every single one of the tables in there. Man, she's like, 48 years old, a one-woman situation tragedy.'

He would have said more . . . but at that moment the Royal family's last unmarried Prince made a dash for his car, and the flashbulbs exploded like New Year's Eve 1999.

31

'There she goes,' Kettle whispered to Mandi, tracking Ethiopia's regal egress towards the tent exit.

'Thanks,' she said, watching the procession of gofers, attendants, assistants, new best friends and celebrity sycophants who were surrounding the West End Diva like stardust trailing a comet.

'Listen, Aitch, I heard a good whisper tonight.'

'Wassat?' Mandi asked.

'I was talking to this bird what does her make-up.'

'And?'

'And she says she's up the duffer.'

'Eh?'

'Awaiting a nappy event.'

'Preggers? Nooooo!' Mandi breathed, her face changing colour with excitement.

'Straight up, Guv,' he said.

'Shit, can you get on that tomorrow? Follow it up on your mobile?'

'OK.'

'And Kettle . . .'

'Yeah, what?'

'Give me an hourly check call, we're going to have to play this one by ear, we might shift you on to the Ethiopia story, see what develops. OK, sling your hook.'

He nodded and slithered off.

'God, your shoes are muddy,' Sir Anthony said.

'And you've got a hair growing out of your nose,' she said. 'Ha ha ha, got ya going, didn't I? Where's the bitch queen?'

Sir Anthony made a movement with his head. 'She never met

a bottle she didn't like, that one. She'll be orbiting Pluto any minute. That was one of the things that attracted me to her originally . . . Zelda can drink any man under the table,' he said.

'Well, she hasn't tried to match this woman yet. You've been moving in sheltered circles, Anthony.'

'I don't suppose you fancy going on for a nightcap somewhere?'

'Where did you have in mind?'

'I'm a member at Tramp,' he suggested, referring to the Jermyn Street nighterie owned by Johnny Gold, one-time business partner of Jackie Collins's late husband Oscar.

'What a coincidence, I am such a tramp,' Mandi laughed. 'Tell you the truth, that's a bit hoity-toity for my taste. Why don't we just go somewhere low-key where can have a quiet jar or several, and not be hassled by the jetsam set?'

'Well, where did you have in mind?' Anthony asked, echoing her question.

'Oh, I don't know . . . I don't really care, come to that. What about the Portobello?'

'You have to book a room, otherwise they won't serve you,' he said.

'OK, so let's book a room,' she said, surprised by her own daring.

He raised an eyebrow as he raised his glass. 'You sure about this?'

'I'm sure,' Mandi said evenly.

Outside, other people were starting to leave.

'You must be freezing,' Anthony said, draping his arm around her.

It was cold, but Mandi didn't feel a thing. It was two a.m. but she was walking on sunshine. She felt like having a rash bet on a long-shot dog; like saddling up a dark horse; like ringing up a complete stranger to say she was glad to be alive . . . It reminded her of the way she used to feel as a teenager: the exhilaration of playing a game with no rules. Standing there, at that moment, Mandi had a sense of living large – like she was suddenly more of herself. As a person. And deeper, as a woman . . . more fully alive.

'We'll have to hurry,' Anthony said. 'Zelda could appear any second.'

They raced across to his Mercedes and jumped in. But the damned thing wouldn't start.

'Come on, come on, come on –' Anthony fretted.

'Don't worry, we can always take my car,' Mandi offered.

'Getting out of here's going to be a nightmare,' Anthony moaned. 'God, all those bloody demonstrations, they'll bomb us . . .'

'There are some cabs across the square . . .'

'Let's go,' said Anthony. Hand in hand, they raced across Berkeley Square like two teenagers. Anthony fancied he could hear the nightingale singing, even though it was still February . . .

'Stanley Gardens, West Eleven,' he told the driver. Mandi got in first, giggling like a schoolgirl as Anthony pinched her bottom.

'TONIIIIIIIII!'

Horrified, they both looked up to see a figure in a mud-stained Southern Belle ballgown flinging herself at the vehicle as it pulled away. Mandi caught a fleeting glimpse of the Confederate flag. As they sped off, Anthony turned round to see Zelda standing in the middle of the road, fumbling furiously with one of her pistols. Mandi, who kept her eyes straight ahead, saw a huge stetson blow into their path. She barely felt the bump as the cab ran over it.

Mira Freer Farmer and her gang were trying to finalise their travel arrangements.

'Of course Ian and I can fit in the back,' Crispian was saying.

'Are you sure? It's only a two-plus-two, you know,' Mira said. 'I mean you're both very welcome and all that, but it is incredibly tight and tiny, the back of that car.'

'Just like me, loverboy,' Crispian teased, swooning at his blond Adonis. 'Give Crispi another little Disco biscuit, darlink. They make me feel positively baroque.'

Mira led the party through the debris of the ball. Caro Buchanan and her new Indian girlfriend roared away in her smart little black Golf. Toby took his fiancée and Gervaise de

217

Groot in his MGA. Wedging Ian's gangling frame into the back seat of the Vendetta proved difficult, but eventually the model hit on the idea of laying down flat on the back seat with his feet dangling out of the front window, and Crispian sprawled himself on top. Brett slid awkwardly into the passenger seat next to Mira.

'What the hell happened at the front there? You run into a garbo truck or something?'

'We were rather late getting here and I clipped some idiot on a bike, nothing to worry about. All set?' Mira said, turning the key in the ignition. The Vendetta's powerful engine roared to life.

Zelda stood in the middle of the road, clutching her battered stetson. In the back of her mind she nursed a vague idea of looking for her son. She was crying, staggering, the wind biting her skin, her mascara running like black rivulets, mingling with the tears streaming down her cheeks. She sensed that something had gone terribly wrong: if only, she thought, I could get to what it is, I could start putting things right again . . .

As she zigzagged down the middle of the road, she was wailing at the top of her voice: 'Stone? Stone? Where are you, Baby? Oh Jesus, Mommy's made such a mess of things again. Oh . . .'

An old British sports car shot past her.

'I tried so hard, I really, really tried to make it right for us, Baby, but . . . you gotta give Mommy her picture back. I'm SO close, Baby, I'm SO close . . . I just want to make everything right between us again . . .'

A futuristically-shaped, low-slung shiny black object raced towards her.

'Well, Zelda ain't out of it yet, not by a long chalk, mate,' Brett was saying. 'The Boss seems very taken with her.'

'Despite that libel suit?' Mira frowned. 'Shit.'

'She turned the *Gazette* around. Letting hookers advertise in those sex education supplements made the paper a real profit centre . . .'

Mira turned hard and the tyres screeched their treads off as the Vendetta missed the figure in the road by about the width of a coat of paint.

'Fucking maniac,' Mira yelled, changing down into third as the lights at the end of Bruton Street turned red ahead of them.

'Didn't you see who that was?' trilled Crispian. 'It was her! It was the Wicked Witch of the Upper Westside . . . Zelda Lee Powers!'

'Was it?' Mira cried. She stopped short, slung the gearstick into reverse with a nasty grating of expensive syncromesh and backed round the corner, her foot hard on the accelerator.

'Jesus Christ, easy there!' Brett shouted.

'I'm going to die in the arms of a dreamboy,' Crispian squealed. 'Valhalla! What becomes a legend most?'

The Vendetta lurched to a halt in front of Zelda, who had collapsed against the railings.

'One thing you admire at INI is utter ruthlessness, correct?' Mira was saying.

'I suppose . . .' Brett hesitated.

'And you think I'm nothing but a dizzy deb, don't you? A silly little rich girl born with a silver spoon up her nose? OK, Brett, I'm going to show you how I deal with a competitor.'

The window went down.

'Tell her to get in,' Mira said.

'Where?' Brett asked. 'It's tighter than a dead heat in here already.'

'It won't be for long, and she won't take up much space. We'll manage,' she said.

'Zelda!' Brett called out, 'we're going for a ride.'

'Huh?' Zelda slurred. 'Brett?'

'We're going to a party!'

Inside, Mira hit a button on the console and the moon-roof lurched open.

'C'mon, Zelda,' Brett shouted. 'Paaaaaarty! Best offer you'll get all night!'

'I don't know that . . . oh, what the fuck,' Zelda hiccuped.

'Climb in through the roof,' Crispian urged her.

'Oh Brett, baby, you've rescued me right on time,' Zelda said gratefully, balancing unsteadily on the transmission tunnel between the two front seats. 'I can't TELL you what a bad night I've been having.'

No, she couldn't – because suddenly the Vendetta was moving again, and the sound system was pumping out an old tune, Joan Armatrading screeching 'I love it when you call me names . . .'

Zelda screamed as the wind ripped through her hair at 60, 70, 80 mph, and she herself was almost torn from the car.

'I love it when you call me names . . .'

At the end of Bruton Street, the lights turned red again, but Mira ignored them, hanging a left on to Bond Street, scattering a crowd of straggling protestors in her wake.

'Over and over and over again . . .' droned the singer's voice. Brett wondered if Zelda knew who was driving. But then he saw how easily he could put his hand up her dress . . .

32

The soothing saxophone of David Sanbourne washed through the speakers like ocean spray. The lights were bright enough to sharpen the glint in their eyes, but low enough to soften the lines which life had etched into their faces.

'I knew Kettle once,' Anthony was saying. 'We used to work together.'

'No,' Mandi said. 'He never told me that.'

'It's true,' Anthony smiled. 'On the old *Sunday Mirror*, years ago. I'll always remember one night at The Stab In The Back . . .' The Stab was the nickname *Mirror* hacks had bestowed on The White Hart, their local pub opposite the paper's old Holborn headquarters, in New Fetter Lane. '. . . I'll always remember one night at The Stab, a group of us had been talking about getting the sack.' Sir Anthony George revealed how his early departure from the *Rochester Gazette* had been accelerated after a member of the Women's Institute had walked in on him locking loins with the paper's tele-ad girl on the editor's desk.

Oh dear – so he does talk about himself in the third person when he's drunk, Mandi thought. But she was conscious of being slightly drunk herself. She felt amusing, so she was ready to be amused, and Anthony's pomposity struck her as endearing – like a crease in an old canvas, say, or a tear in a Buddhist prayer rug. Proof positive that this was genuine, authentic, the real thing.

'Kettle told one of his many egregious expenses stories – something about buying rope from a gypsy to smuggle a message to the Great Train Robbers, if I recall . . .'

'Money for old rope,' Mandi said. 'Yup, we've had that one too.'

'And then there was John Roberts . . . Remember him?'

'He edited the paper for a while, didn't he?' Mandi said.

Anthony nodded. 'When we asked why he'd been given the bullet from *The Sun*, do you know what he said? "Incompetence."'

'Wouldn't you see an angle if he was teaching trigonometry,' Mandi said. 'Whatever happened to him?'

'He publishes desktop porn. Here, have a top-up.'

'It's a nice drop,' Mandi said, raising her glass of exquisitely chilled Cristal champagne. 'Chin-chin! Shall we sit soft?' she said, eyeing the sofa.

'Make yourself at home,' said Anthony, rising and gesturing towards the sofa with his hand. He sat down next to her and leaned back against the smooth wickerwork. 'It's changed, the Street,' he said, with a discreet belch into his hand.

'It isn't the same,' she agreed.

'I miss those days,' he went on. 'I remember once I was sent to Casablanca – there was a flap on about Christian Barnard . . .'

'What, the heart transplant guy?'

'Yes, my news editor had got it into his head that Barnard was doing sex-change ops out there. At nine o'clock I'd been getting off the tube at Chancery Lane and by five I was filing interviews with six transsexuals from the lobby of the Dar el-Beida Hilton. It was a real industry out there back then. Actually, I think it still is.'

'But Barnard wasn't involved in one of those chop shops?'

'Of course not,' Anthony said.

'Then, it didn't matter. Now, you'd have the calculator men in grey suits all over you,' said Mandi, leaning forward to tug at the ends of his bow tie. 'You seem hot,' she said, pulling the handkerchief from his top pocket with the intention of mopping the fevered brow. Out popped three blue-wrapped condoms. As if on cue, the music stopped.

'Oh, er, um,' mumbled Sir Anthony.

'Shall we get another bottle?' Mandi blurted simultaneously. There was an awkward silence, broken only by the cacophonous sound of accordions and drums blaring through the speaker system, as a new tape played some Zydeco tunes from New Orleans. Anthony went to the bar and ordered another bottle.

Mandi reached over and pulled a flower from the vase on the coffee table in front of her, put it between her teeth as she got up and started tap-dancing towards the door.

'Where on earth are you going?'

'Just off to the little reporters' room,' she said.

She staggered upstairs to the main reception desk and booked them a room. As she signed in, she made a point of scanning the registration book, surreptitiously so that the receptionist wouldn't notice. She was looking for tell-tale signs that Ethiopia was there – with her Royal Consort.

33

The first thing Zelda Lee Powers felt when she came to was the cold. The second thing was the pain. Every bone in her body felt as if it had been deliberately smashed and set in small, spiky casts of sulphur.

She remembered . . . after they'd passed Stone's flat, someone had dragged her from the car. She remembered some ex-army officer tying her by her feet to the back bumper with snowchains . . . 'This is what they do in Belfast,' de Groot had explained to Brett Collins. 'It's the only language Johnny Bogtrotter understands.' Everyone had laughed. Shuddering to recall the cold feel of the cobbled stones of the mews beneath her, the terrible roar of the engine as the car took off . . . Zelda burst into tears.

'. . . So how did you get it inside?'

'Oh, they came round with a crane, and hoisted it through the window this morning.'

'Isn't that rather cruel?' Gizelle had asked.

'Oh no – not really,' Mira replied,

'The animal's sedated and all that. It has to be for the performance.'

'What is this performance exactly?'

'Mico's hired these terribly sweet local homeboys to sort of spray-paint it. It's his statement about us all being animals in the urban environment.'

'Spray-paint it? That really does sound nasty.'

'I hope it washes off,' Mira chuckled. 'Gervaise, would you get another crate? We seem to be running rather low.'

'Mirabelle,' said Toby uneasily, 'there's water leaking through the walls.'

'What?'

'Water, darling,' Toby said, pointing. 'Look.'

Even in the low, flickering light from the candles, Mira saw a discoloured horizontal patch spreading across the wall behind her. 'Oh Christ, what a nightmare. We've had a plumber round, he left a phone number somewhere . . . It's all to do with the central heating breaking down or something, they're supposed to come tomorrow, definitely, and fix it. Anyway, Brett, what was I saying? Oh yes, the nepotism . . . I don't think we have to worry about it really, it's a fact of life, isn't it, like Royal families or Derby winners sharing the same gene pool? I mean, look at this table. How many people would you say are here?'

'About 30,' said Brett, with a loud belch.

'OK, so I'm related to 20 per cent of them then . . .'

'Not these two, I hope,' said Brett, with a glance down the table towards Gypsy and Joker, who were burning cigarettes into each other's palms to show Caro how tough they were. 'They look like they fell into the shallow end of your bloody gene pool.'

Mira ignored him. '. . . the same way you're a beneficiary of heredity too, by being The Boss's nephew. Nepotism's one of the wonders of human nature, isn't it? Besides, being absolutely cold and realistic about it, you couldn't expect any of the others to get it, not editing *The Times*, not understanding people like us, our culture – OK? Don't get me wrong. Women like Kiki Cox and Mandi Harry are brilliant journalists within their own remit,' she said generously, '. . . but they're just not conversant with the codes. They don't have the background to understand the way this country works, so they're scarcely qualified to run one of its best-loved institutions really, are they?'

'Talking to you, Mira,' Brett said, wondering whether any food would ever appear, '. . . makes me not so sure about my own credentials, either.'

Toby and Gizelle exchanged knowing glances and rose in unison from the table, bidding adieu to various half-, step- and putative siblings-in-law.

'We have to go to the Embassy tomorrow and pick up my visa,' Toby explained. 'Is Mico upstairs? Perhaps we should pop in and say goodnight?' suggested Gizelle sweetly. Mira caught Caro's eye behind Gizelle's back, and made a mock-vomiting gesture with a forefinger pointing into her wide open mouth. 'I'd love to see his graffitied rhino.'

'No,' Toby said, shepherding her towards the door. 'He gets frightfully stroppy if you disturb him while he's working.'

'It's a question not only of coherence but of continuity,' Mira was still explaining to Brett. 'Assuming that your Uncle isn't taken in by Duncan Campbell's psychotic disinformation campaign, a female editor on the paper is going to create some major ripples, so now we're back to that old saw about a woman having to be twice as good as a man to get the same job done.'

She laughed.

'Mandi Harry and those others can't possibly understand the subtle interplay of the forces that drive British Society. We are sitting here at this table, yah? Well, this is the same table at which my ancestor Sir Phillip Sidely sat, shortly before he and Drake sank the Armada. I mean, one feels a resonance from these things . . .'

'What are you saying? That having a lot of old furniture around is going to boost the paper's circulation figures? Or help you sink pirate fishing fleets? I don't follow.'

'One is attuned to the continuum of history. Why do you think the Editor's desk at *The Times* is the same one John Walter III wrote his Crimean editorials on? It's because one absorbs the same psychological cues, Brett,' she said patiently.

'When the Monarch looks out of a Balmoral bedroom window, she sees the same vista that greeted Queen Victoria . . . they literally see the world in the same way. Do you follow me? It's an onomatopoeic metaphor, just like Judges' wigs, Parliamentary procedure, clan tartans, or the fact that cricket bats are made from willow rather than aluminium,' Mira said.

'Is that right?' Brett replied.

'OK, OK, perhaps they weren't the most brilliant examples,' Mira backtracked, '. . . but you understand the intellectual thrust of my argument, surely?'

'I think I get your drift, yeah,' Brett nodded.

226

'Although to an outsider some elements of British Society are arcane and anachronistic or just completely bloody barking,' Mira continued, '. . . *Times* people understand that these onomatopoeic metaphors aren't merely indulgent eccentricities. They are quintessentials of civilization. They are organic elements of our national identity. They are how we Brits reassure one another of certain enduring values distilled through years of war and strife and change.'

'So what would you say those values are?' said Brett, rubbing his temples.

'Broadly? A sense of tolerance. The kind of fair play that comes from existing side by side on a crowded island. Self-discipline, a responsibility bred from creating and dismantling an Empire. A sense of humour. A certain natural diffidence, a North European prudence, a sort of need to keep things in a safe place.

'You see, that was the *raison d'être* behind our little demonstration with Miss Powers just now. She had an absolute sense of humour burn-out over it – but it's only the kind of thing any little girlie might expect to endure during her first term at boarding school here. It's survival of the fittest, Brett. And if you can't take it, you don't make it. You're Australian, you understand that. The issue here is where to take the paper next. *The Times* has lost a lot of its moral authority, its gravitas, over the last decade – all this price-cutting, promotional gimmickry, flabby reporting, hiring celebrity columnists – TV bimbos who couldn't write home for money – it's all set rather the wrong tone. I think there's support for the contention that the paper should go back – although, obviously, I wouldn't be so tactless as to actually use these words to your Uncle – go back to the Harry Evans-style pioneering journalism of about 15, 20 years ago. Innovative formats, hard investigations, setting the agenda, exploring where we're going as a Society. For instance, I'm very interested in these Animal Rights groups at the moment . . . the whole idea that we treat animals today the way colonials treated blacks back in the 18th and 19th centuries – like slaves, here for our convenience and with absolutely no rights of their own. It's interesting, because if one follows their premise to its logical conclusion, we can see that there'll be a flashpoint over racing, and I think that'll be an interesting test of our core values: which is stronger, the great British love of animals, or our love of gambling – the Grand National and Ascot? It'll be a truly defining moment, I think.'

'Jeez,' Brett said, looking down. 'My feet are bloody soaking.'

Mira turned round. Water was seeping heavily through the walls. Not just a drip, but a steady, insistent trickle. She struck the side of her glass with a spoon. 'Is there a plumber in the house?'

Upstairs, Zelda brooded on the nightmare ride which had ended with her imprisoned in this manky, wood-panelled room. She remembered, just before she'd nearly been thrown from the car at Hyde Park Corner, waiting for the lights to change and overhearing Mira tell Brett that she had one of her staff checking out the competition . . .

'. . . we're very good at exposing frauds, bogus people, you know' . . . and that there was no trace of Kiki's background at all. Zelda had been digesting this snippet and considering what advantage she could gain from it. The process had helped her compose herself enough to explore her surroundings. The house, she had decided, was probably very old, the product of numerous attempts to 'fix it up' that had been prematurely abandoned when their instigators realised the futility of the enormous, all-enveloping nature of the task which they had, in that first flush of enthusiasm, imagined was within the bounds of human organisation and willpower.

The bookshelves groaned under the weight of autobiographies of long-forgotten politicians and once-fashionable photographers. Zelda caught a glimpse of a dusty wooden floor hidden beneath piles of clothes and papers and detritus. A cat had clawed the sofa, next to which stood an abandoned lavatory beneath a pair of giant ivory tusks. A root sprang from a fissure in the wall that someone had once tried to pack with cardboard. In the corner of the room stood an old television set wired to an ancient video recorder.

Zelda switched it on.

'Oh my God,' she breathed, watching for a few minutes with a bilious fascination. She turned it off quickly, ejected the cassette and searched for somewhere to hide it. The tape featured Mira romping stark naked with the tattooed skinhead plumber and a figure who was clearly none other than Toby Freer Farmer . . .

'If the tank's at the top of the house, then you've got a real problem . . .' said Gypsy. Gervaise de Groot questioned whether a correspondence course taken in Wormwood Scrubs constituted a professional qualification in plumbing. But his words were suddenly drowned by a loud whooshing noise and an awesome, explosive rumbling. The kitchen door was suddenly flung open. It was Crispian, banging on a saucepan with a wooden spoon. He was dressed in a frilly maid's outfit. 'Good morning, gourmets and gourmands!' he cried energetically. 'Breakfast is served, baked beans au gratin . . .'

Mira glanced round at the walls. At that moment a massive lump of sodden plaster fell from the ceiling. Then all was mayhem. Amid the sound of scraping chairs, horrified screams and a desperate, panic-stricken run for cover, the chandelier above them dropped on to the ancient table with a huge crash, scattering glass in all directions. The ceiling began to collapse into the room below in a thick fog of dust and a torrential flood of filthy water.

Zelda heard an explosion somewhere in the house. She'd been trying to break the door down quietly with the butt of one of her revolvers, but now, she figured, it didn't matter any more. Woozily, she aimed and fired. The recoil sent her sprawling back against a bookcase. A dozen or so old telephone directories, ancient atlases and obscure Mexican novels tumbled down on top of her. She cussed and swore, and struggled painfully to pick herself up. But her efforts were well-rewarded. Dusting herself down, she saw that behind the books someone had stacked vast numbers of videotapes in boxes, all neatly labelled and dated. With great difficulty, Zelda climbed on to a dusty sideboard and began to explore, pitching aside Victorian biographies, African travelogues and backnumbers of *Granta* with equal abandon, even though her arms ached with every move. The videotapes ran the length of the bookshelf . . . and the bookshelf ran the entire length of the room . . .

As the dust began to settle, and the water to seep through the floorboards, everyone crowded around the kitchen door, gaping. Crispian circulated, offering brandy and baked beans to the stunned and astonished guests.

'Please, someone going to come in here, yes? Is fantastic shot, please, someone be coming in!'

In the kitchen, no-one moved.

'Do you think it's still alive?' Caro said warily.

'It doesn't seem to be . . . moving.'

'Please,' begged the distant, disembodied voice. 'All the refugees in Cambodia and Haiti want to see this, someone got to come, is for my artwork, the camera turning, is for charity, I'm begging you . . . Miabelle? Please?'

'Stand aside,' commanded Gervaise de Groot, crossing the threshold. 'I'm an old Nairobi hand, I'll deal with this.'

The rhino was splayed over the shattered timbers of the dining table, which had collapsed under its weight. The beast, whose hide was daubed with vividly-coloured aerosol paint, seemed to be languishing in a stunned stupor. Gervaise de Groot entered the room with quiet, measured steps. Staring up through the hole in the ceiling, he saw Mira's Brazilian husband, as naked as the day he was born, suspended from the ceiling of the floor above by a harness attached to a huge hook, the red light on his Hi-8 camera flashing.

'Go to the animal!' Mico shouted. 'You cradle him, like he is your son.'

Gervaise looked at the great beast, trying to evaluate the situation. A black eye stared back at him. Suddenly his attention was distracted: unmistakable gunshots rang out through the house. 'What the bloody hell was that?' he shouted.

The noise disturbed the rhino. It rose unsteadily, its beady gaze fixed on de Groot. Gervaise, realising the danger he was in, began to back away, retracing his footsteps. But he tripped over a broken chair, and the wounded animal's response was much faster than he might have expected. The limping beast began to lumber straight towards him, four tons of bleeding, frightened, armour-plated anger. As it dropped its head and made to charge it bellowed, catching the corner of de Groot's dinner jacket on its

230

horn and tossing him high into the air.

Zelda flung open the dining-room door. She saw Gervaise de Groot suspended by his braces from a wall light above the fireplace. Gaping over him was a huge hole in the ceiling. All around him lay the debris of a dinner party that appeared to have been disrupted by a medium-sized earthquake. Beneath him, a bleeding, spray-painted rhinoceros bellowed as it tried to remove its horn from the thickly-plastered wall.

Zelda took another hit from the bottle of Grand Marnier she had found upstairs and walked calmly towards the animal, splashing through water and avoiding the larger lumps of plaster. Just as the beast was about to remove its horn – and in the process bring down the entire wall – Zelda used both hands to hold her gun to its ear, turned away and, with cool deliberation, emptied the chamber into its skull with a series of loud reports.

Gervaise's braces ripped at last and he fell, face down, into the sticky mixture of blood, flesh, plaster and vile water. Zelda adjusted the battered stetson on her head and stared at the goggle-eyed group spilling out of the kitchen. She fired off the last two rounds from her other gun into the air. A strangled cry emanated from above her head. She ignored it.

'Listen up, you wusses' she said, bringing the barrel to her lips and blowing over it, Western-style. 'There's a new Sheriff in town.'

'. . . but you'd look fabulous in it,' Crispian was insisting to the former SAS officer who was trying to find a change of clothes. Crispian was pressing the maid's outfit up against his barrel chest. Someone turned on a boombox, and the lazy, sensual beats of the SOS band drifted from room to room.

'Hey, man,' Joker said lazily, 'she's got a stroboscope.'

Caro was dancing, and shedding her bustier.

'Pain?' Zelda was saying. 'I'm into pain. I spent three years working for Morty, didn't I?'

The hardcore revellers were now gathered in Mira's boudoir. It was the only room in the house which offered any heat.

'Jeez, I don't reckon much on the grub, Mira,' Brett said,

examining the congealed baked beans on his chipped plate.

'Are you sure that's the extent of your appetite?' asked the hostess, sliding the beans into her mouth with her fingers. 'Gosh, it's awfully hot in here, don't you think, Caro?'

'Hey, Baby,' shrugged Caro, peeling down her fishnet stockings and unhooking her leather girdle.

'How can I help you meet my needs?' Zelda was saying, as Brett's attention was distracted by Caro's saucer-like nipples being thrust into his face.

What happened next, she would only recall later as a disjointed mosaic: fragments of conversation.

'. . . Hey, Baby, what do you mean you've never shot speedballs?'

'. . . I thought all you Australians were supposed to be macho . . .'

'. . . are you chicken?'

'. . . but we always cherry-bomb the lavatory at the end of a good party . . .'

She could vaguely remember a terrible taste . . . the salty secretions of sweating flesh as Brett's body intertwined with Caro's and Mira's; a visual snapshot of a red light on Mico's camcorder . . .

Somehow, as she lay there in this strange bed, the light blended into a burning cigarette being forced inside her body . . . a man with gold teeth and something written inside his lip forcing it into her . . .

Was it her imagination, or did Brett really promise Mira the job if she landed a cracking story before the swimming gala?

Zelda didn't know, couldn't tell any more. Everything seemed jumbled and jagged and jumpcut . . .

The phone rang.

Her body screamed with pain.

She remembered Caro threatening to chop Brett's cock off with her switchblade, and making him come and come and come, and Mira crying hysterically . . .

. . . and hitting her with the others.

She looked down at her body. It was covered with ugly puce-yellow discolorations and cigarette burns, and caked with dried excrement. She dragged herself from the bed, every step a monumental effort, her mouth dry, her limbs lead, her torso searing with pain . . .

She staggered into an adjacent bathroom and turned on the shower . . . she picked up a tiny pink bar of soap from the wall-mounted dish, and saw that she was in a Holiday Inn . . . She tried to remember how she'd got there, when she'd arrived, and with whom . . .

Then she started to cry. Slowly and softly at first, but soon the tears were wracking her entire body as the water from the showerhead beat down like rain in a tropical forest, and she heard someone knocking at the door.

34

Three a.m.
     Outside, the moon sat like a fingernail in a blue velvet jewellery box.
     Inside: nightlife.

Kisses are like rainbows . . .
     They come in many colours, never failing to inspire us. From the blazing thrust of young lust, when inquisitive lips are poised on the brink of change, to the tender kiss of commitment, nurtured by a bond of unconditional love that, like an ancient river, flows deep and strong; from the kiss of innocence, that of a mother gently caressing her cherished newborn, spilling sweetness and wonder, to the social kiss that tells the world we know who we are; and the courtly kiss, bestowed on the hesitant hand of a loved one no longer a child, but not quite a woman . . .
     Or – the most exquisite, and all the more pricey for that – the secret, dearly forbidden, ill-advised yet inevitable kiss of a woman who has fallen passionately in love with a man who is married, but not to her . . .
     'When I give my heart . . . it will be completely . . .'
     The songs were ripping through his memory like a Golden Oldies radio show from a lifetime ago . . .
     'Our lips shouldn't touch . . . I like it too much . . .'
     When Anthony kissed Mandi for the first time, it was, of course, like no other kiss that anyone had kissed before.
     'The moment that I feel that you feel that way too . . .'
     Lip to lip.
     Hip to hip.
     Skin to skin.

He moved his body.

She moved her mind.

'. . . Move over, darling . . .'

'Magic . . . moments . . . when two hearts are caring . . .'

Alcohol fumes and stale scent. Crumpled clothes, ripped and torn as sweaty, out-of-practice hands pushed and pulled and probed. He was a blind piano-tuner on overtime. She was Mount Etna, slowly awakening from volcanic dormancy.

'Baby, it's warm inside . . .'

'You can call me a fickle thing . . . but I'm practically yours forever because . . .'

Clothes were strewn across the deep-pile off-rose-coloured carpet. A bottle of pink champagne from the minibar rested upside-down in an ice bucket on the ottoman at the end of the bed. The sheets and duvet had enraged themselves into an impossibly damp tangle as two half-naked bodies writhed luxuriously on the bed.

'Rain in my eyes, tears in my dreams, rocks in my heart . . .'

'You've captured my heart, and now that I'm no longer free . . . make love to me . . .'

But suddenly they stopped.

'It's no good,' Anthony sighed. 'I'm afraid, I've had too much to drink.'

'Don't be embarrassed,' Mandi said, her voice cooing and billing like a bird's, soothing him. '. . . It happens to the best of us.'

'I just wish it wasn't happening to me. Not now, not here, not with you.'

'I'm used to it,' she muttered. Better to turn it into a joke, conceal the pain inside. 'I haven't made love with my husband since Millwall were relegated from the First Division.'

'First Division? It's been the Premiership for years.'

'Tell me about it,' she murmured, beginning to massage his shoulders. 'You're very tense, Babe.'

'Hmmmmm. You should be the one who's tense.'

'Should I? Why?'

'It was the best of *Times*, the worst of *Times* . . .'

'I wasn't thinking about that.'

'You're dealing with the pressure much better than I would.'

'No, no pressure.' She shook her head. 'I'm not going to go creeping round Duncan Campbell or Brett Collins. If they wanted me up their arse, they'd kiss me first. I like what I do now, Anthony. It's fine, it's fun, it's what I used to dream about when I was editing the school magazine 20 years ago. I'm past caring about the bloody *Times*, to tell you the truth.'

'Past caring?'

'Nothing – no man, no job, no dosh – nothing's worth this amount of aggro. And to be honest with you, I'm freaked out by all those International News powerbabes at *The Times*, you know? The women with legs up to their armpits and brains down to their hairspray. Birds who've married a grousemoor and hold "fraffelly" smart dinner parties for Princess Margaret, a shipping tycoon, an Oxford Don and a couple of hundred other of their closest friends. I hate all that shit. They send their kids to the Eva Grabbler Academy of the Motivated Child, and . . . it just isn't me, Anthony, I'm far too ordinary for all that. I can't compete. Can't you see, I'm just not up to it? I like pottering about in my back garden, watching the soaps, going to the dogs, having a little flutter and a bloody good laugh . . .'

'But you are up to it, Mandi. You've got what it takes. I know it.'

'Don't tell me who I am.'

'So you're going to let them walk all over you, are you? They slag you off, they kill your cat . . . this doesn't sound like the Mandi Harry I know.'

'Maybe you don't know Mandi Harry as well as you thought.'

'But I know of you, Mandi, I know of you. Journalism's a hysterical profession. Everybody's worked with everybody else, slept with everybody else . . . or if they haven't, they've got the number of someone who has. You've got a reputation to protect. In this business, you're only as good as your last splash, and today's scoop is tomorrow's litter-tray lining – God, I didn't mean that . . . you know what I mean . . . your reputation's all you've got. You're clever, you're funny, you're sexy, you're very, very lovely, inside and out – and you know how to fight your corner. If you give up now, you'll never know if you were good enough. And believe me, it isn't the things you do that you regret later in your life . . . it's things you never did. Is that how you want to end up?' he asked her, '. . . a bitter, twisted old hack like me, who's condemned to live in the past because he can't face the future? Someone who can't sleep at night because all his dreams have been used up? I'd do anything to be Editor of *The Times*, Mandi – anything. But I'm a boring, white, middle-class man in a suit. A washed-out, beaten-up, broken-down, spat-out tabloid editor, and I'm never going to get the chance. There's a moment in everybody's life, a defining moment which shapes what sort of person you'll become, what sort of life you will lead from that moment on. If you don't seize that moment, there are a hundred eager, hungry kids out there who'll soon be tap-dancing on your face. You mark my words: this is your chance, Mandi, so grab it with both hands. You probably won't get another. Come home with your shield . . . or come home on it.'

Mandi was silent for a moment.

Out in the street a fire engine roared past, its siren tearing through the silence of the stark, cold night like a banshee. Inside the room the air-conditioning whooshed a smooth, soothing, monotonous symphony. Mandi was wondering if he really cared about her – or if he was the sort of operator who could size people up that fast, take what he wanted and get out before dawn, not a bloodstain, not a lovebite, not the tiniest scratch, nothing to write home about . . .

Have I got what it takes, she wondered – honestly? Or is he just geeing me up because he hates his wife so much and fancied a leg-over? Oh no – just suppose this was all some sort of sick game between them? Maybe he was her shill . . . or, she realized with a nasty shudder, maybe Zelda's manipulating him, using Anthony to get to me, wind me up tighter and tighter than a clockwork mouse, so I'll burst and over-react and expose myself – do something that she'll be able to use to her advantage against me, wipe me right out of the game . . .

'What about a family?' Anthony said.

'Bit previous, aren't you?' she said. 'We're only just beginning to get to know each other.'

'You're funny. No, I mean, do kids come into your picture somewhere?'

Mandi's hands stopped moving over his smooth tanned skin. 'I did have a kid when I was a teenager,' she blurted. 'But I lost it.'

'Oh,' Anthony said, 'I'm so sorry.'

'It's too late for all that now,' she said, her hands caressing his flesh once more. 'I just can't see myself getting up every four hours to change a pooey nappy. I'm the wrong side of 30 for all that shit, pun intended. I need my eight hours, you know?'

'It's different for men,' he said, nodding. 'But the same too, in a funny sort of way. I see Stone, Zelda's kid, and I think, Jesus, one day people like him are going to own everything. The geeks shall inherit the earth . . . It just makes me feel old, a has-been.'

'At least you're not a never-was.'

'I sometimes wonder what my new secretary thinks of me. Does she see some ghastly, pot-bellied, middle-aged lech? I'd hate that. I think men fear becoming leches in the same way women fear becoming mutton done up as lamb.'

'Not all men, Anthony,' she said, leaning down to lick his ear. 'But you can lech over me all you want.'

'I keep getting turned on at all the wrong times,' he admitted sheepishly. 'Incongruous times, with women young enough to be my daughter . . .'

'So you want me to get the nurse's outfit on now or later?' she said with a saucy wink.

'No,' he laughed. 'Well, yes . . . but that's not what I meant. Let me tell you something. At John Temple's funeral I was watching you and ogling your tits, as a matter of fact, and trying to imagine what they were like underneath all those clothes . . . and I was fantastically turned on . . .'

'Well, here they are, Big Boy, and they're all for you,' she said tenderly.

He licked and sucked and bit and frolicked.

'Jesus, Anthony, it's harder than Chinese arithmetic. Hold that thought, Stud, I'll be, how you say, two shakes,' she said and,

238

sliding the sheet around her, tossed Anthony out of bed. 'Christ,' she giggled, 'I'm such a slapper.'

Sir Anthony picked himself up and glanced down at his body. 'What you may lack in finesse,' he said appreciatively, '. . . you certainly make up for in technique.'

Mandi grabbed her handbag, made for the *en suite* bathroom and locked the door.

She fumbled around in her bag. Where the hell was it? She ferreted among the tissues and sachets of Elastoplast, the crumpled letter from her bank with the cheque made out to the Cashbox Club inside, the battered box of Lillets and the slip from the bank cash machine with a shopping list on the back, the filthy Mason Pearson hairbrush, the make-up bag caked in foundation and eyebrow pencil, and a parking ticket she suddenly realised would be overdue tomorrow . . .

She suddenly felt tired. As she produced the vital item, she could no longer suppress a yawn.

Mandi removed the contraceptive cap from its plastic container. When was the last time she'd used this thing? It was probably rusty . . .

'Shit,' she said, starting to search for a tube of spermicidal jelly. She dived back into the bag, pulling out a new Fendi *Eau de Parfum* spray, a scrunch of dollar bills, a dusty black velvet beret, a pair of snagged tights, a can of hairspray, a paperback copy of *Full Moon On A Dark Night*, a Canon Sureshot, a roll of Sellotape . . .

She found it, yawned again and began squeezing the goo around the rim of her rubber cap. Methodically, she squashed it and squatted, aiming for the vital part other contraceptives could not reach . . . just as she was about to insert it, Mandi overbalanced slightly and toppled, losing her grip on the device which, suddenly, sprang from her hand.

'Shit!' she cursed.

She looked around for it everywhere. It was so frustrating. She was on the verge of tears and sat down heavily on the toilet seat, flinging back her head . . .

There it was! Attached to the bathroom ceiling.

Mandi climbed on to the toilet seat and placed one foot precariously on the rim of the basin. She caught a glimpse of her thighs in the mirror as she did so, and noticed with a groan that the Miracle Cellulite Pills hadn't done the trick, nothing like, more money down the drain . . .

Not quite high enough . . . Mandi put one foot on the cistern and stretched as far as she could to grab the cap . . . But she slipped, came crashing down, and smashed her head on the basin.

Four a.m.

Sir Anthony couldn't get a peep out of her. The bathroom door was locked. So he booked a seven a.m. alarm call, ordered himself a taxi, used the Gents next to the reception desk to wash his face, paid the bill and left.

The concierge used his master key to open the bathroom door.

There was a little blood on the tiles.

'Mrs Harry, Mrs Harry?'

He wondered whether he should call an ambulance. He dashed back into the bedroom, lifted the phone, dropped it, tore back to the bathroom . . .

Mandi was waking up, and was rubbing at her head.

'Did we do it? How long have I been here?' she moaned. 'Anthony . . .?'

'Sir Anthony George has left,' said the concierge with an embarrassed cough. 'Would you like to see the menu? Shall I get the doctor in to look at your poor head?'

'Oh Christ,' Mandi said. 'He's never going to talk to me again.'

35

There was a long queue outside Doctor Ramish's surgery. All were women. All wore hajibs: long, colourless garments which concealed the body, the hair, and, in many cases, the face. Except for the eyes. Dark eyes, shifting eyes, eyes that never settled on anything, eyes that stared vacantly into space. Eyes of chattels enslaved in an exile which had severed them from their homes and, more cruelly, had transported them to this rainy, English-speaking city where they were stranded, peons of powerless luxury, pampered prisoners of easy money who, when they left the doctor's waiting room, would leave behind within it their last hope of joy. These were watchful and fearful women, mothers and daughters talking quietly among themselves. The most terrified among them were silent.

The doors of the surgery burst open and a dark-haired woman in a fur coat hobbled in. Even though she wore huge sunglasses and a large hat, one couldn't help noticing that she was black and blue. Even her legs and feet were bruised, and one of her hands had been grossly disfigured by cigarette burns. She ignored the receptionist who tried to block her access to the surgery.

As she forced her way inside, the white-coated man looked up from a young woman's body hooked up in the stirrups of his examination couch. 'No, no,' he told his anxious receptionist. 'That's OK.'

He studied his intruder. 'This is quite a surprise.'

His syntax was English, but his accent was American. He mumbled something in Arabic to a woman seated close at hand, who was probably the patient's mother.

'I need a goddamn prescription', Zelda said. 'And I need it right now.'

'I am at a rather crucial stage of surgical procedure here, Ms Powers. If you'd care to wait outside for five or ten minutes . . .'

'I said NOW and I meant like yesterday was fucking 15 minutes too late, Slimeball. Or maybe I should wait, yeah, that's the ticket. See, my son Stone . . . you remember Stone, don't you, Doctor – I'll bet you do, because your nose still doesn't look quite right . . . See, if I'm not home by four, Stone's going to pick up that horn to the AMA and the BMA and give them this address. Like I told you last time we met: some prosecuting attorneys have said some very unpalatable things to me about female circumcision. They seem to have got it into their skulls somehow that it's like assault with a deadly weapon . . . am I resonating, Ramish? Do the words Rikers Island mean anything to you? Or how about Wormwood Scrubs? They'd probably classify you as a sex offender in this country . . .'

Ramish was at his desk.

The patient's chaperone was shouting and the Doctor was shouting back.

'What is it you want?'

'Benzedrine – lots of it. Enough to get through the next 24 hours without even having to think about sleeping. Plus, ALSO, some heavy tranks, Librium, Valium, Nembutal, a pain killer that won't impair any functioning . . .'

'But the pharmacist . . . he might be suspicious . . .'

'. . . or yours, tough guy,' Zelda finished with a flourish. 'Jeez, it's three-thirty already, doesn't time fly? You know, I heard there was serious gridlock up at Marble Arch. It'd be just too goddamn bad if we got caught up in it.'

She tore the prescription from his hand, had the taxi wait while she collected the various medicines, then did what she always did when her back was against the wall. 'Heathrow Airport,' she instructed the cab driver. 'Let's go, buddy.'

The orchestra on the bandstand had taken a break from playing selections from saccharine operettas to talk among themselves. A group of black-frocked priests scurried through the vaulted arches of the bath houses.

242

'Enough with the water already,' said Zelda, waving away an attendant bearing four varieties of bottled aqua minerale. She looked around at the slabs of Roman marble decorated with Kraft durch Freude scenes. 'This place gives me the goddamn creeps,' she told the girl sitting next to her. Her companion seemed harmless enough: a bespectacled freelance journalist of a certain age, maybe 19, tops, who said she was researching *The Time Out Guide to European Health Farms and Spas*. But Zelda didn't want her to overhear the call she was making.

'I'll meet you in say an hour for some hot tub,' she smiled, and walked – past a pair of nuns who seemed to glide, as if on wheels – towards the telephone.

Twenty minutes later, she finally got through to the Mayfair number she was trying.

'Where are you, Zsa Zsa?' Crispian's welcome voice came through. 'I was in the middle of the most ravishing bath.'

'I called in a marker from this guy in Queens I know who owns this spa outside Florence,' Zelda said. 'It's kind of a Nazi health resort. We're talking Merchant Ivory with the vowel sounds in overdrive . . . Crispi, listen up, Baby, I want to play a little practical joke on Kiki Cox . . . you gonna help me out here or what?'

'Oooooo dahling, I love practical jokes, I'm coming in my bath towel,' Crispian squealed. 'Tell me, is it really deliciously cruel?'

'Well, sorta kinda,' Zelda giggled.

'It's such a test of character – as you found out first-hand the other night . . .'

'Yeah . . . and on that subject, by the way, I REALLY appreciated your total lack of support,' said Zelda sternly. 'Now, take the straw outta your nose and listen. You remember that guy you were with the other night?'

'I'm afraid you'll have to be a teeny bit more specific than that, Precious. Crispi's got rather a lot on his plate . . .'

'YOU know, the blond hunk, the modelle, Mr Kiki Fruit . . .'

'Oh, Miss Ian? She's a lovely boy, isn't she? All pectoral and firm buttock . . .'

'ALL right, ALL right, ya don't have to advertise, I'm not interested in his credentials, he's all yours. Listen up, Crispi, what I need from you is to get in touch with him, OK, and for him OR you to go find another hard-bodied hunk, 'cos we're gonna give Kiki a big surprise on her birthday, OK?'

'Ooooooh, dahling, I love surprises,' Crispi screeched. 'What is it?'

'Can't tell ya, otherwise it wouldn't be a surprise, right?' said Zelda, popping another pill. 'Just have Ian and a body double keep the night of Kiki's birthday free, I gotta little stunt for them, VERY classy, LOTSA laughs, you'll LOVE it.'

'You must tell Crispi what it is!' fizzed the decorator excitedly. 'Otherwise Mummy says Miss Ian can't come out to play.'

'OK, lemme see here. I'm looking for this phone message from Stone in my purse, hey, here we are. Kiki's birthday's next Tuesday, in some room upstairs at Sorrell's, Covent Garden. Mean anything to you?'

'Yes, yes, she invited me . . . but I didn't realise she was holding it there,' Crispian said. 'Oh horrors! Sorrell's is the most depressing restaurant in London, dahling. A so-called rival of mine did the decorating there. They hadn't paid the builders on time, so the brutes bricked a family of rats into the wall. My dear, it is positively arse-paralysingly dreadful. You've never been there? You'll die. In fact, a close personal friend of mine who's very highly placed in Kitchenland told me that three people committed suicide there just last week.'

'Maybe there'll be one more if we can pull off this stunt, Crispi, so listen up, OK? You know how Kiki's always so guarded about her past . . .'

'. . . not so much an iron curtain, more net wincyette . . .'

'Right right right. She claims to have these two cousins in Australia – Shane and Wayne, yuh? She's gabbed on once or twice about them, ya know? But no-one's ever met them, no-one can trace them, no-one's even seen a picture. Well my hunch is, they don't exist. I got some information, see, that our sex queen from Oz is phonier than Directory Enquiries, and I gotta little idea to

expose her. Like, what would happen if she was confronted with
Shane and Wayne, for real?'

'Oh, you bitch!' squealed Crispian. 'I love it! It would be so
exquisitely embarrassing.'

'It could be, Crispi, just listen to my plan . . .'

Zelda and her new friend from *Time Out* were chattering
animatedly as they made their way to the hot tub.

'. . . cosmetic surgery is addictive, honey, same way crack is,
cigarettes, booze . . . I mean, LOOK at me wouldya? You'd never
guess I've had THREE total lifts, two peels, a . . . Oh My
GAAAAAD.' Zelda's voice had dropped to a stage whisper. She
stuck out her hand with the sort of reflex mothers employ to
prevent a child careering through a windscreen. 'How much are
Time Out paying you for this book?' Zelda asked the freelance.

'Well, technically speaking I haven't actually sold it to them
yet . . .'

Zelda was reaching into her handbag. 'Here's a hundred,
honey,' she said, patting the folded cash into the girl's hand and
staring hard at the hot tub. 'Don't ask any questions, just get lost
for an hour.'

Zelda adjusted her Oliver People's sunglasses, and did her
best to stride effectively into the room. She slipped out of the pink
gown marked Treasure Island Resort Fiji and into the hot tub,
keeping her shades on, so that a moment later she could drop
them slightly, peer dramatically over the top and, switching into
Southern Belle mode, exclaim: 'Why TINA!' A girlish giggle. 'Tina
Pupkin! Why, I do declare, just fancy runnin' into lil' ole YOU
here! My, ain't that the most extraordinary thing?'

The Boss's wife peered back at the newcomer, trying to place
her. Even at a resort as ritzy as Montecatini, this kind of thing was
always happening. When you are married to one of the top 20
richest and most powerful men on the planet, as well as being a
successful best-selling novelist in your own right, it is somewhat
inevitable that more people are going to know you than you could
ever expect to recognise or vaguely remember. Zelda was already
sliding up to her in the bubbling tub . . .

'Zelda Lee Powers. We last met at that Met fundraiser last

month with Keanu Reeves and George Solti, remember?'

'Er . . .' The Boss's wife began.

'Of COURSE you do, honey,' Zelda said. 'I just have THE best gossip about some of the girls tryin' to land that lil' old job on the London *Times* . . .'

36

Kettle put the hairpin back in his top pocket, eased the door open and got his story ready.

He'd say that he'd been trying to find the old lady he'd seen leaving the flat below 20 minutes ago, that the door had been open . . . sorry, she lives downstairs, does she? Blimey, I'm always doing things like this, sorry, mate . . . then he could tell Mandi Harry that he'd got in, but the blag had gone wrong, complete cock-up, the geezer was only still there, wasn't he – how was I supposed to know there was a back entrance? Look, I'm a reporter, Luv, not a psychic. Then maybe she'd assign him to the Ethiopia story after all, and he could get out of taking his turn working the night shift on the desk that week . . .

Mandi was going soft, he thought, ever since she'd written that cheque for his wife's Multiple Sclerosis treatment.

Dim bird.

Kettle shook his head. The idea of mixing it up in the la-di-da world of *The Times* was making her an easy mark. His wife was actually living with a football coach in Florida.

Scrubber.

Kettle eased himself into the room. He saw a 1968 black and red Fender Stratocaster leaning against a pile of newspapers almost as tall as he was. That morning's papers were scattered unread all over the floor. He spotted a busted motorbike lock; a Macintosh Duo computer on an Ikea trestle desk; a Leica M6 with all its various lenses and accessories crammed untidily into a silver photographer's flight case; £1400 worth of leather jacket, Gap jeans, white T-shirts and sundry hip'n'trendy garments littered all over the worn brown shag-pile carpet.

In one corner of the room, below the Cindy Crawford poster

signed 'To Stone, Hunk Of My Dreams XXXXXXX', and above a black rubbish sack overflowing with dog-ends, crumpled film packs, Kentucky Fried Chicken take-away boxes and silverfoil trays bearing the decomposing remains of assorted curries, a television set flickered on a cheap stand. It was mute. Across one corner of the room lay an unmade futon bed. At the other end of the bedsit, in a makeshift kitchen area, a portion of leather belt protruded from behind a grimy microwave oven. The bathroom was through the scruffy kitchenette.

Kettle looked at the sideboard immediately to his right. He saw an open bottle of Safari cologne, an overdue electricity bill and final demand from the phone company; a buff box with the number '45' printed on the side, a Mega Sega message pad balanced on something, covered in a demented scrawl he couldn't read but could just about make out a couple of telephone numbers. One went into the Allied Media building. The other was his own.

Kettle picked up the pad and studied the name written on it. Kirem, it said . . . no, Karen – that's it, yeah, there was a secretary in the fashion department who kept getting his calls since Nigel Plant had reorganised the office at Christmas. That was his old extension, not his current one. He was replacing the pad when he saw why it had lain slightly skew whiff. It had been balanced on top of a light blue calfskin wallet.

Kettle grabbed it.

Then the telephone rang.

Stone heard the phone ring. He was less than 40 feet from it. But he couldn't answer from the lavatory. So he listened for a message. But all he heard was silence.

OK, he thought, must be the daily report from the agency coming through on the fax. He returned to the matter at hand. Man, is my body ever whacked, he thought. Haven't had a dump in four days. Guess I'm full of shit. Yeah, that's so funny I forgot to laugh. The muesli should have done it by now, but what's the rush? All I gotta do today is meet up with Natalie, find out where the Ice Queen's having her 40th, call Mom at that Spa and tell her, maybe take in a few clubs . . . It's another rocking day on Planet Stone, paparazzo, stud and way-twisted hard dude.

He snapped his fingers, and flipped the *Daily Mail* on the grimy lino in front of him through to the Nigel Dempster page. There was a story about the chick who edited *Verve*. The guy seemed to be saying, what's with this babe? Like, her squeeze wasn't around, but: '. . . Gervaise de Groot, the former SAS officer who's making quite a name for himself as a Debutante's Delight to rival the late John Bindon, was on hand to accompany the sparkling scion of the Freer Farmer clan, who is expected to take up the editorship of a troubled national newspaper soon . . .'

'Motherfuckers didn't use my pictures,' Stone fumed to himself. 'But maybe that's because I didn't send them any . . . Hey, right.'

He remembered what his Mom had told him on the plane over: 'London's the toughest news town in the world. Lotsa writs, lotsa shits. Until you're a known name, no-one'll do anything for you.'

So the syndicators weren't sending his pictures out. OK, let's be real cold here, Stone thought. I could just send them out myself. Remembering Sir Anthony's dismissive brush-off at his pitch during their disastrous dinner – Zelda had ordered him to act like he was real excited at the idea of lining up outside the Hard Rock Cafe – an idea occurred to Stone. OK, if Sir Fucking Anthony Tough Guy George doesn't want my pictures, I'll take 'em someplace that does: like *Verve*, or the *Sunday Post*. That Karen babe had been saying only the other night that she wanted to see some frames so that she could show them to her boss, that she'd get him in with the picture editor.

Yeah, Stone thought. Way to go.

He looked at the snaps from the previous night's party on Dempster's page – the Prince rushing from the tent, *Bounty!* star Ethiopia kissing Sir Andrew Lloyd Webber, Mira and Gervaise canoodling, Crispian Frye and model Ian Parker . . .

Whammo!

He zoned back in on the picture of Ethiopia, and read the caption: '. . . refuses to name the father of her child . . .' and studied the picture again.

He was sure of it.

It was the girl who visited her Auntie, the old lady downstairs. He had some frames of her from last night. All he had to do was buy the old lady some rum – he knew she liked rum, she'd told him so one day – get her talking about her niece, yeah yeah yeah.

The first thing he had to do was find last night's frames. Then talk to the old lady, maybe try and find out when her niece was coming round next, and ambush her, get some new stuff, jack up the price . . . they'd be exclusive. World Exclusive. Stone was seeing dollar signs . . .

Kettle held the blue calfskin wallet in one hand, the fax in the other.

The paper was headed: 'Lozanc Investigations.' Private dicks, Kettle thought, working out of W9, that'd be Maida Vale.

Dear Mr O'Brien,

Regarding your ongoing query, subject Cox – negative hits.

Regarding your ongoing query, subject Harry – can confirm adoption took place 1967, child fostered briefly by family in Bradford before taken into care early '70s.

Regarding your ongoing query, subject Freer Farmer – shoplifting charge, fined £300 1973; drink driving fined £500 1974; driving without due care and attention, licence suspended twelve months 1976; drink driving fined £2000 1986; possession cocaine acquitted 1988. Freer Farmer paperwork will follow with tomorrow's report.

Please remember next month's retainer payable in advance end this week if investigation services to continue. If you wish to discuss progress of investigation please telephone office hours 071 555 1289 Yours sincerely,

D. Smith, Account Executive.

'Account Executive?' Kettle's experience of private eyes had been a story of disconnected phone numbers, unhappy ex-servicemen in raincoats who sold incriminating pictures of other people's wives, legs akimbo, for cash; a world of hurt, pain and sad losers, and Christ I ought to know, he thought.

The lavatory flushed.

Kettle, startled, stuffed the wallet in his pocket and made for the door. But suddenly it struck him . . . should I rip off the fax too? If I do, he'll know I've been here. If I don't, George won't believe I have. But who cares what he thinks, why should I do his fucking dirty work? But it'd look sloppy if I don't, he'll tell Mandi I'm a wanker . . .

Kettle turned round and tore off the fax.

'Big mistake, motherfucker,' a deep voice said.

Stone was on his way out of the bathroom into the kitchenette. With one fluid movement he grabbed the end of the belt protruding from behind the grimy microwave. It was a gunbelt.

'FREEZE!'

Stone half-crouched, his hands together, and clasped around the pearl handle of a silver 45 Colt revolver which he now pointed at Kettle. In all his years as a crime reporter, no-one had ever trained a gun on him in anger before. The firearm seemed to fill the room.

'Put my fax down. Now!'

Kettle did so.

Stone walked towards him very slowly. Kettle couldn't take his eyes off the gun. If he had, he would have noticed that Stone's flies were still undone.

Stone pushed the barrel sharply into Kettle's nose. 'Who are you?'

'I'm from British Telecom . . . BT engineers . . . Testing your line, Sir.'

'Got some ID?'

'Must've got the wrong flat, sorry, mate,' Kettle drivelled. He was trembling all over.

'ID!' demanded Stone, the urgency mounting in his voice.

Kettle reached into his inside breast pocket, felt a bulge and pulled out what was there. There was something wrong. His world began to implode. He looked at the wallet. It was blue, and made of calfskin.

'No . . . that's my wallet, Tough Guy,' said Stone, snatching it from him. He threw it down on the sideboard, then stuffed his hand inside the reporter's jacket and removed Kettle's own. He flipped it open, keeping half a check on his quarry, his face less than twelve inches from Kettle's.

Stone used his free hand to flip through the wallet. 'What's this? Your contacts?'

'Some of them,' Kettle admitted. 'Freephone numbers, direct lines, you know . . .'

'. . . Metropolitan Police Press pass, monga, been hunting up one of these little suckers myself. Jesus,' Stone said, looking up from the laminated photo card. 'Your name's Armistraud?'

Kettle nodded.

'You a faggot, Armistraud?'

Kettle wheezed nervously.

''Smatter, Dude?' His eyes flicked down again. 'You work for the *Sunday Post*? Now isn't that special. I got some pictures you guys gonna be real interested in.'

'Really?' cut in Kettle, animated. 'I can introduce you to our picture editor, Jerry Tibbets, he's a mate of mine, it's no problem, we pay the best rates for good smudges on the Street, everybody knows that.'

'Good, good,' said Stone.

'You mind putting that thing down? It's making me a bit, a bit adged up.'

'I know,' Stone said. 'I can smell it. You shit your pants, didn't you?'

Kettle nodded stupidly.

'Mn Mn Mnnn,' Stone shook his head. 'I don't think so, Armistraud, Old Bean. You see, I got this real thing about people stealing from me. I don't like it.'

He leaned forward until they were eyeball to eyeball, the cold metal still pressing against Kettle's nose. Kettle could smell Listerine on Stone's breath.

'It's a respect thing, yeah, like a question of self-esteem. See,

I let you get away with this, I might as well just hang a sign outside here saying, "C'mon in, everybody, help yourselves to my stuff." OK? Plus, ALSO, your value to me ends with your contacts book, which I now have right here in my hand. Which is where you end, Armistraud . . .'

'Everyone calls me Kettle,' the reporter interrupted, nothing to lose.

'Mister Kettle – for you, it's Stop Press time. You've hit deadline. You're yesterday's headline. Turn around and start walking.'

'You can't do this,' pleaded Kettle, bravado crumbling. 'I've got five kids depend on me . . .'

'Should've thought of that before, Tough Guy.'

'I was only doing my job . . .' Kettle wailed.

'Not well enough I'm afraid – Old Bean. Here, take my billfold, Armistraud, it's gotta look right, see? You broke in, I found you taking my money, I wasted you. Self-defence.'

'It won't wash over here, you know.'

'Oh, pardon me. My stepfather knows people, my Mom knows people. You? You're just another expendable piece of shit. A thief with a Press Card. C'mon, take it,' Stone said roughly, pressing the wallet into Kettle's hand as he turned him around. 'This is your last clipping, Dude, so let's do it right, OK?'

'The *Post*'ll never buy any pictures off you, not after this.'

'After this I'll be directing my own segment for network TV. You're my best career move yet.'

'But you don't have a silencer,' Kettle squeaked.

'So what? The sooner the cops get here, the sooner my Mom gets to edit *The Times* and will be sending me on all manner of fat expenses-paid assignments.'

'You wouldn't shoot a man in the back.'

'I've done it before,' Stone said menacingly, taunting him. 'Try me.'

'But my wife's got Multiple Sclerosis . . . please!'

'Walk! . . . or I'll blow your fuckin' balls off first.'

Kettle gave a little sob and took a step forward. His feet felt like lead. Stone raised the revolver and crouched down, lining up on the back of Kettle's head. 'Walk, you motherfucker, walk. Try and die like a man.'

Stone took a deep breath and squeezed the trigger.

Kettle took a step towards the rail. He closed his eyes. Maybe there was a God . . . Here comes oblivion.

There was a click . . .

'Shit!' cussed Stone. 'Motherfucker!'

Kettle opened his eyes and spun round.

Stone squeezed the trigger, again and again and again. Click. Click. Click. Nothing . . .

Kettle vaulted over the banister like a relay hurdler.

'I don't believe this!' Stone was yelling, as he raced down the stairs in hot pursuit. But despite twisting his ankle, Kettle had a good head start, and by the time Stone reached the front door his prisoner had disappeared completely.

Stone stared up and down Ladbroke Grove and even glanced inside the betting shop. No joy.

Shit.

He turned to go back to his flat, thinking he'd have to give Kettle a call, get his billfold back . . .

Preoccupied, he collided with a svelte figure waiting on his doorstep.

It was Ethiopia.

'Hi,' he said, remembering to smile. 'Didn't I see you at the Shaken Not Stirred Ball last night?'

'Did you?' Ethiopia said, dazzling him with her teeth.

Just then, her Aunt buzzed open the front door, and Ethiopia's lithe body, clad in figure-hugging black Lycra, bounded neatly up the stairs.

Stone raced back to his crib.

He had to make a call.

No way, he thought, whatever she is claiming, no way is Ethiopia pregnant.

37

At the ninth hole, Bruce's Castle, Kiki took in the lighthouse and foam-flecked waters of the Firth of Clyde that lay beneath as her partner drove from the exposed clifftop championship tee. 'Bit short, I think,' she said, taking a wood from her caddy.

Whack! She smacked the ball cleanly down the fairway, and smiled.

Kiki Cox had good reason to be happy. The latest ABC audit showed *YES* magazine's weekly circulation topping 1.5 million. She'd been able to use that as leverage to increase her budget by more than 20 per cent for the next quarter – good news, because it meant more free trips, longer lunches and pay rises for herself, and perhaps even her deputy too.

Earlier in the week she'd won an award for editorial excellence and danced with her cute chief sub afterwards. Now here she was, playing golf with the man who controlled the major block of institutional shares in International News Incorporated. She knew that The Boss would hear about this.

'Ohhhhhh, *kayayzin*,' said the manager of Nomura's Triple 'A' Corporate Pension Fund Investment team, as her ball landed on the green. 'Kiki Cox, *Wa Yoni Hitori*.' The Japanese smiled at her.

Kiki looked down and smiled back. She pulled her designer parka closely around her neck. It was raining quite hard, and not a trace of sunlight could be seen through the thick, dark banks of grey cloud. Her lead increased as they went round the Turnberry course. Kiki was warming up. She removed her golf glove, and putted the hole.

'Very good, Miss Cox, that's three under,' said her Scottish caddy.

'Thank you,' Kiki smiled, returning her putter to the short, weathered man. His battered clothes and ancient leather spiked shoes contrasted keenly with the spanking new designer gear sported by Kiki, Mr Karoshi and his personal caddy. As they played through the next, Kiki begn to check off a mental list: Dummy for tabloid version of *The Times* and business plan Fedexed to The Boss's office in Los Angeles? . . . Check. Duncan Campbell taken to lunch and neutralised? . . . Check. Brett Collins invited to birthday party? . . . Check. Current professional status safe? . . . Check. Current proprietor in sexual thrall? . . . Check.

That left only one more thing to do . . .

Kiki checked the score card. They were at the 15th now, Ca Canny as the locals called it. Well, Kiki thought, it's time to really play the game. Mr Karoshi controlled the swing votes that would determine the success of The Boss's latest rights issue, vital for the growth of his cable interests in China. It was very important, Kiki realised, that when Mr Karoshi talked to The Boss about her, he should feel totally comfortable and genuinely enthusiastic.

Kiki surveyed the hole. There was a grass ravine in front of the tee, and the green was perched on top of a hillock with a gully to the front and right. To the left were three treacherous bunkers at seven, nine, and eleven o'clock respectively. The undulating green supplied the final twist to this difficult hole. Prevailing wind was against the drive, coming in from the right.

'A classic par three,' Kiki observed.

'Normally for a lady I'd recommend a three-iron,' the caddy ventured. 'But since you've been hitting them so well today, Ma'am, I'd say maybe a four- or even a five- . . . you see, you're going into the wind . . .'

'I'll have the three-iron,' she said sharply.

'Are ye sure now?' the caddy frowned.

Kiki was well aware that her caddy knew the course like the back of his gnarled hand. He didn't have to refer to the card to quote her yardage on the holes. 'Quite sure, Angus,' she said. 'The three-iron, please.'

She hit the ball straight into the gully.

'Ah!' her opponent could not suppress a triumphant cry.

256

'Ach,' the caddy said. 'Doon the dunny! Ye'll be doing well if you get out of that in less than three . . .'

Lose at golf to INI principal investor, reassuring The Boss I know how to play with the big boys . . . Check.

38

The TV sets in the *Sunday Post*'s newsroom flickered. In Monaco, they were erecting a monument to Princess Grace. In Los Angeles, Madonna had called a press conference to announce that she was embracing celibacy and, inspired by 'the miracle of Mother Theresa's successful blood transplant', was toying with the notion of entering a nunnery. In Tokyo, 15 per cent had been wiped off share prices on the Stock Exchange in less than 45 minutes after seismic instruments detected a nuclear explosion in North Korea. In Prague, a former Ulster Volunteer Force terrorist was negotiating the sale, with a Reuters bureau chief, of photographs which linked the overweight leader of an extremist Belfast religious group to a child prostitution ring.

In London, Kettle was asleep at his desk.

'Bloody hell,' the night editor said. 'Wake up, man.'

Kettle came to. He was ashen-faced, unshaven, and his breath reeked of beer.

'Have you done the cuts yet?'

Part of the night reporter's job was to plough through the first editions of all the morning papers and compile a comprehensive dossier of cuttings comprising stories that the newsdesk could follow up for Sunday's edition.

'Eh?' Kettle said. He looked around him as if he didn't know where he was, and rubbed his eyes. 'Sorry, Ken, mate, I was just catching up on a bit of shut-eye. Having a bad dream . . . I'm OK, I'm OK . . .'

'Didn't you get the message?'

Kettle looked up at his screen and pressed a button. The Reuters Wire came up instead . . . he'd never really got the hang of bloody computers. He tried again. His messages read: 'WHERE

ARE MY CUTS?' SINGLETON, NIGHTNEWS 02:42. STONE
CALLED AGAIN. CALL 0843 754779 ASAP TO RETRIEVE
CONTACTS BOOK.' 'WHERE ARE MY CUTS YOU LAZY
SOD?' SINGLETON, NIGHTNEWS 03:12. 'WHERE ARE THE
BLOODY CUTS KETTLE?' SINGLETON, NIGHTNEWS 03:31.

'It's not good enough, Kettle, I need them in the next half
hour,' Singleton snapped.

'All right, all right,' Kettle said. 'Don't have a hernia. It's a
slow day, there's nothing in the papers anyway, I looked before I
came in.'

'I didn't realise the Cashbox Club supplied its members with
first editions,' said Singleton sarcastically.

'I picked 'em up at Leicester Square. It's all bollocks, Ken,
apart from that Royal assassination scare in *The Sun*, there's
nothing else, really.'

'I need 20 stories, minimum, and you know it.'

The night editor lifted a Polaroid picture which was lurking
among credit card slips scattered across Kettle's desk. On his
return from the Cashbox, where he'd been asking around about
Ethiopia, Kettle had started rifling through Stone's wallet before
passing out on top of it.

'Hey,' said Singleton, 'what the fuck is this?'

They both looked.

The picture had been taken at night, on some building site. It
showed a man lying on the ground, a flamboyant scarf tied
around his neck, his body half-concealed by earth. In the
background, a familiar skyline loomed. The man's mouth was
open, his eyes closed, and his discoloured head lolled at a spastic
angle to his body.

'You know who that is?' Singleton said. 'That's Brendan
O'Brien.'

'Brendan O'Brien,' Kettle repeated. 'Writer, wasn't he?'

'Where did you get this?' Singleton demanded.

'Contact,' Kettle fobbed him off, his tone terse, his mind
racing.

The hairs on his neck were all standing on end: infallible
antennae to a big yarn in the warp. He remembered how four

years ago, he'd been in at the kill when the Yard had arrested a New Jersey hitman sent over to London to wipe out a couple of unruly Jamaican drug barons. He'd had 20 minutes with the guy in the back of the meatwagon on the way to the nick. The man had told him how contract killers always deliver a Polaroid of the deceased victim to prove they'd kept their side of the bargain before they could collect the final payment. 'It's like offing someone, you know? There's a way to do it. You tie the fucker's hands behind his back and off 'im in the back of the head. It's less messy, more professional, see. And it sends a message.'

'You remember the O'Brien story?'

'That's what I'm developing,' Kettle improvised. 'I was just going to start a backgrounder on the guy, but you keep hassling me about these bleeding cuts.'

'OK, don't worry about it, I'll do the cuts,' said Singleton, taking the unread first editions from Kettle's desk. 'That Polaroid's worth a million, mate. The widow is Zelda Lee Powers. Mandi'll kill for that.'

'I know,' said Kettle, dragging his weary carcass up from the desk. He was trying to remember what he knew about Brendan O'Brien, the man they once called The Shakespeare of the Emerald Isle. He'd won critical acclaim, big prizes and huge money for his compelling tales of life in the fictional Irish border village of Trechtown. And he had seemed that rare thing: a real storyteller who entertained everyone. But O'Brien's early promise had dissipated in a slew of bourbon, bar brawls and bad marriages. He'd gone to live in New York to write The Great American Novel, a filmscript about the Irish who'd left Trechtown during the troubles of the 1870s. But he'd never finished it . . . because four years ago he had vanished from the face of the earth. Until now . . .

Kettle slugged down the black coffee and called Stone's cellular number. Another meeting, he decided, was long overdue. Only this time he'd be the one calling the shots.

39

Mira knew about models.

Her mother had been one, she had been one, and now she saw them almost every day. Not only professionally but socially, too, because they were the cheapest way to decorate a dinner table. When models worked, Mira had found, they were generally required to do some combination of four things: look surprised; look surprised while pointing at something; jump in the air while smiling, on the threshold of pain; and . . . as the editor of *Verve*, she had no intention of doing the fourth, not even with a photographer as hot as Johnny Sprouse.

'That assistant though,' Caro whispered to Mira. 'Hey, Baby, he's on my fancy list.'

'He's interesting,' Mira acknowledged. 'Though not quite like that.'

'How interesting then?'

'Frightfully interesting,' Mira whispered back.

'Places please, everybody,' announced the photographer's assistant, coming back into the studio at that moment and clapping his hands. His own assistant turned the music on again. Mira repositioned herself and reclined in the enormous cane throne. Her secretary Nadia, Caro and half a dozen or so other members of staff who were currently in favour, adjusted their Mesopotamian costumes and began to wave their giant palm fronds. The fronds were authentic, imported by Sprouse from Cairo at hideous expense especially for this shoot. The picture would run at the front of the magazine, alongside the masthead, beneath the Editor's Letter – the last, Mira was confident, that she would ever write.

'OK,' the assistant said. 'Now when Johnny comes back, he's going to want to do something a little bit different . . . so this is what I'd like you to do: Mira, jump up in the air, and as you do so, smile. I mean really smile, fifty thousand watts, OK, you know the form. Now the rest of you, the moment Mira jumps, you're all to point your fronds at her with one hand and cover your mouths with the other. Like one of those old Bateman cartoons, OK?'

The assistant's name was Russell. He wore corduroy trousers, which Mira couldn't quite figure out, and had unruly blond hair, which she certainly could. It hadn't been his idea to go to the Anvil, the notorious nightclub situated in an old City meat warehouse, it had been Caro's . . .

'Hey, Baby . . .'

A pair of hostile eyes glared out through a bar-grilled shutter drilled into the steel plate door. It sprang shut and the door opened. The eyes belonged to a brick-faced diesel dyke who smiled at them and waved the trio through in spite of their inappropriate attire.

'The sketch is that Russell's a sab, OK?' Mira explained, while the photographer's assistant went to the bar for drinks. 'The guy who runs his unit – Ronnie – is a passionate animal activist – and a footman at Buckingham Palace. He's the man who personally delivers the Queen her mail, and I mean personally, OK?'

Caro nodded.

'While I was arranging the shoot with Sprouse's people in New York,' Mira went on, 'I had to liaise with Russell and organise some stuff here, and it emerged that this Ronnie's leaving soon and going on the dole to become a full-time Animal Rights activist. Yesterday, Russell had rather a festive lunch, and afterwards confided in me.'

'What?'

'Something frightfully indiscreet . . .'

'What?' demanded Caro.

'Last week, Ronnie was given a letter to deliver from the Prime Minister's Office. He said he would never normally dream of . . .'

'He opened it,' Caro cut in. 'And?'

Mira flamed up another Stuyvesant. 'Guess what?'

Caro was agog. 'She's handing in her walking papers.'

Caro gasped. 'Her Britannic Majesty's abdicating?'

'Next month,' Mira nodded.

'When next month?'

'What do you mean, when next month?'

'I mean, next month is the day after tomorrow.'

Caro ripped a Benson and Hedges from the pack wedged into the waistband of her leather knickers, and used Mira's Dunhill lighter to torch it.

'Caro, you mustn't breathe a word of this,' Mira warned her friend. 'My future at *The Times* is on the line. Toby and Brett have both had a word with The Boss, but he's being a bit difficult about things.'

'What do you mean?'

'Tobias told me that The Boss told Brett the appointment must have, in Tobes's inimitable phraseology, "the glossy spin of meritocracy".'

'Meaning it mustn't look like an inside job?'

'It's such a fucking drag,' Mira nodded, stabbing her cigarette on the metal table with a grinding lunge that sprayed sparks. 'Being who I am, tied up with my clan, you know, all these Waughs and Murdochs and Chancellors. What's the bloody point in having relations and entrées when the one time I really need all the help I can get, I have to work twice as hard as everybody else?'

Caro couldn't think of a pat answer, so she remained silent.

'It's so pressurizing,' Mira said. 'He wants me to come up with a ballgrabber – and fast.'

'He's testing your contacts,' Caro said.

'And my nerve. It's a fucking nightmare, the story's there, it's mine for the taking.'

'All you've got to do is lock it up,' Caro agreed.

'Well, I called Diana last night,' Mira said. 'And she's doing another one of her charity jaunts in India. I sort of sounded her out a bit, and I don't think she's heard anything, so it'd be an exclusive. But Christ, I'm shifty about it. You won't breathe a word will you, Caro? Promise?'

'Secret Squirrel,' her friend replied. 'I promise.'

'It's going to happen in about three weeks, I think.'

'Jesus H,' Caro said. 'Scoop newsworthy, or what?'

'I've got to stand it up, though. I've got to get to meet this guy. If it's some kind of wind-up, or just old queens gossiping – well, I couldn't bear to think about it.'

Russell returned with their beers.

'Thanks,' Caro said.

'You'd never guess that Russell was brought up in Australia, would you?' Mira said to Caro.

'I've heard better Australian accents in Russia,' Caro said. 'Which part of Australia are you from?'

'New South Wales,' Russell replied. 'My stepfather's got a place about 150 miles out of Sydney. But I've been over here since I was twelve. I only go back at Christmas now.'

'So you must know Kiki Cox,' Caro said.

'Not really,' Russell shrugged. His voice was impeccably Sloane-toned, but his face betrayed residual anxiety.

'Ah, the mistress of the cold kiss,' Mira said.

'Well actually,' Russell said, 'I did do a shoot for *YES* Mag a couple of weeks back: Celebrity Barbecues. You know what I heard from Barry Humphries?'

'What?' said the women in unison.

A pained look crossed his face. 'Nah, it doesn't matter.'

'What?' cried Caro.

Russell appeared to be on the verge of revealing something, but then he shook his head.

'What?' Caro demanded, exasperated. 'What, for Christsakes?'

'It's just idle gossip . . . Nah, forget it.'

'You can't, you can't tease us like this,' squealed Caro.

'It's not fair, Russell,' Mira coaxed, leaning towards him a little with a flirtatious pout. 'Life wasn't meant to be easy. You can tell us . . .'

'Oh for fuck's sake tell it,' Caro snapped, running out of patience.

Damn, Mira thought, we'll never get it out of him now. Caro has such a way with words . . .

264

'Nah, it wouldn't be fair to repeat it . . . it's too fantastic for words . . . nah. So look, when do you want to meet Ronnie?' he asked Mira, changing the subject.

'ASAP.'

'Well, we're doing a drag with the Haverford tomorrow.'

'Tomorrow? But I'm supposed to be at Number Ten, there's a reception, it's crucial . . .'

The purpose of the Prime Minister's gladhandling the press suddenly became clear to Mira. It was fall-out, a breaking-the-ground sort of operation. The PM was trying to assess whose loyalties lay where, to ascertain how smoothly a transition could be made, to look out for his own interests in what was sure to be the constitutional equivalent of a nuclear onslaught. But if she could stand up the story, there was no point in farting around playing pass-the-parcel with a man who could soon be suffering the ultimate embarrassment of being an unemployed politician . . .

'No, never mind, this is much more interesting actually, isn't it? Just tell me where and when, Russell. And, more important – how?'

'Well, probably the best thing would be if you came along with us, I could introduce you to Ronnie, you'd have a couple of hours to get comfortable with each other before the action goes off. Then we'll give you a lift back – provided we don't get arrested.'

'You're ringing,' Caro said.

Mira spent the next ten seconds hastily searching her pockets, to no avail. She trawled frantically through her bag, her desperation mounting, and finally produced her mobile. 'Hallo . . . Nadia? Oh God, yes, what is it, I'm in the middle of the most frightfully important meeting here . . . Who? Hold on,' Mira said, slipping from the bar stool. 'You're breaking up . . . Hallo? Nadj? What? Harry and Mary Beth who? I've never . . . What? Oh God, Gervaise de Groot,' she sighed, rolling her eyes at Caro. 'That man is trouble Cap "T". Look, deal with them in the morning, I won't be there . . . no, all day, something's come up . . . ring Number Ten first thing and apologise, would you, Nadj, I'm going to have to cut that reception . . . say I'm ill, glandular fever or something . . . yah.'

She stuffed the tiny cellular into a pocket and turned back to Russell. 'OK, I'll do it. It could be a bit embarrassing actually, because the Master of Fox Hounds there is a friend of my father's. Still, we'll brazen it out somehow. Now, how are we going to meet?'

The mobile rang again.

Mira repeated her frenetic lost-and-found procedure.

'Hallo? Toby? Oh God, yes, what is it, I'm in the middle of the most frightfully important meeting here . . . what? Well . . . Oh, can't you tell me now? Oh God, Toby . . . this is really . . . yah, yah, well I'm going to be out in the field all day tomorrow . . . no, 'fraid not . . . Tobias, this is life and death to me too. Oh for God's sakes, look, if it's so bloody important then tell me now. Where? Oh hang on, I remember – that place where Nanny Edwards used to take us to play Poohsticks . . . yah, OK, about five-thirty, OK, OK. So weird,' she said to the others, frowning. 'So unlike my brother. He's really shifting about something . . . sorry, Russell, yah, we've got to arrange the meet . . .'

'Ronnie lives in a place called Slough. He's picking me up there outside a pub called the Three Tuns at five-thirty . . .'

'In the morning?' Caro screeched.

He nodded.

'Golly, how exciting,' Mira grinned. 'It's just like being a real journalist, yah?'

40

It was the evening of Kiki Cox's 40th birthday party. In less than a week, International News would announce which woman would edit *The Times*.

Beneath an oily film of fine rain, Covent Garden's sidestreets and backstreets sparkled with a dark, glimmering sheen. Kiki Cox arrived at Sorrell's Brasserie, an austere temple to 'Recession Chic', dressed in a delicious mink-coloured Donna Karan two-piece, through which just a glimpse of scarlet La Perla lingerie was visible. Her gold and platinum necklace, rings and bangles, from the 'Marriage Of Metal' collection, had been hand-made for her specially by chic Soho jeweller Simon Day to mark the occasion.

She took immediate delivery of a small bunch of wilted carnations with a personal note from David Mellor in which he apologised for his absence, and at the same time wondered whether her magazine might be interested, for a nominal fee, in featuring his new digital wrist-watch from which he claimed to be able to programme his CD player.

Celia McNalty, *YES* Magazine's Chef of the Month, had, with the aid of her team of young helpers from the First Church of Christian Nutrition, already unloaded most of the dishes she had made earlier into the private reception room above the restaurant which Kiki had hired for her party.

'What's the matter, Crispi? You look a bit down in the mouth,' she said to the cheerless decorator, who had made his entrance at exactly ten minutes past eight.

'My landlady's got shingles,' he replied, and sat down glumly in a corner.

By nine, most of the guests had arrived. Celia McNalty was discussing 'the vaguely Rumanian sub-text' of the dishes she'd cooked with an old queen who made up horoscopes for the *Daily Sketch* under the billing 'Psychic Suzi: The Astrologer Who Knows The Stars'.

The rest of Kiki's guests were predominantly female, in their twenties and thirties. They had clubbed together to buy Kiki a droll ornamental teapot which, when its lid was lifted, played 'Good On Yer Mum, Tip Top's The One' – a famous Australian sliced bread jingle from the early 1980s. All the girls complimented their hostess on her chic new haircut and perfect highlights.

'Did you have the body rub treatment at the salon?' Kiki's secretary asked.

'No . . . Jazz came over to my flat this morning,' Kiki replied with a practised smile.

She sat as straight as a pew-back in her steel chair and, with small, precise, bird-like movements, ate morsels of raw carp which Celia McNalty had marinated overnight in vinegar, and which was served with pickles in a sour 'peasant-style' sauce of pig's trotter, lard and tripe.

The Birthday Girl watching the door throughout, somewhat anxiously. She was still waiting for her principal guest of the evening to appear.

As favoured patrons, Kiki Cox and her party were spared the eaterie's speciality: the inviting in of the Garden's most repellent beggars to harangue diners on the subject of their media-rare lifestyles. Even so, by the time Kiki's party had reached the dessert course, the strain was beginning to tell.

Crispian continued to brood at one end of the table next to Psychic Suzi, who had fallen asleep. After Celia McNalty had delivered an ode, in her hearty baritone, to the joys of ageing gracefully, an uncomfortably long silence hung over the table.

'I really do like your haircut,' repeated Natalie from the picture desk to Kiki.

'It does suit you,' chimed in Sue Griswood, Kiki's deputy.

'It's just so very . . . you,' added Nell Windus, who'd joined the commissioning desk just three weeks earlier.

'G'day, teenagers!' came a voice from the other end of the

room. It was followed by a loud belch.

Brett Collins staggered into the room wearing Caro Buchanan on one arm. *Verve*'s Investigative Stylist was dressed in something unusual and abbreviated, made from rubber. 'Where's the comestibles then, Sport?' Brett yelled.

'Ah, Seaview,' he said approvingly, seizing a bottle and swigging from it. 'Good on ya, Keeks. Happy 30th, mate. You don't look a day over 29 . . .'

'Hey, Baby,' Caro said to Crispi, leaning all over him and lapping his ear. 'Why so glum?'

'I've had a romantic reversal,' said the decorator woefully. 'It's too sad.'

'What good in sitting alone in your room . . .' Caro began to sing, opening another bottle of fake champagne by smashing its neck against the edge of the table.

Before Kiki could check this unplanned outbreak of high spirits, the doors burst open again. In stalked two tall, burly police constables. Everyone fell silent and somebody turned the music off. The bobbies prowled the room menacingly. Natalie started to giggle nervously. Then one of the policemen removed his helmet . . . and the other followed suit. Then they began to take off all their clothes . . . to reveal hard bodies, waxed chests, and the tiniest of black posing pouches. They tossed each other a meaningful glance, clicked their fingers in unison, and started up a catchy rap:

> *We're Wayne and Shane,*
> *The Strippogram boys,*
> *We've come to add*
> *to all the noise.*
> *Forty's tough, but it's only numbers,*
> *Reverse them if you come from Down Under.*
> *So it's Birthday Greetings of which we speak,*
> *Don't you recognize us – Cousin Keek?'*

Crispian at least, seemed to perk up a bit – especially when Caro suggested he help with her a little stunt involving two empty bottles.

'How disgusting,' said Brett, letting rip another loud belch, 'I came overseas to escape from all these flaming nancy-boys. Seems nowhere's safe anymore. Keeks, you're not gonna tell me these guys are really your young cousins?'

Kiki's blue eyes were shark-cold. 'Don't ask me,' she said. 'Your guess is as good as mine.'

41

The *Sunday Post* was quiet.

Too quiet.

With Brett Collins all set to name the new Editor of *The Times* within 48 hours, corporate anxiety gripped the employees of International News. The tension was contagious and threw all it touched into a collective conniption. The areas surrounding the photocopiers, the watercoolers and the coffee machines were the worst rumour mills.

At lunchtime, anyone who wanted to stay anyone was over at The Evil Star, watching their backs under the wise guise of attending a drinking session sponsored by Worell, the *Sunday Post*'s deputy editor, to celebrate his big Three Oh-Oh. On the newsdesk, only the morose and taciturn Bowles, deputy sports editor, could be found holding the fort. Through the Pyrex-thick glass that partitioned her office, Mandi glanced up at him and watched, fascinated, as he fielded incoming calls stacked up like Jumbos over Heathrow. She wondered how the man had hung on to his placid composure for so long.

Mandi stared down at the Polaroid picture on her desk. 'Well – is it, or isn't it?' she demanded of the fashion editor.

'Definitely is,' the fashion editor replied.

'Agenda, they were called. Had one myself, but I left it in a hotel room in Tokyo last year. They were limited edition, made specially for everyone who went to the show in New York four years ago.'

'What was the designer's name?' asked Mandi.

The fashion editor put her forefingers to her temples and concentrated hard for a moment. 'I can't remember,' she sighed, at last.

Mandi's heavily shadowed eyelids dropped over her irises like hoods. She felt like all her chickens had died

'. . . But I could find out . . .' the fashion editor said hesitantly.

'Good girl,' said Mandi. 'There must be a record somewhere – at the factory, at the packaging company that boxed up the scarves, or at whichever delivery firm sent them out. If worst comes to worst, track down the PRs and get a list from them. But be discreet, we don't want any, you know . . .'

'Inadvertent disclosure?' supplied a wheedling male voice from behind the fashion editor's back.

'Thank you, Kettle,' Mandi said.

'Do you want the whole list? It could be quite long – the show was at the Waldorf Astoria, there were hundreds of people . . .' frowned the fashion editor.

'No, no,' Mandi said. 'Get the whole thing up by all means, if you can, but there's only one name we're really looking for: Zelda Lee Powers.'

'Zelda Lee Powers?' the fashion editor's face furrowed. 'Isn't she that woman being sued?'

'The same. Get on the phone, the Concorde, the Mayor of Manhattan's dick for all I care. Tear the bloody town apart, I don't care what it takes or how much it costs – as long as you let me know one way or the other by . . . what time's he coming in, Kettle?'

'Six.'

'OK, by five-fifty,' Mandi said.

'That's only four hours away,' the fashion editor frowned as she bit on a sculpted puce nail. 'Suppose I can't stand it up in that time?'

'See you at the Job Centre,' said Mandi evenly. 'Go on, go on you're wasting time. . . . Is this the original?' Mandi asked, dismissing her and turning to Kettle. 'Or the dupe we got back from the lab this morning?'

'I wiped the dabs off it and put the original back in his wallet,' Kettle said with a yawn. Through the open door of her office they suddenly heard someone screaming.

'Fuck off, fuck off, fuck off!' Bowles was bellowing, as he

272

smashed the telephone receiver into the desk.

'What's going on?' Mandi demanded, coming out of her office, hands on ample hips. Bowles sat down at once, his face resuming its usual bloodhound composure.

'I don't mind Rocky Ryan trying it on now and then. I don't even mind the psychos calling in from Rampton . . . but this is too fucking much,' Bowles sighed.

'What was too fucking much?' Mandi asked.

'These sick fucks are in the lobby.'

'Which sick fucks?'

'This American tourist couple who were stranded in Italy by some nob. They keep raving on about death camps and executions and abortions and castrations . . . God, I'm sorry, Aitch, I'm really tired, I just can't deal with it at the moment.'

'Why? What's the matter?'

'I'm sorry,' Bowles said.

Mandi noticed at the same time as he did that one or two reporters were beginning to drift back into the newsroom. Bowles was safely back in his shell.

'It was an aberration, it's the pressure . . .'

'Next time just don't make the mistake of giving them your name,' Mandi reminded him. Bowles nodded.

'Aitch,' Kettle said, 'he's here.'

'Who?'

'Stone. He's downstairs at the gatehouse.'

'You said the meet was at six.'

'That's what he said. Seems he's changed his mind . . . says he wants to see us now or not at all.'

'Us?' Mandi raised an eyebrow.

'He says he's got some smudges you'll, quote, kill for, unquote.'

'Check 'em out and stall him,' Mandi said. 'We've got to find out if Zelda's involved. I've got to.'

The stench of manky drains and rank, non-specific decay assaulted her nose with customary savagery. The cloudy sky was grey and forbidding, and heavy with rain. It made Mandi

273

uncomfortable. She click-clicked through the dark tunnel beneath the bridge on her scuffed stilettoes, yanking up the collar of her coat against the bite of the wind. She winked at the commissionaire, and slid down the stairs into The Evil Star.

Against one wall of an adjoining room, a low light hung over a corner table.

'I though you were supposed to be swapping your wallet,' Mandi admonished Kettle, 'not emptying it.'

'We traded billfolds,' said the goatee-bearded boy in a plaid shirt. He wore his baseball cap at 180 degrees. His accent was Californian with subtle undertones of Brooklyn. 'We're just sorting out the contents,' he smiled.

Kettle did the necessary. 'Mandi, this is Stone O'Brien; Mandi Harry, Editor of the *Sunday Post*.'

Mandi studied the youth for a split second, taking all of him in. 'You're related to Brendan O'Brien, aren't you?' she said.

Stone said nothing.

'. . . I loved *Full Moon On A Dark Night*, that bit where all the IRA men are weeping into their Guinness, confessing how guilty they feel about all the killing they've done, trying to get Father Farrel to absolve them. . . .'

'I never read my Dad's stuff,' he said, realising too late that he had answered Mandi's question.

'Oh? Well, what do you read, then?'

'I don't read, period,' Stone said blandly, a bored expression clouding his quite pleasant face. 'I watch,' he said, not looking at her.

'So . . . you've got some pictures you want to sell us?'

Stone took two grainy black and white ten-eights from the silver camera case lying on top of a leather jacket on the seat beside him. Mandi studied them. A slim, svelte Ethiopia going into a building . . . and a bulging, apparently pregnant Ethiopia coming out.

'So?' Mandi said, looking straight into his face.

'So I think we both know what this is about,' Stone said. 'You buying?'

Mandi shrugged. 'Depends how much.'

274

'Two fifty.'

'Twenty-five hundred?' Mandi said with a wince, leaning back in her seat.

'Not twenty-five hundred.'

Mandi gave him a look as if to say, I don't quite follow.

'Two-five-zero,' said Stone patiently.

'Two five zero what?'

'Zero Zero Zero.'

'Two hundred and fifty thousand dollars?' Mandi said incredulously, with a theatrical through-the-front-teeth whistle. 'Bit steep for some totty walking in and out of a betting shop, isn't it?'

'Who's bet?' Stone said quietly.

'You had some frames of them together, that'd be different.'

'That broad's about as pregnant as I am,' reasoned Stone, '. . . and word is she's saying the father is a Prince of the Realm.' He resumed his shuttered look. 'The floor's at two hundred first British Serial Rights. World rights stay with me. Like I say, take it or leave it,' said Stone firmly.

'We'll give you twenty-five grand sterling for a UK exclusive only, fifty for a buyout.'

He shook his head.

'It's not that good, Stone. At the moment they're only pictures. We've got to prove the inferences you are drawing from them.'

'Inferences? You mean, like extortion? I think you could prove extortion.'

'Yeah?'

'Yeah.'

'So how would you go about standing something like that up?'

'Hey – you're the hotshot Editor. You work it out.'

'Listen: the pictures we want to buy are more candid. The Prince And The Showgirl, look Ma, no drapes. These are interesting . . . but it's a bit of a flyer, isn't it?'

Adrian Lin called Stone's bet. The American folded his cards, and Lin scooped the pot. Bad time to bluff, Mandi thought.

'What are you playing?' she asked them.

'Seven-card stud,' Kettle said. 'High-Low.'

'You want to play?' asked Adrian Lin.

'Pass,' Mandi smiled. 'I never play games unless I know I'm going to win.'

Lin shrugged, shuffled the cards and passed them to Stone.

'If you want to sell your pictures, you're going to have to stand it up. Sell it to me.'

'How you guys run a newspaper beats me. You couldn't run a goddamn bath,' Stone said, cutting the cards. 'OK – you leave a message on her answerphone, "I'm calling on behalf of your bank manager, please contact him on a matter of utmost urgency, blah blah blah." You follow the Betty, she goes into the bank, OK?' He passed the cards back to Lin, who began dealing. 'You watch which teller she goes to, then you go to the same one, and say, "Oh, this bodacious black chick just lent me some parking money, she was so nice I really wanna be a boy scout and put the money back into her account." So you pay a couple of bucks in, you've got her bank details, you hack into the system, dial up her number, and . . .' Stone saw the expression on Mandi's face, and shrugged: 'Man, you're real lame.'

'You could do that? What sort of computer do you need?'

'Shit, I do it off my laptop all the time,' Stone said. 'The security in this country is crap. I can hack into anybody's files anywhere, anytime I want. Trust me, it's not that hard.'

'Where did you learn to do that?'

'See, I spent some time at what they call a special school,' Stone said deliberately, pushing some chips across the table. 'You learn stuff.'

'You play Brag?'

'Little kids' game,' Stone said.

'How much to buy in?' Mandi asked.

Lin pushed his cards away from him across the table, and looked at his watch. 'I've done my money,' he said, knocking back the rest of his Becks and decking the green bottle next to a dozen others crowding the table.

Stone drained his whisky glass and shuffled the cards. 'Still in?'

'Why not?' said Kettle. 'In for a penny, in for a pound.'

Mandi looked at her pile of chips and nodded. 'OK,' Stone said. 'I'm going to the can.'

'Get another round in on your way back, would you, mate?'

As Mandi watched him disappear into the Gents, she reached down and flicked open Stone's camera case. She glanced swiftly inside, searching for the negatives of the Ethiopia pictures. But something silky looking and vividly coloured caught her eye. Mandi removed it from the case and held it up. 'Recognise this?' she said to Kettle. He stared at the scarf.

'Let me take a wild guess. Agenda?'

Mandi reached over, stuffed it into Kettle's pocket, and snapped the case shut. 'That's it,' she said. 'Bingo.'

'What about the Ethiopia story?'

'It's not as strong as we'd hoped, is it?' she said. 'Prince is doing the nasty – good. Prince is doing the nasty with West End star, and she's black – very good. Queen's First Black Grandchild – Scoop. But this: she's got a great big prosthesis from somewhere and she's ripping the sucker off – not so good. It's just another hustle, and because the perpetrator's a black woman, I can't see The Boss being too thrilled if we splash it.'

'She's in the frame . . . all we've got to do is stand it up.'

'No, Kettle, no. A story like this is like finding a snowball in the desert. You've got to grab it and lob it home ASAP because it can melt away at any moment. Like it just has.'

Mandi picked up her glass. It was filled with ice, lemon and fizzy water. The others thought she was on gin and tonic. But Mandi tasted only tonic water, because when she'd arrived, she had instructed the barman to hold the gin in her drinks.

'Talk about not letting the facts get in the way of a good story,' Mandi chuckled.

'But it is a good story, Aitch, it's a cracker.'

She shook her head. 'Every day I get some new fucking memo from The Boss's office about positive stereotyping and multicultural bloody sensitivity. She may have done it, but even if she has, it doesn't matter, we can't beat it up, and we can't splash it. If it was me, I'd have one set of rules for everyone – cheat 'em all or don't cheat anyone at all. It doesn't do to play favourites. It isn't fair, and in the long run, it doesn't work. But I don't make the rules. I only play by them.'

'But. . .'

'What are we going to do with this kid? You don't think he's tooled up?'

'I checked him out,' Kettle said. 'He's not armed.'

'Are you sure?'

Kettle nodded. 'You don't want his pictures, then?' he said.

'Screw the smudges. I think we should find out how deeply he's involved in this. He's got the Polaroid, he's carrying the scarf, it's almost like he wants to be punished, he wants to get caught. He pulled a gun on you, right? He's capable of doing it.'

'I don't know . . . I was scared shitless at the time, but now I think he was just winding me up.'

There was no doubt who had played their cards the best this session: Kettle began scooping up the vast pile of chips in front of him.

'No . . . don't,' Mandi said. 'Not yet.'

'You can't play with three people,' Kettle said, 'I'm sorry, Aitch, but not even Brag.'

'We're not finished yet,' Mandi said.

Stone arrived back at their table with more drinks, which he banged down on the table. 'Man, I am just one big bag of bloatation,' said the young American. 'You Europeans, you drink so much. I guess I'm just not used to it.'

No sooner had he resumed his place than his pager started bleeping. he glanced down at his hip to read the message. 'So . . .' he said, 'we've played cards, we've chewed the fat. You name it, we've sung it. Now what's it going to be, dudes? We just talking here, or you want to buy what I've got?'

'We've already got it.'

'Say what?'

Mandi held up the Polaroid. A moment or two passed before Stone's face registered recognition.

'Shit!'

He made a frantic grab for it across the table – but Mandi yanked the picture well out of his grasp.

'We've got copies,' she smiled. 'Look in your wallet if you don't believe me.'

Praying that Kettle really had replaced the original Polaroid, she watched Zelda's son watching them both, wondering, trying to work out just how much they knew . . .

'What's the deal here?' he said nervously, his thumb on the original photograph.

'We get our negatives . . . and you get a plane ticket out of here.'

'Harsh,' Stone said quietly. He dropped his head in his hands, and moaned. 'That is so harsh. Just when I thought things were going into turnaround. I can't believe you'd do this.' He looked across the table at them. 'I mean, it's our word against yours. You can't back it up,' he began.

'The scarf,' Mandi said. She watched for the delayed reaction, saw Stone lunge towards his silver camera case and jerk it open. 'It's in a very safe place,' she smiled, wishing that it were. The jukebox was rattling out an old reggae tune. At the table, all were silent. Mandi had noticed the way Stone's eyes narrowed when she'd told him about the scarf. It flicked through her mind that in some ways perhaps they were not so dissimilar, she and Stone.

'So, I give you the negatives – and you give me a first-class round-the-world ticket . . . and?' asked Stone.

'Your freedom,' said Mandi. She paused before adding, '. . . we'll drop in a thousand quid expenses.'

'I don't think so,' Stone replied.

'What are your choices?' Mandi asked him, 'Take the money, walk away – or spend the next 50 years bashing out registration plates with your cellmates?'

'Bullshit. It's not enough. I could walk right now, Audi 5000, outtahere . . . I'd still be ahead of the cops.'

'No,' Kettle contradicted him. 'If you could've scarpered, you would've done it by now. But you know full well you'd never get past the check-in desk. Face it, son, we've got you by the short and curlies, and we might also have done you a favour in the long run. You'll see.'

'And here was I thinking we were all such great buddies,' Stone said, taking a pull of his drink.

Don't like this, Mandi was thinking. Little bastard's far too cocky by half. But suddenly, she realised that he was crying. Straight for the jugular . . .

It struck her that he'd be about the same age as her own daughter.

She reached into her bag for a Kleenex, but then instinct checked her. The same killer instinct honed by thousands of interviews, on hundreds of doorsteps, during dozens of stand-offs. He's going to cough, she thought . . .

'Why wouldn't she get me a job on Anthony's fucking paper? It would've been the easiest fucking thing in the world. "I'll pretend to make up with Tony and you can have my apartment." That was what she said . . . but it was only so's I could make a dossier on you and those other bitches. She thought it would keep me out of trouble, like she can buy me off or something. I just wanted one chance to show what I could do . . . that was all. I worked my butt off. But it's always the same . . .'

Stone was crying, slumped over the table. Mandi remained impassive. It was Kettle who reached over, patted his arm and urged Stone to pull himself together and have a drink.

'. . . You know she made up all that shit about my Dad,' Stone sobbed, ignoring him. '. . . I was at UCLA, and she did the same thing then – made me depend on her for bank, so I'd have to call her every week and she'd tell me this shit – not straight out, more like a tease, you know? She'd say how she went to the emergency room again, and like how Dad was drinking all the time. OK, so he was no saint, but what she did . . . it's haunted me every day ever since. You know, there isn't one day when I don't think about what happened? You off some guy, OK – shit happens . . . but your own father?'

He sobbed uncontrollably. Kettle took a swig of Stone's whisky himself, and wiped the tears from his own eyes. Mandi tossed him an old-fashioned look. 'So let's get this straight, what are you saying: that Zelda made you kill Brendan O'Brien so that she could marry Sir Anthony George?'

'No, no, not that . . . she hadn't even met Anthony then. Like, she called me up and told me he'd got drunk again, and was beating her, and he'd fallen over. They'd been having rough sex, drinking a lot and shit, he was out of it, and by the time I got there he was just weight. Yeah, right. She said they'd been perchin' . . . it had got out of hand . . . she didn't know, like she was carried away, and somehow strangled him accidentally. She was totally freaked out, I was totally freaked out, it was all totally bended . . .' Stone was regaining his composure a little now, and wiped his tear-stained face on his sleeves. '. . . she told me she'd give me ten grand if I dumped the body. So I drove out to this construction site, upstate, only on the way he started . . . well, I shot him, didn't I? It was cold, it was like Siberia, and it was like it was all happening to somebody else, like a mercy killing or something. So I put him in the ground . . . took the Polaroids . . .'

'Why did you do that?' Kettle asked. He felt reasonably confident that, because of the way they were positioned around the table, Stone couldn't possibly see that he had a reporter's notebook flipped open on his knee, and was writing down, word for word, everything Stone said, in shorthand, with a bookie's pencil.

'She told me to,' Stone was babbling. 'It's all down to her, everything that happened, getting busted, doing time . . . moving out to the West Coast . . . she set me up . . . my own Mom. Can you imagine what it's like having to live with someone like her? To know that she's a part of who you are? It's . . . it's beyond intense. Sometimes I don't know how I get through the day, man, it's . . . hey, how do I get my bank?'

'It'll be waiting for you at the gatehouse,' Mandi said soothingly.

'Cash?'

'If that's what you want.' Mandi shrugged.

'Sideways,' Stone said, pocketing his few remaining chips. 'Let's bail.'

'Just one more thing,' Mandi said, as Stone made to leave.

'Did you really get into Kiki Cox's system from your laptop?'

'Sure! Like I said, it was my Mom's idea, setting up those stunts. She just wanted to throw all you guys a scare. I mean, she's desperate . . . this Morgan trial could send her whole career down the pan. The TV thing, having the others gang up on you, that was just improvised. It was like a free gift.'

'So you broke into my house and put my cat in the waste disposal?' demanded Mandi, her eyes blazing.

'No way,' Stone insisted. 'That was Mom's idea . . . the private dick did it. I refused, no way José . . .'

Mandi wondered what kind of pets he'd had when he was a little boy. Even now, after all these revelations, she really wanted to believe that there was some good, a shred of a scruple, something moral, something she could recognise as human.

'I don't mind strategising, making the key plays . . . but going out of town,' he was saying, 'hey, that's gruntwork.'

'Excuse me,' Mandi said, getting up from the table, 'I've just got to call Nigel Plant, our managing editor, get your ticket organised, make sure your money's ready before the cashiers close.'

'Knock yourself out,' Stone said.

When Mandi returned, she looked at Stone and handed him a beermat. He stared at it, flipped it over, and saw a phone number written in Biro on the back.

'Call us when you get to Kennedy, and we'll send the scarf back,' she told him.

'How do I know you're going to deliver?'

'You don't,' Mandi said flatly. 'But I run a national newspaper. I haven't got time to play games with people. You'd better give me the negatives.'

'But . . .'

'Your ticket'll be at Terminal Four Heathrow, British Airways. You go through Kennedy, LAX, through Fiji via Nadi, then on to Sydney. It's first-class all the way, and you can get off anywhere you want.'

'Where do I get my bank?' Stone repeated, as Mandi took the

negatives from him.

'It'll be in an envelope couriered over with the ticket. Don't worry, it'll be there.'

'But how do I . . .'

'Trust me,' Mandi said, squeezing his hand. 'It's been interesting to meet you, Stone. Call us whenever you get any more pictures. And – good luck.'

'You're losing your mind, Aitch,' Kettle scolded her as O'Brien slunk away. 'He's a self-confessed killer, and he knows where you live.'

'No,' Mandi contradicted him. 'Sometimes you've just got to have faith, give people a chance. He'll go to Heathrow tomorrow because he knows his tickets and money will be there waiting for him . . . and the Feds will pick him up when he disembarks in New York.'

'So who did you call at the Yard just now, then?'

She told him. Kettle nodded. He had introduced her to the guy, an old friend of his, when she'd been a cub reporter on *The Sun* more than ten years earlier.

'How much money would you say you won?' she asked him, looking down at the pile of chips. 'Five hundred quid?'

'About that . . .'

Mandi scooped them up into her purse.

'What's the big idea?'

Mandi reached into her pocket and placed the Cashbox Club cheque face up on the table next to a sealed, crumpled envelope. 'You've had your chips, Kettle,' she said, almost sadly.

Kettle ripped open the envelope. The letter was backdated to what must be ten days after he'd cashed Mandi's cheque at the Cashbox Club.

'I had faith,' she said, not looking at him. 'I trusted you. Gave you a second chance.'

'But . . .'

'Don't bother, Armistraud,' she said, using his Christian name for the first and last time. 'Don't say it. You've done it to yourself.'

'But . . .'

Mandi started to walk towards the door. Oh, yes, she thought to herself, you've always got a reason, haven't you? 'Some days, Kettle,' she said, spinning on her heels to face him, 'it's a dog-eat-dog world. And some days, it's the other way round . . .'

42

Toby stood alone on the little wooden bridge at the end of the path. He was wearing a Burberry trenchcoat and muddy brown brogues, and he was dropping sticks into the slow water below.

'Toby?' she said.

He looked up at her. But he didn't smile.

'I was worried . . .' she began, '. . . you sounded a bit funny on the phone. Is everything all right?'

On her way towards the bridge, as she negotiated a path through brambles and puddles, steep mounds and deep ditches, Mira's impatient anger towards her half-brother had abated, and had been replaced by puzzled bemusement. Ninety minutes earlier, she'd been bursting to tell him of her success with her Royal Abdication issue, which she had just despatched to the printers under Kremlinesque conditions of secrecy. Half an hour before, as she'd clambered up Brecken Hill, the memories had flooded back: of endless happy hours spent playing here with Toby when they were little, the beginning of a deep, unusual bond between half-siblings, a bond forged for life.

Her head had been buzzing with exciting plans to turn *The Times* around; with fantasies of her burgeoning bright career and even more beautiful future . . . but now instinct, a gut feeling, had filled Mira with misgivings, and with dread.

'No,' said Toby, looking up to face his heartbreakingly lovely half-sister. 'Everything's not all right.'

The wind had whipped her flowing red hair into a frenzy, and she struggled to pull it away from her pale face. As she did so, Mira saw a strange look in Toby's eyes, a look of such emotional intensity that she had never seen there before. It disturbed her.

'What is it, darling?' she said soothingly, reaching out to squeeze his wrist.

Toby looked away for a second, then turned to stare at her, his whole face filled with sorrow and dread. 'The results came back from the American Embassy lab,' he said coldly, as he struggled to keep control. But then his eyes overflowed with all the tears he had been too devastated to cry. 'I'm HIV-Positive.'

Mira was silent. She wanted to speak, but her words caught in her throat, almost choking her. 'What?' she whispered, finally.

'I am,' he said. 'So you are too.'

Mira turned away from him, not knowing how or what to feel. She leaned against the bridge's mossy wooden rail for support. She was aware only of a loud, rushing sound – the deep, cold water flowing way beneath her. She saw a bushy-tailed grey squirrel, its movements quick and nimble, darting to and fro along the branch of a lofty cedar tree on the opposite bank . . . the same tree beneath which the two children had acted out their innocently intimate doctors and nurses games ten years earlier. Same old tree, same swirly river rolling along between the same old banks. But it was a totally different world.

'Are you sure?' Mira whispered, at last.

Toby nodded, and dropped another twig aimlessly into the water. 'They've checked. They've double-checked. Twice. That was why I couldn't tell you before. Not until I was absolutely certain.'

Mira nodded. She was quiet for a minute. Then she said angrily: 'It was Gizelle, wasn't it?'

Toby was sniffing as he stared at her. 'Gizelle flew home last night, she needs some time . . . I've told her I want to go ahead with the wedding, but . . .' Toby started fumbling in his pocket for something. 'I don't think it was Gizelle, no,' he said.

Mira took the folded piece of paper he was offering her. It was a newspaper cutting. Mira immediately recognised an old photograph of Michael Orlando. 'It's from some trashy tabloid, you can't believe a word they say,' she stammered, her voice rising in pitch and volume. 'It's just filth and lies, you hear, lies, lies . . .'

'You had another fling with him last year, didn't you, Mira?

You went out to Tuscany and you stayed with him . . . You don't have to lie to me, I know . . .'

Mira's breathing was short and shallow. 'He must've known,' she said with a small sob. 'He must've known. He wanted to get back at me because of what happened to him . . .'

Mira burst into tears. Toby tried to comfort her, but she screamed at him, and began to pummel him on the arms with her fists, the way she had done when they were very young. Toby held her, rocking her gently in his arms.

43

'I heard a terribly interesting rumour at lunchtime,' Sir Anthony George murmured to the Prime Minister.

'Did you?' the PM replied.

'The contract printers for our Saturday supplement also print *Verve*,' Sir Anthony said. 'And I understand from a – source – that the forthcoming issue is quite explosive. The Editor, Mira Freer Farmer, has somehow got hold of details of the Abdication plan, Prime Minister, and has devoted the entire magazine to it. Not really cricket, is it? We've all known from the lobby that this has been in the works for some time. There was a gentleman's agreement to hold off on it until autumn, maintain a level playing field until we could prepare our readers before the story breaks officially next year. We've made substantial deposits into your personal favour bank, and . . .'

'I've obtained an injunction to stop you printing those pictures,' the Minister of Leisure hissed at Mandi Harry, ignoring the two burly men in blue suits standing like dobermans on either side of her.

'Pictures? What pictures?' Mandi asked sweetly, feigning innocence.

She had been button-holed in the narrow corridor on her way to the reception room where the Prime Minister was mingling with his guests. She noticed that Number Ten Downing Street's new pastel colour scheme had softened the more formal, strident decor favoured by some of its more thrusting previous inhabitants.

'You know bloody well what pictures I mean,' the attractive cabinet minister shot back. 'I can promise you this: they won't be appearing in that degrading porno rag of yours – not this month, next month, nor any time in the near future, I fancy.'

'Now, even if I did know which pictures you were talking about, why would that be?' enquired Mandi innocently.

'The vice squad went in this morning,' the minister replied with that winsome smile so popular with picture editors and directors of breakfast TV programmes. 'They seem to have got it into their heads that they've found a major child pornography ring operating from their offices.'

'The miracle of inter-departmental co-operation,' Mandi sighed, indicating to her minders with a silent gesture that it was time to make for the stairs. 'I like your hairdo,' Mandi added over her shoulder, putting significant distance between herself and the woman currently considered to be the Prime Minister's most dangerous rival, 'I didn't realise you were a natural blonde.'

'Well no, neither Ms Cox nor Ms Freer Farmer would be invited,' the PM's press secretary was explaining. 'You see, these functions are restricted to Editors of national newspapers, Lady George.'

'Actually, I go by my maiden name – Zelda Lee Powers.'

'Of course, I'm so sorry,' the press aide replied. He quickly covered his *faux pas* : 'Well, it may be that you'll attend our next little get-together in your own right.'

'Bet the farm,' Zelda said, lowering her voice. 'I got dossiers on these other broads. After this I'm going to pick up a document from Australia House, then the whole lot gets Fedexed to The Boss in LA on the last plane outtahere tonight. Once he's seen what's in that pack, those guys will be flipping burgers at MacDonalds.'

Zelda suddenly spotted a familiar figure entering the room. She glanced over the frames of her Christian Dior sunglasses, and stared disdainfully at Mandi Harry as she tried to ease past her. 'I don't believe it,' Zelda said. 'That's my scarf!'

Mandi turned round to face her. 'This is?' she said, indicating the exotic silk square knotted around her neck.

'I got it at a show four years ago,' Zelda snarled, '. . . how the hell did YOU . . .'

'Zelda Lee Powers?' said one of the burly blue-suited men. With one deft flick of the wrist he discreetly flashed a badge. 'Field Agent David Hughes, FBI, Ma'am. We have a warrant for your arrest in connection with criminal libel . . .'

Frantically, Zelda looked around. She couldn't see her husband anywhere.

Mandi was untying the scarf, which she now handed over to Hughes's partner. 'You'll be wanting this as evidence,' she said, 'if you're going to make the murder rap stick.'

'You have the right to remain silent . . . but anything you say can and will be taken down and may be given in evidence in a Court of Law . . . You have the right to a . . .' Agent Hughes recited the familiar litany.

'Tony!' Zelda screeched. The awful sound pierced the elegant humming of low, refined voices in the room.

'TONIIIIII!'

The murmuring ceased.

All eyes were suddenly on Sir Anthony George, including those of the astonished Prime Minister, who was standing right beside him.

Anthony looked uncomfortable, but managed to force a limp smile.

'Would you excuse me for a moment please, Prime Minister,' he said graciously.

'Don't you push me, goddamn it!' Zelda barked, struggling with the handcuffs digging into her thin wrists as the blue-suited men bundled her out into the corridor. 'Tony! Jeez, get these goons off me, you can't DO this!'

'Hold on, hold on a moment there,' Anthony said, coming up behind them. 'I'm Sir Anthony George, Editor of the *Daily Sketch*. This happens to be my wife. What the hell do you think you're doing?'

'My job, Sir,' Agent Hughes replied calmly. 'Your wife is under arrest for criminal libel. The Bureau, in the course of an ongoing investigation, may or may not press further charges . . .'

'What exactly might those be?' Sir Anthony asked, aware that Mandi was watching them from the drawing-room. 'You can't possibly arrest my wife here. Do you realise where you are? This is preposterous.'

'Sir, as I explained to the, uh, bobbies, downstairs, we are acting on information received in confidence from your Scotland Yard. The Bureau's jurisdiction extends beyond United States borders. In special cases it supersedes formal extradition treaties with nations such as your own. Sir, on behalf of the President and Government of the United States of America we are empowered to apprehend criminal suspects wherever we find them . . .'

'It's that Harry bitch,' Zelda spat, squirming. 'Just look at her gloating . . . well, you'll soon be gloating on the other side of your ugly mug, you squat little turnip-faced toad . . .' Zelda continued to struggle with the FBI men. 'She knows I've found the kid she dumped when she was a teenager . . . and she'll do anything to cover it up . . . I've got the goods on ALL of them, Tony, I was going to tell you tonight after I'd sent the dossier . . .'

'Where are you taking her?' enquired Sir Anthony.

'Well, Sir, there's an 18:30 American Airlines connection out of Gatwick non-stop to JFK. Our instructions are to accompany Ms Powers to the Metropolitan Correctional Centre in Manhattan, where she'll be processed prior to arraignment in the New York State Supreme Court tomorrow morning.'

'It's a set-up, Tony,' Zelda was still howling, '. . . it's a conspiracy, I'm warning you, these people are all in it together . . . I can prove it, I got VT showing Freer Farmer making it with Brett Collins, BRETT, they have ORGIES! They are drunks, sex addicts, substance abusers . . .'

'Can't you just wait a minute?' reasoned Sir Anthony, who had never been so embarrassed in his life, '. . . this is a nightmare . . . please, hold on. I'm in the middle of a very sensitive discussion with the Prime Minister about a major constitutional crisis. Will you please just wait for one minute?'

'Sorry, Sir, no can do,' said Agent Hughes. 'We've got a plane to catch.'

'I demand to see a warrant!' Sir Anthony insisted.

Agent Hughes flashed a piece of paper in his face.

They took Zelda away.

'Where can I get in touch with . . .'

'Call the MCC in Manhattan,' Hughes's partner said as they dragged Zelda down the stairs. 'They'll explain how to make bail.'

Zelda, meanwhile, was still shouting at the top of her voice, '. . . and Kiki Cox? Ha Ha Ha, Kiki Cox, Ha Ha Ha Ha . . .'

Enthralled by the spectacle, and longing for a shutterbug to be lurking out there on Downing Street to capture the caper for Sunday's edition, Mandi stuck her head out of a first-floor window to try and catch what Zelda was saying.

'. . . Kiki Cox isn't REAL at ALL . . . she's not Kiki Cox, she's . . .'

But Zelda was already belted into the backseat of a black saloon, on her way to a court date.

44

'Editors in their underpants!' drawled Dermott Chalmers, doing his swansong stand-up to camera for what was to prove the final edition of *Inside Media*. 'Oh, all right then . . . one or two Editors and many of their minions in their swimming trunks. We're at the annual INI-sponsored Editors' charity swimming gala, where International News Europe's maverick, debonair CEO Brett Collins is about to announce the name of the first ever female editor of *The Times* . . .

'For the candidates here poolside within the swank surroundings of London's RAC Club, this afternoon isn't just about winning . . .' here, Chalmers leered knowingly at the camera. '. . . It's about losing, too . . .'

'I can't swim this afternoon I'm afraid,' insisted Kiki, out of shot behind Chalmers, to one of the stewards.

'But this'll completely ruin the rota. Couldn't you just take a little dip? What's the problem?'

'It's quite out of the question,' Kiki said. 'Personal reasons.'

'Personal reasons? Like what?'

'I don't wish to discuss it,' Kiki said. 'It's personal.'

'Why can't you tell me? Is it a state secret?'

Kiki rolled her eyes.

'If you must know, I'm having my period . . .'

'I'll do the swim for you,' Duncan Campbell's secretary Hanni volunteered, jogging up to them.

'Good,' said the organiser, with a sigh of relief and a snarky glance at Kiki,

'If you come with me, I think we can get the club to sort you out a costume . . .'

'Hey, Cold Type – got any space for a Hot Metal slug in your case?'

'Anthony,' Mandi smiled. 'Great to see you. I didn't think that, well, after what happened, you'd want to, you know . . .'

'Don't be daft,' he said, giving her an affectionate squeeze, and a kiss that lingered a little too long to pass as purely professional or between Just Good Friends . . . just long enough to remind Mandi that there was a hole in her heart the size of Lake Erie, and that something ought to be filling it . . .

'Loved your spread this morning – I thought running those topless smudges of Zelda was a stroke of genius.'

'Best to make a clean breast of things,' Anthony quipped. 'In fact, I'm trying to encourage some other figures in pubic life to write follow-up first-person pieces about their secret shame.'

'Oh yeah? How's it going?'

'Rather disappointing so far, I'm afraid,' he confessed.

She knew what he meant.

'They tried to do it gently,' Mandi said, 'but Zelda would insist on screaming her bloody head off . . .'

Behind them, the tournament was beginning to wind down.

'I feel very bad about it all,' she admitted to him.

'You do? I'm now in the precarious position of having to remortgage my house to raise bail for her, or be branded a world-class rat for deserting my wife in her hour of need.'

'She did it,' Mandi shrugged. 'Don't you . . .'

'Oh yes. Your piece on Sunday convinced me she did it, all right. Her and that little shit of a son of hers. D'you know, from the first time I set eyes on him the day we were married I didn't like the cut of his jib one little bit. Kids today are so bloody unimaginative. Now when I was Stone's age, I'd . . .'

'Have you seen *Verve*?' Mandi interrupted him.

'Yes,' Anthony replied. 'Rather spiked your guns, I'm afraid, hasn't she?'

'I thought that showed so well, our Sunday splash,' Mandi said, 'the ambiguity over his sexuality, it was so easy – and the way we fudged Ethiopia . . . on the one hand, she was another victim of the poverty trap, and on the other a conniving little vixen . . .'

'Yes,' nodded Sir Anthony, making his thinking noise. 'You didn't overplay it, no rancid clichés about Ethiopia's "Black Heart" . . .'

'. . . her "Dark Secret", "Heart of Darkness", . . . I practically had to break Worell's arms to stop him going with that one.'

'The fact she was black seemed almost incidental in the end,' Anthony said. 'I don't know how you cope with the Wapping Wharf Thought Police . . . Mandi?'

But Mandi was gone from his side. He spotted her in the distance, making for the swimming pool like some pre-programmed somnambulist. Something had caught her eye . . .

. . . a bell-shaped birthmark on a young girl's bottom . . .

Mandi knelt down, regardless of the chlorine puddles, and helped the swimmer out of the pool . . . Their eyes met, and a weird moment of recognition passed between them.

'Thanks,' said the girl in the red bathing suit. Mandi tried to find words. She opened her mouth to speak, but nothing at all came out.

Something was going on at the far end of the pool. People were turning round and grouping into a surging crowd. The noise in the room changed . . . the laughter was louder, the speech was softer, there was a buzz.

Sir Anthony George was shaking someone's hand, but it was hard to tell whose, because Duncan Campbell was standing in the way – just one of the milling mob moving towards her.

Mandi heard someone announce: 'It's Brett Collins . . . he's here!'

She scanned the crowd frantically, searching for the girl in the red swimsuit. But she had disappeared.

Brett Collins stepped up to the podium at the poolside. All eyes were on him. Only the gentle lapping of water against tile broke the silence. 'My Uncle has asked me to make a statement,' Brett said.

45

Among the rows of neatly parked Ford Fiestas, once-hot hatchbacks and Volvo estate cars, one vehicle stood out.

It was black. The bonnet had been torn away, revealing the dirty metal of the engine underneath. The off-side wing had vanished, leaving the wheel assembly open to the elements. The surrounding panel had crumpled, the rear bumper had been stolen, the back windscreen shattered, and its tail lights smashed. A gaping envy-scratch ran the length of the passenger door and the moon-roof had jammed wide open. The Cosworth Vendetta's bodywork was filthy, and oil leaked from its engine into a dark, rainbow-hued slick that spread on the tarmac.

Inside the shopping mall, Mira looked around. She saw polished stone, shiny tile, reflective chrome and gleaming brass. From her third-floor vista the mall felt endlessly textured: lifts enclosed in tubes of glass, neon lighting, bridges, balconies, gas lamps, vaulted skylights, all enclosing the people ambling in an endless promenade.

Young mothers with buggies and grandmas and brothers and sisters came and went, in and out of Marks and Spencers and British Home Stores and C & A. Everyone seemed to be buying shoes, everyone seemed to be eating and everyone clutched 'bargains' in thin plastic carrier bags. Kids played with primary-coloured footballs in a specially designated area, like figures in an architect's model, under the watchful gaze of uniformed supervisors near the fountain. The mall was alive with the sound of Muzak: it wafted through the shops selling Must-Have things she had never known she needed: desk putting sets; unique collections of seven-inch floral hats manufactured from the finest English bone china, and painstakingly hand-painted by the craftsmen of The Gridlington Mint, Seoul; sealed jars of Pearl Cream, ground from the jewels of the sea, the secret of the ageless beauties of the Orient . . .

Mira watched the young people darting in and out of the wide-fronted stores; saw a woman smack a crying, snot-nosed toddler covered in ice-cream in Clarks shoe shop; noticed a couple holding hands as they gazed at value-for-money sapphire and diamond engagement rings in the window of H. Samuel, Britain's Largest Jewellers.

'I used to despise these people,' she said quietly, '. . . the riff-raff element. Hell, that was if I could ever be bothered to think about them . . . They were never individuals . . . just lumpenproles . . . and God, how bloody snotty I've been about their bourgeois little lives, with their takeaways and their leftovers, and their joke mothers-in-law who read *Woman* and *Woman's Own* in the bath and on the bus; their Fly-Mos and their shellsuits and the boot sales they cart the contents of their lofts and garages to, and the eight-year-old cars they wash by hand every weekend . . .'

'And now?' Mico asked his wife.

'I envy them. God, I envy them. Do you realise how lucky they are, to be able to worry about their kids catching the lurgi at school, about stretching out their paypackets to cover the gas bill, about how lovely it'll be to get home tonight and put their feet up with a nice cuppa tea in front of the telly, to sit down and watch *Eastenders* over a plate of cod and chips and then go for a nice Radox bath? No . . . of course not.'

Mira blew her nose on a crumpled, blood-streaked Kleenex, and chucked it.

'I had so much more, didn't I? But you get caught up in it, you see. We're the only animals that can rear up on our hind legs and look at ourselves in the mirror, be aware of what we are . . . but we don't, do we? We can't really see ourselves through our own eyes . . . We may think we know who we are, what we're capable of . . . but until I knew I was going to die, I didn't really know what it was to live . . .'

She stopped in the Atrium beside a sculpture of a rampant white horse. Behind her, water was cascading from a gaping ornamental gargoyle in the glass roof. Mira thought of her father, who'd been in a bar in the Philippines staffed entirely by dwarfs when it was buried by an avalanche . . .

'The only thing, the only true thing I know is . . .'

'Shit!' Mico exclaimed, staring at his camcorder.

'Is out of tape. Hold on, I'll go back up Tower Records, buy more.'

Mira watched as her husband ascended the down escalator by leaps and bounds, until he had disappeared.

She hated goodbyes . . .

She dropped the car keys into a Manila envelope addressed to Peter Watson, Cosworth's, and popped it into a gleaming brass postbox set into the wall nearby. On impulse, she wandered into a travel agency.

'I'd like a one-way ticket, first-class, to Port-au-Prince. I want to fly as soon as possible.'

The clerk, who was good on Malaga and Benidorm and a dab-hand at EuroDisney, but who didn't even know where Port-au-Prince was, didn't bat an eyelid. 'How many people will be travelling?' she enquired in her desk voice, cucumber-cool.

'Just the one,' Mira replied. 'There are some journeys that are best made alone, don't you think?'

46

'M y Uncle has asked me to make a statement,' Brett said, the brisk, all-business clip of his tone betrayed only by the upward tilt on the last syllable.

He referred to his clipboard.

'International News Incorporated and its subsidiaries are firmly committed to diversity in the workplace,' Brett read. 'And we actively encourage the appointment of women, people of ethnic origin, the physically challenged and those of alternative sexual preference, for senior positions within our corporation. My decision to promote an experienced female to edit *The Times*, our flagship title, reflects the strength of that commitment. The extremely high calibre and all-round excellence of each of those I considered for the position has reinforced my faith in the consummate professionalism and superior expertise that women bring, every day, all over the world, to the workplace . . .'

Brett looked up from his clipboard for a moment. 'On a personal note,' he said, his voice relaxed, 'I'd just like to add that I foresee a time in the not-too-distant future when women will comprise half of every government instead of three per cent . . .'

'Pass the sickbag,' Sir Anthony George muttered.

'. . . when their earnings will match those of their male counterparts – and when the male of the species will fully comprehend that the global conspiracy to cripple female power damages them in the long run as much as it does the women themselves . . .'

Brett looked around for the approval he felt sure he was winning, and beamed. There was a light, polite ripple of applause.

'. . . So before I, as it were, open the old envelope, I'd just like to say, Good On Yer, Girls. Your presentations were real beauts.

All seriousness aside . . . the winner is . . .'

At that moment, a mobile phone trilled its shrill summons.

'. . . I mean, the new Editor of *The Times* is . . . aw, shit.'

Brr Brrr. Brr Brrr. Brr Brrr.

Brett turned away from the podium: it could only be one person. 'Hello . . . Uncle Ruprecht? Sorry, mate,' he whispered, '. . . it's difficult, I'm just about to announce . . . no, I haven't, Mira Freer Farmer's disappeared off the face of the bloody earth. I called up to offer her the job and her assistant told me she'd gone overseas indefinitely. Haiti? Well, I think there'd be a few bloody problems trying to put the paper out from there . . .

'What? She told you that herself? Jesus. Oh, Jesus Christ. No, mate, no . . . why should I be worried? It does stuff my bloody speech up a bit, though, but that's . . . wait a minute, what's Auntie Tina's return from her little European junket got to do with . . . Oh. Oh. Yes . . . I see. There's just one slight dag in the Vegemite there, mate – Zelda Lee Powers was arrested yesterday at Number Ten Downing Street. Yeah, the Prime Minister's gaff. Well, it was too late for edition, and . . . no, I don't think so. Seems like it's criminal libel, so the men in shiny buttons turned up with a pair of silver bracelets and . . .

'What? Murder? Oh flaming hell, this is turning into a bloody nightmare . . . what am I going to tell them, then?

'. . . What do you . . . OK. OK. Yeah, I'll do it. Love to Auntie Tina.'

Brett folded the phone and slipped it back into his pocket. Then he remounted the podium, drew himself up to his full height, and took a deep breath.

'I am pleased to announce that the next Editor of *The Times* will be . . .'

Brett scanned the crowd. Mandi Harry was nowhere to be seen . . .

'Kiki Cox.'

The chic Australian's porcelain face remained totally impassive. Only the closest observer would have noticed the pinpoints of excitement in her shark-cold eyes, the delighted smile that hovered over her luscious, pencilled-in lips . . .

Mandi sat on a damp wooden bench in the changing-rooms. The girl in the red swimsuit, the one she had helped from the pool – the one with the bell-shaped birthmark on her bottom – was uncomfortably aware that this woman was staring at her.

She snapped off the wall-mounted hairdryer and turned to face Mandi. 'What do you want?' she flared.

'I know this is going to sound barmy . . .' Mandi began slowly, '. . . but I am your mother.'

'I know you are,' said Hanni in a small voice.

Mandi walked over to her, and caressed Hanni's flushed cheek with the back of her chubby hand. 'My baby . . .'

They embraced. They were still crying when Hanni pulled away suddenly. 'How could you do it? How could you give me away? I've been looking for you all my life.' She held her mother's gaze: 'Now that I've found you, I wish you were dead.'

Hanni grabbed her clothes, stuffed them into a black hold-all which she slung over her shoulder, and ran, before Mandi could stop her, across the pool area and out through the reception rooms, pushing her way through the animated throng and making for the main foyer.

The first thing that went through Mandi's mind was: please, don't go outside, your hair's still wet and you will catch your death of cold . . .

Mandi raced after her, but Hanni was younger, stronger and much, much fitter. Mandi saw her running towards the main road, barefoot, still wearing nothing but the borrowed red swimsuit.

The Piccadilly traffic pulled up short in a ragged line, brakes squealing, as the near-naked Lady In Red sprinted across the road as if to make for the park. Mandi stood in the middle of the traffic, oblivious to the irate gestures of drivers and the deafening roar of their honking horns as her daughter disappeared down the underpass. Dazed and devastated, she wandered back into the club.

'Who was that girl in the red swimsuit?' Mandi asked Duncan Campbell, still panting from her ordeal. 'My secretary,' he replied, 'Hannah Slynn. She's an excellent PA . . . Kiki Cox cried off games, so Hanni swam for her. Why do you ask?'

But before Mandi could answer, Kiki Cox was in her face. 'No hard feelings, Mandi,' she said with a smile, extending her hand.

'Of course not. Congratulations,' Mandi replied, through gritted teeth. Her own smile was on autopilot, her mind elsewhere, still out there, somewhere in the traffic. 'We must have lunch when you're settled, we're going to be neighbours and colleagues at Wapping Wharf,' said Mandi brightly. 'So you must let me give you a guided tour of the zoo some time. I suppose you'll be making some changes?'

'Starting first thing Monday,' Kiki nodded. 'And I see you as part of them.'

Kiki cast an eye all around her. It was that reflexive Editor's movement: Who's watching? Who's waiting? Can we talk?

'Duncan Campbell's getting his walking papers this afternoon,' Kiki confided, '. . . so the deputy slot's wide open. I need a top gun number two. You fought a ripping campaign, and you've certainly earned my respect. Harry, you're the best man for the job', said Kiki briskly. 'So what do you say?'

'I'll call you at home before midnight. Give me your number. Why don't we discuss how we could make it work,' Mandi said. 'I need a couple of hours just to think.'

And, she thought to herself, to find her baby again . . .

47

Of course, Mandi had gone back to the office after the reception and checked it out. She'd called two reporters off the I'm Having Julian Clary's Baby stakeout, and tumbled three more hacks from their beds to call in favours from Australia and discover why there weren't any records of Kiki Cox.

Zelda's hypothesis had been that Kiki Cox didn't exist because there were no traces of such a person – officially. Kiki Cox had deposited none of the footprints an individual should leave as she moves through life: birth certificate, health and schooling records, driving licence, credit reports. Mandi was surprised that Zelda's ambition had blinded her to the obvious, logical solution. The reason was simple.

Mandi had thought about it over the weekend, as she tried to work out why Kiki had changed her name. Eventually, she'd come to the conclusion that maybe Noleen Cox hadn't enjoyed a lot of luck in the lunchbox department. Perhaps she'd been teased at school and eventually it had become a self-fulfilling prophecy: No Cox. That was how Mandi had solved it before she went to bed on Sunday night.

When her car pulled up outside Mandolin to collect her at 6:45 a.m. on Monday, Mandi's first thought was that this was a big mistake. 'Ronnie . . . what happened to the car?' she said, getting in. 'Did it shrink in the rain?'

Ronnie chuckled softly. 'On Saturday you were editing the *Sunday Post*, right?'

'Yeah . . .'

'So you got a Jag. But today, you're deputy editor of *The Times* . . .'

'. . . So I get a crap green Rover,' Mandi nodded with a wry grin.

By the time she reached Wapping Wharf, it had got worse. Kiki Cox, keen to impress her no-nonsense regime upon her new staff, had called conference three hours early, thus making Mandi late. Not that it made much difference to her contribution.

From Kiki's office wafted the heady scent of hyacinths, pink, blue and white, planted six-deep in a vast basket, spilling spirals of white ribbon, parked on the corner of her desk. As Mandi stepped in to face her Editor, she found herself picking her way through a colourful forest. Tall vases brimming with orange tiger lilies, yellow roses, blue delphiniums, pink carnations, jostled for space across the rich green, brand new carpet between the door and Kiki's desk. They gave the otherwise stark office the air of some exotic hot-house, or an expensive florist's shop. Greetings cards, hastily opened and discarded along with the envelopes which had borne them, lay in neat piles on the coffee table. Mandi's nose twitched with all the heavy scent and pollen, and she rubbed at it. Looking around, she noticed a collection of sickeningly pristine, just-back-from-the-dry-cleaners' designer suits wrapped in polythene and hanging, ever-ready, on a hook behind the Editor's door.

'You're late,' barked Kiki, her eyes flicking upward.

Workmen were painting the wall behind the Editor's chair where Kiki now sat, taking notes with a Mont Blanc fountain pen which she grasped in her perfect, silky white hand. Watchful, attentive, absorbing every detail, drawing her staff out, reeling them in, never committing herself, nodding, smiling scanning, probing . . .

The atmosphere was a little more formal than Mandi was used to, the staff's wit a little drier . . . but the subject matter was utterly obtuse. *The Times* men – and they were mostly men, Mandi noted – talked not so much to contribute, nor to move the discussion along, but simply to monopolize attention with grandstanding showcases of erudition on esoteric topics. Kiki sat, smiling and nodding, and at last, dismissed them.

'It's like listening to Oxford Dons on acid,' Mandi thought as she tottered back to her office. 'How the hell we're ever going to get a paper out tonight, I'll never know.'

304

Inside her office they were boxing up the sporting prints and computer peripherals. 'Where are you taking all this stuff?' she asked.

Of course . . . Duncan Campbell . . . he would have a grip on things. He'd know the ropes . . .

Maybe she'd have lunch with him, Mandi thought. Sure, he might be a bit prickly at first, he had good reason to be. But he, of all people, would recognise that newspapers have an autonomous life all their own, which transcends any individual and every crisis. If she could find him – perhaps he was at home – she could build some bridges, get a few pointers, establish the infrastructure for getting Kiki out of that office . . .

'This stuff? Downstairs, love,' one of the removal men replied.

Mandi went into the secretaries' office that separated her own from Kiki's. 'Does anyone know where Duncan Campbell is?'

The girls all looked at each other nervously. One or two of them began to blub. Another took a swig from a bottle of Marks and Spencers Claret. Mandi sensed an awful tension. She was about to ask the question again when Joan Winterbloom looked up from her paperwork. 'Mr Campbell committed suicide yesterday morning,' she said, with a small, controlled sob.

'Oh, my God . . . How?'

The senior secretary stared over the heavy frames of her spectacles, her grey bun quivering. 'He shot himself . . . in the mouth . . .'

'Oh God, how awful . . .' Mandi managed to say.

'This might actually be a good moment to introduce you to the team,' came a bright Sloanie voice from a sun-tanned girl standing right behind her. 'That's Joan Winterbloom – she works for the Editor.'

Joan Winterbloom dabbed at her tears with a stiffly ironed lace handkerchief, and acknowledged Mandi.

'And I'm Katherine Ewart. It's nice to meet you, Mrs Harry.'

'Good morning, Mrs Harry', said a disembodied voice, 'I'm looking forward to working with you'.

Mandi looked around and finally saw Alice, the shortest

secretary at Wapping Wharf. 'Katherine will be doing a lot of your work next week, because I'm on holiday.'

Mandi politely asked where. Alice said she was going skiing.

At that moment, Hanni came in with a tray of coffees.

She stared at Mandi.

Mandi stared back . . .

'Hello, Mum,' she said.

'You think you can just bring people in and out of your life like characters from some crap Mills and Boon romance, or the reporters on your paper? You're dreaming, Mother . . . you can't treat people like that and get away with it. How do you think I feel? How do you think . . .'

Mandi sat motionless, saying nothing.

'How do you think I feel?'

'I don't know,' Mandi admitted. 'That was why I thought we should have lunch, I want to . . . get it all out, out in the open.'

'It's out in the open all right.'

'You've got every right to be angry.'

'You bet I have,' Hanni flared. 'And you've got no right to patronise me.'

'I'm not patronising . . .'

'You've ruined my life.'

'I gave you your life.'

'Yeah, thanks. Thanks a lot.'

The waiter cleared away their coffee cups. Mandi handed him her Visa card. Beyond the restaurant's picture window flowed the Thames, propelling boats with places to go on its powerful current.

'You didn't give me any of you, did you? What did you give me?'

'I gave you a chance'.

'Oh yeah? The chance to become a fully qualified juvenile delinquent.' Mandi was going to say something, but Hanni cut in. 'Nothing. No support, no love, nothing. You were never there for me. When I cried, you weren't there to tell me it was all right.

When I fell over, you weren't there to kiss it better. When I had my first modelling pictures published, you weren't there to look at them and say, "Well done, Hanni, you look great." When I was in trouble at home with the police, where were you? Why? Why? Why did you give me away?'

'It was 20 years ago,' said Mandi quietly. 'People were different then. Life was different then. Everyone had old-fashioned values. Nowadays, for example, no one looks twice at a black guy and a white girl together, more the merrier. But back then mixed marriages were strictly taboo, especially in a place like Gravesend. It was unthinkable, Hanni, unthinkable.

'I would have been a single mum. Gymslip Mums, we used to call them. What kind of life could I have given you? I gave you away to give you a better chance.'

'Women have babies on their own all the time,' Hanni said angrily.

'They didn't then. It was different . . .'

'It was your choice. And what you chose was to dump me. Excess baggage. Too much weight around your neck, too much hassle to have a little kid when you had your eye on a glittering career. You could have given me love. You could have given me your time. You could have given me you. You, a mother, my mother. You could have been there, but you weren't. That was what you chose.'

'I just couldn't see any way I was going to make it, Hanni, you must see that. I was a schoolgirl, I was six years younger than you are now, for Christ's sake. My Mum and Dad were very strict, Hanni, they made me put you up for adoption . . . they pushed me, they made me do it, what would the neighbours say . . . They went on and on and on, it was all about how it would look for them. My feelings never came into it. I was weak, I was young and naïve. I had no choice but to give in to them. You don't know how much it hurts. I've never got over it, something inside me died the day I gave you away, and it never came alive again. Until now.'

'But I was too young to have any say in it at all. I was just a baby. My feelings didn't matter.'

'You're angry, you're hurting, you've every right, but I'm

hurting too . . . even though it's myself I'm angry at,' Mandi said.

'Sometimes, Hanni, in your life, maybe someone you love very much . . . maybe someone you love will depend on you for something. They'll be looking to you, and be counting on you and relying on you to come through, to be there for them. But you won't be able to do it. You just can't give it to them, and you can't give it to them because you haven't got it to give. Do you know what that's like? Look . . . I'm not asking you to forgive me, Hanni, I just want you to try and understand.'

'To understand? I should understand? I think you should try and understand what it's like to grow up without a Mum and Dad. Try to imagine how I'd try and imagine what you looked like sometimes, where you were, what you were like, what you were doing. What you felt like, what you smelt like . . . I used to push myself right inside my pillow case every night in my sleep, just as if you were tucked away inside it . . . when I was older I stopped pretending that you'd ever come for me, even though a bit of me always wanted you to turn up and rescue me, like you were a millionaire in a movie or something. I used to sit there in my room at night and read under the bedclothes, all these fantastic stories. I'd pretend my Dad was Keith Richards and my Mum was a beautiful Princess.'

'Better late than never,' Mandi said. 'But I'm sorry if you're disappointed.'

'It's not that kind of disappointment,' Hanni sighed. 'You think I believe in happy-ever-after endings? No, it's not like that. It's – how could you work at the *Post* and write all that crap about single mothers?'

'I don't make the rules,' Mandi said, 'I just play by them.'

'Oh come on, now you're gonna tell me you were just doing your job . . . writing all that bullshit about dole scroungers and mums who get knocked up just to jump the housing queues . . . you're doing The Boss's dirty work. No, you're not making the rules, it's worse than that: you're just the peon who enforces them. That's why I'm disappointed, Mum, finding out what sort of person you really are. I'd rather you cleaned toilets.'

'You work for International News too . . .'

'So what are my options? What choices did you give me?'

'I can't help who I am, Hanni. It's too late for me to change. I'm not apologising for what I do. I just do what I have to, do whatever it takes to get me through the day.'

'You're so full of shit. You're lying to yourself. You're lying to me. You screw everything up and you ignore the pain and crap and you tell yourself it's OK. The world's falling to bits around our ears but people like you go: "No – everything's great!" You just wrap yourselves in bigger cars and more shopping and longer holidays and weekends at Champney's and you say, "Yeah, I'm a survivor", like you're really proud of it. You should take a look at yourself, Mum. A long, hard look. You should feel guilty, you've got plenty to feel guilty about. You spend your life dumping on people and making their lives hell, like you've got the right to judge them because you're so much better? Look at your life . . . look at my life . . . look at the bloody mess you've made of everything.'

'I only did what I thought was the best thing at the time.'

'And who do you think has to clear it up? Oh, what do you care? You might think you care, but you don't really. Why should you . . . you've had your fun? You'll get away on your freebies to Florida, or Jamaica, and you'll get your new car every year, and your new clothes . . . and when you're 60 you'll get a nice fat pension, paid for by me working myself into the ground for three hundred quid a week until I drop. But so what? It's OK for you, isn't it? That's all that matters . . . you've had yours.'

'But I do care, Hanni, I do. What do you want? What can I give you?'

'I don't want anything from you – Mother. Nothing. You're a fraud.'

'Maybe you're right,' said Mandi quietly. 'But that's the way I am. What can I do? I don't know what to do.'

'Nothing. There's nothing you can do. Neither of us . . . it's happened. We're going to see each other every day . . . I'm going to be working for you, for God's sake . . .'

'I could get you transferred . . .'

'Oh, don't go doing me any favours. Why should I change

jobs? I've had to fight for everything I've got, and I got it on my own. I've been doing fine now for 23 years thank you very much, so why should I change everything just to fit in with you, stop you feeling guilty?'

Mandi felt a sudden pang of empathy with Zelda. Not regret about what she had done to expose her: that was business, another fab kill in the universe of media pollution, fake information and toxic hype . . .

No, it underlined how difficult it was to be a woman. Any woman. How demanding it was to reconcile the home-maker with the home-wrecker, the hard-edged career cappo with saintly motherhood . . . it was like attending a dinner where all your multiple roles and personalities turned up in their own right and began gossiping with each other, and you had to play the mediating Mistress of Ceremonies, lubricating the event like a mechanic, keeping all the balls in the air like some scented juggler, watching the clock like a short-order cook in a dead-end town, as short-fused guests became tiresome and querulous, conscious of time running through your fingers like sand, and the food getting colder, and wondering who's on next . . . Oh, it's me again. And again. And again . . . And you could never stop, never let yourself go, not for a moment, because you knew that if you did, you'd break down, and once you started crying, the tears would never stop . . .

'Anything I say, it's going to be wrong,' said Mandi at last, looking out at the river. 'Anything I do . . .'

'Was that why you really came here?'

'You don't think it's the lure of all the fun I'm to have working for the Ice Maiden, do you?'

'I wish I could believe you. I want to believe you.'

'Say you'll try . . . even if you can never love me. Even though you may never like me very much. Please just say you'll try.'

'We don't know each other,' Hanni said dismissively, as the waiter brought their bill and Mandi signed it without checking. 'Not at all. We're starting from scratch.'

'So help me get it right this time. Please. Even though you're angry and upset, perhaps I can help you in future. I don't want to interfere, but if you want something and I can give it to you, tell me. Oh shit,' she said, looking at her Fendi watch and rising from the table, 'I've got to get back and put this Korean advertorial to bed. Will you come back with me?'

'Talk about being thrown in at the shallow end,' Hanni said.

'There are some tricky colour plates,' Mandi said as a woman helped them on with their coats. 'But you're right – it's just a production job really. You know, I can't understand why Kiki hired me at all. Perhaps she thinks I've got something on her.'

'I can't understand why you left the *Post*,' Hanni said, as they left the restaurant. For the first time in a long time, she noticed, the sky was streaked with blue. 'I mean, it's not setting the Thames on fire, is it? But in terms of crap, it's classy crap. And at least you were your own boss.'

'You never are, working for INI. There's always someone with their foot on your neck and their nose up The Boss's crack.'

They walked in silence for a minute, back towards Tower Bridge.

'What I think,' Mandi said, 'is that Kiki wants me inside the tent pissing out rather than outside pissing in. She needs me as her friend because she doesn't want me for an enemy. If things go wrong while she's learning the ropes, I'm the scapegoat. She can blame me for absolutely everything, and then she can throw me to the wolves.'

'You should try and get close to Brett,' Hanni said.

Mandi stared at her as they walked along, as if seeing her for the first time. 'Perhaps that's not such bad advice,' she said. 'Where did you pick that one up – on the secretaries' network?'

'We know everything.'

'Yeah, don't I know it,' Mandi said. 'Do you like it? Being a PA?'

'It's OK,' her daughter replied, slipping on her sunglasses as the sun came out. 'Mind you, it's not what I want to do for the rest of my life. Joan Winterbloom made me realise that. Not for me. Maybe I should travel, see a bit of the world . . .'

Mandi was just about to say 'I'll give you the money', when she thought better of it. Listen she told herself. Just listen.

'I've got a kind of yearning, I want to have what I've never had. I want to feel what I'm afraid to feel. I want to see what's on the other side of the door . . .'

'You said you liked stories . . . maybe you should think about doing some hacking.'

'Journalism? Where would I start?'

'Local paper, like everyone else.'

'I don't know . . .'

'It's all up for grabs. This Abdication doo-dah is a great example of how chaotic everything is at the centre, where news happens. If you can thrive on chaos, live with that degree of uncertainty in your life, you're halfway there. You're working in the right sort of environment, you're in a good position there, a lot of secretaries go over. So start writing . . .'

'Yeah, bits of stuff about street fashion, or subbing aftershave supplements for Weekend City pull-outs . . . no, that's not me either, Mum, I want to be in the thick of it, you know, hard news . . .'

'It takes time,' Mandi said honestly,

'But you never know. One thing being in this game has taught me is that the more you know, the more you realise there is to learn. If you're on the ball, sometimes stories can just pop up.'

'Well, my contacts book is growing by the minute.'

'That's half the battle,' Mandi said. 'You're only as good as your phone numbers.'

'Sir Anthony helped me there. He encouraged me . . .'

'Like mother like daughter,' Mandi said with a wry laugh.

Hanni looked at her. She badly wanted to smile, but she couldn't quite manage it. If only her mother knew . . .

Her mother's look told Hanni she did.

'What you need,' Mandi said, brisk as a Brown Owl, changing the subject, 'is to break a really big story. A scoop and a half, something inside, and hot, that every other Editor will notice you for. They'll start asking "Who is this Hanni Slynn?" That's a great period, when you're on the cusp of success . . . you don't have to worry about staying up there, you're just into The Life . . . everyone being nice to you, your writing getting better and better, people paying you to interview celebrities you would have given your gums to meet anyway, and throwing presents at you like there's no tomorrow. Living the life . . . it's brilliant, Hanni. It really is.'

'So I need a scoop.'

'You and a hundred thousand grubby hacks,' Mandi grinned. 'But at least you have one thing going for you.'

'What's that?'

'Me.'

'What?'

'I'm on your side. Now,' she said, as they stepped out of the fifth-floor lift and made their way towards the executive suites, 'let Mummy treat you to a session in the Editor's bathroom. No, Hanni, I insist . . . my treat.'

48

When they returned from the hospital on Elizabeth Street, her mother had told her to sit down in the kitchen.

So she waited at the small wooden table in the corner of the dark room, looking out of the window through the pink gingham curtains at a crack of blue sky and a strip of yellow grass outside. She listened to the flies buzzing, waiting for one of them to get caught on the thin plaster strip that hung from the light in the middle of the ceiling.

She sat there, a gossamer-haired angel, no longer a child but not quite a woman, absorbing the familiar smells of home. Everything in the room seemed stultifyingly normal: the picture of the Queen hanging above the mantelpiece, the *Sydney Morning Herald* announcing that Menzies was to visit London that summer, the wooden cuckoo clock that her grandfather had left them, going tick-tock-tick . . .

She was bored.

She got up, and switched on the wireless. 'Say Wonderful Things To Me . . .' sang the voice of Ronnie Carrol, '. . . And I'll Say Wonderful Things To You . . .'

At last her mother came out to the kitchen, clutching a glass of sherry. All the way back on the bus, her Mum had been unusually quiet, looking out of the window at the endless tracts of suburban houses of Paramatta and Bankstown that were so similar to their own. In fact, she'd been virtually silent since she'd left the consultant's room at the hospital.

Something was wrong.

Her mother had never really explained why they had to visit the same consultant at the same hospital at the same time every year. This annual ritual never varied. She'd undress down to her knickers, and sit on the examination couch. The consultant, Mr Knowles, would always wink at her as he breathed on the stethoscope which he pressed to her chest, 'to take the cold away first'. Then she would flip over, and then back again. His hard practised fingers would edge along the groin and feel at her two tight little scars . . .

A few years ago, she had asked her mother why they were there. 'Growing pains', her mother had said with a shrug.

The explanation wasn't good enough any more.

That afternoon, her mother had been talking to Mr Knowles for over an hour in the consulting room after her examination was finished, while she waited outside in the busy corridor, reading a copy of *Australian Women's Weekly*. Not really reading, more looking at the pictures . . . She had flicked through its monochrome pages depicting photographs of the Royal Yacht *Britannia* and 'A Hundred And One New Ways With Lamb Left-Overs', looking up from time to time to see bustling nurses with big bottoms in white linen caps carrying trays of blood samples, and frail old folk on Zimmer frames negotiating the shiny lino floor . . .

The floor in their kitchen was lino too. Her mother was staring at it.

'What's wrong with me, Mummy?' she repeated.

'Nothing's wrong,' her mother said. 'Not really.'

'You're lying, Mum, you are. I know it's not nothing. What did he say? What did Mr Knowles tell you?'

Her mother flopped down on a kitchen chair, worn out. She had taken a day off from her job at the local old people's home where, ever since her husband had been killed in a crop-spraying crash when their daughter was three years old, she had scrubbed floors, emptied bedpans and spoon-fed bowls of porridge and oxtail soup to forlorn, incontinent, toothless people waiting to die.

'No one's going to do anything horrible to you,' she reassured her little girl.

She took another gulp from her sherry glass. She looked old.

'What is it?' her daughter said. 'You have to tell me.'

'Well . . . I suppose you were always going to find out one day,' her mother began with a heavy sigh, staring into the dark, sweet contents of her glass. 'I have always hoped, always prayed, that one day things might change. They can do bloody wonders with science nowadays. One day they might be able to do something . . .'

'About what? Do something about what?'

'Darling – not all babies are made the same.'

'Yeah,' her daughter said. 'So?'

'Sometimes when a baby is forming in a mother's belly, it's not sure whether it's a baby boy or a baby girl . . .'

'And . . .'

'So when you were growing inside me, the seed that Daddy put there first made a little boy, then it changed its mind and made a little girl. That made you a very special baby . . . because your father and I, oh good God I miss him, we wanted a little girl more than anything in the world. You were just what we longed for, what we had wanted for years . . .'

Her mother was upset.

The child was persistent. 'But what's wrong with me?'

'Some of the bits and pieces you once needed to be a little boy hung around, and had to be taken away. That's why you have those scars, it was done when you were really little . . . and some of the other bits, you just didn't grow them. Like a plant that doesn't quite get all its leaves . . . But some of the bits you needed to be a girl, you didn't grow those either. It's not as bad as it sounds . . . you know when I told you all about the eggs that Mummies don't need each month to make babies . . . the ones that are washed away with blood, and we call them periods?'

'Yes . . .'

'Well, darling, you don't have the bits on the inside that make those eggs. So, really you're a very lucky girl. You won't ever have to worry about all the mess, or the headaches, or the terrible bloody moods all the time . . .'

She couldn't quite take it all in at the time, of course. But there would come a time when she did.

316

Androgen Insensitivity Syndrome . . . Pseudo-Hermaphroditism
. . . Morris's Syndrome . . . rare genetic defect . . . baby born with
male chromosomes but develops female body . . . no womb, no
ovaries, no fallopian tubes, no childbearing possibilities . . .

She looked like a girl. She walked and talked and cried like a
girl. But inside, she was really a boy. A real boy, trapped inside the
body of a beautiful little girl . . .

These mechanical, medical phrases had at first smacked Kiki
in the guts like boulders the size of armchairs. Get on with your
life as if nothing were out of the ordinary?

Be one of the girls?

Oh, really?

What, when they all started nattering on in huddles in the
playground about tampons and boys and sex? They knew she
didn't have periods.

Sex?

She could have sex with boys.

She knew enough from having explored her body to know
that this was true, as they had insisted at the hospital. What she
didn't really have was the inclination. Oh, she had tried, once or
twice . . . but it was almost as if they knew there was something
different about her.

Some of the bullies in her year called her names. 'No-Cox
Cox . . .'

The words festered in her mind.

Was it really too much to ask, the best of both worlds?
Considering what she had been through? Kiki didn't think so. She
would get her own back. The operation was expensive, but
straightforward. A simple graft. You have the money? We can
build you.

She had arrived at the exclusive clinic in Casablanca and left
three weeks later, for London, a new person. A total person. His
and Hers. Coming out of No Man's Land. Out of No Woman's
Land . . . into a new life.

A pair of white silk briefs fell to the floor of the bathroom
reserved for the exclusive use of the Editor of *The Times*.

She took it in her hands, wondering at the awesome, throbbing appendage. She stroked it gently. It never ceased to amaze her. All it took was a flick of the fingertips, a turn of the wrist, and it sprang to life in her palm, twitching and growing at her command. She ran her long, delicate fingers along it now, comparing the colours: the creamy white of her hand contrasting perfectly with its glistening, moist, heathery hue. Its musky scent intoxicated her. Her nostrils flared as she inhaled dreamily. Her eyelids fluttered, her head rolled, her tongue slid deliciously along her dripping bottom lip . . .

The hot, urgent sensation ripped into the core of her as she pumped frantically, until the creamy juice began to spurt and seep and drip along the back of her hand and into the crisp white cuffs of her starched blouse . . .

It took her breath away . . .

Mandi and Hanni were giggling hilariously at a bad joke as they bundled into the bathroom reserved for the exclusive use of the Editor of *The Times* . . .

Mandi opened the door . . .

The women's smiles froze. Their jaws dropped. They both stared at the Editor . . . the Editor and her penis.

'WOW!' they said in unison.

Kiki tried desperately to shield her awful secret with her hands.

Mandi thought how Kiki must've caught glimpses of herself in the mirror, wondering why the image she saw there didn't reflect the person inside her. She wondered if that warped appendage had reconciled the demons within, if those few inches of flesh, metal and plastic had slaked their rage. The thought flashed through Mandi's mind: Kiki was a woman who wanted it all so badly that she had nothing.

Mandi's reaction was instinctive: this was Fleet Street. These are tabloid *Times*, where everyone's a headline from oblivion. She was already back in her office, and dialling.

'Anthony? This is Cold Type. Yeah great, you? Listen, I'm just about to put Hanni on. Has she got a hot story for you.'

'Hey, Boss', Hanni said, taking the receiver from her mother: 'Hold the Front Page . . .'